EMMA ELLIS

The Invisible Kick

Expose the Poison

First edition

Cover art by MiblArt

1

Prologue

Grace should have written this story. I wrote five years ago of my awakening to the lies that dominate us, all of us. Now it's been Grace's turn to discover the truth, to bring her mind out of sleep and see the hell that we live in. Indeed, what is a society without truth? It is the whispers of the few drowning out the screams of the many. And I have been such a whisperer. For my own gain and for hers, my whispers have circulated and morphed, twisted to suit the agenda of the Centre. My name gave their words a stamp of authenticity, legitimising their deceit.

I kept Grace in the dark for so long, that light switch obscured by my warped sense of morality. But secrets can't be kept forever. The poison coursed through her veins for so long, this antidote was like a shot of adrenaline. When day breaks through the night, those first beams of light are blinding.

I'm sorry, Grace, for what it's worth. For lying to you. For trying to protect your beauty from the ugliness that is this reality. Even I did not fully understand the brutality of our grey world, its lack of integrity as unwavering as its palette.

I have said sorry, of course. Over and over. To Grace. To him. To them, even though they'll never hear my apologies. But there is something more meaningful in writing it down. Spoken words disappear. Rumours are blown away with the wind. The longevity of language is in its printed form. Words written down can last forever.

So I'll leave this book behind, optimistically. In case, by chance, there is anyone left to read it.

2

Chapter one

She died on her birthday.

'Just like Shakespeare,' Maisie uttered with her last breath,
a reference few would understand. His works were cast into
the sea decades ago, or buried under the stone-cold brutality
of progress. But Maisie's nostalgia remained in her heart until
its final beat. At 117 years old, she remembered what so many
had cast aside in pursuit of advancement. Who we were is not
whom we had become. The collective changed. Individually,
though, some were stubborn.

As she coughed, I held one hand and Grace the other. We
grasped tightly as Maisie's grip loosened. Ethan watched
silently as his grandmother passed, showing a level of respect
way beyond his years. His little mouth sank into a frown. His
soft cheeks paled with grief.

'Children should not know such sadness,' Grace said, moisture shining in her dark eyes.

I disagreed. Five years old was a fine age to become ac-
quainted with death.

'What happens when we die?' he asked, his forehead

furrowed in the same way Grace's did.

'We burn,' I said. 'Like the rest of the planet, we burn.'

I'm in awe of him every day. His mind is inquisitive, a scientist from the start.

'He gets that from you,' Grace would say, revealing her own limited knowledge of science.

Not that I was an expert on that side of things, either. What he had inherited from Grace was clear to see, but the rest of his genome was a mystery to me. It wasn't as if we had used a donor. 'It doesn't work like that,' is what the clinic told us. No man had enough squirmers left to make that process worthwhile. 'Modern methods,' they said. Cleaner. More hygienic.

Grace may have been right, though. The nature-versus-nurture debate has never been resolved, and I was but one mother to the boy after all. Some of me may have rubbed off on him. I would read him my papers and science journals and encouraged questions and intrigue. He had jigsaws of biological structures: place the mitochondria in the cell, join up the nucleotides. He drew pictures of us, of boxy apartment blocks, of molecules. When I was a child, I'd had a book about farm animals. My parents would ask what noises a cow makes, get me to do impressions of sheep and dogs. Of course, Ethan had no concept of this. His world was infinitely more silent. Less tactile. Sterile.

Maisie loved him as she would her own grandson, and showed it with her endless sweeties and biscuits.

'What did you do at Granny's today?' I would ask after collecting him.

'She talked a lot, and I ate all her sweeties.'

I'd laugh. 'What else are grandparents for?'

There was no funeral for Maisie. That tradition had ended with the last outbreak all those decades earlier. Who wanted to crowd around a corpse when condolences could be made on social media? No point in instigating a mass gathering or we'd all be joining Maisie soon. We did the usual thing and put a notice out on the national obituary site, in case she had any surviving friends or family on the Raft who remembered her. In case the outside world could see in where we were unable to see out.

Maisie Jones, passed away on 13 February 2118, age 117. She will be missed by her loving adoptive family, Savannah, Grace and Ethan Selbourne.

We kept it simple. The complexities of her persona were our delight. The rest of the Raft wouldn't have cared. Uniqueness wasn't worth celebrating. We all blended into the eternal walls of grey.

Her body was taken away within an hour of her passing, as the law dictated. Corpses risked attracting vermin, so they said. The dead were toxic. That seemed ridiculous to me. No vermin had been seen for years, not a single bird or bug since before Ethan was born. Where would the maggots come from? Even the disinfectant on the street was watered down. It was cheaper but less potent. What was the point in upping the concentration when there was nothing left to kill? On the dry-weather days, of which there had been few recently, the spray was less diluted and the stench of bleach all the more powerful. Our eyes watered within minutes of stepping outside, unused to the potency of the extreme cleanliness.

The drones even gave up patrolling for birds. There were

none left anywhere, it seemed. Everyone was safe.

Maisie was cremated that same day, her ashes thrown into the sea. I imagined her swimming, her energy enjoying the freedom of the water, her elements reaching the parts of the planet she had missed so much. She remembered the sea quite differently. She had vivid, garish blue photographs of her and her family stretched out on golden sands. Her recollections carried with them a degree of imagination and editing, I assumed. There was no way the sea was ever inviting. Not a chance that seeing fish swimming around would cause anything except nausea. Still, she would natter on, and we would indulge an old woman's sentiment. The stinking sludge that laps our shores is best disregarded, anyway. Its putrid waves wash up centuries-old rubbish, the Raft's edge a treasure trove of pollution and filth. No one wants to go near the sea, except those who profit from its contamination. Fishers still cast their nets, scooping up the suffocating fish, their opiate and benzodopamine levels worth the risk.

We didn't need Maisie's apartment anymore. My bargain with the Centre meant we had our own place. But in the absence of her real family, it was left to us, along with all her possessions. In the six years since we'd known her, there had still been no contact with the Mainland. She never knew whether her granddaughter survived. My brother's fate was still unknown also, as it was for so many who'd raced across the bridges before the anchors blew up. No contact in decades. Not a jot.

When we got back to our apartment, the sun was beaming into the living room from a completely different direction to the day before. The Raft was turning on its journey. I watched dust particles floating in the light. Outside, the Centre fence glinted. Grace was speaking but my thoughts were elsewhere, and her voice reached me as if coming from a great distance.

'Savannah?'

'Sorry, I was miles away. What did you say?'

'You remember what Maisie used to say about not hearing from her family?'

'No?'

'She always said, "We can put people on Mars, but we can't speak to the Mainland. Work that one out."'

I looked at her face. Her eyes seemed dimmer than before, like Maisie's death had extinguished some of their sparkle.

'Look.' I pointed out the window and Grace's faraway stare followed my gesture. 'It's not that surprising. We must have spun 180 degrees from yesterday, and the day before it was the same. Phone connections are hardly going to work when the Raft moves so much.'

Grace looked at her arms, her elegant limbs catching the light. 'I swear I can feel it move these days. The dips and troughs.'

'No chance. Not this far inland. Maybe if we still lived near the edge, but not here.'

'I can, I'm sure of it.' She held her arms out as if balancing. 'Where are we now?'

'I'm not even sure. Somewhere turbulent, though.'

'Yet they can launch rockets to Mars.' She waved her finger in the air, doing her best Maisie impression. We laughed, and Grace wiped a tear from her eye.

'It's good to laugh, Grace. It's what Maisie would want.'

'I know.'

We were silent for a moment, then I went to the kitchen and poured us both a Pinot GrigNo, one of our best bottles. The syntho grapes were getting much better these days, with none of the acidity of previous batches. Grace raised her eyebrows when I handed the glass to her, but accepted it and leant into me as I sat down.

'I think Maisie deserves a glass of our finest,' I said.

Grace nodded and sipped her wine. Motherhood had taken any remaining youth from her complexion, but she wore age beautifully. It suited her, as did everything. Her back was more rounded, her curls a little straighter. Little lines framed her eyes. It all fitted together seamlessly. Next to her I must have looked like some hag. Not that it mattered to her. My contribution to our relationship was as provider, protector. My roles came with a responsibility I couldn't smile away.

'You know,' she said, 'I saw a rocket go up the other day. I could see the contrails from here. The strip billboards say the building work is almost done.'

I wrapped my arm around her shoulders and pulled her closer. 'Well, there's not much point in us concerning our-selves with that. That's Centre business.'

'What if they bring something back? Some germs from Mars?'

I squeezed her a little tighter. 'You've seen what the news says. It's the most sterile place humans can go. There's no disease there they can bring back. Try not to worry.'

She tilted her head back and looked at me through narrowed eyes. 'You seem worried, though.'

'Me? Oh, maybe, but not about that.' I retrieved my arm and rubbed my forehead. 'I've just got some work stuff on tomorrow. Archie messaged me. Greg is coming into the office.'

'That's the last thing you need. No day off, even after today.'

'Yeah, exactly. And I've no idea why. He's not been in the lab for months.'

'No point worrying until you know what it's about. You'll just be worrying for the sake of worrying.'

'You're one to talk!'

Ethan appeared in the doorway, the little shuffle of his feet a giveaway as he rarely wore his socks properly. He had crayons in his hand and his mop of golden hair tumbled all over his face.

'I'm hungry, mums.'

'I'll fix him something,' Grace said as she stood and kissed me on the cheek. 'You want anything?'

I glanced over to the kitchen, its cupboards filled with packets of BioLabs synthetic food. The shops barely sold anything except food made in BioLabs these days, such was the company's market dominance. Every time I ate, it was like being at work.

'No thanks, I'm not hungry,' I said, preferring a rumbling stomach to ingesting any more work produce.

Grace picked up Ethan and sat him on the counter, brushing his hair from his eyes. She loved that kitchen counter so much and polished it daily. It was the best imitation grain, she said. Centre quality. It was one of her favourite things about the place, that and the view of the fence.

'What do you fancy, little man? Some SynthoSpaghetti? Or some RealioVeg chunks?'

'What were those biscuits Granny always had?' His cheeky tone almost made me choke on my wine.

'VitaBiscuits?' Grace asked.

'Can I have some of those?'

Grace frowned at Ethan and looked my way. 'Biscuits for

dinner?'

I smiled back at her. 'Just for today, I think biscuits for dinner is fine. Granny would say so, anyway.'

Delighted, he took the packet and put a VitaBiscuit in his mouth, letting crumbs fall down his front. One of Maisie's bad habits had rubbed off on him.

'Will I see Granny again?' he asked, his little smile twisting in confusion.

Grace lifted him and settled him on the sofa. 'No, darling. That's why we're sad.'

He nestled into Grace's arm and continued making crumbs. His forlorn face made me want to cry for him. To him, death was something that happened just for that day. The eternity of it was still too abstract. In his scant years in this world, he had known nothing but joy.

Lucky boy.

A shadow enveloped the room, our sadness mirrored by the sudden gloom. Static tingled every hair on my body until lightning flashed, making us all jump.

'*Another* storm!' Grace said with a groan. 'It feels like they come once a week at the moment.'

'We're probably drifting around some tropical climate,' I said as I got up to turn a light on and peek out the window. The sky was as black as night and rain was hammering in the distance, getting closer. I counted the seconds ... one, two, three, four ... until the thunder roared.

'Maisie thought storms were an omen,' Grace said as she pulled Ethan in closer. 'They mean bad things are going to happen.'

'Shh!' I whispered, and smiled at Ethan. 'No bad things are going to happen. The lightning is what takes souls away to the stars, that's all.' I could allow such childish notions to bring comfort, sometimes.

'I like that idea better,' said Grace.

There was a soft rumble, like waves rolling against the shore. Except we were nowhere near the shore. I assumed it was more thunder as the storm raged angrily on and I went to look. An acrid smell of damp concrete wafted in, even though the windows were closed. The rain picked up and thrashed down, a little river coursing through the street below, and still the rumble continued, getting louder. No more lightning flashed, but the great roar rolled closer towards us.

I looked at Grace, who was frozen, eyes wide, squeezing Ethan's wrist as the apartment began to vibrate. The crockery in the cupboards rattled. Grace's wineglass jiggled along the table and fell to the floor. I didn't hear the smash as the thunderous cracking was too loud by then.

Panic rose in my belly until I was sure it would burst. 'Grace, Ethan, come here now!' They ran to my arms and we cowered in the doorway as the whole apartment shook. Photo frames fell from the walls, shelves rid themselves of their clutter, the sofa bounced across the living room.

'Mummy, what's happening?' Ethan cried out.

'It's okay, it'll stop in a moment,' I said, the shaking of the apartment disguising the tremble in my voice. I buried them both beneath me, making the smallest ball three people could make.

And then: silence. The shaking stopped. I waited, my pounding heart ticking away the seconds, my ears drumming along with its beat. But the silence held. I crept to the window to look for fallen buildings, for the contrails of a rocket that had passed too close, for evidence of an explosion. Anything.

But there was nothing. The only shaking left was from my lungs as I forced myself to breathe.

'Sav ...' Grace's voice trembled as she dared to uncurl herself. 'What the hell was that?'

I took some deep breaths to quieten my thumping heart. 'Just a bit of current, I'm sure.' The quiver in my voice revealed my doubts. 'It's all over now. Why don't you put Ethan to bed and I'll make some calls.'

Ethan's eyes were wet with tears, his crayons scattered across the floor.

'Come on, sweetie,' Grace said, taking his hand. 'It's all okay now. Bedtime.'

Ethan wriggled from her grasp and ran to me, grabbing my leg. 'Mummy, I'm scared. I don't want to go to bed.'

I removed his arms and shook him off. 'Go with Mummy.'

'I don't want to go to bed!'

Grace tried to take his hand again, but he snapped it away. 'Do what Mummy says. She's busy,' said Grace.

'She's always busy,' he said, folding his arms and pouting. 'What if the house falls down and she's busy?'

His words cut me like a dagger in the heart. 'Don't be silly,' I said. 'Off to bed.'

I watched them walk down the hall, holding hands, their bond something I could never match. Ethan stamped his feet the whole way and Grace escorted him, her patience unrattled.

I wiped my sweaty palms on my trousers and went for the bottle of wine, pleased I had put it in the fridge before the shaking started. The bottle had survived, but leftovers had overturned and were now pooled across the bottom of the fridge. After taking a large gulp, I cleaned the fridge then refilled my glass. The mugginess of the storm was suffocating.

I cranked up the air con and sat down, clenching and loosening my fists to force the trembling out of my hands. Another gulp later and I'd calmed down enough to message Archie about what had just happened.

Waiting for his reply, I looked out the window again. The strip billboard opposite gave nothing away.

Prime Minister popularity rating at all-time high! With sterility comes liberty! Mars project nearing completion! Progress is paramount! Disinfectant in street sprayer as effective as ever. Everyone is safe now! Street safety 5/5.

I kept watching but it didn't change. The shaking had been ignored.

Grace returned, looking exhausted and red-eyed. 'Kids say silly things,' she said. 'Don't take it to heart.'

'I didn't,' I lied. The wound from Ethan's words still ached in my chest, but my mind was on work and my busy schedule over the coming weeks. 'She's always busy' was actually spot on.

Grace sat next to me and snuggled in close, the warmth of her body making the stuffiness worse. 'Maybe you can spend some time with him before he starts school?' She looked straight at me with her brown, pleading eyes, full of wishes I was yet to grant.

Time was in short supply those days. 'I've got this meeting with Greg tomorrow. I'll have to wait and see what that's about. But with the new injectable due out soon, I don't think I'm going to have a minute to spare.'

'Maybe you could suggest restarting the internship pro-gramme? To reduce your workload a bit?'

'No way. I'm busy, but at least I'm working instead of babysitting interns. Dealing with those hyper-emotional adult-babies was harder work than my actual work.'

'Ethan just wants to spend time with you.'

'I know. I just don't need this pressure right now,' I snapped. I shouldn't have done that. 'Busy with work and impatient at home' was hardly the best attitude. Being cross was going to make me an even worse mother than I already felt. Grace looked down at the floor, making the same genetically matched sulky face as Ethan. 'Look, I'm sorry. I didn't mean to yell. I'm just tired.'

She didn't reply. Instead, she went to the kitchen, retrieved the dustpan and brush, and started cleaning up the smashed glass on the floor, hitching up her skirt to get into the corners. I hadn't even seen it until then. Shards of glass and broken frames were everywhere. One fallen picture was of Maisie holding Ethan, the crack in the frame dividing them. Grace held it for a minute, then retrieved the photo and threw the rest away. I went to get a brush to help, willing my hands to be just about steady enough to handle it.

Grace sniffed as she tipped broken glass into the bin. 'What was it? The shaking? I mean, I noticed some movement recently, like I said, but nothing like that.'

'I've no idea. I messaged Archie.'

'Maybe an earthquake?'

'Don't be daft. We're floating. An earthquake would mean we were actually attached to the earth by dirt, so no way. Earthquakes are dirtquakes.' I rubbed my eyes and sat on the floor. 'Probably just some turbulent water, like I said.'

'Maybe we crashed?'

'We've not been near land in ages, so that seems impossible.

And it's not like there are any icebergs.'

'An explosion?'

I shrugged. 'Maybe. I guess we'll just have to wait and see.'

My phone pinged with Archie's reply. 'No idea,' was all it said. I showed Grace.

She nodded. 'It's like Maisie said. Storms are bad omens.'

I rolled my eyes at her. 'Maisie was a lovely, wonderful woman, but she was a bit bonkers.'

Grace laughed until she started crying again. 'She was, wasn't she?'

Chapter two

I had no time off to grieve. Better to keep busy anyway. The evening disappeared in the blink of an eye. Time never passes as quickly as it does when I know Greg is due into the lab.

I left Ethan and Grace sleeping as I crept out in the morning. Ethan had woken crying in the night and Grace had sat up with him for an hour, telling him some of Granny's stories to calm him. I heard her doing the voices, a higher-pitched one and a lower one meant to sound scary, Ethan giggling at her attempts. She couldn't match Maisie's skills, of course, but her efforts settled him. When she returned to bed, her muffled sobs made my heart ache. I held her tight and kissed the crown of her head.

'She's at peace,' I said. 'She's free.'

The storm from the day before had left puddles in the street that were still there the next morning, the street sprayers achieving nothing among the rainwater. I felt no reassuring sting as my feet were soaked, the smell of damp concrete stronger than that of the bleach. I shivered to think how ineffective the street sprayers would be against insects and filth. My eyes darted back and forth as I searched the air – old habits are hard to break – but I found nothing. The walls of the buildings were untarnished, the air that far inland was clear enough, and there was no sign of any vermin.

The familiar vibrations of the Autocar rolling towards me made my breath catch in my throat.

Don't be ridiculous, Sav. Dirtquakes aren't possible here.

The Autocar came to a stop in front of me and I climbed in, its climate control blowing the humidity away. I took out my e-pad and looked through some data. The last infusion had been a great success, and working around the pollutants had given the product a better absorption rate than I had predicted. Vitamin deficiencies were much reduced and BioLabs' market share was nearing one hundred per cent. The Selbourne Range was the most sought after of all synthetic food, and the credibility my name carried was well known. Now the injectable infusion was almost ready for launch, with just a few loose ends to tie up.

As was usual in those days, I skipped the Selfie Station by the lab. The beauty aids were more hassle than they were worth, and that snippet of my day could be forgotten. I wore age like a scratchy old blanket, looking threadbare and creased. My complexion had gone from pale to constantly flushed as my body expunged a sticky soup of hormones. Womanhood was testing my temper and sweat glands to the limit, so I denied myself that daily reminder. I had sucked up to the corporate crap for long enough before we got fertility treatment, so now I allowed it to lapse. As Archie would say: screw them!

'How're you doing, Prof?' Archie asked as I entered the lab, handing me a cup of MimikTea, its soothing warmth agreeably bittersweet. He looked at me with pained sympathy as I turned my head away.

'I don't want to talk about Maisie. Need to keep my work head on.' I waved him away. 'I'll take the tea, though. Thanks.'

He nodded. 'Fair enough.'

I took the cup and walked through to my office, sitting on its only chair. Archie followed and perched on the edge of my desk, still giving me a look of concern. His pale face was more crumpled than usual.

'I'm fine, Archie. I really don't want to talk about it.'

'Okay, okay. If you're sure.'

'And stop looking so worried. You look old enough without even more wrinkles. Amalyn won't want you anymore if you look like that.'

He gasped in melodramatic offence and ran his hands through his thinning hair to tidy it.

I decided to change the subject. 'Any idea about what that was yesterday? Felt like an earthquake, but that would be ridiculous.'

'An earthquake would indeed be ridiculous. But I've no idea. No idea what you're even talking about, to be honest. We didn't feel anything at my place.'

'Really?'

'Yep. I've been looking at some online chatter, and it seems only the more central postcodes felt anything. My best guess is a lightning strike or explosion somewhere. Nothing in the news this morning, though.'

'Which probably means the Centre caused it.'

He gave me a little shove. 'Listen to you, the cynic! I've taught you well.'

'The apprentice becomes the master.' I laughed. 'Anyway, any idea what this meeting is all about?'

'Nope. Which means it's not good news. If it's good news, he likes to brag beforehand. Heard a rumour about his new assistant, though. He has four now. And this latest one, her entire job role is to hold his drink, put the straw in his mouth, then wipe his mouth afterwards.'

'Oh, come on! That's nonsense. Even Greg isn't that awful.'

Archie raised an eyebrow at me.

'Okay, maybe he *is* that awful, but that's a bit extreme.'

'And check out this guy.' He pointed towards an exceptionally tall man walking around the lab with his hands behind his back, puffing his chest out like he'd been triumphant in a war. Ribs poking out of an emaciated torso were visible through his shirt.

'Who the hell is that?'

'No idea, but he's been parading up and down the lab for the last hour.'

'*Hour?* Blimey, Archie, what time did you get into work?'

'About an hour ago.' He winked. 'Not my idea. Amalyn rallied the troops to come in early and make sure everything is shipshape for you. In case you weren't up to working much.'

I glanced over the lab and saw Amalyn poring over paperwork and e-pads. Her hair was flying about her face, as unruly as always. She hadn't looked up since I'd arrived.

'She's a gem.'

'Weird how enthusiastic she is, when you consider what kind of mentor she had.'

'Hey! Look what my nonchalance and ridicule have produced. Clearly it's a winning tactic.'

'Yeah, a roaring success,' Archie said with a laugh. 'Five years of internships, one hundred interns enrolled, and we have two from five years ago and three from before that. What are their names again?'

'The ex-intern staff?' I chewed the inside of my cheek for a moment. 'Give me a clue?'

'Ha! You actually don't know?'

'I'm a numbers person. I just know them as 2-10, 4-09 and 8-08. And Amalyn and Mabel are 7-12 and 4-12.'

'You don't seriously call them by their numbers?' Archie put his hands to his cheeks in astonishment.

'I try my best not to speak to them at all.'

'If Amalyn ever hears you refer to her by her number—'

'She won't. She's actually worth talking to,' I said. 'It was better when the others didn't bother coming into the lab. They're only data inputting. Why are they bothering?'

'My guess is because the street sterility rating has been 5/5 for so long now. With no filth spotted in such a long time, they're happier that it's safe and are venturing out again.'

I looked around at the lab, busier than it had been in years. My sanctuary was being disrupted by people daring to walk the streets. I sighed. 'I almost miss the worries about vermin. At least the lab was quieter.'

'Ha! If I find out who the Poison Maker was, I'll give them your details.'

I smiled, but my cheeks blushed with betrayal. Neither Archie nor Grace knew of my deal with Peter the Press editor and the Minister. No one did. My son was the payoff. Archie, like everyone, thought Grace and I made the list for fertility treatment due to our work achievements and persistence. I was still writing propaganda pieces for the National Press. I couldn't bring myself to use the wording the Centre demanded, but the edits were done without my input, skimming over the facts and adding the required hate and hyperbole as always.

The unmistakeable scurry of Penny's heels came hastening up to my office. I cursed myself for leaving the door and blinds open, giving me nowhere to hide. Her perfume preceded her by at least a few metres. I squeezed my eyes shut and groaned.

'Professor Selbourne?' Her voice rasped in the way of all Perimeters, only several octaves higher.

There was no point ignoring her; she'd only shriek louder. 'Yes, Penny?'

'As the wellbeing manager here, I just want to let you know that you can come and talk to me if you feel you need to. Grief can be a tricky companion.'

Talk to Penny? I spent most days doing everything I could to stay well clear of the woman. When she wasn't telling me off for something ridiculously trivial, she was making a drama out of a paper cut or insisting everyone meditate because the street-safety rating had dropped one point. Going to Penny with an actual emotional problem would most likely cause her to explode.

I forced a smile. 'Thanks, Penny. I'm fine and would rather not talk about it right now.'

'Not talking only makes things harder. It is much better to …'

Her voice trailed off as her gaze was pulled away from me to the stranger in the lab. Her mouth hung open and her eyes bulged wide.

'Who is that man?' she asked.

'No idea,' I said.

Penny started fanning herself. 'Oh gosh, isn't it hot in here? How nice to have a new man about the place.' Her face was turning a deep shade of scarlet.

'Are you okay, Penny?' I asked. 'Do you need to sit down?'

Archie and I looked at each other. A silent joke passed between us, and we both bit our lips to keep the laughter in.

'No, no, I'm quite all right. Do I look all right? No lipstick on my teeth?' She opened her mouth and revealed her sepia-coloured teeth. They went on forever.

I recoiled and nodded. 'You're looking fine. Yep, all good.'

'Please excuse me for a moment. I'll just go and freshen up.' And she darted away.

As soon as she was out of earshot, Archie and I doubled over in stitches.

Archie held his stomach. 'Oh, the poor man, whoever he is. Penny with a crush sounds like the worst thing in the world.'

I wiped tears from my eyes. 'I think we'll need respiratory masks with all the perfume she's going to use.'

As our giggling fit began to subside, we both snapped our heads up to the familiar sound of the lab doors swishing open and the thunderous footsteps of Greg. His entourage of buxom assistants tippy-tapped behind him like an echo of an echo. Shockingly, what Archie had said seemed to be true. One woman with almost her entire cleavage on show stood to the side of Greg with a drink in hand, along with a napkin. That appeared to be her entire role. Her face hung nearly to the floor, heavy with humiliation.

I looked at Archie, who mouthed, 'Told you so.'

I shuddered. 'Centre pricks!' I mouthed back, and I shook my head and rolled my eyes.

Greg heaved his extravagant paunch through the aisles, being sure to brush against Amalyn as he walked past. She squashed herself into her desk to give him room, yet her effort was in vain and she was caressed by his insatiable torso. She looked our way and feigned a retch, but Archie was not amused.

His face was reddening, his cheeks rippling over gritted teeth.

I grabbed his elbow and whispered, 'Amalyn can handle herself. She's fine.'

He grunted and walked to his office, slamming the door.

Archie's passive-aggressive door slamming did little to distract Greg as he continued his parade. The new man, as lanky as Greg was round, followed him closely, alternating his attention between Greg's musings and his assistants' chests. Next to Greg walked a younger man, difficult to age through his well-oiled skin and likely collagen injections. He was clearly Centre, going by his height and pearly white teeth. He was walking with his chin high, his lips peeled back in that sinister way all the Centre did. His broad shoulders were packaged into a snuggly fitted suit, embellished with buttons that served no purpose, lapels that used fabric but had zero functionality, and finished off in a bright colour that was like a migraine next to the drabness of the Perimeter.

'All right, all right, quiet down, all of you,' Greg yelled unnecessarily, his speaking voice being loud enough. 'I would like to introduce you all to my son, Declan.' He slapped the younger man on the back. 'Declan will be taking over from me as head of BioLabs. He is here to learn the ropes.' Declan nodded at us, pouted his lips and tensed his chest muscles until his shirt strained against them. At least one staff member stifled a chuckle. Amalyn, probably.

Declan being Greg's son seemed unlikely. Greg was an advert for what overindulgence could do, if you had the money to fund such intemperance. Declan was groomed to such an extent that there was no room for Greg's level of immoderation. With a manufactured perfection and contrived image to maintain, he was the perfect poster boy for a company selling healthy food and clearly knew it.

'And this is Lars Cowley.' Greg pointed at the other man, the weak-looking one who had been there earlier, who smiled at us and picked at the dead skin hanging from his lips. 'Lars is an auditor and cost-saving specialist. He and Declan will be going through the company in every detail, checking to ensure there is no waste. They have my permission to access every computer, and you must answer all their questions.'

A murmur rolled around the lab as Declan blinded us with his teeth and Lars rubbed his hands up and down his thighs. I shook off a chill that crept up my spine.

'Savannah, my office,' Greg said, his bellowing voice causing the furniture to vibrate.

Microbes! I had hoped that speech would be all. After stifling a moan, I followed Greg, his assistants filing in behind me.

'Shut the door, Selbourne, for Raft's sake!'

Greg's female entourage hovering at the door all retreated a few steps. I stared at them, hoping for a clue, a warning, but their helpless faces gave nothing away. My pity was wasted on them. Their eyes were clouded with despondency, resigned to their fate.

'Sit.'

I obeyed and didn't dare speak. The chair was stiff and uncomfortable, its height and rigidity making both sitting up straight and slouching feel awkward. His office felt airless and stuffy, or perhaps it was just the ambience he conveyed. His abundance of real wood furniture had recently had its annual coating of fresh lacquer, entombing the old amoebas within it under a skin of solvent.

Standing next to Greg was Declan, his whole body clenched, one thumb and forefinger cradling his chin as he held it high.

He didn't look my way, directing his gaze instead at the ceiling. The strength of his aftershave, together with the furniture's varnish, made my eyes burn.

'I have a new project for you,' Greg said. 'This must be handled with the utmost secrecy. I've been looking over the files of your colleagues. That young blonde one looks a bit too innocent, if you ask me, but she has the required credentials.'

'Amalyn?'

'Yes, that's her. The tart with the messy hair. You'll need her.'

It took all my strength not to scowl at him. 'Okay, sir, no problem. She's an excellent—'

'Anyway.' He waved his hand to shut me up. 'Just listen for once. We are orchestrating a big new business venture for BioLabs, and we have chosen you to be the lead salesperson. Since you are the head researcher, we thought it would be a good ploy to stick you out in front. You'll need to look presentable.' He frowned and looked me up and down. 'Sort your hair out a bit. And for Raft's sake, look healthy. What is with your skin these days? You look like old pavement.'

'Tiredness, motherhood, overworked ...'

'Well, leave your problems at home. They don't need to come to work with you. You need to look like these vitamins actually work.'

'They do work. But, sir, who would I be selling to? The whole of the Raft buys our products already.'

'Europe.'

I choked on my own breath. 'Excuse me, sir? Europe?'

'Yes, the Mainland. Europe. They're keen to hear all about it. That blonde tart. What's her name again?'

I winced at his description. 'Amalyn.'

'Yes, her. She speaks several languages, doesn't she? That might prove useful.'

I was struggling to find my voice, the enormity of *Europe* taking ages to sink in. 'But, sir, there's no one on the Mainland. Where exactly—'

'I didn't ask you in here so you can waste my time with all these questions. An Autocar will pick you up Wednesday next week to take you to the airport.'

'Next week! The *airport?*' My voice sounded shrill as excitement knotted my throat.

'Yes. You know what one is, don't you?' he barked, and I nodded my reply. 'Don't look so stupid, then. You'll be provided with the appropriate clothing at the airport, and someone will meet you when you land. And, Selbourne, this is highly confidential. Not even that pretty little wife of yours can know what you're up to. This is big business for us. This alone could fund my trip to Mars, so you know how important it is.'

I stood straighter and found my voice, along with my professionalism. 'Yes, sir. Of course, sir.'

'Lars and Declan are here to audit the lab, as I explained.' Declan nodded my way at the mention of his name, putting his hand to his chest and flashing his teeth again. 'They'll keep things running when you're away. Take the reins, so to speak. In the meantime, they need to look through everything. See if any time or money is being wasted anywhere.'

'Right, sir,' I said, as what he'd told me began to sink in. I wiped my clammy palms on my trousers. 'Exactly how long will I be gone, sir? I'm sure the lab can function well for a short time without me.'

He slammed his hand down on the desk. 'Did I not just say I

don't have time for your questions?'

I nodded. He peeled his hand off the table, his excess skin making a sucking noise as he did.

'And there's an article coming out in the National Press,' he said, as he scrolled through something on his computer, avoiding eye contact with me. 'About the ways the Blue Liberation Party are helping the people of the Perimeter. You're far too busy to write it, so Peter will do it and your name will be attached.'

'So I'm not writing the article at all?'

'You'll still be paid for it, if that's what you're worried about.'

'Great, sir,' I said through my still-clenched teeth.

He looked at my pained expression and made a face like he'd smelled some curdled IcyCrema. 'How old is that kid of yours? Four? Five?'

'Five, sir.'

'Well, if you want to have him around for another five years, you'll act a bit more grateful. He's Centre property as much as you are. Show me a smile, why don't you?'

I managed to lift the corners of my mouth slightly, with pursed lips and face aflame with rage. I was sure Greg wouldn't ever take Ethan away. At least, I thought so. What would be the point? His threats were as empty as they were frequent. But he knew how to make my blood boil.

'And tell that Ama-whatsherface, if she does well, I may have an assistant position open up for her soon.' He wiped a line of spittle from his chin.

I certainly was not going to agree to that. I ran out of his office before either of us could say anything else.

The lab staff's sympathetic and curious glances burned

into me as I hurried past them. It was as if I had the words 'highly confidential' branded on me. Surely everyone in the lab could read my expression and knew that Greg had just dropped a bombshell on me. I made the most 'don't bother me, everything's fine' face I could manage and rushed to the safety of my office.

I closed the door and shut the blinds. A few minutes alone to calm down was all I needed. I cranked the air con and fanned myself with my top. When I sat at my desk, it really started to hit me, and I forgot Greg's latest threat as I remembered the rest of the conversation. I hadn't imagined it. I wasn't dreaming.

I was going to the Mainland!

4

Chapter three

I couldn't sit still at my desk, and opted to pace up and down instead. How could I hide my excitement and apprehension? And Amalyn was going to be thrilled. I remembered when she'd been an intern, when I'd read her qualifications and dismissed her language skills as pointless and useless. How wrong I'd been.

Greg and Declan stomped out of the lab at lunchtime, several test tubes falling to their death from the vibrations as they clomped past. Rather than learning the ropes, Declan had succeeded in nothing but striking poses at every desk. By then, Lars had introduced himself to the staff. 'Overseeing and streamlining the business' was how he referred to his role.

'A Centre snitch,' Amalyn translated, directly to his face.

I nearly spat out my tea. Quite why Archie ever worried about her was beyond me. She'd survived the pressures of her internship with ease and since then had become exactly the sort of bad-ass she craved to be. Most days, her brash comments made us spill more tea from laughing than we managed to drink.

I called Amalyn into my office. Archie, predictably, followed.

'This is for Amalyn's ears only, Archie. That comes from the top.'

'Yeah, all right, Sav, as you were,' he said, as he perched on the edge of my desk.

'I mean it, Archie. I've been told.'

'Oh, come on, Sav,' Amalyn said. 'It's Archie. I'm going to tell him anyway. And why don't we go to his office? It's comfier.'

'This won't take long. Lars is doing his rounds.' I grimaced as I watched through the window. 'He reminds me of a bug from my father's book. A praying mantis.'

'Aw, look at Penny following him,' Amalyn said, holding her hands to her chest.

Archie gagged. 'So gross.'

'It's cute! They suit each other.'

'Ahem.' I cleared my throat. It was a conversation that could have continued forever. 'Amalyn, brace yourself. Apparently, we are to head a sales team to sell BioLabs products. To Europe. We leave for the Mainland Wednesday next week.'

She shrieked and put her hands to her mouth. Her whole body was shaking. Tears welled in wide eyes staring at me, unblinking.

At that moment, the distinctive tap-tap of Marcus and his feeble wrist sounded at my door.

'What is it, Marcus?'

'Sorry, Professor, I hope I'm not interrupting.'

'You are. What do you want?'

'The new beaker order. The delivery bot needs a code.'

'Marcus, you ordered them, so the code will be in your emails.'

'Of course, Professor. I quite forgot. I'm sorry.' And he left.

'I swear he's losing his marbles,' I said.

Archie put his arm around Amalyn. 'Europe, Sav? Seriously? You two? Is it safe? I mean, where? There are hardly any communities anywhere.'

'Oh, Sav!' Amalyn's voice was squeaking with excitement. 'We get to leave the Raft! You're not kidding, are you? This is so amazing! We get to go to Europe. Do you know which country?'

'Honestly, that's all I know. Top secret, guys, remember that. And Archie, yes, we'll have full protective gear, people to meet us and I have no idea exactly where we're going. An Autocar will take us to the airport. Ams, you speak other languages, don't you?'

'French, Spanish, German and a little Russian. I'll practise all of them.' Her voice was still trembling.

'She sounds lovely when she speaks French,' Archie said with a smile.

Amalyn grabbed his hand. 'Where could we be going? You must have seen somewhere on the satellite images? Somewhere where people still live?'

'I really haven't. The odd small population, sure, but not enough to bother with for business. It's just desert and floods everywhere.' He scratched his head. 'Sav, are you sure he said *Europe*?'

'Yes, I'm sure. Even if I misheard, is there another continent that would be better? Perhaps the wildfires of the Americas would be preferable?'

'Good point,' he said, accepting my sarcasm. 'Annoying he didn't tell you any more.'

'Well, he did say it's top secret, so maybe he didn't tell me much on purpose, knowing we'd spill to someone?'

Amalyn laughed. 'Maybe, but who cares anyway? We get to leave the Raft!'

'And by the way,' I said, 'apparently Lars and Declan will be in charge of the lab while I'm gone.'

Archie's face dropped and he slapped his forehead. 'Take me with you! Don't leave me alone with them!'

* * *

I managed to avoid Lars for most of the morning, but he eventually found his way to my office. He smiled, or should I say sneered, his top lip curling back, unwrapping from long, yellow teeth. He walked over with exaggerated strides, his waif-like body doing a poor impression of a Centre, and greeted me with a sort of bow.

'Ms Selbourne. As I'm sure Greg has explained to you, I'm here to audit the lab.'

He instantly made my skin crawl. He smelled of cooking oil and had eyes that looked everywhere except where they should. I had far too much to organise to deal with his snooping.

'Nice to meet you, Mr Cowley,' I sighed as I carried on with my work, leaving him standing in the open space, lingering like a string of smog.

'Oh, please, I'm sure we can do away with formalities. You can call me Lars.'

'Great. Lars. I'm *Professor* Selbourne. Now, if you don't mind, I have a lot of work to do.'

His smile dipped to reveal that his bottom teeth were even more yellow than the top ones. His skin hung off him like he was melting. I noticed old scabs that he had tried to hide under his high collar.

'Well, I imagine there will be lots for me to look through. Why don't I pull up a seat and just watch you?'

'I don't have another seat in here. You can loom over there or sit on the floor. I really don't have time to entertain you.'

'Very well, Professor Selbourne. I shall just stand here.'

He placed himself right behind me and leant down, glaring over my shoulder, his rancid breath licking at my neck.

'You do that. Stay exactly there,' I said as I got up and walked out, slamming my office door before a dry heave kicked in. I walked across the lab to one of the workstations and sat there instead.

Amalyn looked over her shoulder towards my office. 'Eurgh. He's so creepy. Looks like a ghost from the famines.'

'That ghost needs to look through everything, apparently. Like I haven't got enough to do. There's so much to plan for you-know-what, plus everything else we have to do for the injectable launch. Now we have to babysit some snitch as well.' I groaned and fanned myself with my blouse, my insides broiling. 'This is ridiculous. I can't have him staring over my shoulder all day.'

'How are you doing, anyway?' she asked, her voice dipping. 'How's Grace and Ethan?'

'Great. Never better,' I snapped. Amalyn's face fell. 'Sorry, I didn't mean it like that,' I said. 'I just can't talk about it here. I need to concentrate.'

'I know. It's fine.'

I sighed as I watched Lars leave my office and return to wandering around the lab. 'Is he here to be the personification of exactly what we don't want the vitamin infusion to produce?'

Amalyn choked back a laugh. 'Reckon he and Archie will

be best buds while we're away. We'll come back to find them sharing a bowl of IcyCrema.'

We were both in hysterics. 'Microbes!' I said. 'Don't make me laugh so much. Look, he's coming over now.'

'Ladies,' he said as he leant in close. Too close. 'Care to share what's so funny?'

'*Ladies?*' Amalyn scoffed at his belittling tone and shook her head. 'Nah, you're all right.'

'It's an inside joke. You wouldn't understand,' I said.

'Enlighten me.'

'Well, once you've finished reading every file on my computer, you'll probably get it. Go on, crack on.'

He scowled and walked off.

Amalyn grinned and stared at me. 'Whoah! Savannah, you're bad-ass!'

'Greg never said we have to be nice to him.'

She laughed. 'We're going out Friday to meet some friends. You should come.'

'The Golden Fifty nostalgic reprobates?'

'Yes, if that's how you want to describe us. But it'll be fun. Come with us.'

'I'm not sure. They all hate me. They think I'm some Centre snitch.' The filth of the bars didn't appeal, either. Why didn't they at least wipe the tables more frequently?

'Don't be daft,' Amalyn said with a laugh. 'No one even knows who you are. And none of them actually reads the National Press, anyway.'

I pondered but could hardly say no. 'Sure, okay then. I guess we have reason to celebrate.'

Lars came sneaking over again, his waif-like footsteps so light that if it hadn't been for Penny scurrying after him, we wouldn't have heard him coming.

'You have been wasting company time for two minutes and seventeen seconds.'

'We were discussing work. And that's thirty seconds *you've* wasted coming over here,' I said, and stormed back to my office.

* * *

Work was non-stop for the rest of the week with the presentations I had to prepare, as well as going through the data for the new injectable. Amalyn was so excited about the launch. It had been her project from the start, and it was to be her first major product release. That alone would have taken up all my time and more, but now we had the extra staff using lab space as well. As I was getting really annoyed with tripping over people and trying to tell them to go back to working from home, Archie confronted me.

'Did you not read the group email?'

'No, of course not.'

'Due to the audit, working from home is prohibited, for a few weeks at least. Lars wants to monitor what everyone does with their time.'

'You're kidding.'

'Nope. He says he can't monitor their hours if they're at home. I tried to tell him that's nonsense as he can monitor what work is getting done from his own computer. But he wants to see their faces.'

'Wants to judge their complexions and health, more likely. Weed out the more Perimeter.'

'I think that could be it,' he said. 'He's a fine one to judge, though! I've seen him hack up black phlegm at least four times today.'

I winced. 'I suppose everyone feels like their job is on the line? That at least explains why 2-10, 4-09 and 8-08 are being so polite to me,' I said.

'Maybe they're just normal and next to you they seem especially polite?'

'If I wasn't so tired, I'd have a good comeback to that,' I said. 'Seriously, though, all day I've had, "Great work, Professor," "Nice to see you, Professor," "Can I get you a cup of tea, Professor?" As if I have any say in staffing around here! It's driving me nuts.'

'Maybe it's: you're their boss, basically famous in the world of nutrition, and they are honoured to work with you?'

I scowled. 'Now you too? What's with all the ass-kissing around here? Where's Amalyn? Surely I can have some banter with her.'

He gestured to one of the lab stations where Amalyn was engrossed in some data. 'You won't have much joy there. She's really busy. I think you're just going to have to behave until this audit is over.'

'I'm too tired to put up with a couple of days of this nonsense, let alone a couple of weeks.'

'Spoken like a true survivor of a pandemic and a famine,' he joked. 'We'll make up for it Friday night.'

5

Chapter four

When Friday evening rolled around, I was so grateful for
Amalyn's invitation. The three of us went out straight from
work. Grace knew I'd be home late. She never begrudged me a
social life and relished in some more one-on-one time with
Ethan. It amazed me how she never tired of him. She found
joy in every tantrum and tear, as well as every laugh and game.
I'd offered to have him to myself so she could have a night out
plenty of times.

'I don't want to miss a moment,' she would say.

Incarcerated by her fear of the outside, is what I knew she
meant. So she stayed in, her usual preference.

I had visited bars with Archie and Amalyn a few times over
the years. I always felt on edge, unnerved, and left feeling
unclean. It wasn't that I disapproved. Not too much, anyway.
The hygiene standards were lax at best. I saw more water
rings than soap dispensers. The soft furnishings displayed
more stain than original fabric. The clientele would wax lyrical
about a time when filth was abundant, and seemed to take
pleasure in sitting amid the grime. An easy act of rebellion.

The storms diluting the street sprayers didn't seem to bother them, though some wore such thick soles on their shoes I suspected it was to keep them elevated above the asphalt.

My main concern was always that I would say something wrong. Lubricated by cocktails, my tongue could easily slip. I knew too much about both sides. My mind was a puddle of truth just waiting for a splash. The secrets I knew I had to bury deep, but the inebriants could dig them up. So I was always careful to drink modestly and chose my cocktails carefully.

Archie had become such a socialite. He was drinking too much, probably, since his hacking abilities had been curtailed by the improvement of Centre firewalls, and spending less time on snooping where he shouldn't and more on imbibing what he shouldn't. Still, it had given him a new lust for life that he had lacked before. He rarely sat in alone playing computer games now. Virtual reality had been replaced with actual reality, albeit slightly reworked through the help of narcotics.

We walked to the bar, about half an hour closer to the Raft's edge, to 'stretch our legs,' Archie said. An Autocar would have been my preference, but I obliged. The smog wasn't at its worst that evening but was still thicker than my cleaner lungs were used to. I kept my face covered as my eyes streamed in the hazy wind. The quantum-cable trenches were still unfilled this far out, and ditches lined the roads and pavements leading to apartment blocks that I knew were mostly empty. The sheer scale of waste for the sake of waste still baffled me.

As we walked further out, the three of us stopped dead in our tracks as the ground beneath us moved, rumbling and groaning.

'Earthquake again?' I asked.

'On the *Raft*?' Archie said, his tone mocking, and I felt stupid for even suggesting it.

The concrete grumbled and creaked. I felt the slight incline and decline as the Raft dipped and swayed.

I stood still for a moment. 'What the ...?'

'Come on, let's keep walking,' Archie said, his eyebrows knitted with resolve.

'Are you sure? Something feels odd.'

'Sure, come on,' Amalyn said as they carried on. I picked up my pace to catch up.

As we walked, I looked at the pavement below and noted tiny fissures criss-crossing the concrete. I had lived in this area for years before and never noticed them. Tiny indiscernible blemishes creeping in. They were easy to miss, as such little flaws demanded no attention. Maybe I had disregarded them. Perhaps now my own neighbourhood was so much better maintained, the defects in the Perimeter stood out much more.

Ignore it, Sav.

It wasn't my business to worry about something so far from home. To judge this rundown area by my own standards. Living away from the edge was making me snobby, that was all.

Archie looked stern, his forehead wrinkled. What was that expression I could see on him? Those lines weren't all from his bracing against the elements. He had a darkness in his eyes. Was it anger? I dismissed the thought. Archie wasn't one to brood on such emotions.

We arrived at the bar. My skin itched and I scratched salt residue from my cheeks. The hours I had spent taming my hair that morning were wasted as it frizzed with the humidity. How unaccustomed I had become to Perimeter air! It niggled at me, though, how different the air felt, how much harsher. When

I lived further out, it was baking hot all the time. Now the weather was more mixed but the variation had done nothing to thwart the callousness of the climate, and only enhanced it.

'Archie? Something's changed. What's been happening out here?' I asked as I watched some Alternates brush salt residue from their own skin.

'Come in. We can talk indoors.'

He ushered me inside with a glance over his shoulder. There'd be no prying eyes in the bar. No spy would risk the unsanitary conditions.

The bars were normally lively and busy places on a Friday night, but that night it was as quiet as the central streets.

'The tax hikes,' Amalyn said as we ordered our drinks. 'Most people can't afford it.'

I selected a lower alcohol drink, free of MDMA and LSD. A sensible start to the night. Amalyn's usual was a potent mix of chemicals and vitamin concentrates. It came served with a glow-in-the dark mixer and ice cubes that fizzed. It didn't surprise me that most couldn't afford to drink in the bars now. The two cocktails alone were eye-wateringly expensive. Archie had a beer.

'Don't be so unadventurous!' Amalyn said. 'You usually love the trippy drinks.'

'I'll have one later. I just fancy a beer right now. We have stuff to talk about first.'

'Sounds ominous, guys,' I said. 'Archie, that might be the most serious thing I've ever heard you say.'

He smirked at me and we made our way to a corner booth, its seats sticky with splattered drinks, the table dusted with snack crumbs and pools of liquid. No one had bothered to sanitise the table. Archie and Amalyn sat without paying the uncleanliness any attention at all.

I noticed it then, more than ever. The turning heads, the scowls. I heard the whispers and the tuts. Then, for the first time, someone actually approached us.

'Ams, I didn't know you kept such bad company.' The man glared at me.

'Leave it out, Obey. She's a friend.'

'She writes for the Press. I recognise her. She makes decent food but then bitches about the Perimeter. Her last article was even in favour of the tax hikes.'

I looked down at the table, not daring to meet his gaze.

'The National Press is full of shit. Sav is no less Perimeter than any of us.'

He leered in closer and inspected my face. At that moment I wished my complexion was worse so I looked more Perimeter. A bit of peeling skin would have been a blessing.

'Not all *that* Perimeter, though, is she?' He sucked his teeth and walked away.

Amalyn rolled her eyes. 'Ignore him, Sav. Most people have a lot of respect for you. There's just the odd idiot.'

'It's fine,' I said, and gulped my cocktail. 'So what's the real gossip?'

Amalyn took her hairband out and let her hair fall down. 'It's just rumours, Sav. You know.'

Archie untucked his shirt and rolled up his sleeves. 'We can't prove anything. But even if we could, who would we tell? I don't have the clearance I used to.'

'What rumours?' I asked. 'What's going on?'

'You can tell, can't you?' Amalyn said, her voice shaky. 'The cracks, the air, the rumbles. It's the Raft. The edge, anyway. It's breaking up.'

I gasped. That couldn't just happen. It was fortified. It was meant to last. I shook my head. 'It's strengthened with iron lintels and god knows what else. It can't just break up.'

'The weather is harsher now,' Archie said, leaning in closer. 'The sea is fierce. Its acidity ratings are through the roof. The Raft was only designed to drift temporarily, but it's been decades. I'm telling you, I know this stuff. It will not last.'

Archie had designed umpteen computer models to predict our trajectories and coming climates, and he knew before anyone else that our land was rotten under the water. If he thought the Raft was breaking up, it was extremely likely it was.

'I knew you wouldn't understand until you saw it yourself,' he said, 'but it's clear, isn't it? The Raft is crumbling out here in the Perimeter. Some remnants of the old docks have all gone. The desalination plants are still there, but they're smaller. I swear a row of high-rises has gone. And no one is doing anything about it.'

'A *row* of high-rises? Really? That would be very noticeable.'

'By whom?' Amalyn asked. 'They're all ghost apartments, anyway. No one would even know. But every inch lost at the edge brings us all a little closer to the sea.'

I scowled and scratched my head. The harsher air, the saltiness, the smog. The edge crumbling into the sea would explain them, but I was now so unaccustomed to the Perimeter, maybe that was all I was noticing.

'I don't know. It's not that I don't believe you. It's just hard to believe. People would be talking about it. It would be so obvious.'

'If the National Press reported it, it wouldn't be so hard to believe,' Amalyn said.

'Be great if people did know, Sav.' Archie's tone was that of a meddling child.

'And here I was, thinking you guys just wanted to spend time with me.'

'That too, obviously,' Amalyn said and grabbed my hands. 'But you have the ear of the Centre. More than we do, anyway. There may be someone you can speak to. Maybe ask what's going on. Write an article for the Press or something?'

Stability. That's all that was important to the Centre. Or at least the perception of stability. The Minister of Impartiality's words were still vivid in my memory after all these years. The last thing they would want people to know was how unstable the Raft was.

'Honestly, guys, they just use my name like a brand, a stamp of assurance. They don't actually listen to me. They certainly don't talk to me about anything.'

Their eyes fell to the table, sombreness replacing expectation.

'But next time I see anyone at the Centre, I'll try. I promise I'll try.' I turned to Archie. 'Is that what I felt the other day? That shaking? All the way at our place?'

Archie shook his head. 'No, that must have been the storm or something. There's no way you'd be feeling the Raft breaking up at yours.'

'It's been happening frequently since then, though nothing as extreme as that first time. It's hard to explain. The ground just feels like it dips, a little vibration every now and then.'

'I wonder if they're mining or something?' Archie said.

'Mining what?' I said. 'It's not like there's anything left to dig for.'

'I'll listen out for any gossip, but I really don't think it's anything to worry about.'

And that was the last sensible thing that anyone said that evening. A nod from Amalyn to the bar staff produced a second round of drinks, vibrantly coloured and mixed with questionable substances. The colours gave me a headache before consuming them actually did. I wiped down our seats with disinfectant and tried not to touch anything. Archie and Amalyn mocked me for my 'mumsiness'. Had I always been so prudent? It was hard to remember life pre-Ethan. I didn't think I'd changed that much, but Archie's lower inhibition barrier set the bar quite high. We drank cocktails laced with mind-numbing, endorphin-creating tinctures that, for one night anyway, took our worries away.

6

Chapter five

Early Saturday morning, Ethan came squealing into our bed-room, jumping on the bed, ready to play and tell us all about everything and nothing. My head hurt and my mouth felt like carpet. Grace took one look at my pitiful, dehydrated face and whipped him away, brought me a glass of IsoJuice, then made breakfast pancakes and MimikTea. She even gave me a two-hour pass to go rid myself of my hangover at the MindSpa.

I stumbled around the apartment, pulling my clothes on, muttering, 'Thank you, love you' as I left to enjoy some recovery time.

By the time I got home, another storm had begun, the rain hammering down. After the Gulf Stream flipped, the currents changed almost daily, pushing us from one weather front to another. The only predictable element of the weather was the wind. It howled most days, rattling windowpanes and SolaArbs. The lines of buildings acted as protection from the wind on some streets and funnelled it on others. By the time I got home from the MindSpa, just a short distance away, my skin stung from the whipping gale and my lips were cracked. I was feeling less relaxed than I'd hoped to.

It had been worrying me for days, how to tell Grace that I was going away. I knew I'd have to lie again, and it meant less time with Ethan.

They were sitting on the living-room floor when I got back. Ethan had his plastic Autocars in front of him. He'd made a little town out of building blocks and was crashing a car into them. Grace rebuilt everything Ethan knocked down, and Ethan destroyed it again.

'Feeling better?' she asked as she laughed at Ethan's car noises.

I walked over and kissed them both. 'Much, thanks. Tea?'

'Just had one.'

'Juice, please!' Ethan said, and I found a carton of red juice in the fridge.

I sat on the sofa and drank my tea, watching their identical hair bouncing with every gesture as they played. Their bubbly laughs blended into one. The ease of their interactions demonstrated the bond between them, which I could never share. Their relationship, their genetic link, was an innate glue. Grace said she knew him so well before he was even born, whereas I was having to learn. I often felt like a spectator or I was in the way, watching their connection blossom as I observed from the side lines.

'Come play too, Mummy,' Ethan cried, his smile making my heart ache.

'No, no,' I said, 'I like to watch.' Better to leave them to it. I didn't understand the game, anyway.

Archie's words from the evening before rang in my head. *The Raft is breaking up.* I watched my little family, satisfied we were far from the edge. But if the sea was creeping closer, how long before the salty air and smog started choking us? Could it ever get that far? I pushed that thought from my head. We were miles inland, and part of an old dock disappearing was no cause for alarm. Instead, I focused again on Grace and Ethan. They looked so delicate, the pair of them. Even enclosed in the apartment, their slight frames and fragile bodies appeared vulnerable. I yearned to bundle them up and have them live underneath me forever, my body as their roof and walls, never letting them away from me. Keeping them safe.

'Grace, I need a word.'

She tied her hair back and came and snuggled next to me, leaving Ethan to rebuild his little city.

'I can still smell alcohol on you.' She laughed.

'I'll shower again in a moment.'

'Maybe brush your teeth again?'

'Hey!' I laughed and gave her a tickle. 'Seriously, we need to have a chat.'

She looked at me, sincerity making her eyes glint under the lamplight. The wind outside had eased, the rain abated.

'Greg is sending me away on Wednesday for work. I have to go visit another lab.'

'*Another* lab? But you never go to other labs. I didn't even know there were any.'

'Something to do with ProLabs. We might be taking over. Greg wants me to go help there, too. It's just a one-off, I'm sure.' It wasn't all a lie. The ProLabs takeover had been in the pipeline for ages and there was always the possibility that I'd have to go to their labs one day, so I blended the truth with the fiction. My exterior held up well, the strong protector as always. Inside, my stomach churned.

Grace blinked a few times and swallowed. 'How long for?

Will you miss Ethan's first day at school?'

The sight of her sadness gnawed at me. I had dived headfirst into those sad, dark eyes years earlier, and since then I'd never been able to climb back out. I grasped her hand, controlling the pressure of my grip. Too tight and she'd know I was lying; too soft and she'd think I didn't care. 'I think it'll just be for a few days. He hasn't been overly forthcoming with information. You know what he's like.'

She nodded and looked at me with sympathy and total conviction, as always. 'You work so hard for us. I'm so proud of you.'

I felt like I'd been winded. *Don't be proud of lies, Grace.* I longed to tell her the truth, years earlier when Ethan was conceived and every day since. Her trust in me was unearned, her love for me a product of deceit, just like Ethan's life. I was reminded of that deceit whenever I looked at him. His innocent face, playing with his toy Autocars. My heart ached with love for him, yet my love for him felt tainted by the Centre's grip on our lives. Greg's reminder that 'he's not *your* son, is he?' came back to me. Grace had carried him, but the Centre owned him. What was my role in our little family? Protector, I justified. But protector seemed trivial when that cushion was padded with lies.

It's just one more lie, I told myself. *One more small lie.*

'You'll be safe?' she asked, her compassion unwavering.

'Yes, of course. I'll miss you, though.'

Ethan came running over. 'Mummies, look, look! My tooth! It's wobbly!'

'Oh my,' Grace said, her face lighting up. 'Our little boy is growing up so fast.'

His big eyes swelled with tears. 'Why is it wobbly?'

I scooped him up and kissed his cheek. 'I've got this one. Science question.' And we sat on the floor as I explained the wonders of human teeth.

7

Chapter six

The days whizzed by with plenty of staff in the lab to annoy me. Their constant compliments were winding me up. They were relentless, and no matter how much I grunted and sighed in response, they didn't get the hint. At one point I stood up and screamed, so everyone could hear, 'I have nothing to do with the audits or lay-offs!'

By the time Wednesday arrived, I was relieved to get out of the lab, but I was a bag of nerves. Amalyn and I had been for blood and swab tests and given an immune-boosting injection, as stipulated by Greg. The idea of mixing with filth on the Mainland made me restless and twitchy. But it would be clean, surely. They wouldn't send us anywhere dirty.

Would they?

The wind was light, which made me feel happier about getting on a solarplane. Archie had said that no storms were due for a week. The address of the airport looked very central, so the smog wouldn't be a problem. Still, I was wiping my clammy palms on my trousers and doing my best not to shake when the Autocar pulled up. Amalyn was already inside and muttering away, practising her languages, unable to contain herself.

'Ams, seriously. Top secret, remember?'

'Oh Sav, I just can't believe it. I mean, leaving the Raft. I just can't. A solarplane, the airport, Europe? I just can't.'

'*Top secret* is what I said. Work on your poker face. Shall we see if we have time for a stop at the MindSpa so you can calm down a bit?'

'What? No chance. No, I'm fine. Really, I'm fine.' She began loudly inhaling and exhaling, counting as she did so.

The Autocar ride was long, about five hours altogether, skirting the edge of the Centre. It would have been a lot quicker just to drive straight through, but that would have involved a lot more leverage. This was the closest to the Centre fence Amalyn had ever been. From some angles, brief glimpses of shiny skyscrapers were visible above the fields of ArbAirs and SolaArbs. Where the grey ended, the gold began. I looked away. I'd been dazzled before.

Amalyn sucked her teeth as her eyes widened. 'Only the best for the Centre.'

I spared her the details of what it was really like behind the fence, though I was sure Archie would have told her. The wide streets, people feeling safe enough to gather, the scrubbed pavements and grandiose buildings. She didn't need telling. We had hours of grey to drive through yet.

Neither of us had ever seen a solarplane before, not even a picture of one. We'd heard they existed, but the use of such things was limited to the Centre, like all luxuries. Even the Mars rockets that went past my apartment were visible only in the contrails they left behind. We craned our necks at the window to get a look as soon as we were close to our destination.

The airport was on flat ground, miles from any Perimeter residences, and clear all the way to the coast. Any solarplane would be high enough above the Raft that it would be only a speck above the smog before any Perimeter postcode got a glimpse of it. I expected some security around it, but there was none. Why would there be? No Perimeter person would even think to come this far just to get a plane that had nowhere to go, let alone have the means to. The secrecy was enough.

Our jaws dropped as a solarplane came into view. A sleek, shiny structure, black and silver all over from the solar receptors. Long, elegant wings many times longer than its body. The underside was covered with the thin tubes of solar thrusters that would silently propel it through the skies. Beyond it were about a hundred more planes.

We stared, wide-eyed and awestruck. 'Why so many, Sav? No one ever leaves the Raft.'

'No one from the *Perimeter* ever leaves,' I said.

She gasped. 'You don't think ...?'

'Honestly, I've no idea. I have a feeling we're going to learn a lot on this trip, though.'

A member of staff had been assigned to look after us. He introduced himself as Jerome, a strong, sturdy hulk of a man, as tall and broad as any healthily raised Centre. As we climbed the steps to the plane, his gloved hand grabbed ours and hoisted us up the final ascent.

'Welcome aboard, ma'am,' he said to each of us.

His face was uncovered, and his skin was smooth and tanned. I doubted he'd ever tasted the ocean's salt. His posture was less sinister than most from the Centre. He kept his chin low and made eye contact with us. He had an openness about him and his smile was just that: a smile. Not a display of teeth worth more than my annual salary.

As we sat, Jerome handed us each a ruby-encrusted crystal glass and filled it with champagne. It tasted more divine than any of the fizz we could buy in the Perimeter. I closed my eyes in pleasure and let each drop circulate in my mouth.

The solarplane interior was a luxurious display of wealth unlike anything we could have expected. I felt grubby as I put my small tatty bag into the cupboard at the side. I didn't own a proper suitcase. Why would I? My bag had been one of Maisie's, unused for half a century. Amalyn had a large handbag – her 'overnight bag,' she called it. The zip was half broken from being overstuffed. She also had a shopping bag with its handles knotted to stop things from falling out.

There were six seats on the plane, but it was just Amalyn and me on board. Each reclining seat had its own luggage cupboard that would comfortably house a bag four times the size of mine. The floral-scented disinfectant was reassuring yet unobtrusive. Each surface shone from being buffed and polished until not a speck of dust remained. The spacious interior was lined with wood-effect panelling, bronze finishing and precious-stone detailing.

Amalyn was aghast. We said nothing to each other except 'Oh my' as we took in every inch of the place. Until:

'Excuse me, Jerome?' Amalyn asked in her sweetest, most innocent voice.

I knew that voice. It was the one she used on Archie when she wanted something. She also used it on me when she had forgotten something. Mischief is what it indicated.

'Yes, ma'am?'

'How many solarplanes fly each week?'

'I am not at liberty to discuss, ma'am.'

'Hmm, I see.' She sat back in her chair and pondered. After a moment, she let down her hair and pulled down her blouse a little. 'So, Jerome, how long have you worked on solarplanes?'

He looked at her, swallowed hard and attempted, somewhat unsuccessfully, to avert his eyes. 'Six years, ma'am.'

'Are you happy with your work?' She smiled as she licked her bottom lip.

'Very. Of course, ma'am.'

'Keep you busy, do they?'

'It's steady.'

She twiddled some hair around her little finger and looked up at him through her eyelashes. 'I'll bet you have some nice colleagues to hang out with?'

'The solarplane staff are all very professional, ma'am,' he said as he stood up straighter, his own professionalism starting to buckle.

I tutted at her. I knew exactly what she was getting at.

'So, Jerome, how come we're lucky enough to get you and not one of your colleagues?'

'Just good luck, ma'am.'

'Do you fly the plane too?'

'Just serve, ma'am.'

'And is this your favourite plane, or do you prefer one of the others? Are they all the same?'

'They are all slightly different. This is the one I'm appointed to most of the time.' His face was getting redder and redder.

She giggled the most girlish giggle I'd ever heard. 'Are any of the planes used more than the others? Has this one done more miles?'

Poor Jerome was trying his hardest to maintain eye contact

to be polite, but his eyes were easily distracted. He cleared his throat. 'I suspect they're all similar, ma'am.'

I interrupted. 'Thanks, Jerome. Give us a minute.' Visibly relieved, he gave me a nod and went into the sealed cabin. 'Amalyn, I know exactly what you are doing.'

She tied her hair up. 'So? Flirting is the only way to get Centre men to engage in conversation.'

'We're here representing BioLabs, remember?'

'Yeah, and the boss of BioLabs treats us like objects. I think I'm representing the company well.'

I rolled my eyes and started to wonder how much trouble Amalyn was going to be on this trip.

'I just want to know more,' she said. 'I mean, look out the window. A hundred of these things, easily, all with their own staff. So they must fly frequently. Let's say once a week, conservatively. That's one hundred trips to the Mainland, to other countries. A *week!* Why? What for? That's just crazy.'

I had to divert my own gaze as she readjusted her blouse. 'The reason we're here is to represent BioLabs,' I said, 'not figure out the logistics of the solarplane industry.'

'Oh, come on, Sav. I know you want to know. I mean, look!'

I glared at her and turned away. Of course I wanted to know, but in the past learning too much had proved to be a burden, not a blessing. I just wanted to do my job. There was no sense in trying to figure out the Centre, and definitely no point trying to change things.

'Knowing won't alter anything. It is what it is. Just be grateful you're here,' I said, a little too mumsy in my manner.

The plane rolled down the runway, picking up speed before taking off. I squeezed my eyes shut and my sweaty hands gripped my seat. When I looked again, we were in the air. It was so smooth and silent, I'd barely noticed the take-off. I leant in close to the window, and as I dared to breathe, my breath fogged up the glass. I wiped it clear and blinked a few times as the Raft hovered below.

Looking out the window, Amalyn got her first proper glimpse of the Centre as we soared above the gleaming, golden skyscrapers. She kept her mouth shut, but her wide eyes gave her away. The awe the city inflicts is inescapable. It glinted below us like the insides of the mussel shells littering the old docks. A swirling display of mother-of-pearl. All that extravagance fenced off, so close yet a world apart from the Perimeter.

As the plane flew over the acres upon acres of ArbAirs and SolaArbs, the contrast with the Perimeter was stark. I noticed Amalyn's shoulders fall heavily as her heart sank. The Perimeter was far from view, but we could make out the smog in the distance. The ring of blackness that enveloped the circumference of the Raft lurked far away, camouflaging the grey streets below it.

As we crossed the Raft's edge, I held my stomach as the sea came into view. Endless green sludge, thick with eutrophi-cation. The acidic currents spewed mists and sprayed the air with its acrid mess. The carcass of a sea beast, likely a whale creature, was bobbing pale and bloated on the surface. How it had survived long enough to grow that large, I had no idea.

'There are shutters to block the view, if you wish,' Jerome said, noticing my pallor.

'I'd rather see everything,' Amalyn said, and I agreed.

The sea went on and on. I saw another Raft, this one multicoloured. Miles and miles of bright plastic, a floating fossil from a century earlier. It left a trail like a comet, an aura of muck in the murk.

After a couple of hours, land came into view. It was the same as in the satellite pictures Archie had shown me over the years. A vast expanse of red, dust devils, smoke and ashes. I could just about make out scorched buildings and roads. No cities, no towns, just the embers of what used to be civilisation. In the distance, a raging river flowed, a torrent of angry brown water hacking through the desert, chopping the land in half.

'We'll be landing in a few moments. Please fasten your seatbelts,' Jerome said.

I looked at him. Surely I'd misheard. 'Seriously? Here?' *In this desert?*

'What land is this? What country are we in?' Amalyn asked.

'France, ma'am, in the south. The city that was once known as Toulouse.'

As the plane dipped lower, I saw the remnants of the old city. The gushing river had swept away bridges, but their towers still poked above the water. Sand whipped up into clouds, shielding our view intermittently, but where it settled lay relics of infrastructure, large buildings and patches of road. There was a burnt cathedral, its spire mournfully on its side, as charred as the earth below. Nothing else was recognisable, just the scorched shells of dwellings, a thick layer of dust dotted with orange sand.

'Is Greg dumping us in the desert to get rid of us?' Amalyn asked.

I laughed, but the fluttering in my stomach didn't find it funny.

The landing strip was dusty tarmac, its grey not visible until we were right on top of it and the plane blew the sand away. Amalyn and I closed our eyes for that part as landing safely seemed impossible. Despite the loose surface, the solarplane came to a smooth stop, and we began to breathe normally again.

'Welcome to France. Please make your way down the steps and continue swiftly on the staircase below. It's fifty-five degrees Celsius outside, so you must get below ground quickly. The plane needs to be in the air again in three minutes. We will collect you when we are summoned.'

Below ground?

He passed us our bags and we thanked him.

'Thank you for flying Solarplanes Progressives. We hope you enjoy your stay.'

He handed us each a dust mask and sprayed us with antiviral spray. When the plane doors opened, the heat hit me like a smack in the face. Each breath seared my lungs. We took the steps carefully, each one hotter than the last, the soles of my shoes beginning to melt against the metal. As we neared the bottom, a hatch in the ground slid open and another staircase appeared. The wind wasn't strong but was enough to blast sand and dust at us, tearing at our faces. I had my hand up to shield my eyes, but the sun was too dazzling to see where I was walking in any case. I had to search for and feel each step with my foot, and all the while Amalyn was pressing against my back, desperate to get out of the heat.

We inched down into the shadow, a hole into the unknown. The handrail was cool when we got below the trapdoor, and I was grateful to be able to steady myself, disorientated as I was. Amalyn entered after me, and as she cleared the trapdoor it slid shut with a loud clang.

We stood in the darkness, waiting for our eyes to adjust. Amalyn held my hand tightly as we waited, blind and nervous, readying ourselves to absorb it all. In the blackness, soft footsteps came tapping towards us, and resonating through the gloom I heard my name.

'Savannah? Is that you, Savannah?'

I squinted, forcing my eyes to adjust. A figure of a man came into view, just a shadow at first, but as my sight adapted some details came into focus. Fine stubble dotting his scalp and chin, simple clothing of sandals and an unfussy smock. He was bald, with a startled look as he lacked even eyebrows. His face was lined, wrinkles set deeply across his forehead and lips – worry rather than laughter lines.

'I can't believe it, Savannah. It really is you.'

I struggled to verbalise a response. Did I know this man? His face was smiling broadly, a recognition in his eyes that I knew mine lacked. I looked at Amalyn and she stared blankly back.

'It takes a while to adjust down here, but you're here, you're safe.' Another voice spoke, in a more formal tone, her accent like velvet. I began to see her outline through the darkness as she approached us behind the bald man. She was smaller and also bald. Her face was more sincere, and she grinned less than the man. She spoke again with an accent that made music from the words. 'I'm Sara, your escort. Here, I'll take your bags.'

'Savannah. It really is you,' the man said again, and this time he hugged me.

I stood rigid, unsure how to react to the unwelcome gesture, not wanting to be rude and certainly not wanting to recipro-cate. He pulled away suddenly.

'You don't know who I am, do you?' His face fell. The glinting light in his eye faded. 'You were a little girl when

I left. Just a girl. But it's me, your brother, Isaac.'

8

Chapter seven

The room spun as my dry mouth gasped for air. I pulled my dust mask down and inhaled, counting my breaths in and out, like the interns did on their panicked first day. Yet the room would not stay still. I reached for a wall and let the stone take my weight. The man in front of me looked nothing like the brother I remembered. We were never close. There was such an age gap between us. How many years had it been? Twenty, thirty, maybe? I remembered him as a teenager, vaguely, causing my parents grief. Shouts from all three of them when he arrived home late, didn't study as hard as he should, dated the wrong girl. In hindsight, I realised he'd been an Alternate, like my father. He also liked the insects, the filth, the vermin that plagued us. Despite their rows, he sympathised with my father's nature sickness. But he did not wallow as my father did. He watched our father sink into despair, stood over him as infection oozed from him. Then he ran.

I stared at him and, as my eyes adapted, I could see it. Those cheekbones, that high forehead, the slightly crooked nose I shared.

I said nothing. Words seemed out of reach. The scant fond memories I had of him had misted during the years apart. I'd been a child when he left. He'd fled Britain with his French wife and their child, before the anchors blew up, before the country became the Raft and started to drift. We never even knew if he'd made it. We saw so many who didn't, who left it too late, their bodies raining into the sea below. He left me alone with my mother to cope with her decline. His absence was the start of her malady, I believed. With her son and husband both gone, she gave up, any remaining joy extinguished. She withered away in remorse, the unknowing as bad as the knowing.

To see him now, I didn't know how I felt. Shocked was all. Just shocked.

'You made it, then. Across the bridge,' I said. The familiarity in his face was obscured by my nutritionist's vision. I saw vitamin D deficiency, vitamin E deficiency. I saw scurvy, the bowed stance of rickets.

'Yeah, we did. All the way down here, too. I wish I could have told you. I tried to get a message home, but it was impossible, you know.'

'I know.'

He had tears in his eyes now, like my father did every day towards the end. That shine of sadness was unmissable. I was too young to feel his loss back then. The anger didn't come until later, when I was abandoned, alone and hungry. I rid myself of it over the years and I prided myself on that. Such emotions were a waste of energy. Ambivalence was more productive, more manageable. Less painful.

'Sav, I wondered about you and Mum every day. I never thought I'd see you again.' He pulled me in for another hug, and this time I reciprocated. I didn't cry – I never do – but

I felt my body convulse and weaken under the strain of it all. Emotions were trying to return, knocking on my chest like it was a locked door.

I have a brother. I have family.

He pulled back and said the words I could see he was scared to ask. 'And Mum?'

I shook my head. 'She died not long after you left. The famine. She grew tired, then she just slipped away.'

He nodded. No doubt he already knew. He must have seen the state she was in when he'd left. How bad was she by then? I struggled to remember. At some point, she'd become a shell of her former self. She'd begun to hollow out years before that, though. The world had taken so much from her. Too much. Everything changed, and she hated it. Her soul had already surrendered; her body simply followed.

'I should have taken you with me. I wanted to – I suggested it – but Mum, she couldn't be without you, and she wouldn't leave. I had to think of my family, my daughter.'

'It's okay,' was all I could manage to say. His justifications weren't needed. I knew how he felt – of course I knew. My own family, Grace and Ethan, they'd always come first to me. I wanted to reassure him more, but my whole body was disorientated as I tried to form words. Instead, I made eye contact and smiled meekly.

'I've followed your career,' he said. 'Everyone here has. The breakthroughs you've made, what you've achieved. You're remarkable. You've done our parents proud. We both have. Wait till you see what we've done here. Come, let me show you.'

I looked at Amalyn, who had her hands clasped to her chest, her eyes wet with tears. 'My god, Sav, can you believe this?'

I didn't reply. Most words were still beyond reach. We followed Isaac through the tunnel. It was dimly lit with sporadic bulbs that buzzed and came on as we approached. The air felt damp and cool, and smelled musty, like what I had imagined dirt would smell like. I suddenly felt very exposed. Weren't we supposed to have protective clothing? We'd been sprayed, but that was all. I was expecting hazmat suits, proper respiratory equipment. Had these people even been sanitised? As my balance steadily returned, I kept away from the walls, my hands in my pockets.

My unease must have been obvious. 'It's okay,' Isaac said. 'You've had your bloods and swabs done, I assume? If you passed that, there won't be anything here that can harm you. We have the same vaccines as you.'

I looked at the walls made of dirt and opted to keep my hands where they were, and give them a wide berth. There were no street sprayers here, no smell of bleach. My skin tingled as if dirt was jumping off the walls and onto me. I swallowed back my worries. *It must be fine. They wouldn't send us here if it wasn't.*

The tunnel ended and opened out onto a vast chamber. Amalyn and I stood and stared, dumbstruck. Staircases encompassing the sides led to mezzanine floors that had more corridors leading to more chambers, all carved into the earth and rock, orange walls and flooring and roofs, with ornate detailing up the banisters and supporting columns underneath. Beams of light came from high up in the domed ceiling over the central chamber. Ventilation tunnels dotted the ceiling, ladders following them up. It all looked so familiar. I had seen this design before. My father. *He* had seen this design before.

'Termites,' I said.

Isaac looked my way and smiled. 'I knew you'd know.'

In sheer awe, I only managed to whisper my reply. 'Dad always spoke about them, about the great structures they built.'

'To regulate the airflow and temperature. He taught me everything I know,' Isaac said, inhaling deeply, a look of pride blossoming. 'He wrote a book on them that I took with me. That's how we've been able to live down here. All from Dad's knowledge of termites.'

We just stood for a while, trying to take it all in.

'We had no idea. We thought there was no one left, that everyone had died with the fires,' I said.

'How big is it?' asked Amalyn.

'Hundreds of kilometres. Thousands of chambers connected by tunnels. Entire cities were moved underground. Come on, let's go have a drink and I'll tell you all about it.'

We loaded our bags into a trailer and Sara pedalled a bicycle attachment at the front. She also wore the same sandals and smock, which she hitched up as she took her seat. Amalyn and I sat in the trailer while Isaac escorted us down a great corridor on his own bicycle. The bikes screeched and creaked like nails scratching render.

'Not much oil around here, I'm afraid,' Isaac said, pointing at components thick with rust, redder than the dirt.

The corridor was several metres high and wide, wider than any residential street in the Perimeter. After a few minutes, we arrived at another great chamber, even more impressive than the last. The walls and banisters had been painstakingly carved to create intricate detailing depicting what the world had once looked like above, the skylines and technology, even *plants*. One carving of a tree was repeated often, its branches reaching skywards, like it was rising up. A hollow eye in the middle of its trunk, watching always. I recoiled from it. So many images of filth, reminding me we were in a city made of dirt.

Amalyn grabbed my hand. 'Bloody hell, Sav, can you actually believe this?'

'I know, Ams. I know.'

'No wonder the satellite views don't show anything. It's just insane.'

'Incredible.'

We cycled across a mezzanine balcony overlooking the heart of the chamber until the road opened out into a square furnished with rock-carved tables and chairs. Strewn across benches were soft cushions, their fabrics alive with colour, all with the same tree-and-eye design. We got off the trailer and Isaac beckoned us to a table. We sat, and he boiled a kettle.

I watched him turn on a plug socket and harness the electricity. 'How do you get power?' I asked.

'Nuclear reactors. Each city has a couple. We tried to use solar more at first, but the solar fields burnt down with everything else. We rebuilt them, but with the dust and ash, they get covered too quickly. It's too hot to go up and clear them.'

I nodded as I looked across the chamber and saw other people walking and cycling around each floor, all bald, all busy.

'How many people live here?'

'Across our tunnels, about twenty million.'

'*Twenty million!*' Amalyn and I said in unison.

Twice that of the Raft, all living underground. Of course, the Centre had us believe that the Raft's population was over ten times higher, allowing them to boast about how successful their control and authority had been. But twenty million in the south of France alone took my breath away. A viable population. The Raft was not the last stronghold of humankind. The Raft was not the last great country on earth, as the Blue Libs claimed. I added that one to the pile of lies.

'And all twenty million live underground like this?' Amalyn asked.

'Yep, in the South here, anyway. Our tunnels stretch to Spain and Italy, their northern regions, and they're spreading further south. Northern France, not sure. There's maybe half that number again, is my best guess. When the temperatures went crazy high, loads of people migrated north to escape it, but from what I understand, that relief didn't last long. They started building tunnels, but they're decades behind. It's too hot for them to make the journey here, sadly. But our tunnel system is growing. We're still digging. We hope to meet them one day. It's possible for us to take more people in, if they can get here. We have room to spare.'

'Room to spare,' Amalyn repeated. 'Blimey.'

I looked at Isaac's stooped legs, pale skin and arched back. He wasn't in the worst shape. Certainly some people in the Perimeter appeared less healthy. But living underground at least explained his obvious vitamin D deficiency.

'What about Sofia? And Clementine?' I asked, remembering his wife and child.

His face fell. 'Sofia died just two years ago.'

'Oh, I'm so sorry.'

'It was an accident. Just an accident, that's all. She climbed up one of the ladders to the chimney to clear the glass. We do that job several times a day. Everyone does it occasionally.

She'd done it a thousand times before. But her safety clip wasn't attached properly ...' His voice trailed off. I watched his eyes mist with remorse, the distant stare of my mother replicated in him. 'But we had a lovely life together. She was so happy to be with her family when we made it here. And Clem, well, she's thirty-four now.'

'Thirty-four! I can only think of her as a baby.'

He laughed. 'She was quite a madam during her teenage years, but she's a fine woman now. She works in the chamber over that way.' He pointed towards a corridor. 'You'll meet her soon enough.'

He poured us drinks and sat at the table. With all of us still, no bumpy, screeching bikes, I took a breath and enjoyed a sense of calm. I sat back in my chair, my shoulders relaxed. The slightest draught swept around me, relieving me of some of my sweat. I felt more comfortable than I had in a long time.

'Oh gosh, I'm so rude. This is Amalyn, by the way,' I said.

He smiled and nodded at her. 'You work with Sav?'

'Yes, I'm honoured to. Her work is quite legendary on the Raft. She's fed the whole country.'

I blushed at hearing her say it. I couldn't recall her ever saying anything like that to me. There were too many jokes between us and Archie to allow for honest compliments.

'I know,' Isaac said. 'We've been after her technology for years. The Raft has kept it quite the secret. Food is the area we've struggled with. We make enough usually. Just. But poor quality. Our nutrition isn't great.'

'But you've built *this!*' Amalyn said, opening her arms wide to the immense space. 'I mean, how did you manage it?'

'The digging was already under way when I arrived. It wasn't the government that started it; it was the rich. They had dug miles and miles of burrows by the time I got here. Nuclear bunkers at first, but the threat changed and they expanded. Billionaires foresaw what was coming and paid for these tunnels, but their planning was wrong – they knew that. They built dark, damp corridors, and that was it. They didn't know about thermoregulation or airflow. Just rich idiots throwing money at a problem the rest of the world refused to acknowledge. I heard about the project and got a job with them as soon as I got here, using what I knew about termites. It cost hundreds of billions. The governments didn't want to know. They kept saying it won't get that bad, it's too expensive to fix, blah blah blah.'

I nodded along. Yep, we knew that attitude too well. Governments around the world buried their heads in the dirt.

'The storm warnings were ignored,' he continued. 'Rising temperatures, the floods, the fires – no one did anything. No government wanted to pay. Then, when temperatures really escalated, it all happened so quickly. It went from getting a bit warmer to full-blown drought and desert in the space of a decade. That was all around the time I left Britain. People fled, or came here. Salvation, that's what the Tunnels offered. The financiers knew. Because they didn't have to win votes or appeal to the public purse, they just did it. They built all of this. They saved us. So the cities and towns are now owned by the families that built them. We work, pay, all contribute. We get by. You should see their chambers, their supplies. I mean, you think this is jaw-dropping, you should see theirs!'

'Sounds much like the Raft,' Amalyn said. 'The Centre live in lavish luxury, the rest of us struggle in squalor.'

'Don't say such things!' Isaac snapped. 'The Select saved us. If it hadn't been for them, we would have burnt to a crisp up there. We're grateful. We owe them everything. They gave us everything that matters. We have jobs. We have no complaints.'

'Wow,' Amalyn said. 'Sorry. I didn't mean—'

'Watch what you say,' he said, with dark eyes and eyebrows raised. 'We're lucky – so lucky. To be alive is all we could have hoped for. Yet we have more than that. We have jobs, income. We have everything we need.'

The sudden icy atmosphere did away with some of my comfort. I shivered as I sipped the drink Isaac had made and almost spat it out. It tasted like filth, like dirt.

'Probably not what you're used to,' he said, warmly again, noticing my expression. 'Our food here, it's basic, you know. That's why we're so excited to have you here. We've been hoping for this opportunity for years. We've been trading with the Raft, of course, but selling our fabrics, materials and metals. All the time we've been asking to buy food. Now, finally, they said okay.'

'Wait, hang on,' Amalyn held up her hand. 'You've been trading with the Raft for *years?*'

'Yes, of course. The materials and the fabric we make.'

'Well, that certainly explains a lot. The Centre. *The fucking Centre.*'

I shot her a look. Why did she always have to be so outspoken?

Just then, a whistle blew, and Isaac stood up. A woman pedalling a carriage along the balcony approached our seating area. The carriage was unlike the trailer Amalyn and I had ridden on. It had a slanted roof topped with gemstones and was cloaked with multicoloured fabrics. The woman pedalling stopped in front of us and stepped off the bicycle, before turning and bowing towards the carriage. Isaac didn't move, and just stared straight ahead. After some moments, a woman emerged from the carriage, long auburn hair flowing to her waist, her whole body draped in fine fabrics. Layers of ornamental silks adorned every inch of her. Her skin was flushed pink, looking radiant with health. She walked slowly in pretty cloth slippers, her posture straight, each step gentle on what seemed to be sacred ground. Isaac bowed as she approached.

'Isaac. A pleasure as always.' She smiled at him with soft lips framing a mouth full of Centre-quality teeth. 'And you ladies must be the two food scientists from the Raft. A pleasure.'

We both stood up and ducked our heads in an awkward version of Isaac's bow. After a few seconds, Isaac righted himself.

'Presenting Lady of Toulouse Chiara Monet.'

'*Enchanté*,' Amalyn said.

'A French speaker! *Magnifique*.' Lady Monet clasped her hands together. 'But English is fine. It's good for us to practise. You'll find everyone in the Toulouse Tunnels speaks a mixture of English, French, Italian and Spanish. Use whichever language you like.'

'*Oui? Merci*,' Amalyn said, looking somewhat crestfallen.

Lady Monet stood tall. Her complexion was clear and radiant, with none of the signs of malnutrition that the others showed. Her hair was glossy, rich in keratin and vitamin E.

'So, the famous Savannah Selbourne,' she addressed me. 'Are you really Isaac's younger sister?'

'Yes, so it seems. Though it's been a few years.'

'Marvellous, simply marvellous. Genius really runs in the family. Isaac, why don't we all take a ride to the larders and show our guests what we've been struggling with.' Her accent was as soft as silk.

We got back in the bike trailer, bumping and squeaking along the corridors with Isaac alongside, following Lady Monet's carriage. Our transport was a ramshackle affair made of plastic and aluminium struts with thin cushions for seats. Lady Monet's was bedecked with detailed cloth and soft furnishings, veiled to conceal its contents.

As we entered the next chamber, the whistle blew again and every person, all of them bald, stood to attention as we passed.

'Why are they all bald?' Amalyn whispered to me. I shrugged a reply.

A few chambers later, we arrived at the larder, rows of cupboards that were buzzing like dodgy electrical cables. Next to them were more cupboards with open tops from which light escaped. The room was hotter than the rest of the tunnels we had passed through, but when I touched the cupboard doors, they felt cold.

'Don't! Don't touch anything. Be careful,' Isaac said.

I snatched my hand back.

'Welcome to our larder. Well, one of many.' Lady Monet alighted and held her arms up to the cupboards. 'This is how we keep the masses fed down here. Not quite what you're used to on the Raft, but I think you can look in wonder at what we have achieved.' Her face was beaming with a smile. We reciprocated with a nod.

Isaac opened the first cupboard door, and Amalyn and I shrieked. We retreated and gagged, shielding our eyes from the view. It was lined with vast glass cages, hundreds of them. Their contents were moving, alive. *No!* Each one was filled with filth, dirt and thousands upon thousands of crawlers. *No!*

It can't be!

'It's okay, Sav,' Isaac said. 'We're familiar with the misconceptions on the Raft, but I promise it's quite safe. Insects don't carry any diseases.'

'Oh god, no, I can't look. The filth!' I said. I couldn't hold back. Where manners should have been, I found nothing but fear and vomit. How could he say such things? Of course they were riddled with disease! The drink we'd swallowed earlier crept its way back up my throat.

Amalyn kept her cool, but she was shaking and pale. She put an arm around me. I couldn't tell if it was to support me or herself.

Isaac continued to open more cupboards, revealing more and more creepers, crawlers, filth and vermin. Each cupboard was infested with the hideous things from my father's book. Locusts, snails, crickets, some grotesque things I couldn't recognise but that had too many legs. Millions and millions of horrible bugs living in squalid filth.

How could they? How have they survived?

The next cupboard was filled with greenery growing in muck. 'Food for the insects,' Isaac said. 'And vegetables for us.'

Vegetables! Actual dirt-grown vegetables!

Amalyn and I withdrew to the back of the corridor, where our legs gave way and we sank to the floor.

Isaac walked over. If our reaction offended him, he hid it well. 'It really is quite safe. The Raft's teachings are strange. There is no disease here with the insects.'

I looked at his face, listened to his voice. It was like my father was coming back to haunt me. His environmental dementia had manifested in my brother.

Lady Monet paid no attention to our reaction. 'As you can

see, we have viable protein sources, but our vitamins ... well, that's tricky. We're thrilled that the Raft is willing to share their food. I believe you have some samples?'

I tried to speak but the words grated my throat, and my voice shrivelled into nothing. *Viable protein? It's vermin!*

'It's okay, Sav,' Isaac spoke softly, the way I do when Ethan has had a nightmare. 'You're here to help, remember? We've survived, but we need your input to take us further.'

I looked at his thin face, his gaunt cheeks, his darkly framed eyes. It was hard to muster sympathy when my insides were screaming, *How could you? How could you?*

I looked around at the termite-style city. Living like bugs, *eating* bugs. How my father would have loved it. How often he'd said the bugs should be saved. But to be consumed, ingested. To be idolised? That was too much to take in.

'This last one,' Isaac said as he walked to the final cupboard in the row, 'is a particular favourite of mine.'

I braced myself, held my breath and kept my back against the wall. Amalyn, next to me, buried her face in my shoulder. Isaac opened the door and showed us. And then I threw up on the floor.

'Sea filth! Oh, no, no!' I cried through retches, and covered my eyes.

Memories flashed before me of when I saw that fish carcass in my freezer at home, its cloudy eyes staring at me. The stench of it. Chunks of flesh removed, consumed by Grace, who had sunk so low in her depression, the antidepressants concentrated in the corpse helping her where I had failed. That memory still haunted me. And now there were tanks and tanks of filthy molluscs. Even the word 'mollusc' sounded like the noise vomit makes as it slithers out of your throat. I heaved some more.

Amalyn perked up, however. She rubbed my back but seemed much calmer. 'What sort of drugs are you harvesting? Opioids? Stimulants?' she asked.

Isaac's face changed, like he'd been blasted by a gale-force wind. 'Drugs? No, it's just food.'

'Eurgh,' Amalyn's shocked pallor returned. 'Oh, that's gross, then.'

Lady Monet walked back to her carriage. 'Isaac, Sara, why don't you take our guests to their room? They can freshen up, get some rest, and we can talk more tomorrow.'

Sara and Isaac lifted us by our elbows, encouraging us back to the bike trailer. I slumped in the seat, its lack of comfort no longer bothering me. We rode for I don't know how long until we came to a room with twin beds and an adjacent bathroom. It was lit by a couple of electric bulbs in the corner. The temperature was a marvel. Cool air circulated continuously, taking some of my nausea away.

Isaac and Sara left us, our exhaustion obvious, and bid us goodnight. Dinner would be brought to our rooms if we were hungry.

After covering ourselves in antibacterial gel, we collapsed onto a bed each, silent, shocked and still. After some time, there was a knock at the door and someone came in. I neither looked up nor made a sound in response, but after they'd gone I saw they had left a tray with a bowl of stuff for each of us. Food – that's probably what they would have called it. It looked like grainy mush. Insects, filth, vermin. Crushed and mashed into a disgusting mulch. Amalyn looked at her bowl and then at me. We both shook our heads before lying back down and going straight to sleep.

9

Chapter eight

An orange glow was filtering through my eyelids. The damp, musty air made me believe I was still dreaming, and the pleasant breeze made me think I was at the MindSpa. Then I opened my eyes and saw that I was actually stuck in some nightmare. I was like a filthy worm living underground. A tunnel in the dirt. Sitting up, I saw Amalyn already awake. She was staring at the trays of muck still on the floor.

'I don't want to get out of bed. I don't want to be near that … that *stuff.*'

I composed myself and wiped sleep from my eyes. 'Just don't look at it. It can't crawl out of the bowls.'

'Can't it? Are you sure?'

'Sure,' I said, my voice wobbling with uncertainty.

After a few minutes of staring at the 'food,' I felt confident it wouldn't spring back to life and slither off its tray. Despite the view of the filth, my stomach growled. Amalyn heard it and snapped round to look at me.

'You're not …?'

'No way! No chance. I'm not *that* hungry.'

She jumped up and reached for her bag. 'We have BioLabs food samples.'

'Microbes!' I cursed. 'Why didn't we bring more?'

'We have a few to spare. I reckon we can survive on them for a few days.'

We sorted a couple of no-cook packets each. VitaBiscuits, FakeyFruits and IsoBakes. It wasn't much, and we had no idea how long we'd be there, but we'd need the rest for our sales pitch so we couldn't take more. We ate one each and stored a couple of others under our pillows.

We left our room, carefully dodging the trays of minced filth on the floor, and were struck once again at the magnificence of the place. The orange rock had been sculpted with time-consuming beauty, functionality bonding with aesthetics. The engravings continued everywhere, the tree with its eye, breaking up the monotony of the colour into never-ending designs and pictures. Clearly we were in a residential wing of the Tunnels. The whole balcony was lined with oval doors, each ornately inscribed with the name of its inhabitant. Brass fixtures bejewelled the sides of the doors, a glimmer of sheen against the matte. Above, like in the other chambers, there was a high, domed ceiling with ladders leading up to windows above.

A hustle and bustle resonated up from downstairs. Chatter, movement, plates tinkering. We followed the noise. Isaac and Sara were in the dining hall and stood to greet us. Sat among the rows and rows of table were other people with shaved heads, wearing the same plain tunics. They all stared for a moment, their curiosity breaking their conversations. We tried not to gawk back and approached the tables once their conversation resumed.

Sara stood next to me and leant in to speak softly. 'Lice. In case you're wondering, we shave to remove the lice.'

I tried to disguise my involuntary shudder. My hair bristled against my scalp, and my skin itched across my shoulders. *Lice!* How awful!

Isaac took hold of my wrist. 'Sav, come with me. Come sit with us.'

My arm was rigid under the softness of his grasp. 'I don't know if I can—'

'It's fine. Don't be shy.'

But it wasn't shyness. It was the plates of food, the sludge, the churned-up filth they were chewing.

'Here,' he said. 'Come meet her.'

As we approached the table, a woman stood up, smiled and pulled me in for a crushing hug. I hesitated before returning the sharing of body warmth, then realised who she was.

'Aunt Sav, I've heard so much about you.'

'Clementine?' I pulled back and looked at her. I thought I'd forgotten what her mother had looked like, but when I saw Clementine, I remembered. The same cheekbones, large blue eyes and little ears that stuck out a bit. 'Gosh. You were just a baby. Now look at you. As beautiful as your mother.' She dipped her head, and her smile sank. 'I'm sorry. I didn't mean to upset you,' I said.

'It's fine, really. I like to remember her.'

'Clem, let her sit down,' Isaac said, and Clementine led me to the table.

The plates of food were mostly finished by now. A few people were still chewing and I tried to block them out, leaning on my elbow and using my hand to shield the view. Talking helped to drown out the noise of teeth chomping on vermin, and as long as I didn't look directly at the plates it was possible to cope. I told them about Grace, our life together, and of course about Ethan, his gorgeous curls and infectious laugh. I told them about our apartment. My work, the infusion, anything and everything to dim the background noise.

I kept talking and talking until I was sure that everyone had finished eating. Then, when I couldn't think of anything else to say, I paused. The empty plates were still there. Luckily, Amalyn was sitting with us with the same neck-tilt as me, keeping her gaze fixed away from the plates. She had been silent while I rattled on, hands fidgeting and crossing and uncrossing her legs.

When they asked what life was like on the Raft, I chose my words carefully. Amalyn, as usual, did not. 'The Centre control everything. Where you live, if you can have children, what resources you have. They deny you healthcare if you don't do a job they approve of.'

Clementine, Isaac and others in earshot looked at each other, a silent conversation passing between them, one I wasn't able to decipher.

Amalyn elbowed me in the ribs. 'What the hell?' she mouthed at me. I scowled at her and shook my head. She shouldn't be speaking so curtly.

'But at least we don't have to shave our heads,' she laughed.

'That's one good thing about the Raft,' I said. 'No lice.'

Isaac half-smiled, then he and the others stood. 'I think it's about time for you to come and meet with Lady Monet and the rest of the Select. They're keen to try the samples you brought.'

I clutched Amalyn's hand as we followed. 'We're here representing the Raft, remember?' I whispered. 'Keep a lid on it.'

'This place is weird, though, right?'

'We live on a concrete Raft, Ams. Everything is weird.'

We walked along further elaborate balconies, the sun piercing through ceiling windows and casting spotlights onto the orange rock. The dancing light reminded me of euphoric nights in bars with Archie and Amalyn. The warm glow welcomed us from one chamber to the next.

There were no other people in sight, but the sound of humming and scuffling resonated quietly. Wherever the rest of the people were, they were busy.

'The tunnels echo,' Sara said, as if reading my thoughts. 'The acoustics are strange. There's no one in this chamber or the next. They're all working on the farms, power stations and factories, but the sound carries for miles.' Each r she uttered rolled like she was blowing bubbles.

'Dad would have loved it,' Isaac continued. 'Thermoregulation of termite mounds he knew all about, but the acoustics he never predicted. It would have helped, though, right? If a predator came to attack the termites. The sound travelling would have been a good early-warning system.'

I was still holding Amalyn's hand and the sweat between our palms was building. Isaac was right. Dad would have loved it. Dad loved everything filthy and creepy. He'd never accepted the modern world. I looked at Isaac, Sara and Clementine, and was shocked I hadn't realised it before. Embracing nature, eating filth like it was normal, the skin contact they all partake in, hugging frequently ...

They're Alternates, all of them!

On the Raft, they would have been demonised for such behaviours. Sterility warnings being ignored like that were a cause for outrage. But here, in the Tunnels, such disregard for modern thinking was habitual. Desperation had led them to this, I was sure. If they'd had sterile food, they wouldn't need to be so unclean.

We arrived at a lounge area consisting of a few chairs around a large round table. Soft cushions and blankets were scattered untidily across the place, adding some disorder to the solid immobile furniture. Isaac set about arranging a projector screen while I plugged in my laptop and got my presentation ready. Amalyn assisted me in laying out the samples neatly, heating on a portable stove the ones that needed cooking. Savoury first, then sweet. We eased into work mode, professionalism overtaking our anxieties. Among the rocks and strange people and echoes, in charge of things, I suddenly felt relaxed and at home.

Just as we had everything prepared, carriages arrived. Out stepped Lady Monet, looking every bit as decorative as she had the day before. Again, we copied Isaac's bow as best we could, and she introduced us to the rest of the Select. The Select, I assumed, were their equivalent of the Centre Elite. They all had the same long, glossy hair, glowing skin and confident stride. A rainbow of shrouds and elegant fabrics were draped on their bodies and carriages. Unlike the Centre Elite, though, they looked straight at us, concerned eyes boring into ours. They smiled sweetly, nodded courteously at our clumsy bows, and we all sat down.

I cleared my throat. 'We have perfected food synthesis on the Raft. Complete vitamin and mineral content, in a variety of flavours and textures that mimic the styles of old-world food. Here.' We passed round the samples. 'Roast potatoes, carrots, fruity snacks, some confectionery even. The IcyCrema is particularly popular on hot days. Spaghetti in sauce, my son's favourite. And some mixed syntho vegetable chunks. All completely balanced and healthy.'

They all set about inspecting the packets and reaching for cutlery. Isaac noticed my name on the Selbourne Range and looked at me with pride. As they ate, the 'oohs' and 'ahs' were plentiful. I smiled. I knew it was good. Judging from what I'd seen so far, they hadn't tasted anything that good in decades.

Amalyn smiled along with them. 'All completely sterile when packaged, free of all bacteria and pathogens.'

'What about the good bacteria?' Lady Monet asked. 'The bacteria important for digestion and suchlike. Bacteria have a lot of important roles.'

I swallowed, stifling my revulsion. These people were prehistoric to think in such ways. If they still considered bacteria important, these tunnels must be crawling with them. I tried to find my voice as my mouth dried. 'There is no such thing in our line of work. All bacteria are bad or have the potential to be so. We have rid ourselves of them. We are aware that it is impossible to be completely free of bacteria, and some sneak through despite our best attempts to block them, but we do the best we can to eliminate, to purify, and we certainly do not require any extra.'

Murmurs rose around the table, quick glances, surprised whispers.

Lady Monet spoke up again. 'But bacteria are everywhere. Surely, the land you live on, any vegetation—'

I held up my hand to silence her. 'There is no vegetation on the Raft. The paved land is sprayed liberally with disinfectant throughout the day. There is not a single leaf, nor a single insect. There is not a grain of filth on the Raft.'

She looked at me with wide, surprised eyes. They had no clue regarding the advancements we had made, the progress. The filth we had eradicated.

'Everyone is safe now,' I said. 'The Great Sterilisation Project ensured that our land is clean and hospitable only for humans, as it should be. No filth, no vermin. We haven't had a disease outbreak in decades. With sterility comes liberty.'

Amalyn gave a little cheer. I knew the other meaning of the Great Sterilisation Project. She did not. My inner conflict was mine alone. But despite the project's more secretive side – to control breeding, to allow infertility to be the norm so *they* could choose who has a child – the foundations of the project were sound. Clean, pathogen free, the project had rid us of disease and filth, and those principles I stood by.

I handed Lady Monet an envelope that Greg had given me. It was sealed, of course, no doubt detailing the finances of the deal. She took it and placed it within one of her cloth coverings.

'Well, that was delicious, and I think I speak for everyone when I say how impressed we are at the advances you have made. Professor Selbourne, your notoriety here is not mis-placed.' Lady Monet beamed. 'Why don't we give our guests a tour of all our industries here? They have wowed us, now let us wow them. Show them how wonderfully resourceful we are and demonstrate the scale of our global trade.'

Amalyn nudged me. 'Global trade?' she mouthed.

I looked away quickly, wishing she would be more subtle.

We took bikes and trailers across more chambers and corri-dors, the echoes of workers growing steadily louder. Nothing clear, just mottled sound, like whispers on the wind intermin-gled with clunking machinery and scratching bikes. Electric bulbs switched on ahead as we travelled along the corridors, a welcoming entrance that instantly darkened after we passed.

Clementine, Sara and Isaac showed us several great rooms that smelled even mustier than the rest of the city. The first high-ceilinged room had walls lined with shelves upon shelves housing what looked like white fluff, perhaps nylon medical swabs, shabbily made and untidily packed. The breeze was only light, and the air left a stale taste in my mouth. We walked around the room, nodding, before wandering into the next room, where reels were spinning thread. Cylinders thickly encircled with the white stuff were piled in the corners. Tons of it. Then we realised they were making silk, from actual *worms*. Amalyn and I both recoiled and stepped back until we found the wall and leant against it, our knees unable to fully support us.

How close we had been to that fluff, to those creatures!

And all those fabrics, everything the Select were wearing, were made from worm shit. Suddenly, their fine fabrics looked like nothing more than sewage.

Heat surged up my neck to my face. My meagre breakfast was inching its way back up, wriggling up my throat like it was one of the awful worms. Amalyn's complexion was sallow and wet with perspiration. She tied her hair up high and shivered from the slight touch of a strand on her shoulders as I pushed my own from my face. It was as if my whole skin was crawling.

'We weave the silk into recycled fabrics,' Sara said, not noticing or ignoring our revulsion, 'making old material stretch three times further and finishing to a far higher quality. Our fabrics are sold all over Europe to other fashion houses, but mostly those on the Raft. I understand you have multiple clothing stores selling our fabrics.'

'*Clothing stores?*' Amalyn choked on a laugh.

Sara stared at us, her brow furrowed with confusion.

I felt bile stinging my throat. 'Where we live, in the Perimeter, we are not privy to such finery,' I said.

'Ah, right,' Sara said. 'Well, on we go.' She beckoned us back onto our bike trailers and we continued, the bumpiness of the ride doing little to settle my stomach. I was glad we weren't in one of the fancy carriages, though. Touching those cloths would definitely have seen me lose the battle to keep my breakfast down.

We arrived at other factories, much cleaner and cooler installations, allowing my nausea to subside. They showed us a nuclear reactor in one far corner of the tunnel system, where the coolest air could circulate. Water was pumped from the flooded river above to add to the cooling system, and the rocky walls were lined with dozens of computer screens giving readouts of data.

'Archie would love this,' Amalyn said.

There were more chambers where they upcycled and mined metals for other cities – the Raft again, primarily, and just for the Centre, we assumed. Precious metals and stones were piled in their thousands, mostly pilfered from above before the fires came.

'And all of this is sold to richer nations?' I asked as I craned my neck to see to the top of a nearby pile.

'Yes, of course,' Sara said. 'The Raft is our main customer, or was. A lot of our most valued products are being flown to Mars now. We have far more than we need, and the trade helps to pay for our food and labour costs here.'

'But all of this stuff is worth billions,' Amalyn said, to which she received no response. Our wide-eyed stares made our surprise obvious. Never in a million years had we imagined such large-scale productions.

We meandered down more corridors, more balconies, more chambers. We passed two huge doors side by side that were closed off.

'What's in there?' Amalyn asked.

Sara cleared her throat and paused a moment before answering. 'In there ... well, the Raft asked us not to show you in there. They said it would offend you.'

'Unlikely,' Amalyn said. 'It can't be any worse than worm shit and vermin.'

I elbowed her in the ribs and she tutted back at me.

'Stop the bike,' she said. 'Let us see.'

The trailer came to a stop, and I stepped out to inspect the doors.

'Sav,' Isaac called after me.

'What?'

He didn't respond. His face looked pained. I dismissed his awkwardness and moved closer to the doors. Among the usual carvings and tree-eye designs were inscribed the words 'Donna's Library'.

'Donna?' I said to Isaac. 'As in our mum?'

'It was a silly request of mine to name the library after her. But you know how she loved books.'

'Wait.' I held up a hand, processing what he had said. 'You have *books* here? As in fiction?'

Sticky fingers on deceased tree flesh, is what I meant. 'Books' sounded too blithe.

Isaac nodded. 'All the greats. The other door is our gallery. Paintings, mostly. We didn't manage to save many sculptures.'

Amalyn screwed her face up. She was too young to remember

such trivialities. 'What's the point? Seems like a waste of space.'

Sara failed to hide her shock. 'Well, it's good for the mind, you see. It's calming to look at paintings and to read. Plus, it's our history, our culture.'

'We have the MindSpas for that,' Amalyn said. 'Do you guys not have those? You listen to swishing noises and little beeping sounds. Works wonders after a stressful day.'

Isaac looked at me, his hands held to his chest. 'I'm not sure why they thought it would offend you, but I'm sorry if it does.'

I shrugged a reply. I wasn't offended. It just seemed odd, that was all. A waste of precious space and resources.

'When the other people from the Raft come here, they often spend hours in the library and gallery, sometimes even trading pieces—'

'Wait,' Amalyn interrupted. 'Centre people come here and go in there?' She gestured at the doors. 'What about the germs? Books are just old tree carcasses, aren't they? Riddled with germs.'

'The Centre people don't seem concerned with that,' Sara said. 'They visit very frequently. Most weeks we have a group or two. None this week, though. You are our special guests.'

'So, what is "Alternate" for a Perimeter resident is "cultured" for the Centre,' Amalyn said.

'Come on, Ams,' I said, and linked her arm with mine. 'There's lots more to see.'

She gripped my arm tightly as we walked back to the bikes and muttered, 'The Centre. The fucking Centre!' to herself.

We made our way down another corridor, through another chamber, the dusky orange light giving the place an ethereal glow. As appalling as the whole setup was, I couldn't help but be impressed. The light coming through high portal windows danced across the chamber. Up ladders, people were cleaning the sand from the windows and scrubbing the glass. Below, several people were organising materials into piles, laughing as they worked. Some cycled past us, their trailers loaded with supplies for other chambers. Everyone was helping, talking, interacting in ways so rarely seen on the Raft.

'What's in those books, Sav? Why don't the Centre want us to see them?' Amalyn whispered to me.

'I don't know. Books aren't any worse than the filth they've shown us. My mum used to read fiction. It was just silly stories and rhyming words.'

'Your mum was an Alternate too? I thought it was just your dad.'

'They weren't Alternates. Not really. And that word wasn't used back then. She was an English-literature scholar.'

'It's a wonder you turned out so normal.'

After a few more minutes on a balcony, we came to another large door, even larger than the one for the gallery. Sara jumped off the trailer to stand in front of it.

'And here is our central bank.' They actually had a *bank* in the Tunnels. 'A busy industry now, with our currency changeover.'

'Currency changeover?' I asked.

'Euros have been the currency for well over a century. It's time for a more modern approach. A new currency, martas, has been announced, and all old currency in the Tunnels has now been discontinued. The proceeds of the changeover are going to fund our nation's tickets to Mars.'

Mine and Amalyn's ears pricked up at the news.

'Mars? You lot are going to Mars?' Amalyn asked.

'It's our honour to work and help send our saviours to the great unknown. Their Excellencies take the pride of our nation with them,' Sara said. Isaac and Clementine, almost silent throughout this part of the tour, nodded along.

'So ... just the Select?' Amalyn asked.

'For now, of course. We couldn't be happier for them.'

Amalyn shot me a look, and I shook my head. *Keep your mouth shut.* I saw her lips twitching, her mind in torment, her inner rebel desperate to be heard. I shook my head again and scowled at her.

As we approached another chamber, the clang of machinery and shuffle of manual labour became louder. The vibrations of bashing rocks tingled my toes. Hordes of people were digging, lugging rock and pickaxing boulders with old-fashioned tools. The methods appeared inefficient given the amount of machinery in the rest of the Tunnels. As we paused to watch, I noted the workers' doubled-over stances, sagging skin and drooping faces. All of them were old, disabled and frail.

'This is the honour of the Undead,' Sara said. 'For years, the frail and elderly were left to boredom. Now, with our Mars ambitions, the great vacation for our excellent leaders, they have found purpose, in digging ore to earn a good wage, to change into martas. So we can say "bon voyage" to Their Excellencies. Everyone is useful here.'

'Everyone is useful here,' Isaac and Clementine repeated.

A chill fizzed up my spine. The motto was so reminiscent of the Raft's 'Everyone is safe now.' Yet somehow, in such an alien place, their culture was unnerving.

Isaac bowed at the 'Undead,' who all stood up – those who were able to – and struggled to return a bow.

'It is a great honour, a wonderful service, to dedicate oneself to the cause of Their Excellencies, even when the body has tried to deny them it.'

'I see,' I said.

Amalyn said nothing, but the stone-hard grip of her hand squashed mine. I looked over and noticed her red face and pursed lips. Clearly she was struggling to keep her mouth shut.

As our tour concluded, we were taken back to the seating area we had been in the day before. Isaac offered to make us a drink. We shuddered and refused.

'It's impressive, what we have achieved, and continue to do so, don't you think?' Isaac said. It wasn't a question.

'Very,' I said.

Amalyn folded her arms. 'Don't you think that labouring away, working hard, when so frail, so that your rich leader can go on holiday to Mars seems a bit ... well, unfair?'

Isaac gasped. His eyes widened, but I couldn't read him. Disgust? Fear? I wasn't sure. 'We owe them everything. We owe them our *lives*. It's thanks to their money that we're here. The governments of the time abandoned us. No one else had their intelligence or resources to plan for what happened. We would have drowned or burned to death if it weren't for them.'

'Right,' Amalyn said.

'You know,' Isaac continued, 'Lady Monet, she wanted us to show you all this, so you would be wowed. To show you what an advanced civilisation we have here.'

'A civilisation that eats bugs.'

'Amalyn!' I gasped at her candour.

Isaac nodded, not seeming the least bit rattled by her brashness. 'There really is nothing wrong with the insect food, except we need more vitamins. But now we can trade that, we can buy the food we need and we can advance even more. Having our own food labs would be the ultimate dream, though. That would really make the world of difference to us here.'

'That would be a tricky thing to start up,' I said, 'especially when you have no one with any expertise.'

'Well, Lady Monet would welcome you, and your families, to stay here if you wanted. You would be so useful here. As I said, we have room to spare. Sav, it would be wonderful for us to be together, don't you think?'

My face felt hot as I struggled to find my words. 'Oh, Isaac … I mean, I know the Raft isn't great, but here, it's just so different. It's just—'

'Shave my head? No chance,' Amalyn interjected.

'Think about it, won't you?' There was a hint of desperation in Isaac's voice. Was it guilt? His eyes were telling me something, like he didn't want to let me go again. 'We could arrange everything. We have contacts in the solarplanes company. Friends who understand the struggles on the Raft and how much better things can be here. And the Raft – it won't last, you know. There's no amount of concrete that can glue the land together forever. It'll crumble.'

I thought back to what Archie had said, those little cracks in the pavement, the creaks and grumbles at the Raft's edge, the salty air creeping in.

'I'll think about it, Isaac. I really will.'

With that, the whistle blew and Lady Monet's carriage came rolling around, the screech of metal on metal making me wince. She didn't get out, but her driver handed a leaflet to Isaac and continued on across the balcony to the next chamber. Isaac looked at the leaflet for a few moments.

'Wonderful,' he said, 'and totally as expected.' He handed the leaflet to Sara.

'Of course.' She smiled as she read it.

'What is it?' I asked.

'Nothing. Just business matters.'

I searched Isaac's face for answers, for some familiarity in his expression. I knew his look. My father often had it when the world began to change. The misty eyes of denial, the lips tightening as they struggled to say words they didn't mean. My father never managed to deceive himself, and his insincerity lasted only moments. There is something in that, being a person of truth, a wholeheartedness that I always lacked. But I could see it in Isaac. Attempting to be cunning was a struggle too far. He couldn't keep up the sham for much longer.

I snatched the leaflet out of his hand and glanced at it, but it was all in French. 'Here,' I said, passing it to Amalyn.

She read and reread it. ' "Due to the increased costs of the new nutritious food, the exchange rate between martas and euros has been halved." ' She paused. '*Halved*?'

'Of course, greater nutrition comes at greater cost. We must all pay our dues,' Isaac said, his voice trembling.

'I'll move to a dorm room,' Sara said. 'The high cost of a private room isn't necessary.'

'Excellent idea,' said Clementine. 'We can share if you like?'

'Perfect,' Sara said. She looked at Clementine. Their eye contact lingered for longer than happy news usually dictates.

'You pay rent here?' asked Amalyn.

Isaac nodded. 'Of course. The investment Their Excellencies made to build this city must be repaid handsomely. We are at their service. We have everything we need.'

'You have everything you need. *They* have everything they

want,' said Amalyn.

'Amalyn! Shh!' I scolded.

'What?' she said, dismissing my shock. 'No doubt they've had the Raft's food for ages. Did you see Lady Monet? She's not lacking any vitamins.'

'Their Excellencies deserve the best. They are our saviours,' Isaac and Sara replied in perfect unison.

Amalyn and I looked at each other. We had thought the Raft was elitist. This was a different league.

* * *

By the time Amalyn and I got back to our room that night, we were both exhausted. I removed my shoes and placed my feet on the cold hard floor, enjoying the chill. The waft of fresh air was circulating around the room and I shivered, enjoying the freshness of it. It was a marvel, the engineering of the place. It was disgusting to live like termites, but I had to hand it to Isaac for his genius. Staying cool when outside was ablaze, circulating air so effectively with no power-hungry air con. Our father would have been proud.

Despite the pleasing temperature, the dampness of the Tunnels had left me feeling clammy, and my skin was still tacky even after a shower. Rubbing on antibacterial gel was like smearing on paste. Nerves, exhaustion and fear of the conditions all made for a sticky soup that I couldn't scrub away.

Amalyn was muttering to herself in French, and the impatience that came with my tiredness and rumbling stomach made me more irritable than normal. I didn't tell Amalyn to shut up, despite wanting to. Instead, I used the last of my energy to ignore her. She had changed into plain nightclothes and lay on her bed staring up at the ceiling, muttering phrases in various accents over and over. Is that how she'd learnt the languages? I wondered. What a time-consuming bore that must have been. And I stood by my opinion that it was pointless. She'd barely uttered a word in French since we'd arrived.

I had so much I wanted to discuss with her, but tiredness overcame me too quickly. I looked over to her bed, and the moment she stopped muttering to herself, she fell fast asleep. I quickly followed.

10

Chapter nine

I was awoken the next day by Clementine shaking me gently. 'Morning, Aunt Sav!' Whatever time it was, her voice was way too cheery for me.

I opened my eyes reluctantly. The strange bed had not offered me the support I was used to, and I had knots all up my back. As barely rested as I was, Clementine's pretty face beaming at me chased the last of sleep away.

'They said your flight is leaving this afternoon. Isaac and I want to spend as much time with you as we can. It's been so wonderful to meet you. I know it's strange for you here. Dad said you find the hierarchy strange, but we're all okay. We manage, and we have each other.' She seemed content, genuine, never having known any different, I supposed.

'Here.' She handed me something. 'It's a satellite phone. The Raft can't trace it. If you decide you do want to live here with us, just call.' She kissed my forehead. 'I hope you do. Breakfast is being served.' And then she left us to get ready.

Amalyn moaned as she woke, her voice sounding gravelly. 'I think I'll pass on breakfast.'

'Me too,' I said, searching for water. The thought of insect corpses itching their way down my throat was worse than the hunger pangs. Then I remembered the rest of the syntho food we had stashed, so we ate that instead.

I sat with the satellite phone on my lap, a large, boxy device that looked nothing at all like the phones I was used to. It looked like a relic from a century ago. Archie would be like a kid at Christmas if he saw it, and Grace would have too many questions if she found it. There was a handwritten phone number taped to the side.

'Ams, take this.'

'Seriously? What am I meant to do with it?'

'Just keep it safe. I can't risk Grace finding it. Where would I even begin if I had to explain things to her?'

She bit her lip for a moment, then nodded and took the phone, stuffing it into her cluttered bag.

We waited in our room until we heard the breakfast things being put away, the clang of plates acting as our alarm, then made our way downstairs. People didn't stare this time. Already we were part of the furniture.

Isaac was sitting at his table, empty plate pushed away from him. I watched him for a moment – the smile of my father, the worry lines of my mother – as he chatted to his friends. One of those features was lying, the smile or the worry. He couldn't have both.

I sat next to him and hugged him, surprising myself. I had actually instigated hugging someone. I was overcome with a familial urge, and my usual resistance to affection fell away. I crushed him with my embrace, hoping for that gesture to tell me a message, to read his thoughts through the hug. Was he really okay? Would he survive the currency change, the expense of it? I knew something on his face was lying, to me or to himself. I just couldn't tell how entrenched the lies were. In that contact I found a warmth, a familiarity that had been long lost. The sort of hug only family can reciprocate. My thoughts went to Maisie and her granddaughter, how she never knew what had happened to her, then swallowed my emotions. I never cry, but it was all starting to sink in. Here was my brother. I had some family left.

'Amalyn, some of the other people would like to chat with you. I understand you speak French?' Clementine asked.

Amalyn's face lit up. '*Oui, d'accord!*'

They walked off with Sara to a table opposite. A group of smock-wearing bald heads turned to greet Amalyn, and I heard the mellifluent tones of French seeping through the room. Archie was right. She did sound lovely.

It was just me and Isaac left at our table. His eyes bored into mine, silently saying something I couldn't interpret, his face a tangle of emotions. 'Let's take a bike to the tearoom across the tunnel,' he said.

I nodded, pleased to get away from the last of the breakfast things.

He walked me to one of the many bike parks. There were plenty of bikes waiting there, some with trailers – the basic kind – some just standalone, two-wheeled machines. Two wheels going round without support looked hazardous to me, but everyone in the Tunnels managed the challenge with ease.

'Want to give it a go?' Isaac asked.

I snorted a laugh. 'Ride one of those things? Ha! No way.'

'Go on! It's every big brother's right to teach their kid sister to ride a bike.'

'Yeah, but I'm not a kid.'

He laughed at my discomfort. 'Well, better late than never.'

He took hold of my wrist, gestured me to a bike and proceeded to adjust the height of the seat. I sat, and the saddle's pointy shape prodded bits that did not want to be prodded.

'Good,' he said. 'Now, feet on the pedals. I'll hold you up.'

He grasped the handles, supporting the bike as my weight destabilised it, swaying from one side to the other.

'Two wheels seems like a daft idea,' I said as I tried to right myself. 'Four, even three, would make more sense.'

'Just start pedalling. The momentum gives balance. Push with your feet, one at a time. That's it.'

His words of encouragement sounded like mine when I'd taught Ethan to pair his socks. Surely I was too old for such jovial remarks. But then we were moving along, slowly, down the orange rock corridor.

'I'm going to let go,' he said.

'What? No! Why?'

'You're well balanced. You can do it. Just look straight ahead and keep pedalling, keep the momentum. Ready?'

He let go. I wobbled, then tumbled to the floor.

He walked over to me, laughing. I didn't find it funny. I'd ripped the knee of my trousers and my hand was bleeding. An open wound, underground, in a tunnel made of dirt.

I stood up and dusted myself off with my good hand.

'Aww, little sis, you okay?'

'Look.' I showed him my hand, a horrid red smudge across it. 'The infection risk here must be huge. What do you use to clean wounds? Do you even have a medical area? Antiseptic? Bandages?' My whole body trembled as I realised I hadn't seen a pharmacy or doctor on the tour. I was suddenly aware once again that the place didn't even smell like bleach.

'Relax. We'll get you cleaned up. We have doctors, but they won't be too impressed if I take you there with a little cut.'

Little cut? It's bleeding! I'll probably get maggots in it soon.

We walked the few metres back to the bike park and this time I opted for a trailer with Isaac pedalling up front. He took us to a tearoom, which looked much the same as the one we had been in before. The endless maze of dusky orange tunnels was becoming indistinguishable to me. As everywhere, the furniture here was as painstakingly engraved. The consistency of detail was repeated across every part of the underground city we visited. *Just like the Raft*, I thought, though there we had endless, homogeneous grey. Here it was infinite, detailed orange. The same uniformity, with a different delivery.

Above the sink, Isaac found a first-aid kit with antiseptic wipes and a plaster. He patched me up like he really was the big brother of a little girl. I tried to sit straighter, to look taller. He must have thought of me as some fragile thing as I felt so small next to him, so delicate. I fidgeted in my seat and winced at the sting of the antiseptic. After years of being a provider and protector of my own little family, being cared for didn't come easily.

When he was done, he handed me a cup of ambiguous tea, which I politely accepted and placed to the side. He sipped his, its steamy tendrils skating round his face.

'Your medical facilities are okay, then? Everyone living so close together, I'd imagine sickness spreads really quickly.'

'We wash our hands. We developed vaccines and exchanged research with the Raft. People get sick sometimes, but nothing of note. Vitamin deficiencies are the main issue, obviously. That's why you being here is so great. We've been begging for this opportunity for so long.'

'Why wouldn't they sell to you before?'

'I was hoping you'd be able to enlighten me. The Raft say they need to have enough to feed their own people before they can sell food to us. It has a big population, I understand. Over 150 million.'

I snorted a laugh without thinking. I was being as indiscreet as Amalyn. 'If you believe what they tell you. They're not exactly forthcoming with the truth.'

'The politics there sound tricky. One good reason why you should come here. Clem gave you the phone?'

'Yes. I've stored it safely.'

He smiled, our conversation halting to clumsy silence. He sipped his tea some more.

I shivered. There was something cold about this place in the Tunnels. Something unwelcoming, isolating.

Isaac noticed my unease. 'It's an audible dead zone here. No one can hear us here. There's no one listening.'

I noticed it then. The ever-present murmuring that came through the corridors, the sound travelling, was absent. There were no echoes. Just silence and us.

He put his cup down and looked over the balcony to the chamber, the columns of light attracting his gaze. *Like a moth.* 'Insects were the most successful animals on the planet. Termites alone had thousands of species, their biomass dwarfing that of humans. Ants were even more plentiful. I think the reason why they were so successful was because of their cooperation. They worked together.'

'They're vermin and they attract even worse vermin.' I was regretting eating earlier as my stomach started to churn. Why did he have to talk about such things? My tone was overly harsh and his expression changed when I spoke. It wasn't his fault. He just didn't know any better. How corrupted his mind must have been to believe such things.

'I think the future for us, in these underground cities, is great. Because we work together. Everyone in here has a vital role to play.'

'That's exactly what the Centre tell us.'

'We're grateful for the Select. They really did help us when no one else would.' He took another sip of his tea and leant in close. 'I know it seems strange, but ... I have my suspicions. I hear things, you know. We have friends, contacts. I think that we're on the verge of great change here. For the better. The Raft is on the verge of change also, but *not* for the better.'

I leant in as close as I dared, considering his cup of dirt tea was still between us. 'I need more details, Isaac.'

'I don't want to say more until I know for sure. Just please, keep the phone. And consider our offer. We have connections. We can get you out.'

Leave the Raft? The idea almost made me laugh. Two weeks earlier I hadn't known there were any other significant civilisations, and now I had a brother who was telling me I could live somewhere else. It was too much to process, too much to comprehend. Despite the coolness, I itched with perspiration and my chest felt tight. I forced a smile, concealing my doubts. Everything was just too much.

'I promise I'll think about it. But my wife – I have to think about her.'

'Just don't leave it too late.'

Too late. Those words rang in my head like old church bells, resonating over and over. How often had I left it too late? It was a trait of humankind to dither and dawdle, like when no one checked the seabed until it was too late, like when people ran across the bridges too late, like when my father refused to give up his insect hotel. Still, what did I need to rush for? I had no countdown clock, no date in a calendar that warned me, marking the day I had to take action. Instinct, a gut feeling – was that all I had to go on? That was the hurried fear of an Alternate. My brother, but still an Alternate.

How happy our parents would have been to know we had made it through those bad years. That we'd found a way to survive the diseases, the famines and the climate going crazy. We lived such different lives, but we were still standing. Both of us.

As he released my hands, a loud gong sounded. Isaac stood without saying a word and I followed him down a short tunnel to the next balcony, where everyone was filing out of the dining hall and along the mezzanine surrounding the central chamber. No one spoke. I found Amalyn, her blond hair making her stand out like a beacon. We asked those around us what was going on, but no one answered. They all stood in muted lines, their faces blank, packed in across the balcony and looking up at the floor above. I whispered to Isaac and gave him a nudge, but he didn't acknowledge me at all.

Lady Monet stood there, high up, surrounded by other Select who I assumed must be her family as they had the same thick, auburn hair. On a plinth sticking out of the balcony was someone wearing a plain tunic with a shaved head. The light from the windows in the ceiling glinted off his smooth scalp.

'Good morning, Toulouse.'

'Good morning, Your Excellencies.' The entire population said back.

Lady Monet raised her arms. 'This person has committed the crime of treason. The crime of speaking out against his saviour. This can never be tolerated. For this crime, he is sentenced to one hour outside. Out in the desert, under the sun, where he would have perished years ago if not for his saviours. Here he can consider his thoughts and repent his treason.'

'Hear, hear!' the crowd chanted.

'He will walk up the ladder towards the glass door, and that walk will be one of shame.'

'Shame!' they all shouted. Over and over. 'Shame! Shame! Shame!'

Guards stood across the mezzanine, their status obvious from their identical vests and trouser suits instead of the pallid smocks worn by everyone else. With rigid postures, they all faced the man, hitting their hands with their batons in time with the chant.

The man moved over to the ladder and started to climb, trembling up one rung at a time.

'Repent. And remember, if it were not for your saviours, the Select, then outside, exposed in that desert, is where you would have died.'

'Shame! Shame! Shame!' the cries continued.

Then, silence.

Everyone hushed as the man neared the final rungs. The light coming through the window was piercingly bright, and his face recoiled from its ferocity as his hand fumbled with the latch. He snatched his hand back a few times. The handle must have been baking hot. The whole chamber was still, breaths held as the window creaked open. A guttural groan escaped him as he was blasted by the heat, and he heaved himself outside. I felt the hot gust even as far away as I was. He stepped out, and the window clanged shut behind him.

I remembered when our solarplane had landed, the few moments outside, my shoes melting on the ladder, my lungs scorched from the heat. And this man had to last an hour, at midday, with nothing more than his smock to shield him. I couldn't imagine anything worse. My skin prickled as I wondered how many decided to fall to the ground instead, a deadly leap more appealing than cooking in the heat.

Isaac was unblinking, eyes fixed in a faraway stare, wet with tears. All I could think about was his wife, Sofia.

As soon as the window shut, a collective exhalation sounded across the chamber. Then normal conversation resumed, as if nothing unsettling had just occurred. Through the rows of people, Isaac spotted Clementine and we walked over. He didn't look my way. I longed to ask more, yet the opportunity did not present itself. To everyone else, it was as if the incident had never happened.

'Aunt Sav, it's so wonderful to have met you,' Clementine said, beaming. 'I never imagined such an amazing thing. All your work, all you've achieved – you really have saved us.'

'Sister.' Isaac held me close. 'You're a survivor. We all are. I'm so proud of you.'

'And I am of you.' My eyes stayed on his face, so familiar yet still that of a stranger. I felt illiterate in my inability to read him. The softness of his features counteracted his despondency, yet tears rolled down his cheeks. Who were those tears for? For me, for the man outside or for Sofia?

* * *

We exited through the same tunnel as our arrival, the heat hitting us the moment the hatch was open. The solarplane was waiting and Jerome was calling us aboard.

'This way, ladies, quick as you can. Sixty seconds till take-off.'

He held out his hand and hoisted us up the ladder. An icy blast was coming from the plane door, and Jerome's grasp was cool and dry. I glanced over my shoulder for one last look at the desert, hoping to see that the man was still alive and coping in the heat. The wind rendered us deaf and blind as it churned up the dust, powdery clouds obscuring the land. I couldn't see him.

Jerome helped us with our bags, stowing them in the lockers behind our chairs. He took mine first and I sat down, then Amalyn's. As she handed it to him, she almost dropped it, and out of the poorly tied top fell the satellite phone, landing with a thud right at Jerome's feet. We all froze for a few seconds, staring at the object. I squeezed my eyes shut, willing for that not to have happened, but when I opened them, it was still there, the abnormal relic. Our silence went on forever, becoming as archaic as the phone. Eventually, Jerome decided on an adequate response and bent down to retrieve it.

'I believe this is yours, ma'am?' He handed it to Amalyn.

'Oh, sure, silly me. Just a kid's toy, that's all.'

Her face was the brightest scarlet. Once she'd sat down, she looked at me and mouthed, 'Microbes!'

A fine mist covered us, smelling of bleach, like the street sprayers only a lot less irritating on our lungs.

'Just precautionary,' Jerome said.

It wasn't until after take-off that Jerome stepped away and we felt we could speak more freely.

'Is it illegal? A satellite phone?' Amalyn asked.

'No idea. I doubt it. It just looks a bit ... I don't know.

Dubious.'

'Well, I'm not going to worry about it. Jerome seems nice.'

'He's paid to be nice.'

'I wish *you* were paid to be nice,' she chuckled, and I rolled my eyes. 'Can you believe we've signed a confidentiality agreement about this? The Centre have us believe there's no one left in the world, but they've been trading with them all this time.'

'I always wondered how they made their clothes. There are loads of fancy clothes shops in the Centre.'

'Unbelievable. But not surprising. I mean, it's the Centre. Every twisted thing is believable. At least that explains the solarplane fleet. Oh, Sav, your brother! Do you think that's how his wife died? Being sent out to the desert, I mean.'

'I don't know, Ams.' I didn't want to imagine. 'Did you see his face?'

'Yeah. Shit. And I thought the Centre were bad. I mean, they are, but that's a whole other level. Sending people outside to bake if they say the wrong thing. Bloody billionaires think they own people.'

I nodded. I didn't tell her what I knew, about the Centre, the thousands and thousands of empty apartments, just so they could keep the Perimeter in need of housing. Amalyn may have coined the term 'ghost apartments,' but I doubt she knew the extent of it. No one did. How the population is a tenth of what they claim it to be, just so they could deny us fertility treatment. How they leave pollutants in the water to make us barren. No, that would be too much. It was still too much for me, and I'd known for years. I'd played their game and let them use my name in their propaganda, dutifully keeping my mouth shut so that Grace and I could have Ethan.

The desperation I saw in Toulouse – I knew that all too well. We were survivors, Isaac had said. Survivors knew when to keep their mouths shut.

Amalyn wittered on, saying everything she had been wanting to say since we'd landed, me telling her to shut up each time. She ranted and vented and got it all off her chest, knowing it could be the last time she'd be able to discuss it.

When she had finished, she took a breath and asked, 'Shall we go, then?'

'What do you mean?'

'France.'

'Seriously? You'd consider it? After all you've seen?'

'I really don't want to shave my head, but they make a good point. Some of the Raft has broken off already. Who knows if more will?'

'The edge has crumbled a bit, probably. That's all we know.'

As I spoke, the Raft came into view, its jagged coastline bobbing around in the sludgy sea.

'Oh my god, Sav, look!'

Below us, whorls of black fog were circulating, blowing up particulate matter, suffocating the Perimeter. The wind blew clear patches in the murk, moments of transparent air fighting against the gloom. As one such clear patch evolved, the land beneath was visible, only for a moment, but a moment was long enough. We saw the crack, the blacker-than-black crevice creeping its way across. As we watched, the crack widened and deepened until the chunk of land broke away, disintegrated and sank into the rancid sea.

11

Chapter ten

During the first part of the Autocar journey home, Amalyn and I sat in silence, disbelief giving way to numbing reality. There was little to say. We had seen enough. That chunk of land, a few miles at least, was lost to the sea. The Raft was breaking up. Of that we had no doubt now.

As anguish eclipsed her initial shock, Amalyn buried her head in her hands. 'There were so many buildings there. All those people must have died.'

'Ghost apartments, remember? Let's just hope they were all ghost apartments.'

'All of them? There were so many. So much land, just gone.'

Images flashed through my mind, images I had tried to barricade beyond my consciousness for so long. Families running across the anchors before they were destroyed, the news reports showing them in too much detail. 'Deserters deserve to drown' on a loop across the bottom of the screen. The callous government who'd lit the fuses. Memories came flooding back of the sound of the bombs landing on the coast, the screams of soldiers as they were buried.

At least we'd heard nothing this time. Distant and detached in our luxury plane, flying above the destruction, those cries had gone unheard by us. Screams for help and justice rarely reach so high.

How fragile our land was, how delicate the underpinnings of trust. We had lived under a security blanket of denial and amnesia for so long. I, like everyone else, took our stability, our strength, for granted. Had we learnt nothing from before? The rot had never left our shores.

'What shall we do, Sav? Shall we go to France? Live in the Tunnels?'

I couldn't answer that. I had no idea. To leave our homes and live underground seemed a step beyond comprehension. Perhaps it was just the edges of the Raft that were disintegrating. Inland was probably strong enough, less exposed. Maybe dither and denial would see us through a little longer.

'It's just the extreme edges,' I said. 'Land broke away when we first started to drift, remember? We lost the whole of East Anglia and Cornwall.'

'Where?'

'Exactly. They're long gone. I'll bet that's it. Just some normal erosion.'

'You're right, I'm sure. Just the edges.'

We sat again in stupefied silence, Amalyn with her head in her hands as I stared out the window, trying to get that image out of my head. They must have been empty apartments, useless land. I put the image to the back of my mind. It could collect dust there for a while.

I got out my antibacterial gel and covered myself with the last of it, then took out my phone to let Grace know I'd be home soon.

Amalyn grabbed my wrist. 'Sav, what happened to your hand? Are you okay?'

My plaster was holding firm, but a little smudge of blood had oozed out the side.

'Just a scratch. Isaac was trying to teach me to ride a bike.'

She laughed. 'It can't be that hard. They all do it.'

'Hey! It's harder than it looks.'

'Yeah, sure,' she smirked. 'A cut, though? Must have been tons of germs about.'

'I cleaned it.'

'Well, clean it again. It still looks gross.'

We arrived at my apartment before Amalyn's, and I left her in the Autocar, telling her not to worry. The lost chunk of land had been miles away from us and it would all be fine. She was half asleep but nodded along, reminiscence masking her concerns.

'We were on a plane, Sav! We were in Europe!'

Ethan was still up waiting for me when I arrived home. 'Mummy, I missed you!' He ran to me and I hugged him so hard he had to tell me to ease up. He was fresh out of the bath and smelled clean and sweet, his soggy hair leaving a wet patch on my shoulder. I kissed the crown of his head, then set him down as he went to get some of his drawings. He ran on strong legs, his back straight, a picture of health. A lump caught in my throat as I realised his trousers were getting too short for him. Had he grown in just a few days?

Grace walked towards me bathed in the light beaming in through the window. She glowed with the sunset as the final rays made patterns across the living room. A golden hue, brighter than the dusky dimness of the Tunnels.

She wrapped her arms around me. The cool dampness of

the underground had been replaced with chafing humidity, yet with Grace close to me I felt nothing but comfort. Her hair tickled my neck. 'I missed you too. Both of you.' Had I only been away for a couple of days? It was too long, in any case.

She kissed my cheek. 'Did you get lots of work done?'

'I did.' I closed my eyes and breathed her in, soaking up her subtle perfume.

'Staff all good, or are they going to cause you some bother?'

'It was fine.'

'You don't have to work over the weekend, do you?'

'Nope. Even if they ask, I won't.'

She smiled and rubbed my back. 'We really need to get on and sort out Maisie's apartment.'

'Sunday, then. We can spend all day remembering her.'

My phone pinged all night. Archie wanted to speak to me, but I couldn't bring myself to talk about it. Any of it. Instead, I silenced my phone and put it in a drawer, locking away my worries and memories. Shutting away what I had seen was easy. I'm a human being, after all. Stalling is our speciality. I could worry about it later.

My physical absence was bad enough at home. A mental absence would have been even worse. I said little about my time away, covering my family in a blanket of silence. How could I even begin to explain to Grace all that I had learnt? Her disbelief would dwarf mine, her worries eclipse any astonishment. I was still riddled with scepticism even though I had been there. I had seen the vast underground city, seen the Raft's land break away. BioLabs' confidentiality agreement wasn't all that kept me quiet; my sheer consternation was also at work. My brother, the Mainland, the Raft, all of it – I wouldn't allow it to penetrate the fortress of the here and now.

Grace, Ethan. They would be my sole focus. For one weekend, at least.

Grace didn't ask any questions, she just held me and showed me some of Ethan's latest drawings. She knew better than to pry.

After scrubbing myself in the shower, cleaning up my hand and checking my hair for lice, I demolished the food Grace had made. For once I appreciated the BioLabs produce. We drank some wine – not the best bottle, but a lot better than weird Tunnel tea.

Grace asked about my injury and I explained that I had stupidly fallen over, and I got to work sewing up my ripped trousers, all the while fighting away the memories of thread coming out of the worms. Every time the needle went in and out, I heard the little squirmy noise of the creatures, felt the heat of the room and saw the thread being harvested.

Forget it, Sav!

'You all right?' Grace asked when she saw the sweat I was getting into over such a meagre task. 'Sewing isn't that tough.'

'Yeah, I'm just always sweating these days.' She raised an eyebrow at me. 'I know, I know. It'll be your turn soon.'

'I don't doubt it,' she laughed, and brought me a bowl of IcyCrema.

* * *

As exhausted as I was, I got little sleep. Ethan was up half the night, his excitement about starting school keeping him awake. 'How many more sleeps? Is it school time yet?' is all we heard every couple of hours as he came running into our room.

'Not yet, go back to sleep,' I'd say as I led him back to his bed and tucked him in.

'What if I sleep and miss it?'

'We'll make sure you won't.'

'But what if—?'

'Big boys need their sleep,' I said as I left his room. *And mummies do, too.*

My patience was wearing thinner than ever. It wasn't like he was even going to a school. He'd just be sitting in the Interactive Cupboard all day. It seemed daft to be excited about something so mundane. But Grace understood children in ways I couldn't. Where I thought he was being silly, she cooed and encouraged his delights.

'He's a kid,' Grace reminded me. She had put a calendar on his bedroom door to count down the sleeps until school started and Ethan had crossed off extra days, hoping it would make school start sooner, then cried when he learnt it didn't work that way. After calming Ethan down on Saturday morning, Grace sat him at the table to make a new calendar.

I was in awe of her serenity, her calmness. She spoke softly through his tantrum, soothing him and settling him into a new task.

'You're an angel, you know that?'

She kissed me, then made some tea. 'It's just the weather. Gloomy days like this get everyone down.'

She may have had a point. Storms had been simmering all week and returning to the humidity of the Raft from the coolness of the Tunnels was suffocating. My brain felt stuffed with lassitude, like the air pressure was translating to actual pressure. I opened the windows, but outside seemed to alternate between stuffy and cold, and was relentlessly humid.

No matter how frosty it got, a layer of sweat clung to me.

After Ethan had recovered from his tantrum, we ate brunch together. I helped him brush his teeth, the wobbly one now hanging on by a stringy bit of gum. I made MimikTea for Grace and myself. We watched some TV. Just a normal family, a normal weekend.

A sadness lingered in our home after Maisie's death. Not a new sadness, an old, chilling flame reignited, its afterburn never really extinguished. We got on with our days, but our limbs felt heavier, smiles did not come as readily, tears never far away. Grace cried and I comforted her, and Ethan cried because Mummy cried. I had a shoulder for each of them, one on either side, me propped up between them. In chemistry, triple bonds are strong. Nitrogen gas, I told myself, my top damp from their tears. Triple covalent bond.

We're as strong as it gets. We'll be fine.

Maisie's apartment was in a low-rise block, a fairly old style but still strong in construction. It was far enough away from the edge that the smog rarely reached it, but when it did, it stuck like tar to everything. The fog's dampness was deposited at the edge. This far inland, it turned to treacle and ash. The apartment block was flecked with black. The rains hadn't been enough to clean it off, and the dappled blemishes were now permanent stains. Every time we visited, I forced Ethan's hands into his pockets and pulled a mask over his face until we were inside. His little lungs were so untainted, his hands always spotless. He was the picture of health, but it's a mother's job to worry.

When we first met Maisie, we had planned to move into her apartment when we inherited it. Our relationship with her, Ethan's so-called grandmother, was the reason Grace believed, like everyone, we were able to get fertility treatment, which was fine with me. Better she lived in the joy of darkness than the pain of knowing.

But so much had changed since then. Maisie was still family, but we didn't need her apartment. The Centre Elite had made me their pawn, the voice of whatever agenda they had. My son was a bargaining chip. I wrote science articles for the National Press, they twisted my words to suit them, and they allowed us to buy a bigger apartment. But it didn't matter what I said now. They had perfected the art of ventriloquism. After six years of my name in print, the Centre dissecting every word, entwining each with their own vociferous plan, I had no voice of my own anymore. When I opened my mouth, it was their voice I heard. My own gravelly tone had been replaced with the dulcet tenor of fabricated authority. My whole life was a counterfeit existence, puppetry in action.

If I did find that voice, no doubt they'd find a way to silence me. Our apartment reminded me every day that I had betrayed my own people, its relative luxury traded for my scruples, the walls tainted with duplicity. Through my articles, the needs of the Perimeter were offset by the desires of the Centre. Our apartment felt like the product of my deceit. Poison lined the walls and floors. The toxins of my past seeped into every crevice.

But where I suffocated, Grace found solace. Moral freedom was something that I could not explain to her. She knew nothing of my deal. I could never reveal the extent of my deception.

'It would feel nice to own, rather than be owned,' I said.

'But our apartment is ours. It's home. It's the only home Ethan has ever known.'

'We wouldn't have a mortgage to pay if we lived at Maisie's. That would save us a lot of money. And with all the recent tax hikes, having a bit more to spare isn't a bad thing.'

Taxes had shot up over the last couple of years. 'Funding our progress,' was how the government justified it. 'Funding the Centre going to Mars,' was what Amalyn said.

'But we earn enough,' Grace said. 'I'm back at work full-time when Ethan starts school next week. And the cost of installing two Interactive Cupboards would negate any savings anyway.'

'But it's Maisie's apartment. We would feel close to her.'

Such nostalgia was not in my nature, and Grace knew it. 'Oh, come on, Sav. I know Maisie's isn't that much closer to the edge, but here we can see the fence to the Centre from our living-room window. We are *that* close.'

Grace would look longingly at that fence. She stole gazes out of the window at the huge spikes poking above the apartment blocks. What appeared as a threatening eyesore to me was a beacon to her. The fence glittered like jewellery. A mind so used to yearning can't easily be satisfied. That craving could not be shut off for long. When Ethan came along, her joy seemed insurmountable. She danced with contentedness, light-footed as her burdens drifted away. Most of her melancholy was abated, but she still nursed a void that had not been filled. I knew her too well, I could see the signs. A niggling itch crept its way back up her spine, a tingle of dissatisfaction, a little voice whispering in her ear, 'Is this it?' When her new delight became the norm, I watched old habits edge back in. The pacing, the sleeping in, the vacant stares. Not so often, but the signs were there. The desire for something just out of reach.

I saw that spark in her eye, that twinkle that imagined what having one of those postcodes would mean for her. Our new apartment brought her so much joy, yet still she imagined what living in the Centre would do. That's what her eyes were saying when she gazed at the fence.

'The smog never reaches our apartment. I know it only occasionally does at Maisie's, but that's still more frequently than never. And we can rent her place out to make a little money. What about Archie and Amalyn?' she asked.

'What about them?'

'Well, they must be wanting to move in together properly by now. His place is tiny and way out towards the coast. They'd love Maisie's place, I'll bet. And you could share an Autocar to work.'

It was a good idea. Good for Archie and Amalyn, anyway. *Further from the crumbling edge*, the barricaded part of my mind was trying to scream at me. And she was right about the cost of the Interactive Cupboards.

'Fitting the extra one was so expensive. To start again and fit two more would cost too much. Not to mention all the work Archie put in installing it. He only finished last month. Could you really ask him to do all of that again? We just don't have the time. Ethan starts school next week, and I'm back at work full-time then.'

All of her arguments made complete sense, and my contentions were pathetic in comparison. I stared at her face, full of innocence and hope, quiet ambition bubbling inside her. She only wanted the best, like most people. And our son deserved the best.

She got up to fold some laundry, stroking the fabric of a jumper, holding it to her face to smell it. 'You know, I think most of these are too small for him now.'

'We can keep them, if you like?'

'That would be nice.'

Then it started again, that distant rumble creeping closer. My toes began to vibrate as the shaking hit us. There was no storm this time. The weather outside was calm. The evening sun had dipped below the high-rises, but there was enough daylight left to see quite far. I ran to the window to look for a rocket but saw nothing.

'Sav, it's happening again!' Grace cried as she ran to the doorway. Ethan was playing a computer game, the shrill music resonating over the rumble. He hadn't noticed, fixated on the addictive tech. Grace and I cowered as the rumbling increased, watching him.

'I'll go get him,' Grace said.

'Wait, don't scare him. It's just a mild one.'

It wasn't as harsh as the previous quake, its ferocity mellower, quieter. The shaking was slight and subsided quickly, and just one glass fell and broke. Ethan never looked up from his game, and Grace and I both sighed with relief.

Across the road, a strip billboard cut through the grey. I watched as it lit up the sky around it, waiting for it to tell us what had happened. It flashed a little when the rumble peaked, but the stories didn't change.

Blue Liberation study finds Perimeter residents more productive than ever! With sterility comes liberty! Mars resort soon to welcome first guests! Progress is Paramount! Japanese knotweed detected at the Raft edge: if seen, stay away – street sprayer concentration increased! Everyone is safe now! Street safety 4/5.

I kept watching, but it didn't change. Nothing at all about the shaking. Nothing about the chunk I had seen breaking off the edge.

'Nothing to worry about, Grace,' I called out to her as she checked on Ethan. 'The Press aren't concerned.'

'I'm sure it's fine, then,' she said. Despite knowing as much as she did about how the Press twisted my words, she still believed in it.

But I knew better. It was what they didn't say that was more concerning. We were all in the dark.

* * *

Maisie's death brought a lot of work with it, and we had put it off for long enough. Her apartment was busy, cluttered with old trinkets and ornaments. Each object had a purpose. They came with stories she had told us, memories that were hers alone but brought to life with her love of reminiscing. Isn't that how legends are born? With one eccentric storyteller? She told her stories with such exuberance, such sentiment, that we felt they were our memories also. Grace especially did. She revelled in a past we all clung to, secretly, but Maisie made it feel like we were still living in those times. When we had our families and fresh air, when we used to play outside. When there was more to the world than the Raft. I'd look at Ethan and his cluelessness about the past. He'd never known any different and was too young to comprehend. His whole world was our apartment or Maisie's.

We had help sorting through her possessions. Sal and Cass came along to help. Grace was still grateful to them for recommending we adopt a grandmother, and for that I held them in high regard, too. They brought their daughter, Jocelyn, with them, now quite the young lady at ten years old. Sticky fingers at the ready, she was keen to search through everything.

'What's in this picture?' Jocelyn asked, holding the frame up to Sal.

'That's what cars looked like when people drove them.'

'I don't know what you mean. How did people drive them?'

'It's a bit complicated.'

'What's this?' Jocelyn recoiled at the sight of another picture, this one of a quadruped. 'Is that a disease?'

Grace laughed. 'It's a dog. Maisie had a pet dog years ago.'

'What's a pet?'

'They were animal friends that lived with you.'

Jocelyn threw the photo on the floor. 'No way! She couldn't have!'

Cass retrieved the photo. 'Joce, sweetie, don't you remember your granny had a cat when she was a girl?'

'No.' She narrowed her eyes. 'Are you teasing me?'

Cass and Sal looked at each other. 'Of course we are, Joce,' Sal said. Some things are too hard to explain to a child.

We cleared boxes and boxes of clothing and possessions. There were other photo frames we piled up, long-lost family and alien landscapes making up the majority.

'I think we could reuse these frames,' Grace said. 'So many of ours broke. We could put our photos in them, but Maisie's would still be there behind.'

'That's a lovely idea,' I said.

'Check these out,' Cass said, lifting a necklace from a shelf. 'Pearls. Quite the rebel, Maisie was. These have been banned for years.'

Grace walked over and took them. 'They're so pretty. Why were they banned?'

'They come from the sea, from shellfish. They secrete them, somehow.'

'Yuck.' Grace threw the necklace on the floor. 'Those pretty beads are made from fish shit?'

'Yep,' Cass said. 'I'm sure they're not dangerous now. They'll be really old. But probably best to chuck them back in the sea where they came from.'

So much of Maisie's old things were destined for the incinerator. Worn-out clothes, chipped crockery, half-burnt candles, curios from past adventures – all no use now and unsuitable for recycling. A few small items we kept, little mementos. Some of the clothing was fine for sterilising and reusing. One hundred and seventeen years of life – all those memories destined to become ash. But we remembered her.

'Her memories are alive in us, Grace,' I said when she was crying again. 'We'll remember her always.'

Ethan sat next to Jocelyn on the sofa, staring at her with curious eyes. He had met so few other children. She shuffled away from him, so he copied her and shuffled closer. She scowled and turned her back to him.

'Sorry, Ethan, she's got a bit of a headache today,' Cass said.

Grace pulled Ethan away and gave him a hug. 'She's not ill, is she?' she said, and felt Ethan's forehead.

'No, she's fine. We went to see the Japanese knotweed yesterday.'

'All that way to the edge? To see *filth*?' Grace's eyes widened.

I was stood right next to Sal and found myself backing away.

'We thought it might be the only time she gets to see a real plant,' Cass said.

Grace looked at me, her face losing colour. I suspected mine was the same as our silent conversation did nothing to reassure her. 'But it's so dangerous,' she said to Cass. 'God knows what germs that foreign plant has been hiding.'

'We didn't get close. I think all that colour has messed with her eyes a bit, though. She's had a headache since.'

'Was it *that* green?'

'Greenest she's ever seen.'

Grace nodded, keeping Ethan behind her. 'They're saying to stay away, that it's damaging the concrete.'

'We were careful. There are just little cracks around it. The sprayers there are so strong, though. Look!' She pulled up her trouser leg to reveal her peeling skin.

Grace winced. 'Ouch. They're not that strong around here. Maybe they should make them stronger?'

'I don't think they need to,' Cass said. 'There's no knotweed this far inland.'

'Hmm,' Grace said, feeling Ethan's forehead again and rubbing alcohol gel into his hands.

Grace gave Ethan the e-pad to go play with in the bedroom and spent the rest of the morning keeping as far away from the other three as possible. Cass and Sal said nothing, though I saw them exchange glances before making their excuses and leaving early. After they left, I disinfected the entire apartment and Grace ordered some ImmunoJuice for delivery.

12

Chapter eleven

Monday morning, my alarm sounded from my phone that was still hidden inside the drawer. After I silenced it, I noticed its little light winking at me, telling me how much I had ignored it. *Microbes!* It was time to brush the dust off those mental images and remember everything I'd seen.

Ethan woke moments later, excitement ridding him of any morning sleepiness. He came running into our bedroom shouting, 'Big school starts today!' Before we'd even had the chance to get up, he was dressed and helping himself to breakfast, getting more food on the table than in his bowl.

Grace looked tired with red eyes shining from fresh tears. 'Our little boy. How is he growing up so fast?'

I had to wait several minutes for an Autocar, an annoying trend of late since more and more people were venturing outside and using them. The peace I'd once enjoyed was becoming obsolete. *Things change, Sav. Adapt!* I chastised myself when I found I was longing for the ghostly, quiet streets and empty lab. The clinking glassware and background chatter were like metal scratching render. Middle age was bringing with it a desire for the way things were, and I was losing my ability to acclimatise. I worried I was prone to mental stagnation, as my parents had been. They remained tortured by their memories of the past when the world evolved around them, nature sickness robbing them of any joy in the here and now. I had to keep reminding myself: *I am not my parents.*

What would they label the likes of me? My parent's environmental dementia seemed unfitting. Noise-phobic? Tranquil-phile? 'General grouch,' Archie would say. As if his character regeneration of recent years was something to aspire to. In fairness, he had seemed quite happy and content when he'd made that suggestion.

The roads became steadily bumpier all the way to work. Then the haze started licking at the windows. With each passing minute, the ring of smog that encircled the Raft became denser. By the time I alighted at the lab, the air was like turbulent soup and the wind tore at my face. Grace was right. The more central, the better. After years of living more centrally, my persistent cough had mostly cleared, the grating sensation in my throat was much less and my skin hardly flaked at all. And I certainly didn't miss dodging fish junkies and Alternates on my walk to work.

Ethan had never known such atrocities. His lungs were unencumbered, and his skin was perfectly smooth. Maisie's apartment was only fifteen minutes from ours, but with every minute the Autocar trundled along the particulate matter whipped up more and more to form black soot-devils rolling down the street. As much as I detested the situation, I knew that, for my son's health, the ownership the Centre had over me would have to remain.

Work was busy when I arrived. As soon as the door swished

open, I was welcomed by the smell of vegetables and disinfectant. All employees were already at their stations and didn't even look up as I walked through. It seemed the lab still functioned in my absence. Lars and Declan were nowhere to be seen. No doubt they'd take the credit for the efficiency while I was away.

The new injectable product launch was finally happening. The pollutants we'd discovered years ago were taken into account (discreetly, of course. No one really needed to know) and, together with our supplemented food, the Raft was going to be bursting with nutrition. And not just the Raft, I kept reminding myself, but the Mainland, too.

'Morning, Professor. How's your tomorrow?' Marcus asked as I got to my office.

'Uncertain,' I replied. The formal greeting seemed needless, given the number of years we had worked together, but it had always been Marcus's way.

I said nothing else to him but sat down, cranked the fan up and logged on to my computer. The disinfectant spray the cleaners used on my keyboard stung my fingertips. One more way living centrally had softened me.

'Morning, Sav.' Archie appeared at my door, as smiley as ever. He looked tired, though, the harsh Perimeter air ageing him quickly. Sleepless nights missing Amalyn too, no doubt. Quite how he'd managed to capture her heart still baffled me. His charm worked wonders, it seemed. She still had the complexion of a Centre, youth holding on for far longer than it dared with the rest of us. For most in the Perimeter, age hit us like a brick.

'Monday morning and already you bring me a cup of tea,' I said, delighted, taking the cup he held. 'My hero.'

'Amalyn told me everything. Crazy.'

'Everything?' I wasn't really surprised. She was never going to stick to the confidentiality agreement.

'Your brother, Sav. God, what a shock. And how they all live underground, and the Raft. We were right – the edge is crumbling.'

'You reckon it's the Japanese knotweed?'

'Seems unlikely, an old plant breaking up that much concrete. But if it is, they've let it get that bad. *That* much of just one weed, though? It just doesn't sound plausible.'

'Cass and Sal went to see the knotweed. It's definitely there.'

'Who?'

'Friends of mine. They wanted to have a look at a plant, to show their daughter, since she'd never seen one before.'

'Seems pretty stupid. A dirty plant and a crumbling Raft.'

'I don't think they know about the Raft crumbling. I mean, I didn't tell them what I saw.'

'Still, you have some weird friends.'

I raised my eyebrows. 'I've met some of Amalyn's friends, remember?'

'Good point.'

'Listen, we were cleaning out Masie's old apartment. It's empty and ready to live in. You and Amalyn should move in there.'

His eyes bulged wide. 'Me *and* Amalyn?'

'Come on, Archie. She practically lives at yours, anyway. You've been together for years. How slow do you want to take it?'

'I don't know. I guess I hadn't really thought about it. And my apartment – I mean, it's my old family turf.'

'It could be at the bottom of the sea soon. You're really close to the edge. Maisie's is a much bigger place, the rent would be peanuts, the air is better ...'

His face remained blank.

'Seriously, Archie. It's sensible.'

I sipped my tea while he pondered, leaning on my desk and staring at nowhere in particular. My office blinds were open, giving me a view of the entire lab as Lars arrived. Everyone sat up straighter, rigidity overtaking relaxation. He sneered as he entered and began to saunter around the aisles. Penny leapt out of her office and ran over to him, smoothing down her hair and straightening her skirt as she approached. A chill crept up my spine and I shuddered.

'There's always the alternative option,' said Archie eventually.

'France?'

'Yep. Their nuclear reactors sound interesting. And that satellite phone is a thing of beauty.'

'We can't emigrate because you like the tech. *Such* a nerd.' I rolled my eyes. 'Anyway, as far as we know at the moment, it's just the extreme edge of the Raft breaking up. Like with Cornwall.'

Amalyn knocked at my door and came in. 'What's the gossip?'

'Ah, Amalyn,' I said. 'Just in time for my proposition.'

Archie held up his hands. 'Sorry, Sav, you're not her type. And that would be too weird for me.'

'Ha! Very funny.'

'This sounds exciting,' Amalyn said. 'Do I need to sit down? On the floor, of course, since you still have no chairs in your horrible office.'

I looked at Archie. 'Are you going to ask her, or shall I ask for you?'

Amalyn stared blankly at both of us, waiting out the silence.

'It's not like there's time to waste, Archie,' I said. 'What if your Perimeter patch breaks up tomorrow?'

'I was hoping for at least a day to mull it over.'

'Oh, drop the sentiment.' I turned to face Amalyn, who was standing patiently with a blank expression. 'Ams, Archie is moving into Maisie's old apartment. To get away from the edge.'

'That's wonderful. You'll be much safer, Archie. And as much as I love your place, it is tiny and dark.'

'But I like my apartment,' he said.

'Enough to drown with it? Stop being stubborn,' she said. 'It's a great offer. You need to be safe.'

Archie's sulk dissolved as he grabbed Amalyn's hands and pulled her close. '*We* need to be safe. You're moving in, right?'

I tried, unsuccessfully, to suppress my laugh. 'That's about the least romantic way you could have asked her to move in with you!'

Amalyn beamed and kissed his cheek. 'I love his style. Of course I will.'

Before I had time to tease them any further, Lars poked his bony head around the door. I couldn't see Penny but she must have been there. I could smell her perfume mingling with Lars's cooking-oil smell.

'You have all been sitting here wasting company time for four and a half minutes.' I could hear his tongue slapping with each word.

'We got here half an hour early, though,' Amalyn said through her teeth.

Lars's nose and top lip recoiled, revealing his crimson gums.

'When you walk through those doors, you are on company time.'

I swallowed my anger as they left my office, following Lars. His smell lingered long after his physical presence had retreated. Throughout the day, he continued to impose himself around the lab, leaning in too close to all of the staff, breathing his foetid breath over them, intermittently licking away dehydrated white goo that entombed itself in the corners of his mouth. His height was off-putting, but he wasn't the intimidating presence he clearly believed himself to be. He was an annoyance, a bit of grime that needed to be cleaned away.

I sat alone with my thoughts in my office for some time, observing the lab through a gap in the window blinds. 2-10, 4-09 and 8-08 were data-inputting tirelessly. Mabel was engrossed in distillation. Marcus was organising and cleaning up after them. Even Penny was being useful by keeping Lars distracted. She was wearing a shorter skirt than usual and made some attempt to calm her hair's frizz. She had also applied makeup by the gallon. Following Lars closely, she giggled flamboyantly at everything he said, licking her lips as his own twitched into a smile.

I scrolled through the news again for any story of the edge breaking up and found nothing except the danger from knotweed. There was no way the lab was at risk. Greg would know, and we'd be moving premises if that was the case. We weren't *that* close to the edge here. Archie and Amalyn could move more centrally, but where did the rest of the staff live? I realised I didn't know. Some of them would be quite near the edge.

What if we lost all our staff to the sea?

Big if, Sav.

I reminded myself it was just speculation. The edges had broken away when we'd first started to drift. A bit of ongoing erosion was surely normal.

Surely.

I left the comfort of my office to walk around the lab and speak to the staff I barely knew. Probably best to make an effort.

'Good morning, Professor,' 4-09 said. She had been typing rapidly all morning. As she glanced my way to greet me, her eyes briefly left the screen but her fingers didn't pause.

'Good morning … erm, sorry, I seem to have forgotten your name.'

'Betsie.'

'Good morning, Betsie.' I'd never remember her name. 'The write-up you did on the data for the children's calcium biscuits was very good, I've been meaning to tell you.'

She blushed and continued to type. 'Thank you, Professor. The product was so good, it was a joy to write up the results.'

Kiss-ass. I smiled. 'Glad to hear it.'

She looked my way for another split second. 'You're looking lovely today, by the way. Have you changed your hair? It suits you.'

'No, Betsie, my hair is as crap as it's always been. Thanks, though.'

I was getting sick of these contrived compliments. Every day they dished them out, sucking up to me like I cared about anything except the science.

Just do your job.

'Professor?' said Betsie.

'What?'

'We ... Well, we're all a little concerned about our jobs. Do you know when Mr Cowley will have finished his audit?'

That explained the compliments, at least. I had to admire her truthfulness. 'No idea. Nothing to do with me. The sooner we see the back of him, the better.'

I spoke loudly, and in my peripheral vision I saw Lars raise his head and grunt. 4-09 immediately commenced typing, her blush deepening.

My week at work was crazy busy, trying to organise the product launch. The final results still weren't in, so I had to chase everyone, nagging and hassling. All the while, Lars was breathing down my neck. My skin crawled whenever he was near, and by the looks on their faces, everyone felt the same. Mabel and Marcus especially shuddered whenever he was close by. He moved like he had the arrogance and pride of a Centre instead of the humility his postcode should have engendered. Where most Perimeters hunched over, Lars puffed himself up. Where we hung our heads, Lars lifted his chin. I noted Marcus's and Mabel's involuntary judders and fidgeting hands, heard the stuttering voices. Their discomfort made them knock on my door every five minutes.

On Wednesday lunchtime, we all breathed a sigh of relief when Lars left. The atmosphere change was instant. Shoulders relaxed, eyes left screens, the stuffy air seemed to thin. Even my sweating noticeably reduced. I grasped the opportunity and took a cup of MimikTea to Archie. I hadn't had a moment to speak to him since Monday.

He took the cup and grinned. 'How's my handiwork going down, then? The IC must be in full swing.'

'It's brilliant. I really do need to pay you. It took three whole weekends. Ethan won't stop going on about it. He thinks he built it himself.'

'He did! I swear, I did nothing!' Archie said, his face a picture of feigned bewilderment. 'And not a chance are you paying me. Spending time with the little dude and you guys made it well worth it. Plus, Maisie's apartment is going to be great.'

'When are you moving in?'

'Boxed up and ready to go. Think we'll do it over a few days, starting this evening.'

'The sooner the better.'

I'd been sitting for mere seconds and had enjoyed just one sip of tea before Mabel knocked at Archie's door. Rather than stepping in, she arched her long neck around the doorframe.

'Excuse me, Professor.'

'Yes, Mabel?'

'You look lovely today. Is that a new blouse?'

'What do you want, Mabel?'

'I was wondering if I could get you to look over the numbers for the placebo group for me.'

'Is there a problem?'

'No, no, not at all. I'd just like it to be checked.'

I sighed. She was thorough, always, but had so little confidence. 'Sure. I'll do it at some point today.'

'Thank you, Professor.'

'Once an intern, always an intern,' Archie said as Mabel retreated.

'Hey, Amalyn was an intern too. And she's more than capable of working without me holding her hand.'

'Yeah, she's the best, though, isn't she?'

I smiled. 'Excited to have her move in?'

'Sure. I mean, it'll be fine.'

'*Fine?* I've told you before, Archie. You certainly could do worse.'

'I know, I know. Love the girl. I am worried she's going to say I have to get rid of some of my computers, though.'

'Hmm,' I held my finger to my chin, attempting my most quizzical look. 'Amalyn or computers, Amalyn or computers …'

'All right, all right. I have two lovers. What can I say?'

'There's a spare room for all your toys. I wouldn't be surprised if your retro T-shirt collection gets lost in the move, though.'

'She loves those T-shirts!'

'Archie, no one but you loves those T-shirts.'

He put his hands to his chest and mimed a breaking heart just as my phone rang. I'd been ignoring it all morning with Lars parading around the place. It was the eighth time Grace had called.

'Jocelyn is sick,' Grace said before I had time to even say hello.

'Microbes! Really? Is it serious?'

'She's got a cough and a fever.'

'It's quite normal for children to get bugs sometimes. Their immune systems aren't fully developed.'

'Ethan sat with her the other day, remember?' she said. 'He doesn't feel hot but he looks a little flushed. And he hasn't wanted any food today. His tooth came out this morning, and it bled a bit. What if it got infected? And what about your cut?'

'My cut is all healed up. And it's all quite normal for kids—'

'Stop saying that!' she snapped. 'It's not! It's not supposed to be, not anymore. We clean everything, don't we? There are no germs or filth on this whole Raft. His monthly injections are meant to stop all of this. What if Maisie's pearls were riddled with something? Or maybe that foreign plant has released some new contagion. The Press said to stay away. I can't believe Cass and Sal were so reckless.'

'Grace, calm down. He's fine. Just keep an eye on him. I'll leave work as soon as I can.' Then I hung up.

Archie looked worried. 'Everything okay?'

I glanced around the lab. Everyone looked busy. They could cope without me for the rest of the day. 'Think I need to go. I'm sure it's fine. Grace thinks Ethan might have got something from the knotweed.' Then a thought occurred to me. 'You know, it's weird. When we went to the Mainland, they didn't even give us hazmat suits. No gloves, nothing. They sprayed us down on the plane, but I didn't notice if any of the people that lived there were sprayed. Isaac says they're all healthy, but living the way they do? We could have picked up anything there. I swear my head has been itchy. I've sprayed it loads, but *lice!* God, can you even imagine?'

'Maybe you and Ams should go to a walk-in clinic, get your monthly injections and swabs done early, just in case.'

'Good idea.'

I realised then that we should have done that straight away, or at least quarantined ourselves before going home. I remembered hugging Ethan, kissing his cheek, after being near filth, living in dirt. Why had I not been more careful? Why wasn't quarantine mandatory? My heart thumped harder and I got up to go.

Lars was gone so I felt safe leaving work early. I went via the clinic and had my tests done. By the time I got home, Grace was distraught. Ethan was crying from a mild fever, but mostly he was reacting to Grace's panic.

'Have you logged on to the doctor's site?' I asked.

'Yes, and I've been waiting all afternoon for a reply. They're busy. It must mean loads of people are sick. There's nothing in the news, but what if—?'

'We would've heard if there was some new outbreak. I picked this up from the pharmacy. It'll lower his temperature.'

She snatched the little packet off me and almost rammed it down Ethan's throat. Her hands were trembling. 'Maybe we should just go to the hospital?'

'Grace, he's fine. It's just a bit of a chill,' I said, as Ethan wriggled onto my lap and gave me a cuddle.

Just then, Grace's phone pinged with the doctor's reply. It said to just let him rest and give him the pharmacy medicine as needed.

'Well, what good is that?' she said. 'They're not even going to come and test him for anything?'

'Let's wait and see how he is tomorrow. We can take him to a walk-in centre if he's no better.'

'Take him *outside*? No chance. That's how this all started. He went near other people and now look at him. No.' Grace took him off my lap and held him tight. 'He's staying here with me.'

Grace and I took turns sitting up and watching over Ethan during the night. He slept a little restlessly and grumbled a few times and I changed his sheets in the early hours as he had sweated through them. The following morning, he was irritable and tired, but his fever had gone. He wanted breakfast and juice, and chuckled as he spilled half his glass on the floor. The sound of his laughter was the most beautiful thing I'd heard in days.

I yawned as I cleared up after him, his giggles telling me he was feeling just fine. After I'd showered, I stared at my wardrobe, uninspired and failing to summon the motivation to get dressed.

'I'll stay home today, Grace.'

'Really?'

'Sure.' I was too tired, anyway.

Grace worked in her IC, but between every lesson she rushed out to feel Ethan's forehead, give him medicine and cuddles or feel his glands. By the end of the day, Ethan was most definitely back to his old self, demanding biscuits, lively and leaving a trail of chaos in his wake. He had the slightest cough but was otherwise fine.

'I'm never letting him near other children again,' Grace said. 'It's a germ-fest, getting them all together.'

I just nodded, too tired to argue.

* * *

The extra day off did nothing to revive me, as I had to listen to Grace's distress all day, and looking after a fully healthy Ethan was no easy task. My work had built up, but not as much as I'd feared, with the other staff taking on the bulk of it. I still hadn't checked Mabel's work and insisted it would be fine in any case, which almost made her have a panic attack. By some miracle, Lars had not returned. I had finally caught up by the end of the week and sat in a crumpled heap in Archie's office on Friday afternoon.

'Tell me something about your work,' I said. 'I'm sick of mine.'

'Oh, okay. Well, we're currently pretty damn close to where Great Britain used to be. Exciting, huh?'

'Yeah. It's like we're home. It explains this horrible wind.'

'Yep. And that rain last week.'

'Can we see the white cliffs of Dover?'

'Erm, the white cliffs of Dover were part of Britain. They broke away and sank years ago when we started to drift. So, no.'

'Oh. So what bits of France could we see when we were anchored?'

'Well, nothing. But if you were sailing the Channel, you'd eventually see the sandy beaches.'

'Sand? Gross.' I grimaced. 'Bet all sorts of nasty bugs lived in sand.'

'Probably. We're the wrong way round, though. The Raft is basically upside-down to how it used to be. Looking at the currents, we should spin round the other way fairly soon. That will calm down the wind at this end.'

'See? I knew coming in here to chat would cheer me up.'

'Well, just for balance, I have some bad news.'

I groaned and braced myself. 'Go on.'

'Greg is coming in this afternoon.'

'Microbes!'

13

Chapter twelve

'Good morning, lab people. Please take your seats.' Greg's thunderous voice rattled the glass beakers.

The staff all went to sit at their stations while Archie and I hovered at my office door. It was the furthest possible point from Greg and his teary-eyed assistants. They all had the look of defeat, downcast eyes searching the floor for reasons why they were working for such a man.

Declan arrived with Greg and paraded around the lab, flexing his muscles and flashing his teeth. As the shuffle of chairs subsided, Declan found a place to stand – predictably, right next to Amalyn. Once she saw his looming presence behind her, she got up and moved to the other end of the lab. With a disgruntled tut, Declan went back to stand next to Greg, shooing the assistants away like they were smog.

Greg cleared his throat, his pristinely healthy Centre lungs so easily tarnished from his thirty-second exposure to the Perimeter air outside.

'It is with great ambivalence that I must announce the passing of Professor Harold Carter from Protein Labs. Not the greatest mind in food nutrition. His dawdling tactics slowed our takeover of ProLabs over the last five years.'

Amalyn gasped and put her hands to her mouth.

Declan's too-snug shirt tightened around his muscles that he continuously tensed and relaxed. Greg slapped him on the back and pushed him forwards.

'Declan will announce the rest of the exciting news.'

Declan took another step forward, pouted his lips and lifted his chin higher. 'With Harold gone, it's now full steam ahead. The papers are being signed this week, which I'm sure all of you will agree is excellent news for BioLabs, as it will increase our profit margins considerably. And since this takeover has some initial costs, we are using this wonderful opportunity to cut some heads.'

Lars appeared as if from nowhere. His stench was dwarfed by the overwhelming smell of Greg and Declan's aftershave. Penny's perfume even seemed somewhat subdued in their combined presence. As Lars walked to the front, Penny took a seat and perched in a prissy, crossed-legged pose. She leant over, as if hanging off his every move.

Lars nodded and attempted to smile at the staff while Declan continued.

'Lars has concluded his inspection, and it is my understanding that two hundred people work on the factory floor. We have acquired some autonomous technology, and so we can cut those employees. We require only five to maintain the equipment going forward.' He turned to face me directly, his cold, hard eyes drilling through me. 'As soon as you can, summon the team leaders from the factory floor and make the excess staff redundant.' He held two thumbs up and grinned at all of us. Lars copied his action. Their smugness sickened me.

'I'm sure you will all have read the news headlines,' he continued. 'The marvellous news of such wonderful progress about our explorations of Mars. You can feel proud that here at BioLabs, we are offering up a substantial percentage of our profits to fund the mission. This level of exploration is the ultimate in progress, and progress is paramount. You in research are all safe in your employment, as Lars has deemed you all somewhat useful. But the assistants need to go. What an honour for you to serve in such a progressive and prosperous company. With sterility comes liberty!'

The slogan that usually roused people into repeating the chant fell on a deathly silence. Yet Declan remained, his teeth blinding us, as if expecting some applause. We were still, mouths agape in the frosty stillness. Greg stood with his entourage of assistants brushing down his suit, giving him a drink and wiping his mouth. Declan stood like some hideous, polished statue.

'Oh, Harold!' Amalyn cried. She buried her face in her hands. I knew of their friendship, though I doubted anyone else did.

'Yes, he was a great scientist. Such a loss.' I covered for her, my tone harsh to wake her up. Such a friendship could cost her dear if it was more widely known.

'All those people getting the sack.' She sobbed some more. 'They'll lose their healthcare.'

Greg grunted and walked away, Declan striding behind him. 'Savannah, my office.' Greg's voice hit me like a blow to the head.

Microbes! I sighed and followed the heavy thump of foot-steps down the corridor, Greg's voice echoing back at me.

'You've been assigned a story.'

'Shall I bother writing it, or just sign my name to whatever Peter writes?'

Greg stopped and turned around, taking one huge step towards me. Declan copied his actions in near-perfect mime. I stood my ground, Greg's hot breath on my face. 'Comments like that are why you are skating on thin ice.'

'Excuse me?' I scowled at him. His massive face looked like a synth roast potato.

'Your name is needed, as you know all too well. But be well aware, that name does not have to be attached to *you*. Do not think that you are not expendable. Every Perimeter is expendable, like the muck they live in.' He looked me up and down, wrinkling his nose and curling his lip.

I swallowed back my anger as best I could, keeping my teeth clenched. 'You expect me to fire nearly two hundred staff, prepare for the injectable launch, and you still want me to write some Press article that I won't have any say in how it turns out?' I shocked myself at the volume of my voice, yet it failed to rattle the furniture like Greg's did.

He backed away, not releasing eye contact as he heaved open his office door. I went in, Declan skipping through after me, and Greg slammed the door.

'I think you forget yourself. It sounds like the Perimeter are getting too big for their boots. Don't you think so, Declan?'

Declan smirked and nodded. 'You didn't even come in for a day this week, I understand.'

'My son was sick.'

'Your son,' Greg said with a snarl. 'Yes, *your* son. Except, he's not *your* son, is he? It was *I* who granted permission for you to have "your" son.' His fingers made air quotes, which Declan imitated. 'It's the wages *I* give you that allow you to raise him. You, Professor Selbourne, are Perimeter. Don't you ever forget that. *I own you.*'

I gritted my teeth. My fingernails cut into my skin as I clenched my fists. My whole body tensed, poised to surge.

'Perhaps I should inform that pretty little wife of yours about the details of your son's conception. I assume she hasn't read the paperwork? He's on loan to you as long as you are useful to us.'

My face flushed with rage and all my muscles tensed. I wanted to punch the smirk off his face. *Hands off my family!*

'The article you must write is about the knotweed. We need photographs, and no one else is willing to go. The other journalists aren't so comfortable around such filth.' He recoiled at the thought and Declan giggled next to him. 'Take an Autocar – be grateful I'm not making you walk – and take a camera to get some photographs. Then write a lovely article about how the Centre is fixing everything. Heroically cleaning up Perimeter mess, as usual. Understand?'

'I assume no one is willing to go because it actually *is* dangerous?' I said without relaxing my jaw.

'Well, you are the most expendable member of the Press team.'

Anger rose in my belly like hot coals until it threatened to burst.

'I think a trip to the edge will be good for you. Don't you think so, Declan?'

Declan was smiling and rubbing his hands together. 'A reminder, I think, of where you and your family could end up. I'm sure your wife will enjoy living among the fish.'

Screw this. Screw him. Screw all the Centre pricks!

He wanted me to sack nearly two hundred people and then

take photos that could further endanger them and me. No. I was not his puppet. Not anymore. I was not risking my family. If he wanted photographs, he could bloody well take them himself.

'No.'

Greg lowered his chins to stare right at me. 'Excuse me?'

'No. If it's not safe, I'm not going. If it's going to mislead the Perimeter, I'm not doing it.' And I turned and left his office. My attempt to slam the door resulted in an unsatisfying sigh, as it was too heavy for me to push hard enough. I groaned, frustrated, and kicked it instead.

I was too tired to kiss that great stinking arse. Perhaps having Ethan had finally emboldened me, though I felt every bit the trembling coward as I retreated down the hallway. I leant against the corridor wall and allowed myself to simmer down. As my heart rate slowed, apprehension crept in. Where there had been anger and adrenaline, a void of fear remained.

Talking to Greg like that was not going to pass without consequences, I knew that, yet after a few deep breaths I had an epiphany. A beam of light shone through the shadow, so bright it dazzled me. For the first time in my life, I had options. Greg's threats didn't have to rile me now, and I didn't have to play along with his sick games. I didn't have to stay in the Perimeter, or on the Raft, even. The satellite phone, that pilfered piece of contraband, was our way out, and I imagined making that call. If the Centre were going to force me to do their dirty work, we would leave.

As I walked back down the corridor, I noticed the lab staff were red-eyed and staring my way. Lars had vanished, likely back to whatever hole he'd come from before the repercussions of his audit impacted him. 195 staff. I couldn't ask anyone else to tell them. I was lumped with that devastating task.

'All right, everyone, back to work. I'll speak to the team leaders downstairs.'

In mute agony, they obeyed, returning to their stations, their work of scientific excellence – the best minds in the world working to line the deepest pockets. What did a few jobs of the poor matter when the rich wanted to go to Mars? We had all seen the headlines, of course. 'Holidays are back!' Sterile holidays. Holidays without fear of germs and pathogens. The biodome they were creating wasn't concreted, so disinfectant wasn't needed. The universe provided the vast vacuum of space to rid the rock of life. And now, soon, the world's richest could frequent it on a spacecraft more luxurious than anyone from the Perimeter could ever imagine. Delivering the Elite to the galaxy's first space spa break. As long as everyone else worked hard enough.

Amalyn was in Archie's office. I gave the door a gentle knock.

'Oh, Sav,' she cried as I put my arm around her. 'Do you know how he died? I just can't believe it.'

Last time I had seen Harold, he'd looked more tired than most, his skin hanging off him like he had some collagen disease or muscle wastage. I hadn't assumed he was sick, though. Overworked, maybe, but not at death's door.

'It's such a shame, Ams. He was a good man.'

'I'm going to have to go see the rest of the Golden Fifty. Let them know.'

She held her forearm with the tattoo to her chest as she spoke. With the symbol of the remembrance group against her heart, she closed her eyes, her cheeks pale with grief and nostalgia.

Archie rubbed her back. 'Whatever you need to do, Ams. I'll go with you.'

She rested her head on his shoulder. 'It's so sad. He really stood up for the Perimeter, you know? With such integrity. He never let those Centre pricks take that from him.'

I squeezed my mouth shut, shame making me blush as I knew how little I had done for my own people, and how much I had profited from treachery. 'He'll be missed,' I said. 'He was a great mind.'

I left them to it. Archie was enough of a comfort on his own.

I went to my office and took my anger out on my computer for a few minutes by drafting an email to send to the team leaders downstairs, full of expletives about Greg and BioLabs and the Centre. I wrote everything I wanted to say, then deleted it. Despite having options, I wasn't ready to rebel that much. My refusal to write the knotweed article was the most insubordinate I had ever been. Defiance didn't suit me. It made my pulse flutter and my back clammy. I made a cup of MimikTea and wrote a more professional email instead.

I buried a sigh. *Microbes!*

Japanese knotweed. I mulled it over and over, my thoughts bouncing from one conclusion to the next.

Just take the photos. Cass and Sal said it was fine.

Screw Greg. Why should I go to the edge?

Do as you're told. You don't know what the consequences will be.

You have less integrity than Harold. Stop lying to the Perimeter.

If I refused, the fallout would make my mind up for me. But could I really flee the Raft and live on the Mainland? In the Tunnels, living like bugs, *eating* bugs ...? I couldn't see it. As nice as it was to have an option, it was a weird, filthy pipe dream. No way could I live like filth. But Isaac ...

No. I had lived this long without my brother. The rest of my life would have to be just the same.

So many pros and cons ran through my head. The Raft was crumbling. I lived nowhere near the edge. Greg was a prick. I had a good job. I could always speak to Isaac on the phone and maybe visit. Grace and Ethan. *Grace and Ethan.*

The smug feeling of getting off the Raft and telling Greg where to go, getting the upper hand, was a major argument for leaving. But letting my ego and rage dictate such a big decision was likely to be a mistake. I should just take the sodding pictures and write the article, to be on the safe side. But the sinking feeling of humility and having to swallow my pride ... I didn't know if I was big enough.

My computer pinged to say I had received an email from Greg containing an attachment from Lars. It was that Centre snitch's detailed assessment of every staff member's usefulness. I printed it out and read for as long as I could tolerate it.

Professor Selbourne: easily agitated, but the staff do work efficiently in her presence. Useful for her abilities if not her personality.

Archibald Reynolds: getting rid of him would be more hassle than it's worth. Finding a decent replacement would be tricky.

Amalyn Blake: a good researcher. Worth keeping just to look at.

I stopped reading after that. His vulgar assessments made my blood boil. What an awful man. How did such cruelty serve him at all? What had Greg promised him?

I fantasised about writing a review of him:

Lars Cowley: repulsive pervert. No skills. No use whatsoever. Clearly has never owned a toothbrush.

I wrote that in my email, and then, again, deleted it. Cursing myself for my cowardice, I sat and imagined all the emails I would send if I got off the Raft. That would be one satisfying day.

Lars hadn't assessed the factory staff individually, only to say that there were too many, and so 195 people from downstairs were to be let go. The whole factory floor was to be taken over by five massive machines, so one person per machine would suffice. That seemed incredibly tight to me. If one person was off sick, then the entire factory would be put under strain. The stupidity of that level of thriftiness was ridiculous.

I read through the email again and noticed that the actual number to be sacked was 196. Reading through the staff assessments more thoroughly, I saw his concluding statement and read it several times. Then I heard the scurry of Penny's footsteps approaching my office.

'Professor Selbourne.' She looked like she'd applied more makeup on top of yesterday's. 'I will be on hand to offer support to all the staff who are losing their livelihoods today. I have some career-advice leaflets and plenty of tissues.'

'Penny, come in. Close the door.' I regretted that request almost instantly. I was about to be asphyxiated by rip-off Chanel.

She swelled with pride. I think this was the first time I had ever invited her into my office. Normally she barged in and I had to tell her to get out. She stepped in and looked around the vast, empty space, her feeling of self-worth way outstripping mine.

'I understand Lars has been very thorough, the poor man. It must have been so hard for him.'

'Penny, we really need to talk about this—'

'Good, good,' she said, overly eager to finally have some real issues to deal with. 'We should work out our rapport. We don't want to leave them feeling hopeless. There are options for them – limited ones, of course – but I have information from various recruitment accounts and will do lots of research to help the poor souls. We need to find the kindest way to tell the staff.'

'Kind words are your thing, Penny, not mine.'

She gave me a triumphant smile and nodded, her frizzy hair nodding with her. 'I am aware of that fact, Professor. I shall be on hand to—'

'Penny,' I interrupted. She was never going to give me a pause in which to speak. 'You're on the list.'

'Excuse me?'

I handed her the printout. 'I'm sorry, Penny. They've decided to let you go.'

Her face froze as she took the printout from me. She didn't look at it, her reddening eyes staring straight at me. I was glad she didn't. Handing it to her was a stupid thing to do. Lars's words were harsh. Even I wasn't cruel enough to write such things.

Penny Jenkins: serves no real purpose. Has too much time on her hands. Unlikeable and all-round waste of space.

'Lars ... Lars decided that *I* am not needed?' Her bottom lip quivered. Her face fell. Even her hair appeared to drop.

It was the one time I wished my office had an extra chair. The one time I ever felt sorry for Penny. 'I'm really sorry, Penny.'

She put the printout back on my desk and held her head a little higher.

'Well, I'm still the wellbeing manager until the other staff have been cared for.' She swallowed, failing to still her bottom lip. 'So I shall continue to do my job and assist with supporting all the staff through their redundancies.'

I shook my head. She didn't have to do that. 'Oh, Penny—'

'No.' She held up a hand. 'I'm still the wellbeing manager. I will be here, supporting others, until the end of next week. I must be here to support the staff, as that is my job. That is still my job.'

She stepped out of my office and went to the kitchen, her scurry sounding quieter than usual as she walked away.

14

Chapter thirteen

Grace rubbed the stress out of my shoulders that evening on the sofa after we had struggled to get Ethan to go to bed. He didn't want my affections, only Grace's. My demeanour didn't seem to hit the right note, my impatience reflecting in him. I sat alone and frustrated on the sofa until Grace had calmed him down. My glass of wine wasn't cold enough, I hadn't slept well in days, I was dreading firing all the staff and the racket of Ethan's vexations was giving me a headache.

'Maybe just try to spend some time with him,' Grace said as I winced through her massage. 'What did Greg say about taking some time off?'

'I didn't really get the chance to speak to him about that, what with everything else.'

'When this launch is over, and the awful business of sacking all those poor people, maybe you could book some leave? Spend a good week at home – over school holidays would be great. Help Ethan with his homework.'

That would have meant a week of sitting in the apartment, enclosed in those walls. Stuffy, restricted, confined. My sulks would dwarf those of Ethan's. I could not be as happily confined as Grace. The storms outside suited her. They gave her more reasons not to leave the apartment. 'Have you seen what humidity does to curly hair?' she would say. I'd laugh a reply, as if mine looked any better.

Where motherhood had sucked away my vitality, it had restored hers. No longer wasting hours staring out the window, these days she ran around the apartment, clearing up after Ethan, playing with him, feeding him. She had tried rather unsuccessfully to teach him guitar. Her whole world was inside those walls. Nothing else was important. The occasional glances were there, though. I'd catch her in brief moments when she would pause and check out to daydream, to look upon that huge iron fence that poked above the high-rises. Glinting in the setting sun, it was like a beacon to her, tempting her. 'We're so close,' she'd say.

Too close for my liking. That fence surrounded nothing but the Centre's indoctrination. It was if it was a filter for integrity. It appeared to me as a barricade for truth, a huge shackle keeping us all obedient and in our place.

Not close enough, is what Grace wanted to say. In her mind, the concrete inside that fence shone.

* * *

I was in bed on Saturday morning, enjoying a rare lie-in as Ethan hadn't woken us up yet. I was comfortable, enjoying my sleep, when my phone started buzzing. Greg's name flashed on the screen.

Doesn't the prick know it's the weekend?

I ignored it, cancelled the call and considered blocking his number. His damned knotweed article could wait until I'd decided if I was doing it. He rang again and again and I picked up my phone to silence it. As I did so, Archie rang.

'What?' I barked down the line. 'It's the weekend and it's early.'

'There's been a break-in.'

'What?' I sat up, suddenly awake. 'Your place?'

'No, the lab. You've not had a call from Greg?'

'About a hundred. I've been ignoring them.'

'Well, everyone has to go in. The place is trashed, apparently.'

'Microbes. Seriously? It's the weekend.'

'Tell that to the burglars. We'll see you in the Autocar?'

I groaned. 'Yeah, okay, I'll be at yours in twenty. Or more like thirty.'

Grace was still sleeping. I envied how well she always managed to sleep. Not even a thunderstorm would wake her. Ethan's cries had a certain pitch that she would pick up even in her deepest of sleeps, but any other noise didn't disturb her at all. I watched her for a while, yearning to curl around her and wake her in a more loving way than by telling her I had to go to work. I watched her chest rise and fall for a moment, listened to her little nose whistles, then got dressed.

It was so typical that the first weekend in ages that Ethan slept in, I had to get up. It would have been my first lie-in with Grace in months. Putting up with work crap at the weekend was the last thing I wanted to do when I was exhausted, anyway. Our family weekend plans were in tatters. I didn't even have time to shower. I wrote a note for Grace and left the apartment, managing to tiptoe out instead of stomping and slamming the door, which would have been far more satisfying.

Marcus and Mabel were already at the lab when Archie, Amalyn and I arrived, as were 4-09 and 8-08, while 2-10 was absent. He had probably left his phone off. I kicked myself for not doing the same and promised myself to turn it off on Friday night and not turn it on again until Monday from then on.

The mess was maddening. 'Trashed' seemed quite apt. Broken glassware, spilt liquids and paperwork were scattered everywhere. There were several smashed computer screens, and even the staffroom hadn't escaped.

'Why?' I cried. 'Who breaks into a food lab?'

'It's a lab,' Amalyn said. 'They probably thought they could find drugs or something.'

'Bloody Alternates!'

'Hey!' Amalyn looked hurt. 'You've had a central postcode for too long. I don't think you realise what it's like for some people around here. It's likely they were just hungry and looking for food. The tax hikes have been crazy lately.'

Archie was inspecting hard drives, making sure no information had been lost.

'Why did they have to smash up a computer?' I asked, unable to moderate my tone.

'Withdrawal, desperation, anger ...' said Amalyn. 'This whole Mars thing that BioLabs is supporting has hiked prices up so much, people are starving. It's like the famines again, only this time there's tons of food, they just can't afford it. Maybe it was some of the factory staff. They must have heard rumours they're getting the chop. No healthcare, can't afford food, tax hikes. I can hardly blame them, to be honest. Reckon I'd do the same.'

'Ruining people's weekends over a temper tantrum is not right, whatever their reasons.'

'Jeez, Sav, that's nice. Really nice.' She dropped some broken glass on the floor and stormed off.

'Good news, team,' Archie said, walking over. 'The hard drives all seem fine.' He watched Amalyn angrily sweep at the floor at the other end of the lab. 'What have I missed?'

'Nothing. Just Amalyn defending the people who did this. I mean, look at this. Thousands of pounds of damage, our weekends ruined, and for what? It's stupid.'

'Ah, I see.' He put the hard drive down and reached for his coat. 'Shall we go for a walk? I want to show you something.'

I looked around at the other staff, all cleaning, the icy ambience doing nothing to calm my rage. 'Sure, let's get out of here for a bit.'

Our walk turned into an Autocar ride as we stepped out and the smog instantly irritated me. Irritated me more, I should say. The wind was cool but still I itched as my T-shirt clung to me. The sticky smog and salty air created a cocktail of vexation. It wasn't even a warm day, but I was sweating, my broiling temper dripping off me, and the Autocar climate control wasn't up to the job of quelling my heat.

After ten minutes or so of silence, Archie said we should get out and stroll to a part of the Perimeter I had not visited in years. I was not in the mood to walk, especially not in the humid smog with the wind ripping at me. I was in the mood for sitting at home, eating IcyCrema and spending time with my family.

'The old fish docks,' I said. 'Lovely. Why have we come here?'

'Just look,' Archie said, pointing at where the docks used to be.

'At what?' I said, my tone more biting than the wind. 'The dirty docks have gone. There are some new apartment blocks and a desalination plant. This was done ages ago. Is this the sort of romantic night-time stroll you and Amalyn go on?'

'Out to sea. Can you see it?'

'There's a massive wall and I'm shorter than you. All I can see is wall.'

'Okay, now don't shout at me.' He stood behind me and then lifted me up by my soggy armpits.

'What the hell, Archie?'

'Just look at the sea.'

I huffed and did as I was told before his hands dug in any more. The sea looked as it always did. A rancid soup of green-black sludge. Several large ships floated off the coast. I kicked behind me at Archie's thighs and he put me down.

'See?'

'The godawful sea and boats. There've always been fishing boats. Fish junkies need to scoop out their kicks.'

'But those aren't the old boats. Those are Centre boats.'

I frowned. 'Why would the Centre have boats?'

'To fish. The Alternates can't anymore. The Centre dismantled their docks and destroyed all their boats. Now only the Centre fish. They extract all the drugs, purify them and sell them to the pharmacies. The Alternates get nothing.'

My face was getting hotter, which I didn't think possible, my cheeks burning. I recalled the sight of that awful fish Grace hoarded in the freezer, the teeth marks, the stench of it on her breath. Too scared to seek professional help, too worried of the implications, she had stooped that low.

'Stopping people eating putrid fish is hardly a bad thing,'

I said. I still believed in healthcare. I still believed most of the Alternates were just useless consumers. A lifetime of conditioning wasn't so easily erased.

'But when it's your only source of medicine, it's a very bad thing. Look now, over this way.'

I followed him a few metres along the shore until the stench of rotten fish hit me. It had been years since I'd experienced that odour and I'd forgotten quite how repulsive it was. It was as if my tongue was decaying. Even holding my breath didn't help. How I'd ever managed to walk the edge streets was beyond me. Had it been that bad before? It must have been. I had just become central-soft.

Archie pushed me forwards, the wind making my hair frizzier than Penny's. I tried to hold it in place but to no avail. I would look like I'd lost a fight with an electrical socket when we got back. We waded through the odour until we saw some crates of fish being unloaded. People in hazmat suits were carrying sealed boxes and taking them from the guarded dock to the trucks. The trucks were armoured, with barred windows, and patrolled by guards sporting tasers and batons.

Archie leant in and spoke softly. 'All of that is bound for a pharma lab, where it will then be handed over to Centre control.'

Lurking in the shadows close to the vehicle were Alternates, their tatty, paint-stained clothes a dead giveaway. That, and having nothing else to do during the day other than hang around street corners. The smog around the edge was thick, but what was happening was clear. They approached the trucks, begging, fistfuls of cash from god knows where, offering their bodies or anything else they had for a fish.

'It's not always to get high,' Archie said. 'Anti-cancer drugs, heart medication, antidepressants – all the medicines are concentrated in the fish.'

I didn't need telling. I knew. Humankind had dumped its waste into the sea for centuries. The oceans hoarded more drugs than any pharmacy. The fish soaked it up like grimy sponges.

They shouldn't have existed anymore, the Alternates, if the Minister of Impartiality's plan had worked properly. Scaring people into conformity, taking away privileges – no, not privileges, *rights* – was meant to make them into cogs in the Centre's great machine. But it had just marginalised them further, pushing them into obscurity. They suffered silently, their sense of self continuing long after their self-worth had gone.

Grace, I thought. *That could have been Grace.* What would have happened to her if she hadn't had the fish when she'd needed it? Her depression had consumed her entirely. I despised the thought that eating that disgusting carcass had helped, but it had.

'All right, Archie. I get your point.' I swallowed my pride. 'It's quite possible that whoever broke into the lab wasn't evil, just desperate.'

'Yep, and this is just that side of things. There are plenty of working people, non-Alternates, who can't access healthcare or afford food. Shall we go see some of them?'

'Poverty tourism isn't really my thing,' I said, feeling terrible. 'Let's go back and help clean up. I won't moan anymore.'

I apologised to Amalyn when we got back. With my tail between my legs, Archie said, which made me gag. What a filthy animal's extra limb had to do with anything, I did not know. She bore no grudge and smiled it away.

'It's okay, Sav,' she said. 'Most people don't understand.'

But I did understand. I should have known better. I was Perimeter, after all.

The lab had been mostly cleaned up by then. Mabel had managed to make most of the workstations useable, while 4-09 and 8-08 were setting aside the bags of rubbish and counting what needed to be ordered. Marcus was making a poor attempt to fix the broken door frame with plastic boards. It was all we had to hand, so it had to do. He actually looked the happiest I'd ever seen him. Perhaps everyone helping to clean up was a pleasant experience for him. Archie even went over to help him with the door.

It was past lunchtime by the time we'd finished. As the last rubbish bag was cleared away and the final desk polished, everyone gave a little cheer and I felt a warming sense of team spirit. We'd all worked together and got a hideous job done. I thanked them all, and they thanked each other, looking relieved the task was finished. With a sense of gratification, I did something I'd never done before and suggested we all go for a drink. I even said I'd buy a round.

The response mostly comprised of mumbled excuses and people running out the door. I was left standing by my office, deflated and dejected. Archie and Amalyn stayed, their faces red from restrained laughter.

'What's so funny?'

Archie doubled over, eventually finding a pause in his laughing fit to speak in.

'I'm sorry, Sav, really. We love you, we really do. The rest respect you. But, I mean, you're hardly sociable with the staff. You don't even know their names. Why would they want to go for a drink with you?'

Amalyn caught her breath and wiped her eyes. 'What would you even say to them? Oh, it would have been so awkward. I wish they had come! Imagine sitting in a bar and saying, "So, 4-09, how's home life?" All the while, Mabel would be having a panic attack and Marcus shedding skin peelings all over the table.'

They burst into laughter again.

I scowled, then laughed too. 'I think I got a bit lost in the moment there. Thinking about it, I'm glad they didn't want to come.'

'Come on,' Amalyn said. 'Let's go for a drink.'

I didn't stay in the bar long. I really did want to get home, but the drink went down remarkably well. The bar was quiet, as it had been the last time we'd gone there. The staff looked worn out, and I felt glad I could give them some business. A few bars we walked past on the way were boarded up. A couple of MindSpas too.

'Loads of places are closing,' Amalyn said. 'Tax hikes are making the little businesses unaffordable.'

Archie nodded. 'Businesses shutting, livelihoods gone, people breaking into labs, scrounging the fish workers for scraps. Whatever's on Mars, it's not worth this.'

'There are protests planned,' Amalyn said, sipping something fluorescent orange. 'Against the tax hikes. But you know, for a protest to be legitimate, you have to have a licence now, and that licence costs more than anyone can afford. Without a licence, a protest is considered a riot, and that's illegal. So, you get jailed, but no one can pay the bail money.'

'And it's not like people can get another job, just like that.' Archie clicked his fingers. 'Tech has replaced so many people.

Where are they going to work?'

'You heard what some people are saying?' Amalyn asked. 'The Centre are blowing up the Raft on purpose. They know where the unemployed and the Alternates live and are just getting rid of them.'

I listened, but that level of conspiracy theory seemed a bit much, even for Amalyn. 'No way. I mean, some of those apartments would have been two beds. For people with kids. That seems unlikely.'

'Or they're just sinking all the ghost apartments, making everyone else closer to the sea. There have hardly been any new developments in ages. It's probably a year or more since I last saw a new block go up. They've got too many and now they're sinking them.'

'But why? They built them – they've gone to that expense. Even empty they're worth more than they are in the sea.'

Amalyn shrugged. 'Insurance?'

'Oh, come on. The insurance companies are all in the Centre. As if they'd sink their own businesses.'

'Well,' – she necked the last of her drink – 'one thing I'm sure of is it's not the damned knotweed.'

I left the bar and got an Autocar home. They'd ordered more drinks for themselves and, as tempting as it was to stay, I'd missed out on enough family time already. When I got back to my apartment, Grace had dinner on, Ethan was playing a computer game and the apartment was a mess, toys everywhere. A frosty wind was blowing through a window left ajar, and a cup of tea had been spilled on the table.

'Erm, hi Grace?' She didn't look my way and continued to stir a pot on the stove. 'Grace?'

'What, Sav? I've had a hell of a day. What?'

'Nothing. Just wondering—'

'What?' Her bitter tone cut through the air. 'Why is it such a mess in here? Is that what you're wondering? Well, let me think. I've been at work all week, Ethan needs constant entertainment, help with his homework, I have lesson planning to do and you're not here.' She slammed the spoon against the kitchen worktop and grabbed a bottle of wine from the fridge. 'You know what Ethan said today?' she asked as she poured. 'He swore. He said ...' She looked over her shoulder to check he wasn't listening and whispered. 'He said "microbes". That sort of language doesn't come from me. It seems the only impression you're having on our son is to make him potty-mouthed.' She took a big gulp from her wineglass.

I looked at Ethan, sat so innocently, playing on his tablet. I restrained a smile, feeling a little proud that at least there was some of me in the little lad. *The cheeky boy!* 'I'm really sorry, Grace. It was an emergency. There was a break-in at the lab.'

'I know.' She poured herself more wine. 'I know it was an emergency, and I'm not mad at you for working. It's just ... This is hard for me, without Maisie, and you're always so busy. Honestly, I don't know if I can manage. And it's only his first week at school and my first week back full-time. Without Maisie, it's so much harder.'

She looked at me, her eyes framed by dark circles. Guilt crept over me as I realised how tired she was. I hadn't noticed. Too involved with everything else going on, I had neglected more than just the truth. I stroked her back, which she accepted but didn't reciprocate with any affection. 'It'll get easier, I promise. It was only this one weekend.'

She pulled her head back and narrowed her eyes, then sniffed loudly. 'Have you been to the bar?'

I bit my lip. 'Just for one. I felt I should reward the team for their hard work.'

'*Their* hard work!' She pulled away from me and stormed off.

* * *

By Sunday, Grace had calmed down enough to talk to me again. I tidied and cleaned the apartment, fed Ethan and helped him with his homework, all by the time she'd got out of bed. I'd even stashed my phone in a drawer so I wouldn't be disturbed. When she got up, I handed her a cup of MimikTea as she sank into the sofa.

'Have you seen his assessment scores?' Grace asked.

'No,' I said, taken aback. 'He's five. He's had assessments already?'

'Every week. To make sure he's keeping up. And you know, even though he had two days off in his first week, he came out on top. Now, I know what you're going to say – all your interns were top of their class, so it means nothing – but he did so well. I really think he's a genius. He's going to be a doctor or something, live in the Centre, cure diseases, maybe. He's going to be brilliant, I know it.'

I joined her on the sofa and kissed her cheek. 'He'll be whatever he will be. As long as he's happy and useful, that's enough.' That same morning, he had attempted to brush his teeth with the handle of his toothbrush and walked into a door frame. I was reserving judgement on the kid's genius.

'Oh, I know,' Grace said, 'and I'm not pushy, just proud. And so handsome, isn't he?'

'I wonder who he gets his gorgeous looks from.'

It was obvious. Some days I'd look at Grace and her beauty would simply captivate me. I was so plain in comparison. But little Ethan, our golden-haired boy, was the most gorgeous of all. Dark eyes that made him look like an old soul, wise beyond childhood. I saw so much of Grace in him. His smile lit up his whole face. He had her bounce, the bounce she'd had in her younger days before the harshness of the world had taken it from her. Her happiness had returned when she'd had Ethan, but she was never the same Grace she used to be. Too astute, yet too naive. But Ethan, he brimmed with angelic innocence and exuberance. Such a good boy, such a delight.

Most of the time, anyway.

He had inherited Grace's anxieties and so allowed any tinge of sadness to consume him. So often, I felt incompetent. I couldn't soothe him the way she did. I didn't have her patience or intuition. She could tell when the tears were coming and knew the right words to make them go away. Excitement could envelop him as well as sadness, and given a few metres of freedom he would devour the space. He was an explorer by nature, yet even after six years of clean streets, Grace still ventured outside so little. Any moment Ethan was out of the apartment, she was terrified for him, of what germs he might pick up, the sharp edges of buildings, trip hazards on the pavement. Everything she saw outside was a danger to him, yet he longed for adventure. His entire existence had been between our apartment and Maisie's, and now even those little excursions would stop. I dreaded the tantrums that would ensue.

On my mind was the Mainland, the Tunnels, the opportunities he would or wouldn't have there. Would there be a place for him? Would he be better off? He'd have more space to run around and explore. Would my stubbornness with Greg limit his choices later if we didn't leave, in the same way my parents' lifestyles had stifled mine? I should just write the bloody article. Not for my vanity, but for Ethan. My pride shouldn't negatively impact him. We still lived under the rule of the Centre. However much I wanted us to break free from their clutches, we weren't there yet. And if breaking free meant living underground like worms, we probably never would be.

I watched him finish his reading and go over his spellings. He had a good concentration span at times, that was obvious. He could apply himself and sit quietly when he wanted. But he didn't look like a genius to me. He looked like my cheeky little boy. A head of curls and the sweetest grin. He knew nothing of ambition or purpose or ladder climbing.

Stay just as you are, please!

That night, tossing and turning in our too-hot bed, my head was plagued with images of the Tunnels. I dreamed I was back there, and it felt real. Too real, still haunting me.

I was in that lumpy bed, eyes closed, but still able to see that orange hue. I heard Ethan laughing and running down the corridor, little Clem running with him. She was his age, always a little girl to me, not the grown woman she had become. Their game sounded like everything a child's game should be. Running free, energetic, all giggles and excitement.

When I opened my eyes, Grace's hair was all over my face. I breathed in its clean scent as it tickled my nose. When I sat up, the hair came with me, detached from her head. It fell in endless thick locks to the floor. I brushed it off me, but it coiled like rope all around us. I looked down at Grace, sleeping, scratchy blankets pulled up under her chin. She looked warm in the orange light, peach-coloured cheeks, soft eyes and mouth. Even her bald head looked rosy. Her mouth was in a half-smile, her face smooth and content. My heart ached with how beautiful she was. She could never look anything but beautiful.

15

Chapter fourteen

Penny and I began the firing process on Monday. I told her several times her input wasn't necessary, but that seemed to hurt her more than getting sacked. I had been dreading it and was unsure whether her presence and the fussing that came with it would make it easier on the staff or just drag it out longer. But she insisted, and I had little will to argue.

We spent all morning in meetings with the two team leaders from the factory floor. The factory was none of my business, so I rarely ventured down there. My job role involved telling them what to make, and they made it. It was not my place to fire them, but Greg had burdened me with the task anyway. Revenge for the knotweed article, I was sure. I was not the poison, but I was the delivery vessel. We left the team leaders with the task of deciding which employees to let go. The weight of it seemed to hang from their faces.

Penny was gracious where I was curt, understanding where I was impatient, comforting where I was awkward. Her frilly words softened the blow. She lacked efficiency with her language and her voice sounded like the rusty bikes of the Tunnels. Ten words turned into twenty, a five-minute meeting into ten. But she shouldered the load with poise, all the while knowing that she was also out of a job.

On top of everything, I was tasked with sorting out Professor Harold's work. We'd had a working relationship over the years – a mutual respect, I thought – but disdain for the country and its Elite had stunted his intellectual accomplishments. He'd let it cloud his progress. I sifted through his research papers. There was so much good he could have done if he'd applied himself to his job rather than the Golden Fifty. I took the hard drive from his desk and left the rest of his untidy office to the cleaners and his next of kin. Someone would be appointed to take his place in ProLabs. BioLabs was buying them out, but their premises were to remain in place. At least that was one team we didn't have to fire.

I stopped by Archie and Amalyn's apartment on the way home on Monday evening. He had something he wanted to show me, to 'celebrate our test results,' as Amalyn had put it in the Autocar ride. *Any excuse for a drink*, I thought. We were both clear from our swab tests after visiting the Mainland, which was a relief. I felt fine, but the filth we had been surrounded by still niggled at me. Had we used enough antibacterial gel? The spray in the plane had seemed mild and it hadn't even irritated my skin. And even mouthing the word 'lice' made me want to throw up. Could it ever be an option to live there, a place where they still ate vermin, with no street sprayers, living in tunnels dug in filth? Still, I was relieved that whatever bug Jocelyn and Ethan had picked up, they at least hadn't caught it from me.

I texted Grace and explained that Archie and Amalyn needed help with some issue with the apartment, and that she could join us if she wanted. She replied: 'OK. Don't be late. XXX.'

I was finding it hard to spend time with Grace. I had too much I wanted to say. It was impossible to articulate the worries plaguing my mind. Where would I even begin? I recalled all too vividly her years of emptiness and depression. I couldn't concern her with my worries and burdens. She was too delicate. The joy of motherhood had given her strength, but it was a brittle exoskeleton that could shatter.

Guilt ate away at me. At home, I had to close off the part of my mind that was deep in deception, and that closure left me quiet, unable to form any words, as my voice was shackled by silence. In Grace's presence, I withered with remorse. When we were physically close, I felt the chasm of lies between us. It was easier to be mute and vacant than to gloss over the lies with small talk and gestures. When I dealt with what I had seen some more, taken more time to process it all, I would be able to be more open again. That's what I concluded, at least.

There were boxes everywhere around Archie's apartment and not nearly enough furniture to fill the place, but Archie and Amalyn looked delighted with the space and the cleanliness of the neighbourhood. We cracked open a bottle of Pinot GrigNo and sat on the floor to toast their new home.

I drank a whole glass before sitting down and immediately poured myself another. My guilt over my absence at home dissolved a little more with every sip. 'I'm so pleased you guys are away from the edge. You'll be much safer here,' I said.

Amalyn nodded, but she sounded melancholy. 'Yeah, *we* are safe, but we have a lot of friends that live at the edge. Most of the Golden Fifty live there.'

I eyed their tattoos. Archie now had one of his own on his forearm, freshly made and still red raw.

'We can't help everyone,' I said.

'Be nice if we knew what was actually going on, though,' Archie said. 'If only I could access some more satellites. I'll bet the Centre knows exactly what's happening. And what the dirtquakes are.'

'Ignorance is bliss,' I said, joking for their benefit, although I meant it in earnest.

'Seriously, Sav, we really need to know what's going on. I can hardly access any satellites these days, only the ones I really need for work. Even the Raft is censored in the images. I can still access some systems, but not like I used to. And none of my old friends will help me now. They don't even answer my calls or reply to emails.'

'Yeah, we kind of rinsed it, didn't we?'

He raised his eyebrow at me. 'Well, thing is ...'

'Oh god, Archie, why do I get the feeling I'm not going to like this?'

'Hey, after all the favours I've done for you over the years.'

'I believe I repaid you well with cups of tea.'

'Anyway ...' He peered into his empty cup. 'Here.' He handed me a little black disc, about the size of my thumbnail, just a little thicker than a piece of paper. On the underside, gold wires were flat against the surface.

'Great. What is it?'

'I've heard you're getting an invite to the Centre imminently.' He bit his lip.

'Where the hell have you heard that?'

'Greg's emails. He's pissed at you for not doing the knotweed photos.'

'Mid-level hacking is still possible for you, then.'

'That little disc,' he continued, ignoring me, 'those little wires go into a USB drive, if you just place that disc over it. It'll stay in place and it's almost invisible. If you could attach that to a hard drive in the Centre, I'll be able to access their systems.'

'Jesus, Archie, I'll get thrown in the sea for having such a thing!'

'We're all going to end up in the sea anyway,' Amalyn said with a sniff.

'I can't.' I tried to hand it back to him, but he put his hands behind his back. 'It's way too dangerous. I'll bet they've got cameras everywhere,' I said.

'You're the only one that can, Sav,' Amalyn said. 'We wouldn't ask if it wasn't important. So many people are at risk.'

'They won't even know what it is,' Archie said. 'It's hacker tech. The Centre don't have such things. They don't need to hack, so why would they?'

I shook my head, handling the thing like it was a hot coal. 'It's not like they're going to leave me to wander the halls or anything. They look at me like I'm vermin there.'

'Just try. Please? If I can get into their systems, I reckon I'll be able to see exactly where is most likely to break away next, *and* if they're doing anything about it. I'll have access to everything. Also, if we go to the Mainland, I'll be able to tell if we've been detected, get us solarplane permits, whatever we need. We're blind right now – it's all guesswork. This could give us everything we need.'

Oh, he could nag.

'All right, all right. No promises, but I'll do my best.'

* * *

The email inviting me to the Centre came on Tuesday after-noon. At least work was a bit calmer since the backdrop of compliments had come to an end. I still had a lot to do, though, and the time out of the lab was going to be nothing but an inconvenience. In true Centre style, the email gave me very little notice and demanded my presence the very next day. Too much time had passed for my recent swab test to be valid, so I had to find time to get tested again.

I knew all too well that, without a swab test, the Centre would deny me entry or I'd risk being turned away or locked in a quarantine box for a week. The invitation didn't name the member of staff I'd be seeing. Minister roles largely went unchanged for several years, barring the odd reshuffle when they got bored, and the lack of clarity made me think it would be someone mediocre with ideas of climbing up. Whichever of them seemed the most intimidating, so they could bully me into taking photos of knotweed, I imagined.

I recalled when I'd met the Minister of Impartiality in the Centre some years back. She'd said that stability was key, that the old world had encouraged greed, which had in turn created a sense of failure. Knowing your lot from the get-go is the key to a functioning country, she'd said. I had often thought she was right, especially when I witnessed Grace's despondency when she stared at that iron fence, wishing and imagining she was on the other side of it. But I had also seen the opulence of the Centre, their new fabrics being woven, their solarplanes, the entrance to their library. And we could all see their Mars project. The sky was the limit for ambition if you were born in the Centre. There was a ceiling made of concrete for us in the Perimeter.

I prepared little for my meeting since I cared so little about the outcome. I had my permit, took an Autocar and tried to relax. It was a short drive to the Centre fence from my apartment, such was the luxury of my address since their last bribery.

What bribery can I expect this time?

I sweated at the gates, Archie's little black disc making my palms clammy. So tiny and discreet yet screaming in my pocket, it felt like an obvious bulge, hot and obtrusive against my leg. To my relief, I passed security checks quickly. The Autocar was scrubbed, and in no time at all I was driving past row upon row of SolaArbs and ArbAirs keeping the Centre supplied with power and the air as clean as could be.

The SolaArb forests gleamed in the sunshine, like the inherited jewellery my mother had kept in her dresser but never wore. 'Too gaudy, too showy,' she'd say.

As the Autocar skirted the gold statues flanking the entrance-way to the School of Politics, I couldn't help but stare. The school was little more than a breeding ground for the Elite. Frightfully expensive to attend, it ensured that only the richest ended up in power. The next generation of politicians, young and already holding their chins high, were standing outside, gossiping, slapping each other's backs, engaging in ways young people in the Perimeter didn't dare. Solidifying their friendships, their acquaintances being their most valuable possessions. Such affiliations would be essential when they took their ministerial roles for the Blue Liberation Party.

Some loved the Blue Liberation for blowing up the anchors, for severing our ties with the outside world once and for all (or so they claimed). But such disuniting had cut the bonds only for the Perimeter. All the time, the Centre still secretly had access. They'd never lost touch with their families. They'd never had to make the sacrifices we had. As I drove through the Centre that day, past the grandiose skyscrapers, the wide, polished streets, the clothing shops and welcoming seating areas, my ambivalence simmered into hatred, more than I had ever felt.

What else have they lied about? How much more are they going to take from us?

As Amalyn said, we have what we need. They have what they want.

I couldn't resist the call of the Selfie Station, and I had a few minutes to spare to brighten my complexion. The Centre's fully staffed and well-stocked outlets were so much more tempting than the dreary fakery of the Perimeter. The beautician commented on my wrinkles and offered me injections if I wanted them (I did not) while the hairdresser added some glitter sheen to my flat hair, by some miracle giving it volume. My obligatory selfie looked polished and professional. *Perhaps they'll start using this one in my press releases now*, I thought. My old one was from six years earlier, and no matter the genius of the staff at the Selfie Station, there was no hiding those years. Looking older never bothered me, but the passing of time did. How months and years fly imperceptibly. The only evidence I had was my lines.

I entered the vast parliamentary building, and the cheerful receptionist took my name and escorted me up the sweeping marble staircase, leaving me alone in the empty office. Unlike my previous visit years earlier, I didn't gawp this time and looked straight ahead, unimpressed by grandiose furnishings as every stitch and lick of paint represented to me a lie, blackmail or a threat.

The varnished filth and glass cages of deceased vermin

weren't the awe-inspiring displays they once were. They were relics of a dead world displayed by the ones that caused that demise. An exhibit of unjust authority. At least the Select had helped their people. What had the Centre done? Wiped their shoes on us on their way up. The Centre could chew on their real wood if they liked. I would not be held hostage to their agenda. Holding my head high and proud, I practised the word 'No' over and over again.

On the desk were some plans, architectural drawings that looked just like the Centre. Grander, though, from the looks of it. The sprawl of luxury buildings branched out beyond where the solar fields and fence lines were. The general layout appeared altered too, a central square with more seating areas. Some buildings had what looked like viewing platforms. The moat around the main building was gone. The whole place was ringed by SolaArbs and ArbAirs, arranged concentrically rather than just in fields. It was like they were planning on bulldozing the whole Centre and rebuilding to a new design.

I took out my phone to get a photograph, but just then the great door opened behind me.

In she walked, her platform shoes clomping firmly with every step. The photographs in the glass cabinets rattled. Her chin was high, as they always were among the Centre. The sagginess of her jawline made her lift her head even higher to compensate. Her conspicuous nostrils were round and plucked. Her eyes strained with the effort of looking down low enough to see me without dipping her chin.

'Behind you!' she blurted, pointing a finger across the room. 'On the floor, by that cabinet. That white step. Bring it here and stand on it.'

I searched by the cabinet and found a flat piece of plastic

that, when lifted, folded out into a box. I did as I was told. It gave me an extra thirty centimetres in height. I stood on display, ready for scrutiny.

'That's better.' She grunted. 'You Perimeter people cause a lot of eye ache among the Centre. We have to strain to look at you. It is quite inconvenient.'

At almost her height, I could note her unblemished skin, her whiter-than-white teeth, her glossy hair scraped back into a towering updo. I absorbed the full, sturdy stature of her. Unaffected by malnutrition, her spine and neck were as straight as a lamppost, her lungs billowing with each breath, her eyes shining with perfect clarity.

'I'm sorry, Prime Minister.' I humbly apologised for the bothersome nature my less healthy upbringing presented to her.

'Yes, quite,' she continued, dismissing my apology with a wave of her hand, umpteen bangles clanging. 'So you are the notorious scientist and journalist Professor Selbourne. Well, I am pleased to finally meet you, although I was expecting someone more impressive.'

'Actually ma'am, we have met—'

'Did I invite you to speak?' she said, so loudly I gave a little yelp. I shook my head and didn't dare to so much as blink.

She walked to her desk and sat, leaving me standing like one of the carcasses in the cabinets. I felt so small I might as well have been as dead as them. She leant back in her chair and folded her arms. Her necklaces collected over her bosom and met in one hunk of gold.

'Now, there is nothing really *wrong* with being from the Perimeter. You shouldn't be so ashamed of your rearing.'

I clenched my jaw tightly.

'Perimeter people are important, collectively. Their bulk makes up a significant proportion of the Raft and, without that balance, this Raft would not be the success it is. We would not be prospering if it was not for the collective usefulness of the Perimeter. Do you understand?'

I nodded, working hard to stop myself from rolling my eyes.

'It's a Raft of counterbalance, you see. Tell me, are you familiar with the pond skater?'

'Erm, no, ma'am.'

'Awful thing from the past. An *insect*.' She shuddered. 'It had a stocky, strong body and awful, scrawny, weak legs jutting out. Those brittle, feeble legs, as infirm as they appeared, were vital for supporting the powerhouse, the most important, strongest part of the lifeform. And that balance is how the pond skater would float across water. You see?'

I nodded, biting the inside of my cheek.

'It's an important equilibrium, and one we have sought to perfect over the years.'

She held her hands out on either side of her, mimicking scales. Her jewellery was evenly distributed across each arm, I noted.

'Now.' She held up a finger adorned with several gold rings. 'While the collective contribution of the Perimeter is significant, a few members of the Perimeter do a lot more than others. Don't you agree?'

I nodded again.

'Speak! Are you mute? I invited you to speak.'

'Oh, yes, ma'am, of course—'

'Yes, yes, well. I am going to tell you something in the strictest confidence. I myself am spawned from Perimeter blood.'

My eyes bulged. The Prime Minister was not a pureblood Centre! Perimeter and Centre relations were unheard of. The fence blocked us physically, but the cultural divide was even stronger to break through.

'It has affected my height somewhat. I lack a few centimetres that the purebloods have, but otherwise I am as superior as any Centre resident. I am fortunate in that I had only one Perimeter grandparent, and I was born and raised in the Centre. My mother was the result of some inter-class fling from before the fence was built. Thank the Raft we have the fence now, so such affairs are less likely. But I tell you this so that you can see I *understand* the challenges of the Perimeter. I am one of you.'

I didn't nod. I just stood on my mount, awaiting instruction.

'Now, I tell you this not to drum up sympathy but to make you aware that, really, anyone can achieve. I want you to know that the world is still changing, modernising. We are *evolving*. And someone like you ... well, you are one of the few Perimeter people who do a lot for the needs of the whole Raft. Your journalism is on point, and your scientific achievements have been well received.'

She paused, and I assumed it was a space for me to reply. 'Well, thank you, ma'am.'

Holding her hand to her chest, eyes half closed, she carried on. 'I am gracious, I know. But with the strictest confidence, I believe it is important for you to be aware. The world is changing ever more rapidly, and I want you to know that we can make room for you. There is a place for you in this world of accelerated progression.'

I nearly fell off my step. 'Gosh. I'm honoured, ma'am.' I felt Archie's black disc burning a hole in my pocket. I had no idea what the Prime Minister was on about, really, but a sense of betrayal crept over me. Archie, the Perimeter, *my* people. That was where my loyalties lay. The Centre and their words had their own agenda. I was their pawn. Whatever she was on about, that's all I was.

'I understand Greg has requested some photographs, which you have refused to take. I have no doubt that he has not been overly polite when requesting such a task. Greg is not known for his eloquence.'

'He keeps threatening to take my son away.' The words came out of my mouth before I could stop them. I shocked myself at my bluntness. I'd clearly been spending too much time with Amalyn.

'Oh, I see no reason why we should do that just over some little photos.' Her attempt at a smile made me recoil.

I nodded, slowly, but did not feel reassured. I knew what was stipulated in the paperwork. Her promises rang as empty as Greg's threats.

'We shan't force you to take the photos, obviously. Blue Liberation is a party that believes in choice. But we also believe in reward.'

'I see, ma'am.'

'Come, sit now. Let me show you something.' She gestured to the stiff-looking chair opposite her.

Relieved to be less on show, I jumped off the step, rolling my ankle slightly in the heels I was so unused to wearing. I thanked her awkwardly as I half walked, half limped into the seat.

She turned her computer round to show me some designs, the same ones I'd seen on the table at the far end of the room. 'What do you see here?'

'The Centre, ma'am, just more developed.'

'Absolutely. Look at it. Isn't it marvellous? Bigger, taller, more beautiful, more room. And don't you think, maybe here or here ...' She pointed a ring-clad finger at some of the smaller buildings towards the edge. 'Don't you think that a bright mind like yours may fit in well in one of the dwellings here? Would you like to be a Centre resident?'

My heart skipped a beat. 'I never even imagined—'

'Of course you would like to be! Anyone would be honoured to live in the Centre, especially someone from such *humble* beginnings. I brought you here today to say that such an invitation may well be just around the corner for you. Now, I hear some disgruntled voices from the Perimeter about cutbacks and staff losses and inflation and taxes and all these necessary things. But you, *you*, are not to be one of those voices. We have plans for you.'

My lungs felt like they were going to implode, and I realised I had been holding my breath.

'How did you enjoy your time off-Raft?' she asked.

'It was ...' I racked my brain to think of the right words. 'It was different.'

'Yes, *different*. But I hear you were a perfectly adequate ambassador, and that your employer has syntho food orders piling up. Such business is an important financial leap in helping us achieve this development project. You are to be commended.'

Memories of the satellite phone played through my mind. Did she know I had been offered a place on the Mainland? Her compliments were over-generous for any Centre Elite, let alone the Prime Minister. She sounded tactful and overly cordial. I had been in this seat before. I knew they'd expect me to sell more than food. They'd expect me to sell my soul for them. But the Raft was crumbling, or the edge of it was, at least. To live more Centre would give my family a fighting chance.

Yet a cold chill crept up my spine as she spoke. Intuition was fighting back. There was something in her tone, something she wasn't telling me. I glanced down and saw the computer hard drive under the desk. A second glance told me where the USB slots were.

I leant in to the computer screen, angling it with my left hand. 'This area looks perfectly lovely,' I said, pointing with my right hand at the edge of the development. As I did so, I dropped my left hand and held Archie's disc over a USB slot. I felt the slightest buzz as the wires woke up and inserted themselves into the socket. When I let go, the disc stayed put.

Microbes. I did it.

'Ah, yes, a sensible choice.' The Prime Minister parted her lips in what was meant to be a smile but served only to display her perfect teeth. 'Well, keep up the good work, Professor, and who knows? Maybe we could be neighbours very soon.'

I stood and air-shook her hand. My technique was unrefined, and I shook frantically, but it served to disguise my actual shaking. I kept my distance, all too aware of how hot my clammy hands were.

I did it! Microbes, I actually did it!

I left her office and bolted down the corridor, straight past the receptionist, who was walking over to escort me.

'Professor Selbourne! This way!' he called after me, startled.

'Oh, sorry.' I stumbled over my words. 'I just really need the bathroom.'

'Let me take you there.' And with the most courteous service, he walked me to the cubicles. I sat, took some deep breaths, then turned and threw up. Bugging the Prime Minister's office. They'd throw me in the sea for that! I took some paper towels and wiped sweat from my forehead and hands, splashed some cold water on my face and rinsed out my mouth. A life of crime did not suit me. I left the toilets to find the receptionist still waiting for me.

'It can be a little overwhelming, meeting her, I know. She must be a source of such inspiration for the Perimeter.' He smiled sweetly. 'I'm sure you've made a marvellous impression.'

I swallowed back a fresh wave of nausea. 'I hope so.'

16

Chapter fifteen

A Speedy Autocar was waiting for me when I exited Parliament, but even that couldn't get me away quickly enough. I slumped low in my seat as it drove away, glancing over my shoulder through the rear windscreen whenever I felt brave enough. I imagined a fleet of shiny black vehicles rushing after me, armed police eager to chuck me in the sea.

What had I done?

The enormity of it hadn't yet sunk in. Not really. Or rather, I wasn't letting it sink in. Denial. That was what would get me through. That was how to appease the panic. That wasn't me … I wasn't the sort to do such a thing. No way would I just hack the Prime Minister's office.

I couldn't have done it. I would never do such a thing.

But I had. I really had.

Microbes!

Treason – that's what they'd say it was. Treason.

I was a rebel, a criminal.

My stomach churned. I bit my fingernails down to the skin. I got out of the Autocar a few streets from Archie and

Amalyn's. I felt the world watching me and I didn't want to be dropped off right by their place in case, somehow, I was being followed. I must have been followed. Surely they'd have seen me.

It's fine, no one noticed.

I couldn't catch my breath, and hot air lodged in my lungs as I gasped. My head pounded as I felt blood rushing to my brain. I tried to reassure myself all the way to their door while still trembling and looking over my shoulder.

It's fine, no one noticed, I kept telling myself all the way to their door while trembling and looking over my shoulder.

It didn't matter how many times I said it to myself. The actuality of my actions reverberated through my trembling hands, my shuddering jaw, my dry mouth. An icy chill wriggled its way up my neck and across my shoulders. The feeling of arms coming up behind me wouldn't go away. I felt hands on me, breath tickling me. The walls had eyes. So did the street. Everywhere I was, they were watching me.

Of course they saw you. The Centre sees everything.

I skirted the shadows with muffled footsteps, searching everywhere for spies, sweat pouring from every part of me until I was smothered by my own sour smell.

It's fine, no one noticed.

With one last look over my shoulder, I buzzed their apartment and ran up the stairs, the stupid heels killing my feet. Amalyn met me at the door, fresh from a shower and smiling. She saw my red face and wide eyes.

'Oh my god, you actually did it!'

I rushed in and shut the door behind me, collapsing against it. 'I did. Oh shit, I did it!'

She gave a little yelp and pulled me in for a hug, too excited to care about how damp I was.

'Sav, you're amazing.'

I didn't feel amazing. Nauseous, weak, faint maybe. I took my shoes off and threw them on the floor. I needed a drink. Ten drinks. A shower and a sleeping tablet.

'Microbes,' I said. 'I did it.'

Archie darted out from the bathroom, dressed in a robe. 'Am I hearing this right? Sav actually did it? She's gone total bad-ass?'

'Shut it, Archie. I was fucking terrified. I still am.'

He did a little skip, his robe only just hiding his modesty. 'You utter legend! Let me put some clothes on and I'll log on.'

Their apartment was still barely unpacked. Boxes were piled up everywhere, some open with their contents strewn around them. Somehow, the place looked dusty already. Grey wisps puffed up from the boxes as I walked through to sit down. The windows needed a clean, and the floor felt gritty underfoot. It still had the musty smell that Maisie's apartment always did.

I couldn't help but remember her. She'd have been so pleased with me, with my illegal behaviour. 'Misbehaviour is a word for bravery in the face of subordination,' is what she would say with a grin. That calmed me somewhat, to think that Maisie would approve. I was not a spiritual person – who was? – but at that moment, I felt my son's grandmother watching over me, smiling, handing me a sweetie and telling me, 'Well done, dear. Well done.'

Despite the lack of unpacking, Archie's computer desk was up and fully functioning. Five monitors, three hard drives and a load of other devices I could not identify. They all buzzed and emitted more heat than was comfortable.

Archie joined us wearing a hastily assembled outfit of joggers and a stained T-shirt. He hadn't dried himself properly, though he was far too excited to notice. His office chair was in the middle of the whirring screens and he rubbed his hands together, in his element.

'Just a minute. Got to get onto an untraceable server,' he said as his monitor showed a blank screen with a spinning circle.

'So what did the Centre want, anyway?' Amalyn asked.

'I met the Prime Minister, and she wanted to moan at me about not taking the knotweed photos. It was weird, though. She showed me some plans. They're redeveloping the whole Centre. A new layout. Expanding it.' I didn't mention the Prime Minister's unspoken invitation. No point mentioning something that wasn't going to happen.

'You going to take the photos?'

'Probably not. I don't know. Perhaps I should behave, though, just so they don't get suspicious of me. Oh god, what if they saw?'

'Relax. They'd be here already if they had.'

Amalyn was right. She had to be right.

'I'm in! I'm in!' Archie said, punching the air.

We all stared at the monitor.

'Blimey, this hack is better than I imagined! I have access to everything.' He licked his lips as he opened file after file, loading up satellite shots and press releases. He even gave a little clap. 'This is like the old days!'

Amalyn rolled her eyes. 'Such a kid.'

'Search for this new development. Let's see what that's all about,' I said.

A few clicks and he'd found it, and the monitor displayed the whole site. The expansion and scale of it took their breath away, as it had mine.

'Bloody hell. They're spending a ton on this. Look.' Archie pointed at spreadsheets filled with zeros after zeros. I had no idea what that many zeros even added up to. A lot of the money was coming from BioLabs by the looks of it.

'That's trillions,' Archie said. 'Hundreds of trillions. And for what? Slightly fancier buildings and a few more kilometres. Why bulldoze the lot just to rebuild slightly differently? What a load of money for nothing.'

Amalyn and I shrugged.

'Hang on, look. It says here that it's almost complete. The deadline for full completion is just a couple of weeks away. Most of the work is done.'

'Well, that can't be right,' I said. 'It looked the same when I was there. I know I've only been there a couple of times before, but I'd definitely notice if it looked that different. The SolaArbs, the ArbAirs, none of it looks like that.'

We all stared, scratching our heads.

'Maybe they're just behind schedule?' I said. 'Or the completed bits are on the other side?'

'So much money, though,' Amalyn said.

'Loose change to the Centre,' I said.

After a few moments, Amalyn slapped her forehead and her jaw dropped. 'Oh my god. They've built a whole new city. This isn't on the Raft at all.'

'No way.' Archie started searching, clicking file after file. 'But where? It's not like they can build something like this underground. Can they?'

'This looks way more advanced than Toulouse,' I said. 'And why have SolaArbs underground?'

'Go back to the plans. I think I saw it, look.' Amalyn pointed at the top corner of the screen. In tiny font, but clear as day: 'Mars.'

We all shook our heads and spoke over each other.

'No way.'

'Not a chance.'

'As if.'

A moment of silence punctuated our denial.

'Seriously?'

'Oh my god.'

'That's it. That explains it.'

Our thoughts went from total denial and disbelief to shocked affirmation.

Archie leant on his elbows. 'The Raft is screwed, and they know it.'

'The whole bloody Centre,' I said. 'They're all moving to Mars.'

'It's not some holiday camp. The rich are jumping ship.'

'I'll bet that's why they've made the factory totally autonomous. They're taking the lab with them.'

'But everyone else!' Amalyn sobbed. 'The whole Perimeter! The Centre knows the Raft is screwed and they're leaving everyone else here to sink.'

'Shit.' My throat tightened. 'This is too much. I can't take this in.'

My phone buzzed, some message from Marcus. He was working late and had questions. Stupid questions that he should know the answer to. I ignored the message and tucked my phone away. We all sat in silence for a while, just staring at the monitor. A whole new city, leaving the Raft, none of the 'Perimeter balance' the Prime Minister had talked about. A pond skater without legs. That's what they really wanted.

My phone buzzed again and I silenced the call. What was the point in even speaking to Marcus? The whole country was doomed.

'Well, that confirms it.' Archie stood. 'We have to leave. We have to jump ship too.' He grabbed Amalyn's hands. 'The Mainland, Ams. It's the only way for us.'

She kissed his hands. 'I know. I know it is. But everyone else, the rest of the Perimeter. They're all going to die.'

'We can't save them all.' He squeezed her hand tighter.

She looked to the floor, his affection giving her little comfort. My head was spinning. The Raft screwed? All of it? It seemed so unlikely, improbable, implausible. But those plans ... It was the only explanation. The Raft was crumbling. If we stayed, we'd be fish food. We had to leave.

'What if we can?' Amalyn stood, her arm encircling Archie's waist. 'Save everyone. What if the Mainland would welcome more people? They said they had room. Sav, we could phone and ask. At the very least, we have to tell everyone, let them know they need to get as far away from the edge as possible. We can't just leave them.'

A dull ache throbbed through my head. I rubbed my temples. 'This is all too crazy.'

'It's crazy but it's really happening,' Amalyn pleaded.

'Okay. It's really happening.'

'We can't just run away and leave everyone else to die. How could we live with ourselves?'

Ethan. Grace. They were all I cared about. Saving the whole country was never going to be on my radar. But maybe Amalyn was right. We'd be as bad as the Centre if we jumped ship without so much as a warning. 'Okay, Ams. But we have to be careful. We need to play this sensibly, discreetly.'

My phone buzzed again. Mabel this time. A message asking more questions that even an intern would know. And wanting to know where I'd been, what work I had done so she knew what she could do.

'Oh, piss off, Mabel,' I said out loud.

Amalyn retrieved some wine and glasses from the kitchen and poured out the entire bottle between the three of us. 'I'm not even sure I want to live on the Mainland. Have you told Sav what you learnt about the Monets?' she said to Archie.

I looked at Archie, his face a picture of apology. 'No, not yet. Sorry, Sav, I got side-tracked.'

'Oh god, how bad is this?'

'Well, these Monets ... bit of a bad bunch, really. A generation or so back, earnt their money in carbon trading, weapons, fraud. All the bad ways, basically.'

'Doesn't everyone?' I said. 'No billionaires would exist if everyone was decent and honest.'

'True. But these are a particularly nasty bunch. Especially with what Amalyn has said about them. They were the richest on the planet and their carbon trading caused most of the fires and floods. Now the Tunnels worship them as their saviours, when it was the Monets who caused the problems in the first place. It's like they orchestrated the whole thing to be in power. They lit the match, and their house was one of the few left standing.'

'Much like the Centre.'

'But at least we'd survive there,' Amalyn said.

I sipped my wine, but it couldn't take the edge off. I was a criminal. The Centre was moving to Mars. Grace.

Grace.

I drank again. It wasn't the best bottle, some imitation

Zinfandel from syntho dried grape powder most likely, but its sourness snapped my consciousness back into focus as my mind drifted off.

The apartment wasn't there, I hadn't just been to the Centre, the Raft wasn't crumbling. Then I'd have a sip and it would hit me again.

The entire living nightmare was true.

'You know,' Amalyn said while passing round some crispy synth veg slices. 'On Saturday, Archie and I stayed in that bar and spoke to some Golden Fifties. I've been spreading the word about poor Harold. He was on to something, you know. Some think he was rubbing the Centre up the wrong way. They think they had him killed.'

My mouth dropped open. 'No way. Do they have evidence?' Amalyn's Golden Fifty friends were hardly the most reliable sources of information. Too many of them were Alternates with creative imaginations.

'No. But a man like that doesn't just drop down dead. Think about it. The entire Centre moving to Mars. Mars needs protein. Harold was holding up the takeover. His death is way too convenient, if you ask me.'

I sighed and took a large sip of wine. The Raft was sinking. We were going to have to flee, to either the Mainland or Mars, or else end up like Harold. It was all too much.

I eventually broke the silence that engulfed us. 'Well, I'm definitely not taking those knotweed photos now.'

Archie laughed, spilling the last of his wine before his computer screen caught his eye. He disregarded the puddle he'd made on the floor, as well as Amalyn as she handed him a towel, his attention solely on the screen.

'Archie, clean up your mess,' Amalyn said, to no response.

'Raft to Archie?'

'Shut up, Ams, just a minute.' He loaded up another satellite image and zoomed in to one edge of the Raft. The opposite end from us, but it could have been anywhere. 'Shit.'

Amalyn and I squashed in on either side of him, peering at the screen. The smog had lifted, in patches anyway, and the edge of the Raft was in view. Archie had zoomed in close so that apartment blocks appeared as an outline among the grey, people's homes blending in with the asphalt. Desalination plants looked like great dark blocks at the edge, dots of streetlamps scattered along the roads.

Among the grey we saw the crack spreading across the land, the black vein creeping forwards, eating away at the fortifications. We all held our breath as we watched the crevice fingering its way across the land, dividing streets and apartment blocks. When it met the shore again, the crack thickened and convulsed, before ejecting all that had once held on into the murky sea.

'Microbes!' I gasped under my breath.

'That's putting it mildly,' said Amalyn.

We stood still for a while, unblinking, barely breathing, all of us unable to take it in. Had we just witnessed hundreds, possibly thousands of people dying?

Archie reached for his empty glass. Amalyn passed him hers.

'I feel sick. That chunk was huge.' She wiped her eyes. 'You reckon they were all ghost apartments?'

'I don't know, Ams,' I said. 'I hope so.'

So many apartments had sunk, such a huge chunk of land lost to the sea. The Raft was breaking up, it really was. And the Centre had known about it for ages.

I swallowed the last of my wine and sat back down. 'Shit.'

'How long before we can organise getting the hell off the Raft?' Archie asked.

The room spun. I just couldn't comprehend it. How long to organise moving, running away, getting all my research together, telling Grace, uprooting Ethan, leaving everything behind, moving to a strange place? It was all just too hard.

I have a place on Mars.

No! No way could I leave them. No way could I go and live among the Centre. It's what Grace would want, though, I was sure of that.

But no one had to know.

If I don't tell Grace, she won't ever know it had been an option.

My conscience creaked and fretted. Could I really keep it from Grace? I had already kept so much from her. But I knew the consequences if she was given the choice. A life on Mars, among the Centre, was in store for us. Our boy would grow up to be one of them. Conceited, entitled, cruel, yet still an outcast. Too short to ever fit in, he – all three of us – would be seen as vermin on Mars.

'Sav?' Archie prompted, snapping me out of my thoughts.

'I guess ... a week?' I said. 'We can call Isaac and see how many we can take. I'll need some time to talk to Grace, and Amalyn can round up as many people as possible. I need to get my notes and research. Ams, we'll need everything if we're going to start the lab up again. The Mainland needs our food.'

'A week, though?' Archie said. 'You want to wait that long?'

I glugged back the last of my wine and looked at the computer monitor. 'That chunk was the opposite side to here, right?' Archie nodded. 'Maybe just keep an eye on the images? If it looks dodgy at our end, we won't go to work. We're central enough here, we should be okay for now. Right?'

'You're still going to go to work?' Archie said with surprise.

'Yes, of course. We all should. They can't know we know. Everything has to be normal. Plus, the new injectable results, the product launch—'

'Seriously, who gives a crap about work?' Archie said. 'Everyone on the Raft is fish food.'

'But the products are going to the Mainland. Our work can still help them. It's still important. It's still needed. I'll try and download as much of my own research as possible, save all the science we can.'

Amalyn was nodding in agreement. 'She's right, Archie. No one can know. We have to act normal. What if the Centre tries to stop us from leaving or from taking any research? And we have to take all of it. We're still going to need to make food.'

Archie sighed. 'Fine, but I was looking forward to having some alone time with my computers.' He eyed each of his screens forlornly.

'Oh, for Raft's sake, Archie, I'm sure you can pack a hard drive in a bag or something,' Amalyn jeered as she went to retrieve the satellite phone. 'Time to call him, I guess.'

I took the phone and dialled the number written on the receiver, each digit making a pleasing beep, before a hissing and beeping sound began that hurt my ears. It sounded like the thing hadn't been fired up in decades. Eventually, I heard a voice.

'Hello? Savannah?'

'Isaac! Oh my, it's so nice to hear your voice.'

'Hey, great to hear from you. All okay?' The line was crackly, but he was there, my brother. I was talking on the phone to my brother.

'No, not really. It's Mars. The Centre are going to live there forever. It's not a holiday thing. You were right when you said the Raft won't last. How many of us can you take? There are so many here who are going to die.'

'Oh wow, I don't know. God, that's awful. I suspected as much, but still … Okay, well we certainly have room. We can dig more tunnels. The Monets have said everyone is welcome. With the lab food, it won't be a problem feeding everyone. We just need to organise the solarplanes. Transport is the issue. We can start doing trips. I guess a solarplane seats up to twenty. If I speak to our friends with Solarplanes Progressives, I think we could do a trip a day, most likely, without ringing any alarm bells too soon. I'll have to check. Can you call back in a day or two?'

I'd missed it when we'd met in person, deafened by the familiarity in his appearance, but on the phone I heard the rhythm of my father and the softness of my mother, melting my fear away. Familial arms folded around me.

'Of course. Thanks, Isaac. Thanks so much.'

And the line went dead.

'Your brother sounds nice,' Archie said. 'And helpful. Weird that he's your brother.'

I scowled back at him.

'We're really doing it, Sav?' Amalyn asked, hope buoying her up. 'We're really going to live off the Raft?'

'Yeah.' The cogs in my brain were turning, clicking into place. We could get off the Raft and away from the Centre. I could stick two fingers up to them after all. 'Good thing you guys didn't bother unpacking.'

17

Chapter sixteen

I went home to a quiet house. Both Grace and Ethan had gone to bed. I sat and ate a bowl of food she had left out for me. Some BioLabs SynthoSpaghetti and RealioVeg chunks – Ethan's favourite. The spaghetti curled round my fork, and I fought away images of slithering filth on my plate, of worms making fabric, of living in dirt.

We would be alive. We would be together.

That thought rid me of any doubt. I had so much to organise, I didn't know where to start. And I had to tell Grace, to somehow make her understand that the Centre were evil, that her ambitions would go unfulfilled. Telling her the truth, coming clean about all the lies over the years made me nauseous. Everything she believed in was going to implode. Lies were the mortar holding the bricks together. Lies were the render that they plastered on the buildings so we could ignore the salt. Lies laid by the Centre made up the foundations of the Perimeter. And now, those foundations were cracking. *Again.*

The apartment seemed hollow, everything in it temporary, a time filler, soon to be at the bottom of the sea. Photos that

Grace had put by for framing showed pictures of a life we were soon to discard. The stiff pleather chair, dented from the hours my mother had spent sitting in it, reading books that no longer existed on the Raft. All of it could soon be gone. Every memory, every trace of our life here, of their lives, washed away.

I hated so much about the Raft, but it was the only home I had ever known. It was clean, it was where I'd had success, I understood the culture. Over the years, I'd learnt how to read between the lines here. The Mainland was so different, so many silent conversations that I couldn't understand. A society tinged with tyranny like the Raft, but different. So different.

But to live on Mars with only the Centre? With no Perimeter to feel at home in? To be constantly surrounded by the glares of the oppressors, the people who were willing to let a whole country sink? No. I couldn't do it.

The moon was high and full, and the Centre fence glinted its silver glow. A lighthouse, warning me to stay away. Boats sink if they get too close to a lighthouse. Best to steer clear.

The next day, the strip billboards on my way to work were hard to miss. By the time Archie and Amalyn had jumped into the Autocar with me, I had already read and reread the headlines a hundred times:

Chunk of Perimeter broke away. Thousands of lives lost! Prime Minister vows to secure the rest of Raft. With sterility comes liberty!

I opened up the National Press site on my e-pad and read the whole article. Knotweed, they were blaming it on. 'Invasive,' they called it. 'The roots of the foreign plant destroying our country.' They also stated that the bombings from our drifting close to Gibraltar years earlier had weakened that section of the Raft. The memories of our alignment were still evident in the cracks on our land. 'But no more,' they said. The government was ensuring it wouldn't happen again, and we were to work hard as normal. 'Everyone is safe now,' they reminded us. The scourge of foreign tyranny was a thing of the past.

'I wonder how many people will realise that the bombings came from the other side?' Archie said as soon as he got in the Autocar. He looked more well-rested than he had in ages. The idea of escaping the Raft evidently agreed with him.

'Are you sure?' I asked.

'I'm sure. I was there on the front line. This bloody Raft has spun round so many times since then, though, I'll bet most don't know or remember. Most won't even know where the lost land was.'

I stared at him, his face full of solemnity. He hated remembering.

'Don't dwell,' Amalyn said as she squeezed his knee. Her hair was even messier than usual, her shirt still untucked, her usual near-perfect complexion sallow. Where the idea of fleeing the Raft agreed with Archie, it appeared to leave Amalyn troubled. Where Archie lost himself in the past, her anxieties were pinned on the future.

Archie's distant stare remained for the rest of the journey. Even the Autocar colliding with the ditches in the road wasn't enough to snap him back.

'I couldn't bear it, seeing that again. The rubble from the bombs. Soldiers buried. The sight of people running across the bridges to choose a side before it was too late. People holding their babies and jumping into the ocean, knowing they'd likely never come back up, rather than stay on the side of the divide they didn't want. It's going to be like that again, isn't it, when the Raft breaks up. But much worse. So much worse.'

We all know what had happened, of course. Amalyn was too young to remember much, but I did. There'd been a countdown, but little notice was given, and anyone foolish enough to have made their escape too late was a victim of their own indecision. That's what they told us. I wondered what excuses they would give this time, what story the Centre would create to justify their actions. None, most likely. They'd be long gone, sipping cocktails below the Martian sky.

My memories were blurry, mainly clouds of dust and the rubble kicked up by the bombs. I remember protests giving way to a haze of shouting and panic. I remember my mother's defeated sobs as Isaac had left and the hollowness that re-mained. Archie had been too close to the anchors and he'd had a front-row seat for the despair. His memories were too vivid, too clear. He stared out the little window, the beams of light contrasting with the darkness he still saw.

* * *

My shoulders slumped when I entered the lab. There was work I needed to do, sign off and oversee. All so pointless, a ton of work for nothing more than a charade. I had research I needed to smuggle out, recipes and data. Would they even have chemistry kits in the Tunnels? Amalyn had a list too, and together we hoped to save everything, decades of work. But before that, before I left the Raft along with as many people as we could save, before I found my way to safety, I had to sack nearly two hundred people.

The team leaders dithered for days over which staff members could keep their jobs. Their hands trembled as they handed me the note with the names of the three they were saving, the other two slots going to themselves, naturally. Since it was all to be automated, the ones with the most mechanical engineering experience were favoured. They were the most educated, the highest up the pecking order. The ones most likely to get new jobs if they were sacked. Being sought after is not a crime, I reassured them as they tried to justify their choices. BioLabs wants the best, the same as everywhere else.

The team leaders sniffed away sobs as they left my office.

What does it matter anyway?

Penny walked slowly over to me, her makeup minimal, her perfume mercifully subdued. I was expecting enough tears today without the added eye sting. An apathetic stride had replaced her usual frantic pace.

'Good morning, Professor. How's your tomorrow?' she greeted me, sounding more woeful than formal.

'Uncertain, as always.' I didn't follow with the usual 'and yours?' Such a question seemed redundant.

'Such awful news about that chunk of land breaking off.'

I nodded a response. Small talk felt like a waste of energy.

'Shall we get this over with?' she asked, her usual high-pitched shriek now only a mutter.

'Sure.'

There was anger, tears, raised voices. All totally justified. The redundancy pay-outs were pathetic, the legal appeals process not in their favour. They called me a traitor, a pawn for the Centre, accused me of having renounced my roots.

A few understood. Some went quietly with faint utterings of 'What am I going to do?' I emailed them the standard careers-guidance literature, links to job adverts, training courses. Penny gave them leaflets, tissues, hugs if desired, arm rubs if not. They knew that their experience was in a field that was dying out. We had designed technology that didn't need us anymore. Some of them had helped design and build the factory equipment, the old generation and the new. Their own skills and successes had engineered them out of a job. What was next for someone in a world where machines had overtaken them?

The lack of healthcare was the main worry. Their families relied on it. Without a job, they had no access to it. They'd wind up like the Alternates, begging for scraps.

I wanted to tell them they'd all likely be dead soon enough anyway, so what the hell did their jobs matter? That knowledge made my sympathy inept, as they already seemed like ghosts to me. Pale manifestations of humans ready to haunt me.

The morning dragged on and on as batches of factory staff came and left, but eventually it ended.

'Well,' Penny said, her red eyes ridiculing her stiff upper lip. 'I guess my work here is done.'

I sat looking at her for a time, her frizzy mop of hair smoothed back. Styling it out until the end.

I breathed a long sigh. 'Thanks again, Penny. That can't have been easy.'

'Nonsense. Compassion has always come easily to me.'

The cutting edge to her tone made me wince. 'Pleasure working with you, Penny.'

And then I showed her the door.

She walked out of the lab without a wave, head held high. Off to find some other company that still felt the uneconomical need to look after their employees' wellbeing.

Good luck, Penny.

* * *

Every moment I thought I had to myself, Marcus or Mabel would knock at my door, sniffing around, asking questions they damn well knew the answer to. It was like having interns again. As well as a lingering smell of cooking oil and trails of skin flakes, Lars had left behind a sense of job insecurity for those still there. My absence for two days the week before had rattled them and their lack of confidence. They flapped around me, rudderless, confused, nosey. The lab had mostly been restored since the break-in, although new deliveries of equipment hadn't arrived so glassware was in short supply, creating some backlogs and wait times.

'The deliveries are late,' Marcus said. I doubted the order had been processed at all. No way BioLabs would waste the money on new equipment that wouldn't get used.

'Just make do,' I said to Marcus for the hundredth time that day.

'But we only have ten conical flasks, and we're down three computer monitors.'

'Marcus, there really isn't anything I can do about it. Just tell everyone to do what they can, and if they have to wait around for some equipment, then so be it.'

My instructions did nothing to soothe his anxieties, and he fretted and shuffled around the lab making little whining noises. Maybe he lived close to the edge and was worried about the news. I tried to be understanding but his waddling about the place and lost expression were driving me insane.

'Samples!' I shouted over to him when his sulking had made me about ready to smash up the few beakers that remained. 'We have a lot of samples ready. Why not taste test?'

That was always everyone's favourite job and one we saved for morale-boosting moments, so it would do.

Marcus's face lit up. 'Really? You think it's the right time?'

'Just get on with it, Marcus. Along with anyone else. Write notes on one of the computers that wasn't trashed. Just use some initiative.'

His pathetic shuffle transformed instantly into an excited stride. I suspected he'd been hoping I'd say that. Mabel joined him, the two of them tasting early-batch syntho food. If they hadn't been wearing lab coats and goggles, they would have looked like they were on a date.

Amalyn gave me a nudge as I walked past. 'We doing samples?'

'They are. Feel free to join them, but you might be a third wheel.'

She looked over at the sample station. 'Aww, it's cute but also so gross. I think I'll pass. I've been copying the information for the injectable all morning. How are you doing?'

'I've shown the door to 196 staff and told Marcus to leave me alone.'

She looked at the floor and whispered, 'Pretty harsh Greg is sacking people before the Raft breaks up. Maybe they think it'll last a while yet?'

'More like Greg doesn't want to pay even a week's more wages than he has to. And he wanted to test the autonomous equipment before taking it to Mars.'

'Sounds about right.' She sighed. 'Hey, what do you reckon?' She scraped all the loose bits of hair back into her ponytail and covered as much of it as she could with her hands. 'Reckon I'm going to look good bald?'

I laughed too loudly and alerted Marcus, who was otherwise busy tasting some new-flavour IcyCrema.

'Shh. Act normal, yeah?'

She rolled her eyes and walked back to her station as I retreated to my office. To my room of peace and quiet. Alone, with a few minutes of calm, I tried once again to process the enormity of it all. It was too much to comprehend. The transience of the land. How fleeting the Raft was to be. All the effort in building anchors, in hardening the land, in burning bridges – all of it such a waste of time. A project so short-lived, it made me wonder if it had been planned all along. The Raft was designed to be some temporary home while the rich waited for Mars. A great experiment of isolation, to test if living apart from the rest of the world was possible. We were their lab, their test subjects. Their first biodome before their next adventure. And now we were to be disregarded like bad-flavoured synth veg.

4-09 came knocking on my door, their knock the firmest of all the employees. It got my back up.

'Excuse me, Professor. My work is up to date, so would it be okay if I join in with the product tasting?' The question sounded rhetorical. Perhaps my absences of late had eroded some respect.

It doesn't matter.

I nodded half-heartedly. I didn't care in the slightest about the staff's little projects, their worries and insecurities. None of it mattered.

I exited the lab for some fresh air, though it failed to lift my spirits as the smoggy fog made me feel unwashed. But the hammering rain was less of an annoyance than the constant knocking at my office door.

I decided to jump in an Autocar, go to the edge and take the photos of the knotweed. I was a few days late, and I wasn't even sure if the Press still wanted them, but it kept up the farce and gave me some time to myself. Business as usual meant doing what I was told. Still in the back of my mind was the thought that at least complying with the Centre nonsense kept our options open. I wasn't considering going to Mars with the Centre – not at all. But just in case, I thought.

Just in case.

The coordinates for the knotweed led me right up to the edge, and the only barrier between me and the sea was a low wall. Beyond that, nothing. If something had once existed there, something that had crumbled into the sea, I had no idea. If some land had broken away, there was no evidence, no sudden cliff drop or damaged infrastructure. It just looked like the rest of the dingy Perimeter.

There were no docks in that part of town, and from what I could see there never had been. A fish-treatment plant was there, obvious from the trucks parked outside. Instead of reeking of rotting fish, the plant smelled of chemicals for pulverising and cleaning, the sort of smell that burns right up to the top of your nose until it feels like it's hitting your brain. The trucks carrying the hygienic drugs, free of the fish contaminants, were lined up close to the wall. Waiting in the shadows were Alternates, twitching, fidgeting, itching. Some approached the truck, presenting a fistful of coins and cash.

Centre trucks, right up to the edge, by the knotweed!

My mind swam with doubt. Why would the Centre risk their own trucks? Surely they could take the fish to other processing plants where knotweed wasn't growing. Even if it wasn't causing the Raft to break up, it was still filthy. I took out my e-pad and made some notes.

I watched Alternate after Alternate approach the hazmat-suited truck drivers, and saw the drivers' shaking heads responding to the hands begging for fish carcasses and the drugs they contained. Sheer desperation pushed the Alternates to ignore the stench of chemicals and the putrid sea, its contaminated spoils worth the disgust. They fell to their knees, begging, pleading. My insides went cold as their cries echoed through the streets.

That could have been Grace, just a few years ago. That could have been her.

It didn't take long to find where the knotweed was growing. Coiling up through the concrete, it looked menacing, looming up out of the dark below, the headache-inducing green contrasting with the grey. It was only a few metres in width, such a small amount for the destruction they claimed it was causing. The street sprayers were working normally, the slight sting on my ankles telling me that the concentration here was actually higher than elsewhere, its smell camouflaging that of the vegetation.

Archie was right. If they had wanted to, it could have been sprayed with something even stronger, cut back and re-concreted. I couldn't see what lurked below the concrete, but it seemed obvious that more could have been done. Negligence had caused the growth.

I kept my distance, utilising the zoom function on the camera, and walked the streets, looking for more. I found another small garish patch poking through, this one surrounded by people. Alternates, all sat cross-legged on the floor, candles among them, looking at the filth. Their backsides were damp, and they were seemingly unconcerned by the storm that was brewing. Despite the strip billboards flashing warnings down every street, they paid no attention. They were humming at the weed, eyes half closed.

One Alternate was standing away from the group, watching. I took a deep breath and approached.

'What are they doing? Do they think humming will get rid of the plant?' I asked.

'No, they're hoping it will make it live.'

My eyes bulged as I backed away, swallowing down my breakfast as it clawed at my throat.

Make it live? For Raft's sake, why?

Among the Alternates I was sure I saw Cass, sitting and humming with the rest. She looked grubby, sat on the ground without even a mat between her and the tarmac. Her eyes were open and looking at the filth.

I knew she was as good as an Alternate!

I grimaced and backed away. To think I'd let her near my son! Maybe it was the knotweed that made the children sick. An Alternate lifestyle was bound to cause infections for poor little Jocelyn. My eyes widened with rage when I remembered us all at Maisie's old apartment in such close proximity, my little boy infected by her filthy habits.

How dare she!

I doused myself in antibacterial gel and retreated further.

I took some photos of the group, of the knotweed, the buildings around to show that none of it had succumbed to the sea. Then I took the Autocar back to the lab. I'd been gone only an hour, yet it was as if I'd been absent for a month, judging by the pestering I received when I returned. The few minutes of bliss resulted in hours of hassle.

Not worth it.

'Go away,' I yelled at my office door as someone knocked on it.

'I'll take this cup of tea with me then?' Archie said.

'Oh, sorry, Archie. I thought it was someone coming to annoy me.' He handed me the cup. 'Thanks. You're a lifesaver.'

'Can you believe the bullshit in the news? Trying to tell everyone that it's the knotweed, that they're taking care of it. Nonsense. They'll do nothing to preserve the Raft for those who can't jump ship.'

'Shh!'

'Yeah, yeah, all right. Ams keeps telling me to watch my mouth too. I don't see why. The Press can bullshit, why can't we?'

'Because the Raft is the Raft. At least they're reporting it, unlike the times before.'

'This bit was too big to ignore. Thousands of lives lost. Can you imagine a worse way to go?'

I shook my head.

'You take those knotweed photos yet?'

'Yes.' I hid my face in my arms. 'Don't judge me. I had to get out of this place. Marcus and Mabel were doing my head in.'

He laughed. 'Annoyed into conformity. That's a new one.'

I scowled at him.

'How'd it look?'

'Weedy.' I shrugged. 'I didn't get that close. There really isn't that much of it, anyway. Just a couple of shoots poking through.' I showed him the photos.

'It's the evil you can't see that's the worst.'

'I really think it must be nonsense, though. That the weed is causing the Raft to crumble. There were Centre trucks right up to the edge, collecting fish. Heavy trucks. Why would they risk their own trucks if it's that dangerous?'

'Exactly.' Archie nodded.

'I saw Alternates chasing the chemical trucks again. They had fistfuls of cash, but they were all turned away, like their money was worth nothing. And get this. There were Alternates sitting around the knotweed, worshipping the stuff. Check out the photos. They're sitting and humming at it. Crazy.'

'I can believe it,' Archie said, sympathy softening his voice. 'They have to cling to something, anything, to make their lives better.'

'I guess there's no point in me saying they should just retrain, since they're all screwed, anyway. Worshipping the damned thing that's no less useless than anything else, even if it is causing the problems.'

'I really don't think it's the knotweed. The Raft has just had its time. They didn't look after it properly. No one cared enough. It's all rotten, and now it's done.'

I rubbed my temples. 'I just can't take it in. You know how fragile Grace is. But she's been good lately, really good. She keeps thinking we're progressing, maybe to live in the Centre one day. How can I drag her away, to a whole other country, to live *underground*? She won't understand. But Ethan. *Ethan!* Everything is different now. He *has* to have a future. We can't have done all of this for him not to have a future.' Tears were coming. I levelled my breathing, keeping them at bay.

Archie walked over and hugged me, something I wasn't sure he had ever done before. Alternates hug. We don't. Usually. His association with the Golden Fifty was making him more demonstrative. Bodies don't need that much warmth. A hug wasn't nourishment. It was fine when Grace or my estranged family shared their warmth. With Archie, it felt more inconvenient. I knew it was meant for support, but I pushed him away. I wasn't weak. I didn't need it. Hugs were for people on the verge of breaking. That was not me. He wasn't offended and he knew he hadn't crossed a line. He just had no verbal response.

There was a knock at the door.

'Go away!' Archie and I said in unison. But the door opened anyway.

'Sorry, Professor.' Marcus's feeble little voice came into my office. 'But the final results are in. I thought you might like a look.'

'Fine. Send them over.'

Archie left me to it, and I looked at the results on my computer. The injectable was exactly as we'd hoped, and, together with the Selbourne Range, we had increased vitamin absorption by nearly fifty per cent in real human trials. I remembered the days of famine, after the last pandemic and the anchors had blown up, watching my mother's face slowly melt into nothingness. Right then, I felt proud. I had achieved what I had aimed for. Enabling the nation to be healthy. And not just the nation, but overseas as well. My brother. My niece. They would also receive healthier, vitamin-enriched food. However bad things seemed for us right then, I knew that at least I had helped some lives.

18

Chapter seventeen

The Perimeter losses dissolved into background noise when the Press started reporting on the achievements of the Raft, Perimeter deaths being not nearly as important and news-worthy as a big company's balance sheets. 'BioLabs' New Injectable,' the press release I was commissioned to write, was headline news for a day. The photo they shared of me looked so unfamiliar now, a polished and well-groomed woman, Centre-photo quality, smiling and looking kind and competent. Not the washed out, sleep-deprived middle-aged woman I really was. For once, the article was accurate and word-for-word what I had written. No hyperbole was needed for what this formula meant. The absorption increase *was* huge. It didn't require an extra layer of gloss. But after a day, even the excellent health news for the nation could not compete with the Mars updates.

Everyone at the lab received an email from Greg that morn-ing. He thanked us – actually thanked us – for our hard work. 'Our eulogy,' Amalyn said to me. His excitement with the new formula, the money it would make him, had given him and his family the funds to visit Mars. It was a dream come true, he said.

At least we'd made his dreams come true while we were in a living nightmare.

The autonomous factory was working well, he said. Sacking all those employees was an excellent idea, apparently. We were producing twice the amount of product we would have normally for a fraction of the cost. 'Progress is paramount,' he said. The article didn't say why the Raft needed so much food. It didn't imply that it was to be sold overseas, or that they were making stockpiles for Mars. I wondered if anyone would question it. Probably not. Most just believe whatever garbage they are told.

At the end of the email was a quick note to say our wages would now be paid in the new currency, martas.

What the—?

No sooner had I read the article than the news flashed across my screen with an update.

New currency, the marta, goes live from midnight!

How had we not heard about this?

Like the Tunnels, we were to start using martas. All old money would be invalid. It had been a 'long thought-through plan,' said the article. *Long thought through!* But the Perimeter was given just a few hours' notice. It cited progress, and how daft it was that we were still using the same old-world currency we'd had for centuries. The article failed to tell us any benefits of the marta, except to say it was 'new,' as if the people would simply be attracted to shiny new things. It said that the currency would be a different colour, and that was something we should all be very excited about. As if anyone was actually that stupid.

The article explained that we could change our money over online, so it was easy enough, but everyone's balance was reduced by about twenty per cent for the privilege.

That's why the Alternates' money was turned down.

'They're banking it all to take to Mars.' Amalyn came marching into my office when she finished the email. Her normal pale complexion was purple with rage. 'They're literally robbing people to fund Mars.'

'Same as always,' Archie said as he joined us.

I couldn't get as angry as them. 'What does it even matter? We'll need martas on the Mainland, anyway. And everyone else is going to drown. They don't need their money.'

Amalyn slumped onto the floor against my desk. Her eyes were red and her hair was more of a mess than usual. 'It's just ... taking everything from everyone before leaving them to die. How stressed are they all going to be, right up until the end?'

I rubbed her shoulder. 'You spoken to any Golden Fifty yet? Rallied anyone to come with us?'

'A few. It's hard. I'm trying not to cause a panic. But then sometimes I think, fuck it, why not tell everyone and cause a massive panic? Why are we all playing along like this?'

'To secure our places. I know it's selfish, but I have to make sure Ethan is safe.'

She nodded. 'I have a plan, then. Let's get Grace and Ethan on a plane. You too, if you like. We won't judge if you want to go with your family. Then Archie and I will spread the word. Like, *seriously* spread the word. Maybe people can take boats. There are all those Centre fishing boats that they're not going to need anymore. Sure, some won't make it, but some might.

It gives people a chance, at least. Isaac said he can do a plane a day. We have to give everyone a chance.'

'It could work. If you can get anyone to believe you. We have the knotweed photos and the Mars plans for evidence.'

'Thing is, we're close to the Mainland now. If people leave it too long, who knows how much longer that will make their journey? Archie, what's our trajectory?'

'Not sure. I've not really been paying attention.'

'It's supposed to be business as usual,' I said. 'We've got to maintain the image that we don't know anything.'

'I know, I know. You can stop nagging. I've just been busy.'

'Busy? With what?'

Amalyn rolled her eyes. 'Honestly, Sav, you don't want to know.'

I most certainly did want to know. I frowned at Archie. 'Okay, okay,' he said. 'I've just been playing around with a few low-key hacks.'

'Hacks for what?'

'Nothing, really,' he said, blushing. 'Just making the most of being able to do it while I can.'

'I told you, you don't want to know,' Amalyn said. 'Dumb, isn't it? Just playing with his toys. Hacking for the sake of hacking.'

'Oh, Archie,' I chuckled. 'That is a special kind of stupid.'

I spent the rest of the afternoon plodding around the lab. Despite its success, morale was low, unsurprisingly. I wondered if they all knew their fate. They may not have read much about the Raft breaking up, but they must have suspected. No one could be that blasé, surely? But then, Grace had no idea. Cass and Sal clearly had no clue, since Cass was loitering at the edge, humming to filth. I had seen it and still barely believed it.

It was too abstract, too far-fetched. Every so often I chastised myself for believing it, like I was an Alternate or a full-blown Golden Fifty.

This can't be happening.

But it was.

With the sackings and no Penny to pick them up, the team were anxious, desperate to prove their contribution, scrabbling round the lab and systems to find something to report on and new ideas to pitch. Plus, the new currency had knocked the wind out of everyone's sails, not that they would say it out loud. Twenty per cent worse off was better than having no job at all, so they didn't dare speak up.

But their eyes and forlorn faces gave it away. They knew they'd be worse off, for no reason at all that they could tell. The new currency and the tax hikes were pushing everyone to the brink. And for all the staff knew, it was merely for the Centre to indulge in luxuries. The hardworking Perimeter people were picking up the bill.

I remembered Isaac's face when he'd been told of the new currency exchange rate, how his expression had been so hard to read. He wasn't so dumb as to think it was a good thing to be worse off so that the wealthiest could indulge themselves. He'd understood, however much he tried to hide it. But the people in the Tunnels had no complaints, just like the lab staff were not complaining. Carrying on with their jobs, their worries hidden behind the facade of employment.

Isaac and the Mainland population saw their leaders as their saviours. Ours, the Centre, were our jailors.

Soon we'll be free of them!

But not all of us. There were more people in the lab than just Archie, Amalyn and me. The nervous atmosphere was nothing compared to what it would be if they all knew how screwed they were. Once they found out, it would be as Amalyn said: full-blown panic.

2-10, 4-09 and 8-08 were still there despite Lars's absence. It seemed they enjoyed being at work rather than at home. 4-09 was typing as fast as ever, 2-10 was poring over some printouts and 8-08 was staring at some spreadsheets.

I walked over, trying to tread softly to be less intimidating. It was way too late to befriend them, but at least they might not fear me. If I went to the Mainland and the Raft lasted a while yet, the idea of being remembered among the damned as someone to be feared, some ogre, was unsettling.

'Everything okay?' I asked 8-08.

He pulled at his red hair and frowned. 'I'm looking at the billing. With the new currency, all the accounts are wrong. This really isn't my area of expertise, but I put my name on the jobs list for this one since no one else wanted to do it, and they laid off the person who actually knows how it worked.' He folded his arms over his chest and pouted like a sulky child.

'Well, just do the best you can.'

'There's so much stock being sold to "Fr-Tol". That's all it says. Where is that?'

I shrugged and angled my head away slightly, hiding my flushing cheeks.

'They've paid for tons of food, and other "miscellaneous", whatever that is. But only seven small shipments have gone there. After that, none. Zero. But so much is going to Mars. They're basically sending millions of kilos to a holiday camp, and by using the new currency, they're banking trillions. The box on the spreadsheet can't even fit that many zeros in.'

I rubbed my forehead as it sank in. They were taking the

Mainland's money but not sending them the food they had ordered. They'd be long gone to another planet before the Mainland knew they'd been ripped off. I clenched my jaw so hard my temples throbbed.

'If you get it wrong, it's Greg's fault, not yours,' I said.

Everything is Greg's fault.

'He won't see it that way. If I get this wrong, I'll probably be sacked. I can't lose my job, but I really don't know how to do this.'

'Just do what you can and I'll sign it off, okay? If it comes up as wrong in any way, I'll say it was me.'

His astonished face stared at me. 'Really? Why would you do that?'

I watched his perplexity, but what could I say? *Just fill in the boxes with whatever. None of it matters anyway*, is what I wanted to say. Instead, I said, 'Because I'll happily tell Greg what an arse he is at any opportunity. Seriously, just do your best and leave it at that. Don't stress about it.'

His eyes followed me as I walked away. Grateful or suspicious, I couldn't tell. The Raft's culture of trampling over each other to climb the ladder, be noticed, be rewarded and advance did not lend itself to such acts of valour. I suspected my reputation had gone from 'feared' to 'insane'.

I saw Amalyn at the next desk, listening. She gave me a little nod, as if I was saying such things for 8-08's benefit. Him stressing less was a good thing, obviously. But wouldn't it also be nice if our last days in the lab were peaceful and hassle free? Full-blown panic was around the corner, after all. But not yet. Grace and Ethan first, then everyone else. As many as we could fit on the planes, plus the boats.

How were we even meant to get control of a boat? Amalyn's

idea seemed poorly thought out. And was Toulouse anywhere near the sea? I didn't think so, judging by what I had seen from the plane. No one was going to last in the heat for long. Perhaps there were more coastal entrances to the Tunnels? The more I thought about it, the more impossible the task seemed.

I walked around the lab some more and had to admire the staff all working hard. They were the best at what they did, and they deserved a place on the Mainland. I'd get the staff to safety, I decided. Amalyn could concentrate on her friends, the Golden Fifty, but my staff, this team, were my responsibility. I'd nurtured them for their whole careers. They were annoying but hardworking. As I watched them, I felt a sense of duty to protect them and their bright minds. 2-10, 4-09 and 8-08 deserved a chance to live and thrive. Even Marcus and Mabel deserved a shot at survival.

I sat at my desk to write the article but just stared at the blank page. I flicked through the knotweed photos again and again. What was I meant to write? I supposed it didn't matter, really. Peter would edit the article however he saw fit. But I had to act like I was playing along. Too much conformity would give me away, as would too little.

There is a place for you in this world of accelerated progression.

The Prime Minister's words came to me. I hated her and everyone from the Centre, but to have that backup option, in case it all went wrong, was the main reason I felt pressured into playing along. The thought of going to Mars and living somewhere even more isolated, surrounded by those people, made me want to heave. I would spend the rest of my life being blackmailed. My son would grow up surrounded by them, and would adopt their habits and attitudes. The Centre may not have used corporal punishment in the same way as the Monets, but we were hushed. If we did not obey their rules, do the jobs they assigned us, we were denied healthcare, stripped of accolades, financially ruined, left to starve. We were barren until we proved ourselves.

No, the Centre were not like the Monets. Their methods were slower, but the pain was as severe.

However hard I stared at the blank page, the article refused to write itself. I went into the staffroom to make some tea instead. Archie came running over.

'Greg is coming in. As in now! And he's not alone. They'll be here—'

The doors swished open, cutting him off. The thump of Greg's footsteps was amplified by the entourage with him. His assistants (only three now, I noted) fussed around him. Declan was standing by his side, preferring to watch the assistants from close range, and behind them came six Centre residents, all men with thick torsos wrapped in surplus clothing, noses pointing at the ceiling. They made a display of ducking under a doorway that was clearly high enough for them to pass under and skirted around the tables as if they were twice as wide as they actually were. They emitted a mist antiviral spray ahead of themselves with every step and looked around the lab as if it were creating germs, not food.

'This is the lab, where the food is designed and tested,' Declan said, pointing around the room with extravagant gestures, being sure to flex his muscles with every pose. He gave all the staff a wink as he walked past.

'This one here,' he said as he stood behind Amalyn, legs wide. 'This fine bit of skirt, has been working on the injectable formulation.' A few mumbles came from the onlookers. 'Get a look at her while you can, that's what I say!' Declan laughed, and the others laughed along.

Amalyn stood up, sending her chair flying back as she did so, hitting Declan directly in the crotch, then stamped on his foot as she walked off. Archie, who had been standing silently making fists, spat out a laugh and put his arm around Amalyn as she joined him in his office. Declan's eyes bulged as he tried to conceal his pain, his cheeks ablaze.

'So unruly, these Perimeter people,' one of the Centre said. 'Quite feral. Greg, have you not managed to train them?'

Greg cleared his throat. 'Well, they produce good results, though their behaviour is more challenging.'

Declan smirked. 'Luckily their work will outlast them.'

They all laughed again. A haughty, hollow laugh.

My face was burning hot, and my jaw ached from my grinding teeth.

'And which one is Selbourne?' one asked.

Declan's face fell and pointed at me. 'That one. She's not much to look at, though, hardly worth bothering with.'

I heard 4-09 tut and 2-10 gasp. Their years spent working from home had left them inexperienced around Centre arrogance. They looked at me, their faces displaying the hurt I didn't feel. I glared at Declan. I imagined padlocking him and Greg to the edge and leaving them and this shitpile to sink.

'Well,' one Centre said, 'it's simply wonderful that you have been able to give such, erm, *people* employment. Greg, your generosity never ceases to amaze me.'

'Absolutely,' said another, holding his hand to his chest. 'You could have employed Centre people. Your charitable actions will earn you a knighthood, I am sure.'

'Not to mention the profits are better, since it's not necessary to pay Perimeter residents a high wage.' The Centre prick nodded in approval.

'You're like some secret hand, an invisible hand for good out here.'

And all six of them gave a 'hear, hear!' as they patted their old chum on the back.

I'd hardly have described Greg as 'an invisible hand for good'. A massive, exploitative pervert, maybe. And his charity started and ended with his own net worth.

'Let's go see the factory floor, then, and take a look at this wonderful new machinery.' Declan said as he led them away.

I stamped my feet as loudly as I could all the way to Archie's office.

'You okay, Ams?' I didn't need to ask. She was in stitches.

'I really hope I damaged his cock. He is just the worst.'

Archie was still angry. 'What are they here for? One last gawp at the Perimeter before it sinks? Just to feel superior? I can't believe how blatant they're being.'

'Centre engineers, apparently. To check the factory equipment is the gold standard Greg says it is.'

'Doesn't surprise me that they don't believe a word he says,' Archie said. 'They still didn't need to come up here, though.'

'Just for a gawp? No, you're right. Pricks. And I've just learnt that they aren't even sending food to the Mainland. Not much, anyway. Seven small shipments. They're taking millions of martas from them and shipping all the food to Mars.'

Amalyn and Archie shook their heads. 'We shouldn't be surprised, really. They'd happily get richer while everyone else starves,' Archie said, clenching his fists.

'Well, it doesn't matter,' I said. 'We'll be there to make food. And we'll take as much stock as we can carry.'

Amalyn was still laughing. 'It's quite refreshing, knowing that I don't have to worry about keeping my job or my health-care. What other mayhem can we cause before we leave?'

'I could hack into their systems and reallocate all the mar-tas,' Archie said, a little too nonchalantly for something so high risk.

My mouth hung open. 'You could do that?'

'Sure. I think. I don't know what purpose it would serve, though. If they suddenly had less money, they'd probably just value it differently.'

'That depends. They're still trading with the Mainland, so it would make that harder,' I said.

'Hmm ...' Archie's eyebrow lifted. 'It would be fun. Just before we leave. Some hack like that, they'd probably trace, eventually. We'd have to be gone as soon as it goes through. Maybe I can send all the martas to your brother, Sav?'

'Maybe not all. It needs to be discreet. I don't want him getting in trouble. Maybe just distribute it to all the accounts on the Mainland?'

Amalyn sighed. 'Can't we do something more fun, like burn down the Mars rockets or something?'

'Ams!' I cried. 'That's a bit much, really.'

'Is it, though?'

'Well, there'd be a good chance that they'd all flee to the Tunnels then.'

She screwed up her face. 'Yuck. We don't want that.'

'How about,' Archie said, 'instead of just taking the research, we change it. Leave them with dud recipes, or infected supplies. Like the Poison Maker from before, remember?'

'I think the Poison Maker was a load of hype about nothing,' I said. My pulse quickened at the sound of that name.

'Yeah, but the idea is sound. Screw with their food.'

I held my hands up. 'I hate them, I really do. But to make them all starve to death is too much. We're not their sort of evil.'

'Can't we be, though?' Amalyn said with a sigh. 'I'd love some sort of revenge. Not murder-style – just a tiny little bit.'

'Maybe just make it so the food gives them spots or itchy crotches or something.' Archie rubbed his hands together.

I snorted a laugh. 'You computer engineers literally know nothing of our science. I have no idea how to make SynthoSpaghetti give someone an itchy crotch.'

19

Chapter eighteen

My inbox was filling up with emails from the National Press editor, Peter, nagging me about the knotweed article, attempting to guilt me into complying. I ignored all of them, deleting them as they arrived, and dodged several of his calls, but his persistence was getting hard to snub. I clicked to open the latest email and instantly regretted it.

We need that knotweed article ASAP. There are riots in the Perimeter and people are putting themselves at risk of exposure to knotweed. That's on YOU.
   Peter

A riot? I scoffed, wondering what sort of hyperbole he was feeding me this time. I had a look through the headlines and articles to find out what Peter meant by a 'riot'.
   It appeared to be a peaceful protest about the extortionate tax hikes and currency exchange. Destitute people protesting about their pockets being picked to fund the extravagances of the Centre. The Perimeter weren't as stupid as the Centre

thought. They were sucked into most of the lies, but robbing them blind had been a wake-up call.

Since no one had paid for a protest licence, it was designated a riot. I was used to the defamatory pieces the National Press printed, but the riot drivel was in a different league. It labelled the protestors as 'criminals,' 'causing havoc,' 'threatening the good people,' 'selfishly endangering everyone,' 'time wasters,' 'junkies,' and any other derogatory terms they could cobble together. I looked through the pictures, taken from the safety of the other side of the fence. They weren't even Alternates, most of them, anyway. With their sad faces full of hunger and desperation, I guessed they thought they had nothing left to lose. At least in jail they'd get fed.

I was sure I recognised a couple as ex-factory staff. Guilt niggled at me, though it wasn't my fault. Greg had made me sack them, though I doubted he'd have felt any sense of remorse if he'd told them. He'd have bellowed at them, telling them what a wonderful thing they had done, helping ensure his ticket to Mars. He'd have taken pride in their suffering, felt bolstered by their tears. However much of a pawn the Centre had made me, I knew I was not like them. I could never be as heartless as they were.

I'd missed several calls from Grace, too. She'd messaged to say she was worried about my journey home, and the danger of the riot was upsetting her. I'd replied to tell her not to concern herself with it, that it would be fine, but her worries were as tenacious as ever and I called her back.

'It's too close to our apartment. The news says they have weapons.' I could hear the sound of her pacing up and down the living room, Ethan's little cries in the background asking, 'Mummy, what's all the noise?'

'I don't think the Press is being very accurate, Grace. Can you see any fighting or trouble?'

'No, but it sounds awfully loud.'

Ethan was starting to sob in the background, feeding off Grace's anxieties.

'Can you see any Centre police or anyone trying to break it up?' I asked.

'No, but there are a lot of people.'

'So it's just a lot of Perimeter people walking.'

'The news says it's dangerous. Even that many people gathered together is dangerous. What if Ethan gets sick again? There's that knotweed about. Who knows what germs it's spreading?'

I muted a sigh. Her complete faith in the Press never faltered. Despite knowing they had twisted my words countless times, her trust that they told the truth was as stubborn as her worries.

'Just stay indoors,' I said. 'You'll be fine. Stay calm. Your fretting only upsets Ethan.'

'They don't even have a licence to riot like this.'

'Protest, not riot.'

'Whatever,' she said. 'Listen to it.'

The scratchy sound of the window opening came down the line along with the chime of the Centre fence rattling, accompanied by chanting: 'Mars is theft! Mars is theft!'

'Sounds like a riot to me,' Grace said. 'They should just write to the council like the government says.'

I rolled my eyes, grateful she couldn't see my face. 'I'm sure that would be very effective. Listen, Grace, I've really got to go, but don't worry and I'll be home when I can. Give Ethan a cuddle from me.' I hung up.

The protest was miles away from the knotweed, I told myself. The plant couldn't grow that quickly. In any case, there were zero reports of it growing anywhere near the Centre fence. I held my head in my hands and rubbed my temples. As if the knotweed was going to crawl out of the cracks at the edge, walk to the Centre fence and gobble them up.

Plants can't crawl on their own. Can they?

I kicked my desk, annoyed at the nonsense, and tried to write the article Peter wanted. However much I willed it to, that blank screen would not fill up. Something had to be written. I needed to maintain my smokescreen, but it was hard when they wanted not an article but a work of complete fiction.

After making a cup of MimikTea, I sat again, willing the words to write themselves. I flicked through the knotweed photographs, hoping for some lightbulb moment, but nothing came. The photographs turned my stomach. I winced at the sight of the filthy plant, but saying it was causing danger so many miles away was absurd. It looked spindly and barely alive. As if that gangly thing could break up the Raft.

Instead of writing about the Alternates, I pondered how it was that the Centre trucks thought it was safe to drive around the edge, and the reason for the protest. That was the article I wanted to write, but it was pointless, I knew.

After what felt like hours of staring at the screen, I sent the photos. No article, just the pictures. Peter could write whatever he liked. The moment I clicked Send, Archie came barging in.

'Next time you moan at me for "hacking for the sake of hacking", you should instead tell me what a clever man I am,' he said. 'Come into my office, let me show you something.'

Glad for the distraction, I followed. On his desk were several empty bowls and old tea mugs.

'You're not even bothering to clear up after yourself these days?' I asked, grimacing as I moved all the dirty stuff to one side.

'What's the point?'

'General cleanliness?'

Amalyn was sitting on one of his chairs, playing with her hair. It seemed her motivation for work was about as lacklustre as mine.

I took a seat. 'What unexciting bit of hacking have you been up to, then?'

It was then I noticed Amalyn was crying. 'It's bad, Sav. I knew something wasn't right. I just knew it.'

Archie leant over and rubbed her back as she sniffed into a tissue.

'Nothing is right,' I said, dismissing her melodrama. 'What's new?'

'People don't just drop down dead.'

'Harold's hard drive,' Archie said. 'I finally got round to having a peek. He had it all encrypted, but I think a child must have done it because it took me about five seconds to get in.'

He looked at me as if expecting applause. He received a blank face instead.

'And?'

'Dodgy, dodgy, dodgy stuff. There are some pretty long email chains between him and Greg and other BioLabs board members. All wanting to buy him out. Offers getting higher and then stopping and being replaced with threats.'

'Threats on his life?'

'No, nothing that obvious. Threats to tank the company.'

'I would imagine that's fairly standard haggling among the

Centre.'

'Yeah, for sure,' Archie said. 'But Harold knew about the Mainland.'

Surprise hit me. 'Seriously? How?'

'Get this. ProLabs was *owned* by the Mainland.'

'No way!' I almost shrieked. 'But they eat *bugs!* Why eat filth when they could have ProLabs food? I mean, why eat *insects* when you don't absolutely have to?'

'They had filth available and just stuck with it, I guess. ProLabs was a money earner for them, that's all. And Harold had a theory.'

I narrowed my eyes. 'The sort of theory the Golden Fifty come up with?'

Amalyn shot me a look. 'He's dead, Sav. Show some respect.'

I apologised, and she resumed her sobbing. 'It's awful, Sav,' she said. 'He had this video blog. Watch it.'

'*Harold* had a video blog?'

Archie nodded, wheeled his chair closer to his computers and pressed Play. 'Yep. The old boy knew something was amiss. It seems he wanted to get word out.'

The screen filled with Harold's round face, wobbly chin and toothless mouth. His glasses sat wonkily on his face, and his stare was as awkward in the video as it had been in real life. He looked down or beyond the camera, never straight at it.

'I'll cut to the good bits,' Archie said as Amalyn gave a whimper. 'He goes on a bit.'

He fast-forwarded, making the footage of Harold's face look like some hilarious film, his swaying cheeks like some windup toy. Even Ams giggled a bit at that.

'What you must realise,' Harold said, his voice breathy and strained, 'is that BioLabs is the Centre's most profitable company. The man at the helm, Greg, is among the greediest in the Centre. He caters to every political event, threatening to withhold food production if he doesn't get his way. His extreme wealth and power hold the whole Raft to ransom. He is a close friend of the Press editor, and his number-one staff member, Savannah Selbourne, writes many defamatory articles for the Press and pioneers food synthesis – a very unethical combination, if you ask me. She is also not to be trusted.'

'We're ignoring that bit, obviously,' Amalyn said. 'I told him years ago that you are a good one, but he never really believed me.'

I tried to shrug it off. 'He was a bit of an oddball,' was all I could think to say.

'It is therefore a logical assumption that Greg would want control of all the world's food to increase his profit margins and exercise greater control,' Harold was saying. 'The Mainland makes their own protein through farming insects. A marvellous achievement, and one any scientist would hail as remarkable.'

My face contorted at that, as did Amalyn's.

'Self-sufficiency in such difficult circumstances would be very difficult, but the cooperation across the Mainland has achieved a lot. They do not require synth proteins but have been gracious enough to support our work here. But since Greg wants further domination and seeks to take over ProLabs, he wants to sell protein to the Mainland.'

Archie fast-forwarded a little more, and Harold looked in worse shape than he ever did when I'd met him. His eye bags hung lower than his spectacle rims. He had zero teeth left, from what I could see, and his face was ashen and dotted with hives.

'Part of the deal of selling BioLabs food to the Mainland is that Greg buys ProLabs. I have resisted and resisted, but it's not a fight I can win. And now, I am certain, the insect populations on the Mainland are under threat. Visitors from the Centre have been contaminating their supplies with pollutants to make breeding impossible. They're starting to see the effects of this. There is no reason why their insect populations should be declining unless human interference is purposefully causing a problem. The only explanation is that the Centre is behind this. I am trying to get word out to the Mainland, but my communication links have been tampered with. I'm being followed—'

Archie fast-forwarded some more.

'My blood test today shows, again, increased levels of arsenic. The threats from the Centre are continuing. Greg will not rest until I'm gone and ProLabs is in his hands for his greater profit and control. The government has no power. The Press has no power. They are all at the mercy of the big-money businesses, of which Greg is on top. The Mainland making their own food is against all they believe in. They intend to wipe out the Mainland food supply and sell synth protein back to them. Please, if anyone sees this, get a message to the Mainland. Warn them about their food supplies.'

Archie fast-forwarded again. When he pressed Play, Harold's face was bloodied and bruised, his glasses smashed. Harold was never a friend, but he was a decent colleague. It was hard not to feel sorry for him. He coughed and wheezed as he tried to speak. Amalyn held her hands over her face as the video played.

'I know I haven't got long now. I'm not strong enough to

survive another attack. A lot of people on the Mainland are going to starve if their insect protein gets wiped out. Please, someone get a message out.'

'That was the last video he did,' Amalyn said, reaching for a fresh tissue.

Archie put his arm around her. 'He posted his blog on the dark net frequently, but it was always taken down immediately. I can't tell if he knew or not. He kept trying anyway. Nobody saw it until today.'

'Why didn't he speak to the Golden Fifty?' Amalyn cried. 'We could have helped him! We could have gotten word out!'

'Oh, Ams.' I pulled my chair next to her, and she cried into my shoulder.

All this time, Harold had known about the Mainland. Had he known about the Raft breaking up? About Mars? Why hadn't he told people, the Golden Fifty at least, that the Mainland existed? I had so many questions I wanted to ask him, but they would be forever unanswered. One thing I knew for sure was that he hadn't trusted me at all.

'Maybe he thought your association with me had left you compromised?' I said.

Amalyn lifted her head and sniffed. 'As horrible as that sounds, you may be right. He was always suspicious of this place. He probably thought I'd become a Centre snitch. I'll bet he didn't trust me.' She blew her nose and tears poured freely again. 'Oh, poor Harold. How alone he must have felt.'

'Maybe he tried to get a message to the Fifty, Ams. Look how beaten up he was. That was probably from trying to reach you. But I doubt anyone could have helped him. The Centre get what they want, always.'

Was that what would have become of me if I hadn't agreed to

play along with the Centre's plans? I shuddered at the thought. I'd been thinking of them as on a par with the Select, the lack of corporal punishment being the one thing in their favour. But they really were the worst of the worst. If they'd done that to Harold for trying to speak up, if they would cut off the Mainland's food supply for their own greed, they were as rotten as the land under our feet.

'We have to warn your brother, Sav,' Archie said. 'There's a good chance Harold was right. I wouldn't put it past Greg to tamper with food supplies for his own financial gain.'

I nodded. Greg was the vilest, most malicious person I had ever met. If he thought he could starve people to make a buck, he would.

'God knows how good the food supplies in the Tunnels are,' Archie said, 'but I suspect it'll be ages before they totally switch over to synth food. A lot of people will go hungry if the insects fail.'

I shook at the thought of the insects, their hideous little bodies, all those wriggly legs. Why did they need so many legs? But I had to think of Isaac, not my own squeamishness.

'We'll call him tonight,' I said. 'Did Harold say anything else about how they're contaminating the food? It might be useful for the Mainland to know.'

'There are some soil-sample studies I've been looking through on Harold's hard drive. I suspect the Mainland will understand all of that better than we do. We need to get it to them, along with as much synth food as we can.'

'And we need to get there as soon as possible, to start building a new lab and factory for them,' Amalyn said. Her sobbing had abated for now.

'Microbes!' I cursed. 'I hadn't even thought about the

factory. They'll need all the equipment, too.'

'That's a big job,' Archie said. 'No way do we have the expertise to build and use those machines.'

'We need to get the factory staff off the Raft too, then.'

Archie snorted. 'Yeah, they love us down there. What are we going to say? Hi guys, remember how we had all your friends sacked? Come join us in another country!'

Microbes!

I rubbed my forehead. Fleeing the Raft was starting to seem more and more impossible.

'Well, what choice do we have?' I asked. 'Kidnap them?'

Amalyn sat up when she heard that. 'Sounds exciting if nothing else.'

'Ams, we are not kidnapping people. We need to find a way to convince them. Their families, too. We can hardly leave their families behind.'

'Harold has a nephew,' Amalyn said.

I nodded. 'We'll get him too. And any other family he has.'

In all my years of working for BioLabs, I'd been down to the factory floor only once. Why make that journey when we could email? I didn't know the staff down there at all except to fire them, and they certainly didn't know or trust me. I had no idea what I could say to convince them. Although it was likely they hated Greg and the Centre more than me, and distrusted everything that came from behind that fence, it didn't mean they'd listen to us.

The three of us debated how to tell them. Threats, blackmail, a brief discussion of kidnap again, duping them into getting on a plane by saying it was a work trip. In the end, we figured honesty was best. But not yet. We couldn't risk it getting back to Greg as we were sure he had more arsenic to hand.

'Why those five?' Amalyn asked.

'They're the best at using the machines.'

'The 195 people who were sacked will be desperate to pay the bills. I reckon they would be easier to convince, since they've got nothing to lose.'

Archie nodded. 'That's a really good point.'

'Can you access their details? Their addresses, email addresses, phone numbers?' I asked.

'Easy-peasy,' said Archie.

'We really only need a handful to come. So, if most don't believe us, that's fine. But obviously, if even more want to come, then that's okay too. We just need to open the offer up to all of them and hope a few bite. Be honest. Tell them exactly what's happening.'

'Agreed,' Amalyn said. 'As soon as we're ready to let the whole Raft know, we'll make sure they're first to find out.'

Archie copied Harold's video blog and drafted emails to all two hundred factory staff and former staff. He explained about the Mainland, the Tunnels, where the airport was, the solarplanes, and then pleaded with them to come. He planned to add images of the Raft breaking up and the Centre's plans. Everything we knew, they would know too.

We planned to send it all as soon as Grace and Ethan were on a flight – to 'shout it from the rooftops,' as Amalyn put it. Archie also downloaded the machinery plans, just in case. The files were huge. We debated printing it all out, as who knew what computer systems or pen drives they had there? Archie was shocked we hadn't checked out their hardware when we'd visited the Tunnels (seriously!). We decided to gamble on a USB drive, since Archie would try and take a computer anyway. As long as a few of the factory staff agreed to come, we could manage. We could train more people eventually. They were to be the first people we evacuated.

Our plan was beginning to form: flee the Raft, feed the world, screw the Centre.

What could possibly go wrong?

20

Chapter nineteen

Archie, Amalyn and I were the last ones left in the lab. I told Marcus to go home earlier than usual, commending his efforts, saying all was taken care of – whatever it took to get rid of him. Luckily, the rest of the staff were more amenable to the idea of leaving early and packed their bags instantly.

'It's the weekend,' I said. 'Go. Be with your families. We'll work more next week when all the equipment arrives.'

'Phew!' Amalyn mouthed as Marcus left and the glass doors swished shut. We had too many documents to smuggle out to be discreet about it. Their prying eyes of the staff were not welcome.

'Have you finished saying goodbye to your computers yet, Archie?'

He stuck his tongue out at me. 'Yes. Well, almost. Anyway, if you'd like to know, our trajectory is really tricky to predict right now as we're stuck between fronts. It's most likely we're going to swirl around here for a while.'

'The Raft wants to go home,' Amalyn said.

'Maybe we could anchor?'

Archie laughed at me so loudly he almost dropped a hard drive. 'Yeah, good luck convincing people of that one.'

After half an hour, we had a few bags of documents and data ready to take away. I'd made a list of everything I wanted to take, and we had copies or the originals of everything, in triplicate so we could take it all on three planes. 'Just in case,' was what Archie said. Luckily, his pessimism was not catching.

'I just can't wait,' Amalyn said, gazing into space. 'I know it was weird there, but I'm so bored of the Raft. And I barely got to practise my languages at all last time. I'll make sure I do when we live there. I'm even looking forward to checking out the room of books. What did they call it again?'

'Library,' Archie and I replied.

'Yes, the library. And the room of art pictures?'

'Gallery,' we said.

'Just imagine. Have either of you ever seen a real book or painting?' We both nodded, and her eyes widened. 'Really? I mean, it all seems really pointless, but maybe it'll be wonderful.'

I laughed. 'Maybe.'

She smoothed back her loose bits of hair. 'I think I'll look good with a shaved head, don't you think, Archie?'

'You'd look better shaved than dead.'

'Well,' I said, throwing some rubbish at him, '*you* won't look much different.'

We laughed and joked as we carried on rearranging the lab so the stolen items wouldn't be missed, for a few days anyway. It gave us enough time to make up excuses, but we hoped to be off the Raft before anyone realised. Amalyn went to the staffroom and came back with a bottle of wine.

'What?' she said as I rolled my eyes, her face full of

innocence. 'It's Friday night.'

She handed around tea mugs. The pleasing glug of the bottle relaxed me even before I'd swallowed any wine. The red liquid was sweet and comforting. My muscle knots eased with my first sip.

'I never even found out whether they have wine in France,' Amalyn said.

'They certainly used to,' Archie said.

We all sat and drank for a while, looking around the lab, taking it all in. Who knew how much more time we'd spend there, how long it had left before it sank beneath the waves? We had achieved so much in that building. We'd been feeding not just the Raft but the world.

'You know the people Greg laid off?' Amalyn asked. 'A couple of them were in the bar last night.'

I gasped. 'That bar by the edge? Amalyn, you have to be careful.'

'Yeah, yeah, I know. We were checking the satellite cameras, and it was fine. But anyway, they told me that some of the others knew there'd be no work for any of them, and so no healthcare. Five of them jumped straight into the sea.'

'Shit, no!' I held my face in my hands.

'They can't afford rent or food, and that was before the new currency. I reckon more will have done the same since the martas announcement.'

I finished my wine and poured myself another glass. 'That's just awful. So much sadness, right up to the end.'

Archie and Amalyn nodded and refilled their own glasses.

'I don't know what's worse,' Archie said, 'jumping in the sea now or waiting until the Raft forces you in.'

Amalyn bit her lip, fighting away tears.

Guilt rose from my stomach to my chest, threatening to make me heave. Maybe if I'd been kinder, if I'd told them in a different way – why had I bothered telling them anyway? – they could have worked a few more weeks, or however long the Raft had left. Greg would have gone mental at me, but what did that matter? All their faces burned into me, their looks of hatred, seeing me as a conspirator, a defector of the Perimeter, enforcing their misery. What had the Centre turned me into? Their evil messenger. The sound of my voice spread their words. The hideousness of what I had become over the years, their ownership of me, forcing me to do their evil bidding. I hated the Centre and how they asserted their power.

I slammed my cup down. 'We have to make sure we pull this off. Sod the Raft. Sod the fucking Centre pricks. I'll get Grace and Ethan to France ASAP, then we can tell everyone. Inform the masses, give them all a chance. Even if they don't survive, they can withdraw all their money and stop the Centre taking everything. Everyone should have some dignity, some self-belief, instead of just being another leg-up for the Centre arseholes.'

Before we could say any more, Mabel entered the lab, her eyes widening when she saw the bags.

'Oh, hi, Mabel,' I said, jumping in front of the bags. My courteous tone reeked of guilt. 'Can we help?'

'Erm ...'

'We're just having a clear-out. Old notes and things. Stream-lining.' Amalyn almost had me convinced.

'Right.' Mabel nodded, eyeing the wine. 'Well, I just came back because I realised I hadn't said congratulations, Professor. About the results for the injectable. A great achievement.'

'Yes, thanks, Mabel.'

And then she left. We all looked at each other.

'What the Raft was that all about?' Archie asked.

'She's getting weirder by the day,' I said. 'Do you think we got away with that?'

'Have you noticed her lately, always sniffing round?' Amalyn said. 'Her and Marcus suit each other, always sticking their noses in.'

'They want to be annoying and can't just get on with their work,' I said.

'Anyway, when I was in the bar—'

'I really wish you wouldn't hang out there so much,' I said again.

'You sound just like Archie! Anyway, how else am I meant to spread the word? I have to see them.'

'Just be careful.'

'Anyway, there were loads more grumbles and creaks. Everyone can feel it, even if they won't say it out loud. They don't want to believe it. But I reckon it won't take much to convince them.'

'Aren't they freaking out about it enough to stay away from the edge?'

'Where are they meant to go? Their homes are all near the edge. They might as well be in the bar, spending their martas before the Centre run off with the lot.'

'She's right, Sav,' Archie said. 'Are they meant to camp out near the fence until the end, or until we can get them a flight? They have nowhere else to go. We need to get moving.'

'I want to take the staff as well,' I said.

Archie raised his eyebrows. 'Even Marcus and Mabel?'

'Yes, even Marcus and Mabel. They're weird, but they don't

deserve to drown.'

Amalyn rubbed her eyes. 'No one deserves to drown. No one but Greg and his Centre-prick friends, anyway.'

'We'll save as many as we can, Ams,' Archie said, squeezing her knee. 'Promise.'

We left the lab and walked a while before getting an Autocar home. The wind was calm and the sun was low, and despite the smog I could feel its warmth. I wondered if I'd ever see or feel the sun again after we'd left the Raft. It's funny how we don't appreciate what we have until it's gone. The grey beneath my feet, the monotony of it – I hated it, but it was there. Solid, dependable, familiar, its colourlessness predictable. It was all we'd ever known. I'd acknowledged that we had to leave, recognised the necessity of it, admitted to myself that the Raft was screwed, but the fear of the unknown, of moving to a place so strange, I was finding hard to accept. Could I really see myself living underground among people who ate filth?

Blue Liberation had burnt down the bridges, yet the Mainland were ready to welcome us back. It niggled at me, how convivial they were. We were aliens to them, our worlds were that different. But they had room and we were useful, so the maths was simple. However, after years of reading Press articles labelling anything off-Raft 'invasive' and 'foreign filth,' I had my reservations. Open arms where ours were shut. How was anyone that forgiving?

I arrived home late, as was becoming the norm those days. The short walk from the Autocar to my building left me soaked from the rain, the storm lashing down early. The sky was as black as night. *One benefit of living underground*, I thought. No rain, no howling wind, no frost. Just that cool, cool breeze.

I had left all the bags of research at Archie and Amalyn's.

There was no point concerning Grace just yet. Little Ethan crawled onto my lap as I sat on the sofa and put his arms around my neck.

'Hey, what's this for?'

'I missed you, Mummy,' he chirped, melting my heart.

His little cheeks were rosy, his hair in disarray. Drawings were inked up his arms, smudges of biscuit crumb around his mouth. He deserved a life full of adventure and mayhem. I imagined what he would get up to if he had the run of a whole city instead of being cooped up all day. I smiled at him. Mischief, that's what he'd get up to.

Isaac would adore him. Ethan would have an uncle and a cousin, as well as Grace and me. An entire family, almost. It was the best option for him, I was sure.

Grace came into the living room and scowled at us. 'Well, this is great, isn't it? I'm home with him all day, feeding him, working, entertaining him, and you get all the hugs.'

I lifted Ethan off my lap. 'Go play in your room, little man.'

He grabbed his toy Autocar off the floor and skipped off.

'I'm sorry I'm late. It's just work—'

'I know it's work. It's always work. But this is too hard. Working full-time, Ethan full-time. I haven't had a minute to think. I've not made us dinner, I haven't even shut down the IC, and I'm shattered. And you're *always* late. This is actually relatively early for you. At least you made it home before bedtime.' She huffed and sat next to me. 'I can't do this on my own.'

'At least it's the weekend,' she said. 'Can we have a relaxing one, just the three of us?'

I backed away from her, bracing myself. 'I do need to do some work over the weekend, probably Sunday. Amalyn—'

'Again? Amalyn? That's all I ever hear. I've barely seen you at all this week. You spend all your time with her and Archie. And I can smell wine on you. Have you been for a drink again?'

'We just had a glass in the lab after work.'

'Maybe if you spent less time drinking at work, you'd have your weekend free to spend with your family.' Every syllable was enunciated like a slap.

'It's the new launch. Just work stuff.' The untruths were getting easier to say. My heart barely raced when I spoke. I didn't even fidget, hardly sweated. I was acclimatised to dishonesty. Yet the guilt remained, stronger than ever. The drink kept it at bay for only a few moments. Grace's sad eyes tore my heart to pieces.

'Are you having an affair?'

'What?' I shrieked with surprise. 'No! God, no, Grace! Of course not. I love you. Everything I'm doing is for you and Ethan.'

Her big brown eyes filled and her mouth twitched as she bit the inside of her cheek. I hated seeing her hurting, but I couldn't tell her the truth, not yet. Where would I even begin? Tell her about my deal with the Centre to get Ethan, and that, on paper at least, the Centre owned Ethan? Tell her about all the lies I'd allowed the Press to say using my name? About the businesses that queued up to dominate the headlines and line their pockets? That I'd been to the Mainland, had a brother, had lied and lied and lied again? That her dreams of going to the Centre would never come true? I'd built her dreams, and now I had to crush them. She would spiral again, fall deep into despair, withdraw from life. Until we left, she would have to continue living the lie. I would have to rely on Grace to go along with our plans when all it would do was serve as notice for her to run away with Ethan. I couldn't trust her not to do that, could I? I wasn't sure. The only thing I was sure of was that her world was going to collapse, and I had to time the news carefully.

'We need you at home. Or else I need to reduce my hours. Maybe I'll go back to part-time. I miss Maisie. She did so much for us. This is too hard without her.'

'Okay.'

'Really? Part-time?'

'Sure, I don't see why not. Makes total sense.' *It doesn't matter anyway. We're leaving.*

She collapsed back onto the sofa and started sobbing.

'Grace, it's okay. I'll have less work soon, and part-time will work fine.' I put my arm around her and she nuzzled in. My insides were screaming at me to tell her everything, to explain how everything I was working on was to keep her and Ethan safe, that it would all be worth it to survive. But still my deceptions dug in deeper.

Not yet. I can tell you soon, but not yet.

She wiped her eyes on her jumper. 'I'm just so relieved. If we can manage, that really helps. I'm so tired. *Can* we manage, though? The tax hikes, the new currency ... Even food is so expensive.'

'We'll manage. I have a surprise. I can't tell you what it is yet. But soon, trust me, you'll be really happy.'

I don't know why I said that. I think it was just seeing her struggle and then her relief. I couldn't leave her like the staff I'd sacked, miserable until the end. Their pain and worry must have been unimaginable. No way could I do that to Grace. She had to be happy. She had to know I was looking after her, both of them. That I would do whatever it took to keep them safe.

The rain started hammering down, deafening us. I got up and found some music to put on and cranked the volume. A tune from a century ago, with lyrics about love and hope.

'What are you doing?' Grace asked.

'Sounds nicer than the rain. Come here.'

I took her by the hands and pulled her up, her lightness making it easy. I held her close to me, feeling her soft chest against mine. I put one hand round her waist and kept hold of the other, swaying to the music.

'You never were a good dancer,' Grace said with a smile.

'Hey! Bad dancing is better than no dancing.'

She leant in close and whispered in my ear. 'Tell me about this surprise.'

I smiled and shook my head. 'Nope. Not yet.'

She feigned offence, her dark eyes deep and wanting. Then Ethan came running over.

'Mums, it's too loud! What are you doing? I'm hungry.'

We laughed and I turned the music down. 'I'll get dinner on. Why don't you have a nap?' I said, and Grace snuggled down on the sofa. I pulled a thin blanket over her and took off her shoes, wanting to rub her feet, but Ethan was pulling at me, reminding me he was hungry.

I put some food in the oven and left Grace dozing, her face soft and relaxed. As dinner was cooking, I went to Ethan's room. It was chaotic as always. He had a messy mind, like Grace. He showed me what he had built with his building bricks, his drawings of tower blocks. 'New designs,' he said. They were all crooked and impractical, his imagination running away with him.

'I like your designs better than the real buildings,' I said.

'This one is from the Centre.' He showed me a drawing

of a larger building. He'd drawn little stars on the corners, twinkling away. 'Mummy says the buildings there sparkle. See?'

I saw. His vision of the Centre matched Grace's. Her ambitions were also inhabiting him. Untarnished. Gleaming. He would forget, soon enough. With no fence to remind him, his memories of the Centre and the Raft would fade quickly. But Grace ... How was I ever going to convince her?

Ethan climbed onto my lap to show me more pictures, telling me all about his designs and who would live there. He had a kindness that he shared with Grace, and none of my bad moods. His tantrums came with the frustrations of childish powerlessness, not the constant vexations that incite my own short temper. With his blond ringlets and rosy cheeks, he was her little likeness. His smile had the same energy as Grace's in her younger years, his laugh as infectious. His eyes were so dark and deep, it was as if looking at him meant looking at the whole world. I got lost in his eyes the same as I did with hers.

In my mind I saw what new pictures he would make – tunnels, chambers, balconies. No more straight lines, instead swirls of mezzanine floors, engravings, stone staircases. Much harder pictures to draw. Even harder to imagine.

I ran my hands through his hair. It'd be shaved off in the Tunnels. Termites – we'd be living like termites. I held him close. *My little boy.*

After they'd gone to bed, I crept through the apartment and took my father's book from the shelf, sliding it out of its plastic vacuum sheath with gloved hands. His work in the field of entomology. Pages and pages of the awful vermin he'd loved so much. The disease outbreak that had ruined him, blamed on his insect collection. The Press had written the most callous things about him. I'd believed them then, as everyone had. His fascination with filth cost so many lives. I managed a short glimpse of each page before I had to turn away. He was wrong. The Great Sterilisation Project was right. It had to be. There was no way vermin were a good thing.

But the Tunnels ...

I washed and tiptoed back to bed, too tired to think anymore.

Ethan's adventurous nature kept him busy at all hours, often denying Grace and me a full night's sleep. But even when he did sleep, often I could not. My mind churned with worries of the Raft, the Tunnels, escaping, convincing Grace. A deceitful mind is not a rested mind. For the odd hour when I was able to sleep, my dreams left me agitated. I sweated like I'd never sweated before. Even when the Raft had been meandering around the Equator, I hadn't sweated like that. Womanhood at my age brought more hassle than joy. I would soak through the sheets, irritable from the moment my eyes opened, sleep deprived and sticky.

'Dreams are our subconscious reconciling with ourselves,' Maisie would say. If that were true, I would have forgiven myself a long time ago.

I went back to sleep and dreamed of the bridges. Their solidness and sturdiness, built to last. All turned to dust.

I was running across, barefooted and panicked. Surrounded by termites, cockroaches and birds. Butterflies whipped at my hair and bees buzzed past my ears. The entirety of my father's book swarmed with me as I ran, a praying mantis scampering to catch up. I ran and ran as the bridge behind me smouldered and burned and turned to ash. Bald, dehumanised, dewomanised, scared. All the creepers and crawlers scurried around me as we bolted for the end of the bridge, their colours a kaleidoscope of swirls around me. Alien textures and hues, like a mess of broken crayons. Then we made it to the end of the bridge, but I was still on the Raft. It had taken me nowhere. The colour dissolved into nothing and I was left with the ceaseless dull grey. Greg's awful face grinned his whiter-than-white grin, matches in hand. The dust never settled on him, and he remained pearly white.

Chapter twenty

On Saturday morning, I got up early to give Ethan his breakfast and make sure he was washed and dressed. After cleaning the apartment, I got food prepared for the day. I needed more sleep, but I also needed Grace to be happy. Grace distracting me with worry was only going to cost me precious time. My head was stuffed with too much else. There was no room left for wife dramas. I'd save her, but that meant, for the time being, I was going to be busy. She'd understand soon.

When she got up, she seemed much more at ease. A good night's sleep and the knowledge she could reduce her work hours rid her of some stress. The apartment was clean, food was prepared and Ethan had done his weekend's homework already.

'He really is a genius, Sav,' Grace said, looking at his maths and spelling. 'Way above where he should be for five. And his assessments yesterday were top. I know. I know all parents say that, but I really mean it. He's learnt up to his seven times table and can recite them like that.' She snapped her fingers.

So far that morning, he had drawn on the walls and missed

the toilet with his pee, which was fine with me. I loved the kid, but until he could at least do algebra, I'd consider him just a kid and not a genius. Grace, however, saw nothing but perfection, a future more golden than his hair, a life of opportunities. I hoped that would still be true.

I smiled. 'I'm sure he's doing marvellously.'

'I'll prove it. Ethan!'

He came galloping over, grinning from ear to ear.

'What's five times seven?'

'Thirty-five.'

Grace clapped her hands. 'Good! Really good! Now, what's three times six?'

'Eighteen.'

We both clapped that time.

'All right, Grace. Ethan, well done. Now go play.' He trotted off, looking very smug. 'He really is clever, but he also just needs to be a kid.'

'He'll be our ticket to the Centre one day, I know it.'

I squeezed her tight and looked out of the window. The Centre fence lurked like prison bars above the high-rises. Which side of it was the prison was where Grace and I disagreed.

'All right if I go to the MindSpa?' I asked.

'Sure. Home for lunch?'

I kissed her forehead and left.

The MindSpa was where I would normally go to unwind, to realign any twisted thoughts and rid myself of any tension. But that day its rustles and cheeps felt strange to me. Where I normally found solace, I found discomfort. I fidgeted in the chair, my clothing prickled and I scratched as the breeze spread the irritation all over me. The rustling noises weren't soothing. They sounded like the larders on the Mainland, or the silkworms squirming in their trays. My skin crawled and my forehead tensed. When the orange hue lightened my eye mask to end the session and rouse me, it was as if I were in the Tunnels, stressed and confused. Instead of feeling reinvigorated, sweat pooled along my hairline and my skin itched.

Is that what the MindSpa is meant to represent? Filth?

I left feeling unclean and tired. My nails scraped at my skin to try and get rid of the crawling sensation. The walk home didn't comfort me as vaporous threads of smog licked at my ankles. The street sprayers didn't sting enough, and the wind wasn't strong enough to blow the grime away. It was a dry day, but I begged for rain. The trickle of sweat down my back made me think some filthy creature was slithering on me. The humidity made my hair frizz up, the soft wind gluing it in place. I remembered the days when I'd spent ages teasing any bit of volume into my lank locks. Now I was constantly trying to flatten it.

You'll shave it all off soon.

The thought almost made me happy. One less hassle, at least.

As I approached my apartment block, I froze for a moment. My breath caught in my lungs. Outside my building were two shiny black Autocars, obsidian like jewels against the grey. I had seen those cars before. Nothing from the Perimeter gleamed like that.

I slowed my walk, heart racing more with every step. As I got nearer, I noticed two heavily armed guards standing outside my building and two across the street, hazmat suits disguising any hint of their intention.

I flapped my T-shirt, asphyxiated from sweat. My heart

thumped in my ears.

'Name?' one guard grunted at me as I approached the building.

'Savannah Selbourne.'

He typed my name into a mini e-pad, held it next to me to scrutinise the photo, then stepped aside.

I took the stairs, dragging out every pulse-quickening minute until I reached my front door. Outside was another armed guard, who stepped out my way as I approached. The door was ajar and from inside came voices, female, Ethan's giggles, then—

'Mummy!' He was at the door and hugging my leg, ruining my plan to eavesdrop.

I picked him up. 'What's going on, little man?'

He leant into me to whisper, his angelic voice making my skin tingle. 'There's a big lady here.'

Microbes!

I put him down. He was getting heavy these days. The voices from the living room hushed and Grace appeared in the doorway, her face radiant, eyes wide, giggling like a schoolgirl.

'Sav, we have a visitor.' She grabbed my elbow and dragged me in.

'Uh-huh. I figured that much.'

'It's the Prime Minister!' She clasped her hands together.

The 'big lady' was sitting on our sofa, posture straight, her head towering above the headrest, her knees bent to her chest from sitting so low. Her jewellery caught the light from the window, casting little lasers across the room.

I clenched my jaw to stop my lip trembling, tensing every muscle. She had invaded my home! Most likely to tell us about Mars, and Grace would then never be convinced to go anywhere else. If she'd told Grace before I'd had the chance to tell her about the Tunnels, I had no hope of convincing her. The Prime Minister would sell Mars like a gift-wrapped present.

'Good afternoon, Prime Minister,' I said through my teeth. I didn't bow. She was in my house uninvited. Screw bowing.

'Professor. Wonderful. Please sit.' The flash of white from her smile-cum-grimace made me recoil.

'Sav, she's been telling us about how well Ethan is doing.'

'Right.' The Prime Minister's head seemed huge now she was down at my level, like when the sun is on the horizon and looks so much bigger than when it is up in the sky.

'She says he's the best-achieving five-year-old on the whole Raft. Can you believe that?'

My boy was none of her business; that was all I could believe. 'Okay,' I said, giving her a side-eye, waiting for the real reason she was in my home.

'She says he's been chosen. *Chosen!* Can you believe that? As a gifted child.' Grace's voice was all jittery, and she cupped her face in her hands.

'Uh-huh.' Suspicion gnawed at me. I stared at the Prime Minister's face but she looked only poised and serene. She'd practised that look, I knew it.

'*Chosen*, Sav! Can you believe it?'

'Sure. For what?'

'For a scholarship to the School of Politics. In the Centre!'

'He's five years old.'

'Ahem.' The Prime Minister cleared her throat. 'It is the best school on the Raft. For the best students. This scholarship is offered to one Perimeter pupil per year, so the school can diversify and represent the whole Raft.'

'We'd have to move to the Centre, Sav,' Grace said, eyes moistening with excitement.

The Prime Minister's face was blank and still, but her hands were fidgeting. Not nervously, more of a cool, calm fidget. They turned themselves over and over, while she sneered in the way they all do. I sat and eyed her with distrust.

Then I saw what was in her fidgeting hands.

A little black disc.

'You see, Professor Selbourne, we have eyes and ears everywhere. Gifted children like Ethan, and their families, do not go unnoticed. We always knew Ethan would be special since his very conception. As I have told you before, Blue Liberation is a party of reward.'

'Can you believe it, Sav? Isn't this the most wonderful news?'

I swallowed. There was no offer in the Prime Minister's words. I heard exactly what they were.

A threat.

I smiled back, sickeningly sweetly, those barely used muscles pulling my lips up but also making me ready to bite.

Stay away from my family!

'Why don't you spend some time in the Centre?' the Prime Minister said, her arms opening as if she was about to crush us. 'My cars can take you there straight away. We can put you up in the finest accommodation and give you a tour of the school and the parliamentary buildings, to see how at home our young man Ethan will be.'

'Our' young man? He's mine, you bitch!

'No,' I said, too quickly.

'Sav!'

'No, Grace. It wouldn't be right – not right now.' I wanted

to launch at the Prime Minister, to wrap my hands around her thick neck and kick her teeth in. She was in my home, threatening my family and trying to sugar-coat it as a favour to us. I'd die before I'd let her take them. 'It was only a few days ago Ethan had that illness, remember? He really shouldn't be mixing with other people yet.'

The Prime Minister's posture straightened even more, and the armed guard stepped a little further from us.

'Obviously this is wonderful news,' I maintained my smile, nauseatingly saccharine, 'but I'd say we need a few days, just to be sure. Next weekend would be better, don't you think, Grace?'

'You're right,' Grace said, face reddening. 'I'm so sorry, Prime Minister. With all the excitement, I totally forgot. I should have warned you as soon as you arrived. I was just so blown away. I really am sorry.'

The Prime Minister stood quickly and backed away towards the door. 'It wasn't anything serious, I hope?'

'Just a bit of a fever.'

'*Fever!*' she choked out through an audibly dry mouth. 'This really should have been brought to our attention.'

'I'm so sorry,' Grace said again, her voice sounding desperate. 'This won't affect the offer, will it?'

The Prime Minister paused in her retreat to turn and smile at me, achieving a level of menace I could not compete with. 'Of course not. We will see Ethan in a few days. I am looking forward to having you all in the Centre.'

She left, her security spraying themselves with antiviral spray.

We watched from the living-room window as they got in their cars and drove away. Only then did either of us dare to exhale.

'Oh my, Sav. Do you think the offer will stand?'

'I'm sure it will,' I said, unable to hide my anger now. 'But Grace, the Centre?'

'She was so nice, wasn't she? Can you believe the Prime Minister visited us? And she knows about Ethan!' She spun around the room, as if floating on a cloud of glee.

How could I explain? Where to begin?

'They're evil, Grace, all of them. She has an agenda. This isn't the offer it seems.'

Grace stood still and frowned at me. A hurt silence passed between us, happy tears turning to sad. 'Why would you say that? I told you he's a genius. They want the Perimeter represented.'

I rubbed my temples. How could she not see this for the trap it was? 'First of all, the scholarship is nonsense – she made that up. Second of all, if they wanted the Perimeter represented, they'd have more than one Perimeter in the whole school. The School of Politics? He's five years old, for Raft's sake. I'm telling you, this stinks of rotten fish.'

'This is what we've been dreaming of, Sav. The best for our son.'

I pulled her in close to me and kissed her forehead. 'Just please don't get your hopes up. Let's just wait. I'll do some digging. I really think she's being devious.'

'Devious? She's the Prime Minister! The Press is always saying about how good and thorough she is. She actually comes to visit the Perimeter.' Her naivety made me bite my lip. 'What could she possibly be being devious about?'

'Please, just a few days.'

Looking at Grace, the moisture collecting in her dark eyes,

my boiling rage calmed. The biting cold thawed, and all that was left was her warmth. It wouldn't happen, what the Prime Minister said. Grace would understand. She'd see sense. She *had* to see sense. I still didn't know where to begin, but I knew I had to start thinking about what to say. The Centre, or rather Mars, could never be our home. We could never live among those people.

A few days. That's all you've got.

Panic tingled through every inch of me.

'I need to see Archie and Amalyn for a bit tomorrow.'

'*Again?*' her pleading cry hurt. 'Can't it wait until Monday? Come on, Sav, it's the weekend.'

'I know, I really am sorry. I told you yesterday I had to do a bit of work over the weekend. It's something big we're working on that I'll be able to tell you about soon. A big surprise.'

I searched her face, but her emotions were hard to read. She was too far away from me. Then I realised that it was the first time I'd ever seen that look on her. She wasn't listening to my reasons. Instead, she was searching for the truth. Her trust in me was faltering.

'I'll tell you all about it next week. I mean it,' I said, feeling my chest crumple with the weight of it all.

Ethan came running over, his socks trailing behind him as always. 'Look, mummies, the big lady threw this at me! And I caught it!'

'Well done, little man,' I said as he handed me the thin black disc. For a moment I'd convinced myself I'd imagined it. My heart froze. There was no denying it. I was busted.

'Please, Sav. Tell me what this is all about.'

Tell her? Tell her I'd hacked the Prime Minister's office and now the Centre was threatening our son? Tell her I may have blown our chances of being safe if the Tunnel plan didn't work out? Her kind naivety deserved better than that. Better than me.

'Just a few days, Grace, please. I have a lot to figure out.'

I felt those arms reaching for me again, the eyes in the walls watching my every move. Had they bugged my flat? I longed to call Archie but didn't dare. Anyway, I needed time to process it all. We had an escape all lined up and ready. I was so relieved I hadn't told Grace the truth yet – she would have been in bits if she'd had to lie to the Prime Minister – but my deceit was hovering over us like the smog at the edge, a dark cloud over our relationship. She knew I was hiding something, I was sure of it. She didn't hassle me, she didn't ask what was going on, but I saw it in her distant eyes. A scepticism towards me, eroding trust that I would have to claw back.

For now, though, her excitement eclipsed that cloud. She'd had a glimpse of the Centre, an offer she'd been dreaming of. However much I'd tried to tell her not to get her hopes up, she did.

* * *

On Sunday I promised Grace I'd be home by dinner time as I left to go plot with Archie and Amalyn. She held me before I left. I breathed in the scent of her, nestling into her hair. The indulging scent of ignorance. When I looked at her, I was home. She had to feel the same way about me, that I was her home, not the Centre. Soon she'd know the truth. Soon I would crush her dreams.

Please don't hate me, Grace.

The sooner we had a workable plan, the better. The more

lives we could potentially save, the sooner I could get Grace and Ethan off the Raft. My gut wrenched with guilt over the factory workers throwing themselves into the sea, keeping me up all night. I saw their ashen faces, hopelessness draining them of colour, their backs bowed, heavy with despair. They hit the water with a thud, like rocks, doomed to sink to the bottom. The sea left a putrid smell in their wake. Decay, rot, the entrails of life.

You can't save them all.

I reminded myself of that over and over, but their blood was on my hands. It was me who had told them the awful news. Me who had supported this evil company for years. I poisoned the Perimeter with my words. Saving more people wouldn't wash that immorality away – I knew that – but it was the best I could do. Every single life saved was worth the effort. Ten million corpses was too much to bear.

Years earlier, the Minister of Impartiality had told me how dangerous hope was, and the importance of stability. Well, we were going to turn that upside-down. If the Centre could jump ship, so could everyone else.

I went to the MindSpa again before meeting Archie and Amalyn, figuring it could be my last time, as I couldn't imagine the library or gallery would produce the same endorphin-inducing effects. I had to wait. For the first time I could recall, every station was taken. More and more people were feeling safe and leaving their homes, just as the Raft was becoming the most dangerous it had ever been. I watched them all for a moment, lying still, their faces serene, relaxed, no clue that their entire country was disintegrating. Burying their heads in the dirt.

I reserved a slot for an hour later and went for a walk. I

approached the fence and stared through the bars. The protest having long since dispersed, it felt abandoned and desolate. Rows of high-rises had been built right up to the fence, most likely empty. No lights on and windows bolted shut. The fence wasn't electrified. It had been mentioned over the years but had never happened yet. Each long bar was set a fist's width apart, stretching almost as high as I could see, ending in a vicious point. Protecting its precious Elite from the likes of us. I walked along the fence line. On the floor around each post was a little pile of dirt, like it had been freshly drilled. I guessed they'd let the maintenance slip and had had to make repairs.

When I finally got to my MindSpa room, I was able to relax. It was more calming than the day before. My thoughts could unwind and the tension seeped from my muscles. The rustling noises, the cheeps and chirps, weren't meant to be filth – of course they weren't. What stupid ideas I'd had yesterday. Filth noise could never be relaxing.

Often when visiting the MindSpa I thought of my father, his environmental dementia, his longing. Those subtle tweets and chirps ignited the part of my memory that normally stayed hidden, folded up in the way that Grace folded away Ethan's baby clothes, collecting dust until the MindSpa breeze blew it away.

That day, though, through the hypnotic noises, the soothing rustles, I thought of my mother. Seeing Donna's Library had not filled me with nostalgia at the time. Fiction had turned her mind to ash. What was the point of imagining when the glaring reality in front of you needed so much attention? She'd given up on me. I was not enough to live for, her love of books more important than her love for me. But the delicate sounds in that moment reminded me of brittle paper pages, the thinnest of thin tree carcasses, her humming as she read, the whistle of her tongue as she whispered a poem to herself. Words inaudible, just a hint of sound. Her dark eyes widening, full of reverence at every word, engrossed in a way I could not imagine. Isaac said she couldn't leave me, but she did. Not physically, but long before she died. So rapt with stories about mothers and daughters, poems of love, fantasies a million miles from the here and now. I resented her for her escapism, but there, in the MindSpa, enjoying a few stolen moments to distract my anxious mind, lying to my wife as time together eluded us, I realised how my mother and I were not so different. Perhaps her own MindSpa, her books and her art, would be relaxing after all.

Nonsense, Sav.

When the lights eased back on, the orange hue came through my mask, making me think of the Tunnels again, and my relaxation was tinged with sadness. Perhaps there were some parts of the Raft I would miss.

As I walked out of the MindSpa, I couldn't shake the feeling that the greyness, the bleakness of the Raft, had killed my mother. She'd lost her voice when her ability to imagine had become obsolete. Reading fiction wasn't just escapism for her. It was also her hope. The Minister of Impartiality had told me that hope was deadly, but she was wrong. In this barren world, hope was all we had. If my mother and I had left with my brother, maybe she would have survived. She would have had her library to nurture that part of her brain that had died first. The Centre and their agendas had killed her. They were not taking my wife and child, too.

22

Chapter twenty-one

I arrived at Archie and Amalyn's with the black disc in my pocket. I was looking out the Autocar window for the whole journey, watching for someone following me, that creeping feeling of eyes on me. But as I alighted, I saw I was alone, not a soul on the street.

Maisie's old place looked more cluttered than ever, scattered with never-to-be-unpacked boxes, dust that would never be cleaned, photo frames soon to be forgotten. There was meant to be a new life in that apartment, a fresh start. Instead, it was to be left behind to rot with the rest of the Raft.

We cracked open some beers, and I showed them the black disc.

'Where'd you get another one?' Archie asked.

I shook my head and tossed it to him. 'It's the same one. I had a visitor yesterday.'

His eyebrows went as high as they could go. 'Someone from the Centre?'

'The Prime Minister. She was at my house. Speaking to Grace.'

'Oh shit.'

'Yep.'

He paled and immediately glugged back half his beer. 'Well, I guess that means they're on to us. I'll be first on the suspect list for providing that. What did she have to say about it? How are you here and not in the sea? How are we *all* not in the sea?'

Amalyn cleared her throat. 'Are you a spy, Sav?'

'Don't be daft. She didn't say anything about it, she just left it behind. Although she made it clear she had it, sitting there fidgeting with it in front of me. She was talking to Grace about Ethan, sickeningly smiley, clearly threatening us.'

I told them everything, about Ethan's apparent genius, his school offer, how they wanted to take him away there and then, about her hinting about Mars at our earlier meeting.

'Mars? Seriously?' Amalyn's voice went almost as high as Penny's.

'She never said Mars, just the Centre. "A place for us" was how she put it, in her threatening and devious way. Wowing Grace with her offer. She's clever. She knows that with Grace head over heels about the idea of living in the Centre, I'm screwed now. How am I going to convince her they're evil when they've just presented her with an offer like that? You should have seen Grace, her eyes lit up, all excited like it would be something wonderful.'

'Wait. Grace *wants* to go live in the Centre?'

'Yep. She thinks because it's shiny, it must be glorious.'

'Microbes.' Amalyn drank half her own beer.

'I'm just so glad Ethan was sick, so I had an excuse, and Grace not knowing anything about anything was the picture of truth. But this means I now have just a few days to get them off the Raft.'

'You still haven't told her?'

'She knows nothing, absolutely nothing. I don't even know where to begin. And now this!' I put my head in my hands.

Archie and Amalyn both sat back in their chairs and loudly exhaled.

'Okay, fine.' Archie went to his keyboard. 'I can still get into their computers. The disc was only for initial access. I can still search and view everything.'

'Well, as long as you can continue playing, that's okay,' I said.

'You're particularly grouchy these days,' he said as I flapped my T-shirt to make a breeze. The humidity was getting to me. 'Access is still useful. For information, not just playing.'

'Fine. So, what shall we do?'

'We obviously need to speed things up, but that could draw attention so everyone else needs to be lined up and ready to go.'

'Definitely,' Amalyn said. 'We should call Isaac and get it confirmed. Aim to start evacuating people tomorrow.'

Their pragmatism calmed me remarkably, but the room still spun. The enormity of it was drowning me. I could barely lift my head with the weight of my thoughts.

Archie started taking notes. 'Get Grace and Ethan and whoever else is ready off first.'

'My family,' said Amalyn. 'I want them on the first flight.'

'Definitely. And we'll start writing the articles now. Sav, that's on you. I'll carry on downloading all the proof we need.'

I nodded slowly, my brain like a knotted muscle. Where the Press had spewed out the Centre's propaganda for decades, we were to spill the truth. Straighten out those twisted minds, undo years of Press-led brainwashing. Could that even be done? 'Everyone is safe now' – that's what they all believed. The lies were like a thick blanket, woven together, and unravelling that was going to take a miracle.

But we had to try. It was time to bring people out of the dark. We were going to turn the lights on.

'We'll start from the edge and work our way in,' Amalyn said. 'The furthest out in the Perimeter go first. That's how we'll be discreet. No one will miss them.'

Archie handed me the satellite phone. 'Time to call him, Sav. Time to find out if we can pull this off.'

I took the phone and dialled. After a few moments of static, his voice came through.

'Sav?'

'Isaac, thank god. Listen, we need to hurry things up. Long story, but I need to get my family off the Raft tomorrow. Do you think that will be possible?'

There was a pause for what felt like an eternity, some background voices that we couldn't decipher, then: 'Yes, that will be possible. I can sort a solarplane for the evening, eighteen hundred. Can you make that?'

'Yes! Yes, thank you. Whatever it takes, I'll get them there.'

'It's happening here too, Sav,' Isaac said, his voice sounding low.

'What? The Tunnels are breaking up?' My heart froze. *Please, no!*

'No, the Select. They're leaving for Mars.'

'Why are they leaving? Are the Tunnels still safe?'

'I think Mars is just more luxurious. They told us the truth, at least. And they're making sure we're provided for.'

'So, you've got no leaders? No one in power?'

'We're going to have proper elections and run things our–

selves.'

'No way!' Amalyn and I said together.

'So you're going to be a real community?' It all sounded too good to be true.

'Yep. Govern ourselves, free and fair.'

'Oh, Isaac.' I held my chest as if it were going to burst. 'I can't wait. I really can't.'

'Me too, Isaac!' Amalyn yelled.

Isaac laughed. 'Hi, Amalyn. Listen, I have to go. This signal doesn't last long. I'll see you all soon.'

I hung up, and we sat silently for a few moments. A free and fair society, run by the people, not just the richest. The situation was really starting to dawn on me. I really would have to crush Grace's dreams. I would have to tell her we are going to live underground, like worms, and shave her and Ethan's heads. So much I would have to tell her. But how much better it would be! No rich idiots telling us what to do, a truly liberated community, no oppressor, with real elections. A country where the people had a say, not just the wealthy. There was a home beckoning me and it glimmered with hope. I opened another beer.

'It's so weird that Grace wants to live in the Centre, after everything they take from us,' Amalyn said. 'Does she not understand how nasty the Centre can be? You should tell her, explain to her that living among them would feel like being a bug in the Perimeter.'

'I will, but she's so fragile. She needs to have something to cling to, you know? And she could never lie in the face of the Prime Minister, so it's much better if her mind stays innocent for as long as possible.' I sipped my beer. 'It's going to be horrible when I tell her. I never really noticed it until recently, but she stares at the fence like the ultimate prize is in there. I think the Raft is just so shit, and as far as she knows there's nowhere else, so she figures the Centre must be better. And she'd never met anyone from there before yesterday, when "the big lady" came round, as Ethan called her.'

'Oh wow, that's so funny. To her face?' Amalyn laughed.

'Not exactly, but definitely within earshot.'

'Brilliant!'

'So, that is literally the only time Grace has met a Centre, and it was the bloody PM giving her all sorts of compliments about her genius child. Plus, we waited so long for fertility treatment, and she wanted a baby so much. To her, the Centre is the key to getting things quickly. If you live in the Centre, you can have whatever you want. She sees it as the answer, not the problem.'

Amalyn handed me another beer. 'Well, I'm glad you don't want to go to Mars with all the Centre pricks. The Tunnels would be rubbish without your moaning and nagging.'

'Thanks, Ams.'

Archie's computers were fired up, as always. I sat on the floor with an e-pad on my lap as I drafted the emails, explaining just about everything I could think of. Archie was at his desk searching the Centre files to find out more on the dirtquakes. That part still didn't make sense.

'Would knotweed make that noise?' I asked.

Archie snorted a laugh. 'It's a plant, Sav. No.'

'Maybe the Raft is breaking up more centrally first,' Amalyn suggested.

'No way. They'd fix it.'

We sat and pondered, drinking bottles of the worst synth beer I'd tasted in years.

'Maybe it's them reinforcing the Centre?' I said.

'You know what, that makes sense,' Archie said. 'If they're drilling in, adding more iron, that could do it, for sure.'

'Seems stupid to reinforce a city you're about to abandon,' I said. 'But I saw at the fence that some of the concrete around the main posts is loose, so maybe they've stuck them in deeper.'

'Everything the Centre does is stupid.' Amalyn said.

'Maybe they're trying to save it for the Perimeter people, once they're all gone.' I couldn't tell if Archie was being genuine or sarcastic.

'Yeah, right.' Amalyn almost laughed. 'Imagine the Centre being so thoughtful.'

'This beer truly is revolting.' My lips tightened from the sourness as I finished my third bottle.

'Yeah, my dad gave us his stash as a moving-in gift,' Amalyn said.

'Your *dad?*' I gasped. 'Shit, Ams, I forget you have family.'

'It's okay. They're on the first flight, remember? With as many others as we can. I'm putting them on the plane with Grace and Ethan.'

I smiled. 'Last days on the Raft and we're drinking this shit.'

'Ha! Anyone fancy breaking into the Centre and raiding their wine cellar?' Archie said.

'Don't tempt me!' said Amalyn. 'My family never wanted the anchors to blow. I don't remember when it happened. They probably protested. They moaned about it for years afterwards. Not that they bother mentioning it, now. They've just gotten used to being stuck here, I guess. My dad had a business selling pharmacy medicines. It folded when the anchors blew. And my mum has family on the Mainland. Did, anyway. Who knows if she still does.'

'Maybe you could find them?'

'Maybe. I think they both hoped the world would work together to fix things, not section itself off.' She swallowed the last of her latest bottle and sank lower in her seat. 'Then they saw the floods and the fires and figured we were better off here. But it was all a lie. The rest of the world has been there the whole time. Thriving cities and countries, working together. And we've been drifting in the stinking shit of the sea, cut off this whole time. Lies upon lies. The Centre would have us believe we are the only ones who didn't vanish. The Centre took our ... What are all those books together called again?'

'Libraries.'

'Libraries, even though they still use them. It's like they don't want us to use our minds. They don't want us to imagine. They just want us to do what we're told.'

She was sounding like all the Golden Fifties at the bar with a bit of drink oiling their vocal cords, but I couldn't disagree. 'Lies upon lies' was about right.

'I'll bet it's all been a lie,' she continued. 'The whole "sterile Raft" bullshit, and insects being bad. They just told us those things because they were dying out anyway and they couldn't be bothered to save them.'

'I think that's going a bit far. Filth is still filth,' I said, scrunching my nose.

'Maybe,' she said, 'but your dad liked the creepers and crawlers. I'll bet he was more trustworthy than anyone from the Centre.'

'He had good intentions, at least.'

'They just didn't like it that the insects and birds could fly to other countries, and we couldn't. The filth connected us to the Mainland.'

'They also brought diseases with them.'

She sighed. 'I find it so weird that we used to be connected with dirt. The country's foundations were made of dirt. The rich, dirtying their hands in each other's pockets. It's all the same. The grime of greed, that's what it is.'

I nodded. 'Dirt may have linked us, but poison broke us apart.'

'Poison?' she asked. 'How?'

The beer was making my tongue loose. Why did Amalyn have to get so philosophical? I cleared my throat. 'You reckon they'll believe us at the lab? Marcus and Mabel and the others?' I asked.

Archie swallowed the last of his bottle. 'How is it you know Mabel and Ams's names but not the other ones?'

I rolled my eyes. 'Ams because she's great, obviously. Mabel because she's just so *weird*. Also, she's always in the lab, never a home worker. You know, she even said on her internship that she thought bacteria would *help* absorption.'

Amalyn gasped. 'I never would have pictured her as such a renegade. I almost like her now.'

'I know, quite the sly one. And the others, well, they're not usually in the lab. They're not remarkable in any way, a bit too normal. They just blend in with the paint.'

Archie laughed. 'I can imagine when you tell them: "2-10, 4-09 and 8-08, you need to flee the Raft!"'

'It'll be like when you invited them for a drink,' Amalyn said, crying with laughter.

And we all laughed, wincing down the last of the rank beer, holding our bellies when the laughter cramps came. We raided the cupboards for all the synth junk food we could find and sat around, not saying anything particularly sensible for a long time.

The wind was howling outside, but in that apartment, between our giggle fits, we felt a peace. The excitement of the adventure ahead was not exhilarating, more like a satisfying stretch after a long yawn. We were ready. We were going to be free.

That was it. That was why I was escaping to the Tunnels. The offer of Mars was meaningless, *life* would be meaningless without my friends. Without freedom. Grace could be happy anywhere. She understood the importance of friends and family. I'd tell her everything, come clean about the Centre's control, the poison, Ethan's conception, the whole lot. I'd open her eyes and let her see the Centre for what they really were. The Tunnels were weird, but less awful than the Centre. And we would be free.

I hadn't needed to bother taking the knotweed photos, didn't need to keep my options open. I had the only one I needed. A life with family – more family – and my friends. The Press hadn't even used the photos. It had been just a test, requiring me to shred more and more of my soul every day, proving to me and themselves that I was their loyal puppet. The Centre wouldn't be happy until I was a robot, at their bidding, whatever planet they were on.

Screw them!

I clicked Save on my articles. No doubt there would be some beer-induced mistakes, but I could read them over tomorrow. The gist was there. I emailed them to Archie as backup and checked the time. *Microbes!* How was it that late already? My phone was flashing with a message from Grace asking when

I'd be home. I needed to get an Autocar.

'Guys, I've got to get going or Grace is going to go nuts,' I said as I grabbed my bag and coat. I was going to tell her everything as soon as I got in. The beer had given me a bit of courage and I actually felt excited about telling her, getting it all out in the open so we could start our new, honest life together. I was prepared for the tears and denial, but also ready to tell her everything, to explain it all, the years of deception, and come clean about how shrewd and cunning the Centre really were. The chains of truth that weighed me down for so long would be released.

Tomorrow, we'd be free.

I said my goodbyes. We had our strategy sorted, the articles had been written and Archie was compiling the proof. We'd decided when we would release it all, unleashing the truth in successive but rapid increments. There was no time to waste. Building trust, not piling on too much information at once. If there was one thing I had learnt from the National Press over the years, it was how to manage propaganda. I had learnt how they twist words to suit their own schemes, and now it was our turn. Only this time, we were telling the truth. The beautiful, untarnished truth.

Our articles wouldn't serve the Centre's agenda. They would help the Perimeter, our people, to save themselves. We had enough evidence to convince the majority. Some would never read our messages – our reach went only so far – and of those who did, some wouldn't believe us, naturally. Some brains cannot be unwashed. But we had a viable plan. A bid for freedom, for true liberty.

'Good work, team,' I slurred as I made to leave.

Neither replied. Neither even moved. They stood staring at

the computer screen.

'Bye then?' Still no response. They didn't even look my way. I walked over to them and looked at the computer screen.

Then my whole body started to shake.

The satellite image showed the smog thinning at the edge, just a fine mist over the concrete, and the coastline in contemptible detail, the black slurry of the sea licking at the shore. But an even blacker artery was creeping in. A crack was skulking across, a thick finger of darkness feeling its way across the concrete.

'Is that …?' I couldn't finish the sentence, couldn't say it out loud. I didn't want to hear those words. *Please, no!*

Amalyn quivered a nod. 'Yes. Oh, god, it is.'

Archie said nothing, his hands either side of his keyboard clenched into fists, his jaw trembling.

It was the same image we had seen from the air. The image I had locked away. Now it was replaying in front of us, bigger, clearer, sharper. It was like watching an old film, a horror film where you're left screaming at the TV, 'No, no!' Hoping your sheer will could change the outcome.

But none of us screamed.

We all watched, dumbstruck, as the darkness widened, and the huge crack ripped the land and a chunk of it broke away. It held its shape for a short while, drifting for a few moments, then sank, taking the solarplanes, and our hopes, with it.

The airport, our route off the Raft, had gone.

23

Chapter twenty-two

We remained silent for several minutes, the only sound the drizzle at the windows, each drop ticking the time away, ticking away the seconds until the entire Raft sank.

Drip. Drip. Drip. Three seconds less.

'We left it too late,' Archie said. 'We should have gone straight away, but we left it too late.'

'I just ...' Words eluded me. My mind was hollow.

Drip. Drip. Drip. Three more seconds gone.

How had it gone? The airport, all the solarplanes, just disappeared.

'I need to be with Grace, and ... and hold my son.'

'Bet that Mars offer isn't seeming like such a bad idea now,' Amalyn said, her bitter tone making me wince. She didn't look my way, but I saw her jaw tense.

Mars? I couldn't even think about Mars. The Mainland, our escape, all the food that was supposed to go there ... Surely the airport hadn't just sunk.

My knees nearly gave way as I tried to walk away. 'You know that's not what I want.'

Amalyn's body sagged, and she dropped to the floor. Archie's eye's left the screen and looked down to his lap with an expression of hopelessness.

'At least you have an option. My family doesn't.' Amalyn blinked and tears spilled down her cheeks.

Archie rubbed her back. 'This is awful for all of us, Ams. Sav, too.'

'I'm going to go. I ... I need to go,' I said as I backed away, leaving them suspended in the moment, the air thick with a sense of demise. I needed to be out of the apartment, to someplace away from that monitor, from what had just happened.

Surely that hadn't just happened?

Drip. Drip. Drip.

We left it too late.

I stumbled out of the building and threw up on the pavement, adding some colour to the grey. The rain and street cleaners would wash it away, but what did that matter? Nothing mattered anymore.

I walked home, forgetting that time was getting on. The wind groaned against the buildings and tore at my face. The smog rarely came this far inland, but there it was, ghostly grey, pale wisps snaking through the roads, licking at the high-rises. Had the wind forced it further inland?

Don't be stupid, Sav.

We were getting closer to the sea. Or rather, the sea was getting closer to us. When the time came, if Grace didn't believe me, that was sure to convince her. The proof was making its way up our street. Our central apartment would soon have a sea view.

The rain had stopped and night had arrived. A full moon was

visible above the ethereal tendrils of grey, like the dead were grappling for the land, for the buildings, for all of us.

Grace didn't greet me when I got home. She was red-faced, dark-eyed and shattered. My rain-soaked appearance and apologies did nothing to quell her rage. She spoke to me with an angry voice. She was tired, and Ethan had been a handful.

He was mid-tantrum when I arrived, but I scarcely heard his wails. His fists thumping the floor could not grab my attention. He was an echo, the faintest sound of life where soon there was to be none.

I sat on the sofa, doing nothing in particular. Staring out the window in the same fashion as Grace when she thought that everything was hopeless. I couldn't eat, could barely form words. Everything around me looked like a morgue-in-waiting. How could I articulate that? How could I explain to Grace that no one would survive?

She stomped around the apartment, blaming my mood on the beer. 'Drinking again.' I didn't argue, and let her think it. *Hate me instead of despairing. It's kinder. I can take it. A hundred and ninety-five other people hate me, what's one more?* It didn't matter. They were all dead, anyway. Grace could hate me, too. She was going to leave me. I could feel it. She would survive on Mars and live happily there, among those people, blind to their evil. But I would die inside. Where she would blossom, I would wither.

Ethan went to bed without too much trouble. His tantrums had worn him out. I watched him sleep, heard his little snores, saw his tiny twitches as he dreamed. He deserved more, so much more. More than the Raft, more than Mars. More than the contrived existence the Centre would offer. I wrapped my arms around him. He stirred and gave a little sob as he awoke from his nightmare.

'Go back to sleep, son,' I said. 'Your nightmare can't be that bad.'

The real world is worse. Much worse.

Grace didn't react when I tried showing her some affection. I needed to feel her warmth, her love. There would be something reassuring in that, I was sure. The world couldn't be that bad, the situation not so dire, if I could feel her comforting embrace. She was pretending to doze on the sofa, but I knew she was awake as there was a frostiness to her fictitious sleep. The cold shoulder I was snuggled against reciprocated nothing.

'I'm sorry, Grace,' I whispered. 'I've been trying so hard. Everything I do is for you and Ethan.'

By the time we went to bed, Grace's anger had turned to pity. She sat next to me on the bed, her kind nature wanting to release me of the burden she knew nothing about. She began massaging my shoulders. Her bony hands did nothing to relieve the knots. If she released one, another came to light.

'I'm just trying to protect you,' I said as she jabbed her thumb into my shoulder blade.

She stopped prodding me, and I turned to face her. My face was hot, but I shuddered, a cold chill inching over me, like the smog. It was the dead, pulling me towards them.

'Protect me from what? We have everything we ever wanted. Almost everything.' Her eyes darted out the window to the top of that spiky fence.

'I don't want that, Grace.'

'Why not?'

'I've met them. I've worked with them. There's an evil beyond that fence that I can't describe. I've seen it.'

I shouldn't have said that. It was our only option now, *their* only option. I should have rejoiced with her and helped her get used to the idea. But I despised them. I was stuck with them, trapped, captive, while everyone else would die. To be a prisoner or to perish. Those were my options now.

'That evil wants to give our son a scholarship to the best school in the world.'

I shook my head. 'It's just not us.'

'Maybe it's just not *you*.' She got up from the bed and went to brush her teeth.

My desire to tell her everything had sunk with the solarplanes. What would be the point now? It was a useless truth. I might as well kill my inner voice and succumb to her desires. The shallow, malicious ways of the Centre were to become us. I should have been kinder to Grace. She had no idea what fate awaited the rest of the Raft. And if she did, she'd feel so grateful that Ethan had a chance to survive. But my son, my golden-haired little boy, was to grow up Centre-reared. His boyish innocence would be replaced with entitlement, his kindness thwarted by evil. They'd ruin him, and Grace. My little family would be duped into becoming just like them. Shorter versions of the same wickedness. My perfect family was to be transformed into Centre.

I slept heavily, from sheer exhaustion or just succumbing to failure. Maybe I'd wake up and this would all have been a nightmare.

* * *

Archie and Amalyn weren't at work the next day. I didn't blame them. The injectable was done, and we had smuggled out enough research and plans to be able to start again, to build a new lab. Only now that wasn't possible. It had all been a waste of time. Our optimism turned to ruin.

I hoped they'd thought to phone Isaac, to warn him that the food wasn't coming, that we weren't coming. We had to find a way to get him the plans for the machinery, the recipes and research. They could survive without us, perhaps, but I would never see my brother again. He was so excited, so hopeful. It would crush him.

The strip billboards on my way to work glared with good news:

Mars ready to welcome its first guests! Progress is Paramount! Knotweed all gone, the Raft is 100% safe. Everyone is safe now! Marta currency boosts Raft economy by nearly 200%. With sterility comes liberty! Street safety 5/5.

It didn't matter what panic we spread now. The Centre would all be leaving. They were to start flying off to Mars that very day. That told me one thing: the Raft had only days left. They would come for Ethan soon.

Normality was my disguise and coping strategy. If my world looked normal and I acted normal, surely everything was normal. As I arrived at the lab and alighted the Autocar, the smell of salt hit me and the smog was worse, as if we were now closer to the edge.

This can't be happening.

I walked straight to my office and shut the door. I didn't say hello to anyone. Marcus's greeting of 'How's your tomorrow?' went unanswered.

You don't have a tomorrow.

I sat and wallowed. I pulled at my hair and bit my nails. Then my phone pinged with a message from Grace: 'Don't come home tonight. I need some space. Maybe some time apart will realign your priorities. Love you.'

The last two words felt more automatic than heartfelt.

I needed to tell her. I had to decode the Prime Minister's message for her and tell her everything. If we were going to live with the Centre on Mars, she should do so without any naivety. She had requested a night alone and I would grant her that – no point aggravating her more – but I would tell her the next day. I'd tell her everything as I'd planned. She should go to Mars with open eyes. She hated me enough already. The truth couldn't hurt us anymore.

I stood up and peeked through the blinds. The staff were all working hard, just a regular day at work. If they'd noticed Archie and Amalyn's absence, they didn't say. They all wore soft faces of obliviousness. Their expressions serene, placid, unruffled in their ignorance.

How could they not feel it? How did they not know? Tunnel vision – that's what every human is cursed with. Blink-ered from the truth, maybe? Constrained by hope? Some unrestrained belief in the government? Denial? Whatever. Humankind simply doesn't want to look around and see the glaring reality or hear the screams. We paid no attention when our roots rotted away, when the foundations cracked. Didn't notice when our heads were filled with hate and lies. We ab-sorbed what we were told with the efficiency and intelligence of a sponge.

Dirt connected us, but poison broke us apart.

I knew then as much as I had ever known, and too much knowledge is no good. When you have no power or control to change things, what's the point in knowing?

For the second time in living memory, the ground beneath us was failing. Or rather, *we* were failing *it.* Generations of disregard and inclement care had washed our land away decades earlier. We'd dug and mined every last piece of the land beneath the sea, then blown up what little was left to extract gases and ore. Plastering over the problem, shoving it under tarmac and high-rises and development. We'd ignored the land before, and this time we'd buried it out of sight.

We never learnt our lesson. Those in power left it too late. Like us, Archie, Amalyn and me. We'd left it too late.

I sat at my desk without turning my computer on. I had no paperwork in front of me, and Grace and Ethan's photo was the only personal item I allowed on my desk. Their smiling faces reminded me of why I did this, of what the point was.

I was squashed, weighed down with the affliction of knowl-edge. An over-awareness of incarceration and mortality. What would Maisie say? 'Don't let the buggers get you down,' most likely. But down is how I felt, and I was sinking lower and lower. Hunched and slow. Suffocating before the sea washed over me. Every time I tried to help my family, to move forward, I was jerked back. 'An invisible hand for good,' was how the Centre had described Greg. What nonsense. An invisible boot, worn by him and the rest of the Centre Elite, was kicking us back into this hole. This cage. Hitting us, hurting us, the boot stamping on us like we were the vermin they believed us to be. Enslaved to this life to do their bidding. Being born in the Perimeter was to be born bruised. However hard we tried, they kicked us back harder.

There is a place for you in this world of accelerated progression.
The Prime Minister's words turned in my head all morning.

I still had options. My little family, we could go, but Archie? Amalyn and her family? I'd be leaving them to die. My mind was more turbulent than the sea. I shook the thought from my head. How could I leave them, but also, how could I not? My wife, my son – how could I doom them to a fate they could avoid?

Grace would be happy, I was sure, to live the lifestyle possible within that fence. She didn't know the ugly truth of it. I groaned, sluggish from despair, forehead resting on my desk. I didn't even have the energy to shout when Marcus knocked at my door.

'Yes?' I whispered. I sounded more feeble than he usually did.

'Am I disturbing you, Professor?'

'No.' For once, I meant it. Alone, I was spiralling.

Marcus looked particularly tired. His lab coat needed a wash, and he had a few days of stubble on his face.

His voice quavered, like he was expecting me to bite his head off. 'The press releases are all done, the papers submitted to journals. We have no new product testing currently. The factory is taken care of. Professor, we don't have any work to do. I've cleaned everything, and the new stock still hasn't arrived. We are awaiting your instruction.'

I rubbed my eyes, but the world was still there. The lab without a million jobs to do was reality. It was like we were shutting up shop.

No point developing anything new now.

'Do you have any family, Marcus?' All these years working with him, and I didn't know. I'd never bothered to ask.

He jerked his head back, flummoxed at the question. 'Oh ... erm, a cousin. We're not close. An aunt.'

'No special someone?' I paused and saw his cheeks blush. 'You do.' *Mabel. I knew it!*

'Well, I guess so.'

I smiled. I think that was the first time I'd ever smiled at Marcus. He shouldn't be wasting his last days in the lab. None of them should.

'Tell everyone they can go home. You included. Take the rest of the day off. I'll message when the stock arrives and you can come in then, or until I've got us another assignment. For now, go spend time with your families.'

His eyes widened with surprise. 'Professor, it's only ten a.m. And it's Monday. If Greg finds out—'

'Tell him it was my idea.' I waved Marcus away. 'I'll email you to confirm, so you have proof for Greg. Go on, get out and enjoy some free time.'

Go be with your families while you can.

I considered telling them the truth then, starting the panic that was bound to come later. Worrying about their job security seemed so trivial. But I still had Grace and Ethan to save. Mars wasn't saving them, not really, but they'd be alive at least.

Uncertain, the staff took nearly an hour to leave. I was not known for being a generous boss, so they probably thought I was having a breakdown. After a final array of compliments from 2-10, 4-09 and 8-08 (you are truly kind, Professor, don't you look lovely, Professor), I was alone.

I shut down each computer, one by one, the space quieting a little more each time. The hum reducing, the muted silence intoxicating. Peace. Blissful peace.

My footsteps echoed around the deserted lab as I walked around, turning off timers, alarms and e-notifications. The shelves were still mostly empty from the break-in, but that didn't matter now. It was all sparkling clean and sterile. Just how I always liked it.

I made sure all bottles had lids on tightly and the gas was off. No point in causing more drama when the lab fell into the sea. It wasn't that far from the coast, close and getting closer. It wouldn't be long.

I'd email Grace, I decided, and tell her everything by email. Archie, too. Tell him to say goodbye to Isaac for me. I'd tell Grace to get to the Centre, tell her I'd meet her there and hope she'd leave without me. Hope they'd take her. I'd explain that I couldn't go to Mars, couldn't live among the Centre, but she should live, her and Ethan. They deserved to live the life she wanted. *My boy.*

I would stay in my lab, my sanctuary, where I had achieved so much. Where we'd ended the famines and fed a nation. Where we'd cured vitamin deficiencies. I'd helped some people. I'd been useful, for a short time at least. Perhaps that's how I would be remembered. So that's where I would stay, until the end.

Grace could access my emails. All the research was there. No one would starve without me. The captain would go down with her ship.

I sat at the product-testing station, where some samples remained. With a fresh cup of MimikTea, I ate some synth roast potatoes (one of our best sellers), allowing every bite to linger on my tongue. I ate some synth carrot chunks, bright orange and sweet. Then I finished the last of the IcyCrema, a new green-fruits flavour. Archie's latest favourite.

Archie.

I remembered the times I had spent with Archie, in his

office and mine, drinking tea, moaning, gossiping, laughing, whingeing. The times we'd all been in the bar, drinking, scowling, dancing, giggling. Archie playing with Ethan as he built the IC. I remembered until ... voices. I heard voices.

'What the hell is going on?'

'Someone's wallowing.'

'Where are all the staff?'

'Sav? Sav!'

What the ...?

'We don't turn up for work for one morning, and this is what the place turns into?' Amalyn's voice pierced my mind fog.

I must have dozed off. Was I dreaming?

'Wakey wakey, Prof.' Archie shook me. 'We've got a plan.'

24

Chapter twenty-three

I hated Noffee, but Archie insisted.

'MimikTea's not strong enough,' he said as he handed me the cup of tepid sludge. It was either a strong Noffee or an adrenaline shot from the medical kit, he said. I couldn't work out if he was joking, so I swallowed the bitter stuff with a frown, and Archie nodded and smiled. Whether it was the bitterness or the caffeine, I wasn't sure, but it did the trick and a few minutes later I was alert enough to form sentences and generally moan, although my self-pity was not appreciated, it seemed.

'Quit your whingeing and give us a minute to explain,' said Amalyn as she started looking through cupboards. 'I need some food first. We had nothing at our place.' She found some VitaSmoothie in the staffroom and I drank some of that too while she continued to search for more.

'What the hell?' she called out. 'This is meant to be a food lab and there's no food. As in nothing, not a single bite.'

'Try the freezer,' Archie shouted from his office. 'There should be some IcyCrema in there. My favourite one.'

'Nope, nothing.'

'Huh?' Archie came out of his office looking perplexed.

Amalyn made her way to the tasting station. 'Not even any samples. Bet Marcus cleaned us out.'

I quickly changed the subject. 'Are you going to tell me why you interrupted my perfectly enjoyable wallowing?'

They came over to me with joyous smiles, laughing at me and my dismay. Archie looked less cheery when he started turning his computers back on, all the while sucking his teeth and muttering, 'No one turns my computers off but me.'

I scowled. 'Diva.'

'Anyway,' Amalyn said, her face glowing. 'Guess who just called? On the satellite phone. I didn't even realise it was ringing for ages, it's so tinny. But it was ringing and guess who was there? No, don't, you'll never guess. But go on, try!' She clasped her hands in front of her with a wide grin. I couldn't tell if she was actually happy or she'd gone insane.

I rubbed my forehead, not in the mood for games. 'Isaac?'

'No. Okay, you can have three guesses.'

I huffed. This was not how I wanted to spend my final days. 'Or you can just tell me. There's a good chance we'll sink before I guess.'

She didn't have the demeanour of someone about to die. Maybe it was good news.

'Just two more guesses. Go on.'

'Father Christmas, or Greg.'

'Ha! Wrong and wrong. It was Jerome.'

I shrugged. 'Who's Jerome?'

'You know!'

Her chirpy voice was really starting to grate on me. I shook my head.

'You do. Think! Charming, handsome, well-fitted shirt, very informative.'

'Ams, I'm shattered, depressed, I have too much on my mind and those clues are rubbish.'

'The nice man from the solarplane.'

I looked at her, then Archie, and back to Amalyn again. 'You guys want a threesome or something?'

Archie chuckled. 'I told you, Sav, you're not her type, and that would be too weird for me.'

'I mean with Jerome.'

'What?' Amalyn's eyes lit up. 'No. Well, if Archie is up for it …' Archie gave her a little shove and she laughed. 'No, anyway, that's not why he called.'

'Are you sure?' Archie asked, raising one eyebrow. 'You've got me wondering now.'

'Oh, for Raft's sake. Sav, just listen. Jerome is Golden Fifty.'

I snorted out the last of my horrible Noffee. 'Don't be daft, Ams, he's Centre.'

'There are loads of Centre in the Fifty. Not every Centre is an arse.'

'Yeah, right.'

'It's true,' Archie said. 'A lot of Centre are sympathetic to the Perimeter. They're caged in just as much as we're kept out. They long for travel and like to reminisce too. It's only the Blue Libs and the Elite who are the pricks. They're the only ones we ever see out here, the only ones who get to visit the Mainland. But they haven't got everyone's support. Plenty of Centre never wanted the anchors destroyed. They had family over the bridges too.'

I grabbed his forearm with the tattoo. 'So because you wear the scabs of this shitshow, you know so much now?'

Amalyn gasped. 'Harsh, Sav. Just listen.'

I tutted and released Archie's arm.

'Listen, we have a way off the Raft. A load of planes transited to some makeshift airport yesterday, before the land was lost. Seems like they knew what was happening.'

'Seriously?'

Archie nodded, 'Yup. I went over last night's satellite images and over half the fleet was transferred. They knew. Which is weird, because I looked and looked, and there was no clue that that bit of the Raft was going to go. It was ridiculously sudden. So either they've got some kit at the edges, monitors or something, that feed them information that isn't uploaded to their main computers, or ...'

'Or they blew it up themselves,' I said. I froze, realisation washing over me. 'Is that even possible? Why would they destroy their own planes?'

'It's not like they're going to need them on Mars. They've lost nothing.'

'But why?' I knew why, it was obvious, but saying it out loud felt like a commitment. After a moment of silence, I dared to whisper, 'They know we're monitoring them. They're trying to stop us from leaving. They're going to take Ethan to make me go to Mars.'

Amalyn held her hands up. 'That is worst-case scenario. Maybe they had other reasons.'

'Since when did you give the Centre the benefit of the doubt?'

'Since we have no choice.' She sighed. 'Anyway, that's not important. What *is* important is that there are scheduled flights every day, mostly taking stock orders over to the Mainland. I know most of their orders aren't going to be met, but a few are, enough to keep them quiet until Greg and his chums are on Mars. And there's room for people, too, especially BioLabs people. It'll be easy to blag. Archie can make permits. Jerome reckons that, over the next week, we can get over a hundred people off the Raft.'

My jaw dropped. 'You're kidding. Are you sure we can trust this guy? How did he even get the number for that phone?'

'Isaac said he had friends in the solarplanes company, didn't he? And Harold knew about the Mainland. The Golden Fifty reaches further than we knew.'

I groaned and rested my forehead on the table. 'So now all our hopes are pinned on the Golden Fifty.' *The sodding Fifty!* A group of Alternates and weirdos. Bloody thespians and artist wannabes were meant to save everyone.

'If it doesn't work out, we'll just be in the sea sooner. We literally have nothing to lose,' said Amalyn.

Not true. I had my family's ticket to Mars to lose.

'Look,' she continued, 'we'll do exactly as we planned. Get our families on the flight tonight, and then we'll follow with as many others as we can over the following days. A week, max, and we'll be off this shithole.'

I shook my head. I couldn't risk this being a bust, not when I had an alternative. An alternative I couldn't bear thinking about, but which was mildly better than death, for Grace and Ethan anyway.

'I'm not sending Grace and Ethan first. I can't risk it. Sorry, but they have another option. A shitty one, but I don't want them to get busted. The PM will still be worried about his illness, I think. Another day should be okay. Send someone else first. I'll put Grace and Ethan on a flight tomorrow.'

Archie walked over and put his hand on my shoulder. 'It'll be fine, Sav, seriously. I trust this guy, even if he does want a threesome.' He gave me a playful shove. 'Also, get this. Jerome says the main Centre population don't know the Raft is breaking up. Why would they? Jerome knows because he sees it and he's Golden Fifty, but the rest, well, they think they're going to Mars to be cleaner and have more space. To get away from the climate going crazy. They don't know that the whole Perimeter population is screwed. They don't even know that there's much of a Perimeter population. They think there's only a few million.'

I breathed in, not revealing that much was true.

'They also don't know that they're basically stealing food from the Mainland, and all the machinery from us. My guess is the Select also don't know. Despite what we think of them, the majority of the wealthy aren't anything like as evil as Greg and the Blue Liberation.'

I took a moment to ponder that. The only people from the Centre I had ever met were Blue Liberation and their supporters. Could it really be that the Centre were not all evil? I had never considered that their access to information was as filtered as ours.

'Sounds possible,' I said eventually. 'About the Mainland, at least.'

'So I'll put all the evidence onto a USB and make us a copy each, just in case. If all this turns out to be dodgy, then we have it as blackmail. We'll tell them we'll spill their dirty secrets. Mars has contact with the Raft – I've seen it on their systems. I could hack in and transmit all the evidence, reveal them for the pricks they are. We'll let all the Centre know, the good and bad, how evil the Blue Libs are. If they want us to keep quiet, they have to let us get people off the Raft. I'll set it up so everyone will find out if anything happens to us.'

I nodded. 'Okay, that could actually work. The Centre Elite would hate to lose face. If there really are non-pricks in the Centre, that truth could cause a lot of problems.'

'I'll send my family first,' Amalyn said. 'I'll tell them everything. They could be ready in an hour, I reckon. I'll call them now.'

'You sure, Ams?' Archie asked. 'We could send anyone else first.'

'No. I trust Jerome. Let me prove it. It should be my family first. I don't want to leave it too late again, and then everyone else will trust me, since I'm willing to send them first.'

'Okay,' Archie said. 'I think we have ourselves a plan.'

Archie forged BioLabs solarplane passes within half an hour, and then we were on our way to collect Amalyn's family. They lived further out to the edge, so no wonder she wanted to get them off first. Archie stayed behind to get working on other forgeries, badges and permits, anything we might need over the next few days.

'Watch the ground, watch the satellites,' Amalyn said to him as we left. Archie didn't need reminding.

Our Autocar followed Amalyn's family, staying a little way behind theirs. I still had a niggling feeling that we were being followed. There was no way the Prime Minister would let us roam freely after knowing I'd hacked her office. I kept watching all around, but no car followed.

Amalyn told her family the truth and, through tears and hugs, they agreed to go. Her family surprised me. They looked so normal, nothing like the reckless risk-taker Amalyn was at all. Her mother had her hair tightly pinned back, making her forehead look higher than it was. Her dad wore a shirt buttoned all the way up and tucked in. He looked stern, but he had spent a lifetime dealing with Amalyn, so that seemed about right.

I didn't get out of the Autocar to greet them; it was their time together. Amalyn didn't need to beg. They were ready in minutes. I remembered what Amalyn had said about them not wanting the anchors to be destroyed. I wondered if they were relieved to get off the Raft, to have a chance at finding the rest of their family. Their faces looked expressionless as they walked to the Autocar. When it drove off, they looked back at their apartment block, watching until the car turned a corner.

The solarplane airport was close to the Centre, hugging the fence, but the opposite side to the one we had used. It was smaller, with about thirty planes lined up ready to fly, each vast wingspan in the shadow of another. Another ten or so more were rammed in next to each other, a tangle that would take hours to free up. Amalyn's family had their BioLabs permits ready and like the previous airport, there was no security. No one from the Perimeter even knew the airport existed, let alone had any desire to leave the Raft. As far as everyone knew, leaving the Raft meant flying into a fire.

I watched as Amalyn's family and their meagre luggage were bundled onto one plane, where Jerome was loading boxes and boxes of BioLabs produce. Their hugs lingered and Amalyn had to peel their arms away. She walked backwards, likely savouring the sight of them for as long as possible. Even from my Autocar I could see their wet eyes glisten in the moonlight.

One small bag each. I wondered what was in there. Clothes were a waste of bag space. Just a few photographs, most likely.

Amalyn waved as the solarplane started to move across the tarmac.

'I'll be there in a few days!' she promised, shouting over the engine noise. 'Archie too. We'll be together then!'

Jerome waved and shut the plane doors.

'See you soon!' she shouted as she got in the Autocar, and kept waving as the solarplane moved away.

We kept watching until the plane became a dot and then disappeared. Amalyn wiped her eyes.

'You saved them,' I said. 'Well done, Ams. You'll see them soon.'

'I'm just a bit emotional at the moment.' She found a tissue and blew her nose.

'That's not really surprising. It's been a tough couple of weeks.'

'Yeah. Glad they believed me. You said anything to Grace yet?'

I held my head in my hands and groaned. 'No. I can't even imagine telling her. She's mad at me because I said the school offer is a sham, and now I have to explain all this to an angry Grace.' I groaned again. 'It's going to be tricky.'

'I reckon when she hears you have a brother, she'll be up for it. She'll understand then. I mean, family's family, right?'

'Maybe,' I said, uncertainty making my voice quieter. 'I don't even know if she trusts me anymore. I used to be able to look at her and know exactly what she was thinking. Now she's so mad at me, she seems distant.'

'She's felt the dirtquakes, right? I know they're not the Raft breaking up, but we could imply they are. We don't know for sure either way, and it might help persuade her. How about Archie and I come with you, with all the evidence we've got? We can be your backup.'

'That could help, thanks.'

She started crying again, wiping her face with sodden tissues. 'I'm sorry, I'm just so emotional about everything. I'm sure Grace will be happy and everything is going to work out.'

I squirmed in my seat. Was this to be some kind of heart to heart?

She blew her nose again. 'Sav, I'm pregnant.'

My breath caught in my throat. I coughed it free. 'Really? Oh, wow. I had no idea you guys were having fertility treatment.'

'We weren't. We're not.'

My eyes bulged, and my jaw hung open. 'You mean you got pregnant the *old-fashioned* way?' I couldn't hide my grimace.

She laughed. 'Yeah, what are the chances? No one gets pregnant that way anymore. Well, almost no one. I never even considered it, really.' She looked down at her belly, eyes glowing through her tears. 'I haven't told Archie. I'm not sure how to. It's not like we've even talked about having kids.'

'Oh, Ams.' I grabbed her hands. 'Seriously, he'll be delighted.'

She smiled. 'I think he will too.'

I let go of her, realisation hitting me like a brick. 'But this changes everything. Ams, you can't hang around here. You should have been on that flight! You're not just risking your life, you're risking your baby's too.'

'I know, but we have to let other people know.'

'Then we do it by email. Ams, seriously, you need to get off the Raft.'

'Microbes, you're right. I know you're right. But there are so many people …'

'The most important thing is saving your child, trust me. You need to get off the Raft straight away. Tomorrow. You can get on Grace's flight.'

'I know. I know it's not just about me. I'd just feel so awful leaving everyone.'

'We'll let them know, I promise. We'll spread the word.'

She pondered for a moment, the focus of her gaze alternating between outside and her belly. 'Okay, let's do it. I'll go to the bar tonight, speak to as many Golden Fifties as I can, give them the airport address, and then I can leave tomorrow. With Archie – I really can't leave without him. And you too. Our families need us.'

'Reckon all six of us can get on a flight?'

'Let's ask Jerome, but I think so. But there's only five of us. Who's the sixth?'

I pointed at her stomach.

'Oh.' She laughed. 'I think six should be fine.'

The Autocar trundled along, the smooth roads kicking up gravel as we approached Amalyn and Archie's apartment. She looked radiant, a half-smile piercing her despair. She didn't say anything else about her pregnancy. She didn't have to. I could see it in her glowing cheeks, the same as when Grace got the news. Visions of the future, of the joy to come, were playing over and over in her mind.

'You know, when we get to the Tunnels, I think I'm going to go full-on Alternate.'

I laughed. 'Really? I still need scientist Amalyn, you know.'

'Yeah, yeah, I'll still be in the lab, but otherwise I'm going to get creative. I'll be bald anyway, might as well try out some new hobbies. I'm going to check out that painting room and do paintings myself. What sort of things are paintings, anyway?'

'They're just pictures.'

'Like photographs?'

'No. Well, sometimes. They don't always look like what

they're capturing.'

'I don't get it. What do they look like, then?'

'I guess whatever you think looks nice. Abstract. Like your tattoo.'

'Oh, I get it. Symbols. I'm looking forward to it. Maybe I'll even read untrue books about fake people. What do you call that again?'

'Fiction.'

'Yeah, fiction. I mean, the world is full of lies anyway. Might as well jazz it up a bit.'

I smiled. 'That's one way of looking at it.'

Archie wasn't back from the lab yet but was on his way, so we went up to their apartment to wait for him.

'Sav, I have to show you something. Don't laugh!' Amalyn ran to her bedroom and came out with one of Archie's vintage T-shirts, cut up and re-stitched on either side. 'I made a baby T-shirt out of one of Archie's crappy retro T-shirts. You think he'll like it?'

I held the tiny little outfit and remembered Ethan. Had he ever been that small? 'It's the most beautiful thing,' I said as I swallowed back my emotions.

'I'll show him tonight, when I tell him.' She took it off me, held it up. 'Are babies really this tiny?'

'Yeah. For about a month, anyway.'

Archie's footsteps were approaching the front door and Ams quickly stashed it in her pocket.

'So, you fickle women have changed your mind and we're leaving tomorrow?' he said as he came in, a big grin across his face. 'If we are, that's great. I don't want to leave it too late again.'

'Yep,' I said. 'We'll tell whoever we can, leave emails and

post articles everywhere just before we get on the flight. Ams's family left, all very easy. Let's get off this concrete shithole.'

Archie beamed from ear to ear. 'Any more of that beer left? I feel like celebrating.'

25

Chapter twenty-four

After we'd had a look through the satellite photographs to make sure it was safe, Amalyn took an Autocar to meet some Golden Fifties while Archie and I stayed at their apartment.

'Be careful!' I shouted as she exited the front door.

'No point telling her,' Archie said. 'She never takes advice.' He had checked the satellite images. They showed a weather front coming in and the smog was pretty bad, but nothing too dramatic.

I should have gone home to Grace. I needed to tell her that night, but I still couldn't imagine doing it. She'd asked me for space and instead I was going to shatter her world, reveal my deceptions, tell her she was not safe, that Ethan was not safe. In the end, I decided to wait until Amalyn was back. Her and Archie joining me seemed like the most sensible idea. Archie would have his e-pad with the images in case she didn't believe me. Moral support, really. And she wouldn't go too ballistic at me with them there. Archie could keep Ethan entertained while Grace cried. We had it all planned.

Archie was putting together the USBs of the big reveal. All

the truths we had discovered, all the evidence, ready to upload to the Perimeter and especially the factory staff to convince them to join us. It would also serve as blackmail.

'I still find it hard to believe anyone from the Centre would give a toss about us.'

'Being born on one side of the fence doesn't make you a prick,' Archie said. 'Being a prick makes you a prick.'

'Well, it's worth a shot, anyway. Did you know that the Prime Minister has Perimeter blood?'

He looked shocked. 'You're kidding!'

'It's true. She told me. I think it's one of her grandparents. Some scandalous affair from before they put the fence up. That's why she's not as tall as the rest.'

'Wow. That's crazy. And she's the top boss. Why'd they put a hybrid in the top spot, I wonder?'

'It probably makes her easier to manipulate, that's my best guess. Do as you're told or big money tells everyone you're part Perimeter.'

'Sounds about right. The most powerful aren't the puppets, it's those who pull the strings.'

On other memory sticks were the machinery plans, my research and recipes. A copy each. Plus all the hard copies, which I'd condensed into one rucksack. Just the highlights and most complicated stuff I wouldn't remember. We had everything we needed to start the lab from scratch, except the staff.

'You going to eat the filth food?' I asked.

'Nah. From what Harold said, it's dying out, anyway. I'll leave it for the natives.'

I gasped. 'We never called Isaac to tell him what Harold said! About their food being contaminated.'

'Me and Ams meant to last night, but we heard from Jerome and then got too excited and forgot.'

'Not much point now, I guess,' I smiled. 'We'll see him tomorrow. I wish we'd thought to give a USB to Ams's family, though, just in case.'

'Hey! None of this "just in case" attitude. We're all going to the Mainland. Tomorrow.'

The lack of beer meant we were drinking whatever dregs we could find in the apartment. Archie poured us some glasses of something that was once wine from Amalyn's dad's archaic booze collection. It was worse than the beer, syrupy and a mottled red with darker streaks rather than a pleasing ruby colour.

'Thanks, I think,' I said, as I took the glass and winced through my first sip.

'I've just realised we'll never see Greg again!'

I laughed so hard at that, some drink came out my nose. 'I would have shaved my head years ago if I'd known that would be the outcome.'

'Me too,' Archie said, rubbing his almost bald scalp.

'No fish on the Mainland.' We clinked glasses to that.

'No street sprayers.'

I hiccupped. 'I actually like the street sprayers.'

'No way!'

'I do. They smell clean.'

'What does it smell like in the Tunnels?'

'Damp, musty, like dirt.'

'Gross.'

'Yep.' I poured myself a drink of something brown and sour, as the wine was too unpalatable to finish. 'I guess we'll get used to it. No weird narcotic cocktails, either.'

'Oh, thank god! I can't handle those anymore, Sav, seriously. Ams loves them, but I need my sleep.'

'Well, she probably won't be wanting them anymore,' I said without thinking, and immediately put my hand over my mouth.

Archie didn't notice my slip-up. The news was going to be such a surprise to him, and I realised it wasn't on his radar at all. He'd be made up, though, I was sure of that. He was such a big kid himself and loved spending time with Ethan.

'It's the only time the age gap is noticeable, I swear,' he said.

I laughed. 'What about when you look in the mirror?'

Archie didn't notice my joke as he was engrossed in his computer screen. Some instinct told him to look, to pay attention to the image rather than our chat. A moment later, he stood up, his eyes still on the screen. Then his arms went limp and his glass smashed on the floor.

'No!'

'What, Archie? What is it?' The room swam a bit as I turned to see what was on the screen.

'Look!'

The satellite image showed the edge of the Raft as usual, the weather-beaten coastline bobbing around in the putrid sea. He leant over his desk and zoomed in closer to the edge. Live images showed a fine line, that was all. The smallest of imperfections. He zoomed in more, and then it was obvious. There was a great crack creeping over, encroaching across the edge. Just like we had seen before. The crevice invading the concrete, a deadly shadow against the grey.

'Microbes! *Another* chunk breaking off! Please, not the airport again, please no!'

Archie zoomed in and out, rotating the image one way then

back again. It all looked too symmetrical either way round to me, but he knew what he was looking at.

'It's not the airport. The bar Amalyn has gone to – it's right there!'

I looked at him. We paused for a second in shock, but even a second was too long. We ran out of the apartment, down the stairs, hailed a Speedy Autocar. It clipped Archie's leg as it pulled up but he didn't even notice.

'Bar Fifty-five, Perimeter. Hurry!' he screamed at the thing. He got his phone out and called. It rang and rang. 'Come on, come on!' He said, biting his nails. 'Answer, Ams, come on!'

'Hi, hon. What's up?' Amalyn's voice sounded cheerful, happy.

'Babe, the Raft is breaking up right by you. Get out, get inland now. Now!'

'Really? You sure?' Her voice was as chirpy as ever, so oblivious to the danger. 'I've barely felt a rumble this evening.'

'I've seen the satellite images. Get out. Run, now!'

'Oh shit! Okay, I'll let everyone know.'

'Just run, Amalyn, fucking *run! Now!*' he screamed, a vein pulsing in his temple. Then: 'Amalyn? Amalyn? Ams?' He looked at his phone. 'Amalyn?' His face was rigid. 'The line went dead.'

It was a windy, dry evening. The storm hadn't arrived yet. The Autocar was going at full speed, throwing us from one ditch to the next, but it was still too slow. No one took Speedy Autocars this close to the edge. The bruises weren't worth it. Except for this journey.

The smog was closing in. The wind howled. Archie tapped his feet on the Autocar floor constantly. 'Come on, hurry up!'

'I'm sure she's fine. Battery just died. She's sensible, Archie.

She'll be fine. Storms cause problems with phones, and the signal is always dodgy at the edge. She'll be fine, I'm sure,' I rambled, filling the silence. Trying to convince myself as much as Archie.

'I know Amalyn too well. She wouldn't just run, would she? No way would she just leave everyone. She'd risk her life to save them all. She's too good like that.'

I didn't say why, but I knew that she'd run. She had precious cargo. A mother's instinct would make her run.

She'd run. She'd save her baby.

She had to.

We followed the route on Archie's phone, watching the little icon that was the Autocar get closer and closer, counting down every metre, willing it to go faster. The asphalt got worse, our collisions with the insides of the Autocar more painful. My shoulder smacked against the door and my neck ceased from being flung back and forth. Archie rubbed his head as a bump threw him against the roof of the Autocar.

'Come on!' Archie screamed at the vehicle. 'Fucking hurry up!'

He tried calling Amalyn again, but there was no ringtone.

'She's running, Archie. She's not going to pause to check her phone. Her battery probably died.' There were so many reasons why she wouldn't pick up. So many good, normal reasons.

That must be it. She wasn't in trouble, she was running. I was sure. I held onto the door handle, squeezing it tightly, eyes closed, willing her to run, to be okay.

Run, Ams. Run!

My heart was pounding so hard I could feel it in my stomach. We got closer, three streets away, two, so close, then *screech.*

The Autocar came to a sudden stop, jolting us forwards, before politely saying. 'Unable to make destination due to obstruction.'

Microbes!

We leapt out, but there was no obstruction. There was the total opposite of an obstruction. There was nothing. Blackness. Smog. The stench of salt. Just a cliff where land used to be.

'No, no, no,' I whimpered.

There was perhaps ten metres of land, then nothing but sea. The slurry of waves beating against the precipice was all around us. I could smell the rot.

'Amalyn!' Archie called, running straight to the edge, just inches away. 'Amalyn!'

'Archie, be careful!'

It was a stupid thing to say. He ignored me and carried on, running up and down the cliff where the road should be, where the bar should be. Where Amalyn *must* be.

Half-buildings clung to the edge, exposed brickwork ripped in half. Chunks of split render scattered across the ground, sharp edges making trip hazards, my mind's eye making every one of them deadly.

Archie was close to the edge, ignoring the uneven floor. He peered over at the remnants of buildings below. 'Amalyn!'

An assault course of plumbing and cables was sticking out of the tarmac. I edged away from the Autocar as far as I dared, the ground wobbling with every step. The tarmac felt soft underfoot, spongy, forgiving.

My heart was racing as fast as my body was shaking. I searched the land, what was left of it, for any traces, peering into the blackness while watching out for Archie. I got my phone out and called her. We'd probably just missed her. She'd already run further inland, and she was waiting for us a few streets away.

Her phone went straight to voicemail. I sent a text and an email: 'Ams, where are you? Call me back.'

The rain started, just a drizzle at first. I heard the life of the Raft ticking away once again.

Drip. Drip. Drip.

'Amalyn!'

Drip. Drip. Drip.

'Amalyn!'

I called again and again, and there was no answer.

This can't be happening. She must be here somewhere.

My knees gave way, and I sat on the tarmac, paralysed with fear. I was propped up against the Autocar, its engine still humming softly, vibrating against my back, saying that we were too late. We must be too late.

The rain was pelting now, each chilling drop letting me know that this was real.

Archie was still scouring the edge, close, too close to the cliff, screaming her name over and over.

'Amalyn!' he screamed, helplessness breaking his voice.

'Archie!'

He heard it. I heard it. The faintest cry, a whisper being carried by the wind. He snapped his head round to look at me. I hadn't called his name. That hadn't been my voice.

She was there, somewhere.

'Help! Archie!' The cry came again.

I stood, not daring to get any closer, the concrete turning to gravel all around us. The rain was getting heavier still, weighing down the smog and making the ground slippery underfoot.

Archie zeroed in on the cries and dropped to his stomach, lying on the edge, both arms disappearing over the cliff. Angry swells of sea sprayed up all around him.

I held my breath and watched as he shuffled closer to the edge. The whites of his shoes were all I could see against the murky sky. 'I can reach you! Hold on, I can reach you!'

Be careful, Archie! Please!

The ground around was loosening, grumbles giving way to dips and troughs.

I tried to step forwards, but the ground softened beneath me. I backed away, pressed against the Autocar and watched, frozen to the spot, blinking away tears as Archie reached over the edge.

'Archie!' the cry came, louder now.

'Reach!' he screamed. 'I can reach you, just grab my hand!' The pain in his voice, the desperation. 'Fuck's sake, Ams, grab my hand!'

And she did, somehow finding that strength that exists in such rare times. Archie groaned a deep, guttural groan, using every bit of strength he had, until he had lifted her over, heaving her over the edge and dropping her to the ground beside him.

There she was. Cut and dirty, muddied by the sea, but she was there. She was alive. Archie lifted her clear of the edge and held her. Sobbing, on his knees, holding on so tight. There was no one in the world but them.

'Archie!' This time it was me shouting. The wind was howling, its whistle louder than my own voice. 'Archie! Amalyn!'

I stepped a little closer, as close as I could, until the cracks started to deepen. I called again and again. But I wasn't there. I didn't exist to them, so absorbed were they in each other. So in love. Their embrace slackened as Amalyn leant back, pulling from her pocket the too-tiny T-shirt. I saw his face, the moment he realised, happy tears replacing sad, joy replacing fear. All panic, gone. They leant into each other again, holding on so tight.

The wind picked up, and the rain was lashing down. They never heard my screams.

'Archie! Amalyn! Run!'

But they didn't. The instinct of love is stronger than that of survival. Locked in an embrace, they never saw the crack, that deadly vein surrounding them, penning them in, didn't notice the ground slacken and release. They never even looked my way.

With a rumble that was barely audible through the wind and rain, the land around them broke away, floundered, then sank. What was there one moment had disappeared the next. In the blink of an eye, they were gone.

The wind quietened for a moment, and the whole world fell silent. I stepped towards the edge, as close as I dared, trembling uncontrollably.

'Archie! Amalyn!'

My voice sounded pathetic. Under my feet the cracks spread again, getting closer, and I backed away.

There was another gust, carrying that too-tiny T-shirt. It danced in the wind, swirling and spinning, before landing at my feet.

26

Chapter twenty-five

I had no memory of getting in the Autocar and pulling away. I was simply there one minute, and elsewhere the next. As my mind fog eased, I found myself a few minutes from home, my knuckles bleached around the tiny piece of cloth I was holding.

The Autocar stopped at my building, but I couldn't get out. My body wasn't working. A tinnitus screamed through my head, a thundering din echoing like I was in a bubble. Everything was so far away. I was so far away.

I heard a voice, calling my name maybe. The surrounding space looked different, not like the Autocar anymore. I was home. I didn't know how I'd got there, unsure how my legs had carried me. The apartment was so bright it was blinding, yet I wasn't there. My mind wasn't there. I was somewhere else, left behind with the smog. But I could see it. The windows, the floor, the walls, all in soft focus. A deafening quiet with ears clogged with salt. The bellowing sea overriding all else.

I wasn't there. This wasn't happening.

I still held that little piece of material, a scrap really. Crum-pled in my fist, soaked and muddy. Then it wasn't crumpled anymore. It was laid out, faded green with a little logo. Dainty buttons underneath, like the tiny outfits Ethan used to wear when he was a baby.

A baby.

Amalyn. Archie.

Things began to sharpen. I squinted to bring the room into focus. There was that voice again. Less muffled now. Closer, then closer still.

'Sav? Sav? Talk to me!'

Grace.

I stood and looked at her face. Clear now, glaringly clear. Everything was sharp, dazzling. I squinted from the clarity. She stood in front of me, flawless, unblemished perfection shining at me. We couldn't stay.

'Get Ethan. We have to go.'

'What? Sav, talk to me.'

'Now.'

I grabbed her wrist firmly. I shouldn't have been so rough. She snapped it back, eyes wide like she was afraid. *Afraid of me?*

'No. We're not going anywhere until you tell me what's happening.'

'Maisie's.' Not Archie and Amalyn's, not any more. Not Maisie's either. 'Get Ethan. We have to hurry. I'll get the keys.'

I didn't know what convinced her – the trembling flatness of my voice, the terror in my eyes, the general state of me – but she got Ethan out of bed and carried him, grizzling and moaning, out of the apartment block and into an Autocar, the same one I had just been in. The seat was still wet and muddied from before. I could still hear Archie's voice screaming at it to go faster, his foot tapping on the floor.

'Okay, Sav, we're in the Autocar. We're on our way to Archie's. You have to tell me what's going on.'

I couldn't say it. How could I say it out loud? Saying it out loud made it real, and it couldn't be real. I handed her the little T-shirt.

'Baby clothes? Sav, I don't understand. Why have you got baby clothes?'

'It's Amalyn's.'

She gasped and smiled. 'She's expecting? Oh, that's wonderful news.'

Wasn't it? Wasn't it just the most wonderful news?

My ears filled with the roar again, the grumble of the ground, the wind whipping my face, my ears searching through the smog.

Amalyn. Archie.

I cried. Like no one had ever cried before. I took the scrap of material back and cried into it. The baby T-shirt that would never be worn. Made by a mum who would never be a mum. Shown to a dad who would never be a dad. Their joy had lasted only moments. I cried until I couldn't breathe, until I wanted to be sick, until it hit me, it really hit me.

The Autocar arrived at their apartment and we went in. Grace followed me with Ethan.

'Shh, little man,' she whispered. 'It's okay, don't be scared.' Her eyes didn't match what she was saying. They looked abandoned, lost, the colour of the sea. 'Where are they, Sav? Why are we here?'

I took Ethan from her and put him down on the bed. He fell asleep instantly. He was too young to hear what had to be said. Let him keep his innocence for a while longer, at least.

I walked back to the living room, an empty space, a vacuum where they should be. Surrounded by their boxes never to be unpacked. Archie's computer was still on, the satellite image still showing the Raft, only now with a bit more missing. Gone. They were gone.

'They're dead, Grace. They died.' My voice was steady. I had no tears left. I grabbed the glass of sour brown drink from earlier and swallowed what was left of it.

'What?' Grace's voice quivered. 'No! Oh god, Sav. How?'

We sat on the sofa, her one end, me the other. Not in an embrace. Only the truth could bridge the chasm between us. I had Archie's e-pad in my hand, his favourite one. 'Best graphics,' he always said. I loaded up the file with all the evidence. 'Centre pricks' he'd labelled it. His voice was still fresh in my ears. He still sounded alive in my head.

I told Grace everything. I told her about the Poison Maker, my bargain with the Blue Liberation, their blackmail. About what Ethan's school offer was really about. I told her about the Raft breaking up, about Mars. About the Tunnels, my brother, Greg taking their money and spoiling their food. The Golden Fifty, Amalyn's friends, the bar, how they'd died.

She didn't ask questions. She looked at what I showed her on the tablet, the satellite images, the Mars plans, the order sheets. The sales to the Mainland. I showed her the satellite phone. She listened. She listened until her tears flowed freely, until her body shook, until her face had lost all colour.

The years of lies, the years of my deceit, all laid bare in front of her.

I didn't wait for her to respond. I took the USBs and sent all the information to the two hundred factory employees.

'What are you doing?'

'Sending all the information to the BioLabs' factory staff, so they can get to the airport. Hopefully, some will believe us. It's timed. They'll get the email in an hour. We have to go.'

'Go where?'

'To the airport. To the Mainland.'

She didn't move.

'Grace, in an hour this is all going to come out. I have to get you and Ethan on the next flight.'

'To the Mainland? To live underground?'

'Yes.'

She bit her lip and looked at the floor. 'I don't want to live underground.'

'You don't have a choice. If we stay, we'll die. The Raft is crumbling. I'm not lying.' I went to take her hand, but she pulled away.

'I know you're not lying. I believe you. But we have another option.'

She went to the bedroom and got Ethan. He was fast asleep and didn't stir. He was such a big boy, far too heavy to carry these days, especially for Grace. I went to take him from her, but she turned away.

'No,' she whispered.

'Let me take him. He's heavy.'

'No.' She kissed his forehead. 'You're not taking him away from me.'

My impatience was becoming hard to hide. 'I don't want to. I'm just helping you carry him.'

She stared at me, her arms faltering. I reached for him and she conceded, her face falling as I took him.

Ethan in one arm, I used the other to stuff my pockets with USBs and handed Grace my rucksack of hard copies. Just as we were about to leave, a photo of Archie and Amalyn caught my eye. They looked so happy, so in love. A lump caught in my throat as I grabbed that, too.

We sat in the Autocar consoling a grumbling Ethan.

'It's okay, little man, we're going on an adventure,' I said.

Grace sat slouched, vacant, eyes searching through the window. As the Centre fence came into view, she straightened, her face becoming full of resolve.

'We're not going, Sav. Ethan and me. I'm not going to live underground.'

I gritted my teeth. 'Grace, you have to. *We* have to.'

'No. We can go to Mars. You said so yourself, it's grander, cleaner, more space. You showed me the plans. Why give all that up to go live like filth?'

'Because it's still the Centre, Grace.'

'Yes, the Centre, but even better.' She was looking straight at me now, her dark eyes so wide and deep, I was lost in them, unable to read her, unable to understand.

'*Better?*' I spat. 'The Centre can never be better. It just becomes a whole new shade of worse. Have you not heard me? How the Centre blackmailed me into spreading their words so that we could have Ethan.'

'They gave us our child. That opportunity is a blessing worth repaying.'

I shook my head. She couldn't be saying this. *No, no, no.* 'They *loaned* us our child. The paperwork says they own him. He's ours for as long as I keep being useful to them. They are literally jumping ship and leaving everyone to die. They're not even attempting to save anyone.'

'It would be impossible to save everyone. That's a hundred and fifty million people.'

'No, ten million, remember? They lied about the population to control us.'

My voice was getting louder. Grace held her finger to her lips to tell me to hush.

She whispered, 'Even so, they can't save everyone. We should feel honoured to have a place there.'

'This is insane. Grace, they blew up the airport!'

'Shh!' she hissed, as Ethan stirred. 'That's only speculation. In any case, you said so yourself, not all of the Centre are evil. Only a few. We could fit in well.'

'If we go to Mars, the Mainland and everyone there will starve.'

'I'm sure you can find a way to send them the plans. Mars is in contact with the Raft. The Select are going to Mars. It sounds easy enough,' she said, like it was that simple.

I held my head in my hands and groaned. 'You can't be saying this, Grace. You can't be. Archie and Amalyn died for this. That's how much they believed in it.'

'Amalyn was as good as an Alternate. You've said that before.'

I swallowed back more tears. 'She was kind and caring and loving. Grace, please. We have to go to the Mainland.'

She sighed. 'You go.'

'What?' I blinked and went cold. My lungs froze. *She didn't just say that.*

'You go. Ethan and I will go to Mars.'

'Grace, they only want you on Mars because they want me.'

'They also want Ethan. He's a gifted child.'

'No, Grace. That was a threat.' She scoffed. 'I'm not saying he's *not* gifted, but they want me, too,' I said. 'They're using him to get to me.' *She doesn't see it. How can she not see it?*

'Well, let them think you're coming too. But just don't go.'

The Autocar stopped at our building. I carried Ethan up to our apartment and put him on his bed. I didn't tuck him in. We'd be leaving soon. I tiptoed back to the living room and found Grace on the sofa, not even attempting to pack. I sat next to her.

'I can't leave you.'

She grabbed my hands and looked me in the eye. 'You're not. I'm leaving you.'

My whole body went stiff, a cold chill slamming into my chest.

She can't. She just can't.

'I love you, Sav, really. But we want different things. Your mind is so poisoned against the Centre, you can't see the good in it, what opportunities lie there. We could have a bigger apartment. Ethan could go to a really good school. All the fine things they have there, we could have those too.'

'None of those things matter, Grace. None of them. Especially not when you consider what you have to give up to get them.'

'We wouldn't be giving up anything.'

'Truth. We'd be giving up the truth.'

'Sounds like we gave that up a while ago.' She took her hands back and put them on her lap.

'Freedom,' I pleaded. 'We'd be under their control, complying to their agenda, supporting their claim to power.'

'You were willing to take us to that in the Tunnels. It was only very recently you heard the Select wouldn't be there. Even though they torture people. Without the Select there to keep order now, who knows what sort of chaos we'd be walking into?'

'My brother is there. My family.'

'*Your* brother. *Your* family. Mine all died years ago. I'm delighted for you, Sav, but your father was an Alternate. Your brother is the same. They're not the sort of people I want my son growing up around.'

'You'd rather he grew up around the evil people in the Centre? The manipulative, power-hungry, profit-hungry, greedy sort that are leaving everyone here to die?'

'The ambitious, forward-thinking sort that have overcome all the obstacles this planet has thrown at them.'

I groaned. She couldn't believe that. She mustn't. 'Remember what they did years ago? They blew up the anchors with people still on them, before they'd made it to safety. They gave them no warning. Just to get us clear of the Mainland because of some twisted idea of nationalism.'

'Deserters deserved to drown.' Her voice was flat, toneless, parroting the crap the Centre had fed us for years.

'That's what the headlines said, Grace. That's exactly what the Press told you to think. Remember?'

'I'm quite capable of thinking for myself. Just because the Press said it doesn't make it untrue.'

'It doesn't make it true, either.' I grabbed her hands again. 'I'm not leaving you.'

'Then come to Mars. Let's live our best life. With luxuries and space and cleanliness. Free of all the muck and grime here. A truly clean place. With the best technology. You've read the Press articles. It sounds amazing there. Sav, do you really think you can start a new lab from scratch? The best lab is already waiting for you there. The Centre have given us so much.'

'They denied us so much for so long. They hoarded empty

apartments and denied us fertility treatment for nearly ten years.'

'Surely it's only right that the best people get the best housing, and the chance to have children. There's no harm in profiting from that.'

'They held our lives to ransom, is what they did. Don't you remember that article, the first really bad one where they twisted my words when you were eating fish?'

She turned away from me. 'Don't throw that back in my face. I still squirm when I think of it. I did what I had to. You know that.'

'Yes, I do. But remember how awful they made it sound? How awful they made *you* sound?' *Please remember, Grace. Please just listen!*

'They were right, though. I should have been stronger. I should have resisted and held faith. They did give us a child. I should have known they would.' She held her chin higher. She'd been practising, I could tell. Rehearsing the prideful posture of the Centre.

It was no use. I saw it then, looking at her as she arched her body to stretch her back straighter, to hold her chin higher, looking out the window to catch the moonlight glinting on that garish fence. So stubborn in her resolve. I wasn't going to convince her. She didn't understand. She would never understand. The poison still coursed through her. *The mind most poisoned is the one I love more than any other.*

'Maisie would say to go. You know she hated the Centre.'

'Maisie's dead, Sav. I miss her, but she's gone. What she would want is irrelevant.'

I shook my head. It was hopeless. Her mind was made up. For too long she had idolised the Centre, seen that wealth as the key to winning at life.

I had to choose. Go to the Mainland to live in filth, away from the Centre and all the crap that had been forced on me my whole life but without my wife and child, or go to Mars, the sterile planet, and live a family life under the Centre's scrutiny and control.

I went to the shelf to find my father's book again. Somehow the pages of filth brought me comfort. Grace recoiled and edged away from me.

'God, I wish you'd get rid of that hideous thing.'

I ignored her, slid it out from its plastic sheath and flicked through it. The pictures weren't so awful, really. What if Amalyn was right, that they'd killed all the creatures and said they were so dangerous only because they couldn't be bothered to try and save them?

I flicked all the way through, lingering on each page without flinching. Maybe dad had been right. Maybe the bugs weren't so bad. I made it all the way to the end and stopped on the last page. I'd never noticed it before, the writing on that page. My mother's writing. A few lines she had written. A note left at the end for me, or my father, or anyone to read.

As we walk in the shadows
    Try not to see what lies before
    Instead reach for the handle
    To find what is behind the door.

A tear rolled down my cheek. The darkness they lived in, the despair they felt. I felt it too, now. The hopelessness as my world dissolved around me. Love is as brittle as concrete.

I had seen the Centre. I had seen the Tunnels. Grace was

living blind, dazzled by the shining light of the Centre. She had been in the dark for too long. The lies infused every inch of her. She was saturated with them, unable to see past them. I had left it too late to tell her the truth.

Once again, I had left it too late.

Reach for the handle, Grace. Please.

How could I leave them? That wasn't an option. I couldn't leave them alone in that awful place. I had to be there to raise my son to be better. My brother had left me, my parents had left me, stuck in the past, lost in their own desires, abandoning me for their memories. I couldn't do that. I wouldn't.

I needed to call Isaac and tell him I wasn't going.

I stood up to walk to the bedroom, my body heavy, lethargic, dragging my feet across the floor. As I neared the hallway, I froze, shocked.

Standing in the shadow of the doorway were two people.

'Hello?' I called out.

The shadows walked forwards, entering my living room.

'Marcus? Mabel?'

27

Chapter twenty-six

They both stood there, Marcus short, his thin face pale and gaunt, Mabel arched over, wilting, staring at the floor.

'What the hell are you doing in my house?' They hadn't even knocked. How had they got up here?

'I'm sorry, Professor,' Marcus said, his meek voice sounding as irritating as ever. 'You need to come with us. The Prime Minister wants you all to go, now. She has an Autocar waiting for you.'

What the hell?

'Please, Professor,' Mabel said, hardly above a whisper. 'She'll be mad if she has to come up here. She's waiting downstairs.'

'I'm not going anywhere. Why are you two up here giving me the Prime Minister's messages? What the hell is going on?'

Marcus took out his phone and turned his back on me. His voice was quieter than ever, but in the silence of the room it was as clear as day. 'They won't come, ma'am ... Okay, I'll ask ... Professor, does your son have a fever? Any sickness signs at all?'

'What? No, he's fine. What is this about?'

He ignored me and spoke down the phone. 'The child is healthy, ma'am.'

He hung up, and we stood in silence, both of them looking weak and keeping their eyes fixed on the floor. Yet in their meek presence, in my own home, somehow I felt powerless.

'Get out!'

'Can't do that, Professor.' Marcus's voice trembled more than ever.

Grace walked over and stood next to me, her wet eyes staring with confusion. 'Sav, what's going on?'

'I've no idea. These two have invaded our apartment and they won't leave.'

Marcus gave a little cough. 'It's not your apartment. It belongs to the Centre. And they tell us we have to stay.'

Behind them another shadow appeared, larger, stockier, getting closer until once again, she too was in my living room. More figures appeared, two security guards, tasers in one hand, the other hovering over their batons.

'If you want something done, do it yourself,' the Prime Minister said as she stomped into my home.

'You can piss off too. I'm not in the mood for games.'

'Savannah!' Grace shrieked. 'That's the Prime Minister you're talking to.'

'I don't care, Grace. You like her so much, you deal with her.'

'Glad to hear your son is healthy. Now, you are to come with me, Professor.' The Prime Minister was smiling that syrupy smile again, oozing sweetness like she had it to spare. 'We are going to Mars tonight.'

'I'm not going anywhere with you,' I said. I realised I had no choice, that I'd been going to Mars only to be with my family, but agreeing with the Prime Minister, being forced like this, felt like surrendering. I wasn't quite ready to surrender.

'You'd rather end up like those renegades Archie and Amalyn?' she said as she snorted a laugh.

Rage boiled up inside me. *How dare she say their names?*

'It's a flick of a switch to get rid of you, any of you. If you don't come, I'll see to it that this bit of Raft is the next to fall into the sea.'

My whole body tensed. 'You did it,' I said through my teeth. 'You blew up the edge. You're making the Raft break up!'

'No, the sea is doing that. Mostly. We just help it along when we see fit. It's crumbling, anyway. We just make sure it crumbles at the most appropriate time. The explosives were buried in the concrete years ago, just in case of an invasion of filth.'

'You killed them. You—'

'They knew the Raft was breaking up and they went to the edge anyway. Stupidity killed them. Plus, they were aiding your escape. I was hardly going to stand for that. Now get that boy and let's go.'

'No.'

She smirked. 'Listen, the Raft really is going to break up, with or without my help. It has served its purpose. Our sterility experiment is over. We have proved that we can survive in a sterile environment, and so Mars awaits. Our time on this lifeboat is finished. If you don't come now, you will die. Even the Centre will flounder eventually. We have been drilling to fortify it more, of course, but that will only last a few more years.'

'But the knotweed,' Grace said. 'The Press said the knotweed was gone, so the Raft won't break up anymore.' Her voice still had such admiration when talking to the Prime Minister. She held her chin high, stretching up on her toes. *Oh, Grace.* So gullible, still. So oblivious to evil.

The Prime Minister choked on a laugh, like she didn't imagine people actually believed what they were told. 'Yes, the knotweed is all gone. Stay here and live happily, if you like.' Her sarcasm was exaggerated, so even Grace couldn't miss it.

Grace sagged slightly, her face starting to redden. 'Why are you fortifying the Centre if you're all leaving? For the Perimeter to live there?' she asked.

'Oh god, no,' the Prime Minister said, with another laugh. 'The fortifications will make it impossible for the Perimeter to cross the fence. We're hardly going to leave our great city to *that* sort. It's just in case we get to Mars and realise we have forgotten some belongings. It gives us time to come back. The shaking from the fortifications may have weakened the Raft elsewhere but needs must. Now come on, let's go. We don't have time to waste.'

The dirtquakes – that's what they were! The Centre were shaking our homes to protect their own. *The fucking Centre!*

I stood my ground. The sight of her made me realise for sure that I couldn't go. I couldn't live under Centre control anymore, without any Perimeter to dilute their wickedness. Without my friends for backup. 'I'm not leaving. I can't leave all these people to perish. I can't believe that you, of all people, could just leave the Perimeter to die.'

'Why should I try and save them? The Perimeter never votes for me. So few of you even bother voting at all. Their meagre wages contribute hardly any tax. They have not paid their fair share for Mars. I'd have to take a Perimeter's entire wage packet to make it worth my while in martas, and even then it would be several decimal places short. The Perimeter are worthless. *You*, however, you are my prize. An example of a person from an Alternate upbringing who has learnt to conform. A shining example of Centre conditioning. A useful and productive person who came from nothing. You are to be showcased. The only Perimeter on Mars.'

A little whimper came from Mabel, her flimsy neck bowed, sunken eyes flickering from side to side.

The Prime Minister laughed. 'Oh, come on, you two. You didn't seriously think I meant it? Lars just told you what was necessary.'

'Lars?' All this time, they'd been supporting Lars!

'He will be making it to Mars, sadly. He's not really the sort. But his grandfather was Centre, and he has done his job well. These two, though.' She grimaced at Marcus and Mabel. 'They have not one drop of Centre blood. And look at them. To think that I'd actually give *them* a place on Mars for spying on BioLabs staff.' She laughed. 'Oh, how stupid Perimeter can be.' She straightened her face and turned to face them, towering over their heads. 'The Blue Liberation would like to thank you for your service. We will remember you fondly. With sterility comes liberty,' she finished with a smirk.

Mabel held on to Marcus's hand as she wobbled. Marcus propped them both up against the door frame.

The Prime Minister took another step towards me, displaying her teeth, twirling her necklace round a finger. 'Survival is a privilege, not a right. You'd all do well to remember that. The demise of the lesser people was inevitable. We were merely the catalyst. Stop being so bloody sentimental about it. This is progress, and progress is paramount. Now, let's go. I mean it.'

'Pearls,' Grace said, almost whispering.

'Excuse me?' the Prime Minister said, her eyebrows raised.

'Pearls. That necklace. You're wearing pearls. Like Maisie's. We threw them out … I thought they were banned. They're filthy, made from fish.'

'Only for those who require rules. Rules are for those without the breeding to make their own decisions.' She let the necklace hang loose and curled one corner of her mouth up. 'Such decorations are required for the Centre. We are not as easily tarnished as you. Filth is a matter of perspective.'

Grace gave a little gasp and backed away. 'You, the Centre Elite, you decorate yourselves with dirt.'

The Prime Minister only sneered in response.

'I'm not going,' I repeated.

She cleared her throat. 'You forget yourself, Professor. We own you. That child of yours is Centre property. I shall take him from you, if that's what it takes.'

'No!' Grace yelped. 'He's my child. If he goes, I go.'

The Prime Minister laughed. 'How sweet you are. But really, he is not your child. He was created by the Centre. One of our experiments. He is Centre property. The first child born from the DNA of two mothers. We produced the gametes from both of you. Your looks and your brains, so to speak.' She indicated Grace and me in turn. 'What a breakthrough, producing male gametes from female stem cells. We are hardly going to let our little experiment slip through our fingers.'

Grace sobbed and grabbed my hand.

The Prime Minister's words hit me and took my breath away.

Ethan is my boy too! Not just Grace's.

'Check your clinic paperwork, if you like. It clearly states that he is our property. He does not belong to you at all.'

'It says he is Centre property,' I said. I knew the bargain. 'The Centre is on the Raft, not on Mars.'

'Well, you can argue that point when we get there.'

'I'm not going. Nor is my son. He will not be raised by you, with your sick ideals.' The USB was burning through my pocket. I could feel Archie and Amalyn pushing me forwards, goading me on.

'You're not as popular as you think. I know there are Golden Fifty in the Centre. I know that a lot of the Centre population have sympathy for the Perimeter. And I know you are lying to them, too. Telling them that the move to Mars is to have more space and be cleaner. They have no idea the whole Raft will sink. They have no idea that you're stealing from the Mainland and leaving them to starve. The Select are joining you and they don't even know you're killing their own people.'

'So?' she said, still holding her chin high. 'It is the right of those in power to let people believe what we want them to believe.'

'You are more vulnerable than you know.' I squeezed the USB, felt it giving me strength. 'There will be an uprising when word gets out. It's already simmering in the background. You know it is. Your perfect image will be destroyed.'

'Well, luckily we will be on another planet, so they will believe whatever I want them to believe. Get the boy. We're leaving. Now!'

'No,' Grace said.

I gasped and looked at her. In her hand, she too held a red USB, with all the evidence that we were to send to Mars.

I smiled at her, then turned to face the Prime Minister. 'We've set up communications links. Emails have been sent, on timer. Marcus, check your email. You should be receiving it soon.'

Right at that moment, his phone pinged. Mabel's too. They looked at them and scrolled through.

'She's right, ma'am,' Marcus said. 'Everything is here. Proof, all of it.'

'Give that here.' The Prime Minister snatched the phone. Her face grew red, her white teeth disappearing between pursed lips.

'That has gone out to two hundred present and former BioLabs staff,' I said. 'And it's set up to go to Mars, too. Everyone will know. The entire Centre will know what you are doing. What you have done.'

She lowered her head to glare at me through narrowed eyes. 'You wouldn't dare.'

'I have nothing to lose. That information is due to be sent tomorrow.'

'You would rather stay here and die than come to Mars?'

'No. We'll go to the Mainland. Start a new lab and live in a free society, with free elections. Live by our rules, not yours.'

'You think I will allow you, my prize, to go and live among that filth? That leaderless pit is so corrupt, they'll have some unqualified, inexperienced leader, bred from grime. Mixing nations and backgrounds like some cesspit. No, you will come with me, where you will be forever housed in appropriate conditions, in a sterile lab. Or I will have the Centre starve.'

I took a deep breath. 'You have all the factory equipment. And you should take Marcus and Mabel. They're excellent, as good as me. And we can communicate. We can have a relationship across borders and share research and ideas. We do not have to work against each other. We can work together.'

She looked over at Marcus and Mabel and drew her chin back, turning up her nose. 'They cannot be my prize.'

'Then say I'm there too. Lie. You're good at that. I don't care. I'll let you know how Ethan gets on, I will aid the science however I can, but I will not go to Mars.' Grace grabbed my hand. Her teary eyes looked at mine, and she nodded. 'We will not live under the control of the Blue Liberation. We want to be free.'

The Prime Minister looked at me, at Grace, and back at me again, her black eyes scrutinising every inch of us. 'And that evidence?'

'Gone,' I said. 'I will not share it any further. It starts and ends with BioLabs.'

'And the rest of the Raft? You will leave them to die?'

'Leave the Centre fence open. Give them some time. I will not send any more emails. I will take whoever has already heard and wants to come, but I will not share the proof any further. I will write your articles, or you can use my name. As far as the Centre will know, I'm on Mars.'

She stood for a moment, Grace's grip tightening on my hand. I heard Ethan stir in the bedroom and one of the security guards moved to go and get him.

'No,' the Prime Minister said. 'Leave him.'

Grace dropped my hand and ran to Ethan.

'You will be the name attached to press releases and food products. Marcus and Mabel will work under your supervision. You will give me that USB.'

She held her hand out, steady despite the weight of gold that adorned it.

I handed her the USB. 'I have copies, naturally.'

'How will I know you will keep your word?'

'Trust.'

'Trust?' she replied, her voice high-pitched.

'Yes.' I nodded. 'You have to trust me. I know you have the means to seek revenge if I go back on my word.'

She shifted her weight from one foot to the other, never taking her eyes off me. 'I have ears and eyes everywhere. You know that?'

'I do. That is how I know our communication links with Marcus and Mabel will work.'

'You are willing to flee to the Mainland, without telling anyone else, and leave the rest of the Raft population to die, to go down with the Raft?'

If Amalyn were here, she'd say no. She'd sob and say we had to try and save more people. But Amalyn was gone. Grace and Ethan were all that mattered now.

I swallowed and nodded. 'If it means saving my family.'

She turned on her heel and made for the door. 'You may take the moral high ground when it suits you, Professor, but we are not so different.'

And then she left with her armed security, Marcus and Mabel trailing behind her.

Grace was stupefied, solemn in the hallway, staring at her feet. Ethan was still in the bedroom behind her, fidgeting and restless. We had not a moment to waste. It was time to go. I had my rucksack containing all my research, a few photographs and a couple of Ethan's favourite toys. That was all. I went to the bedroom and picked him up, his little sobs quietening.

'Grace?'

She didn't answer.

'Grace,' I said louder. 'I'm sorry I didn't agree to go with her. I'm sorry that I stopped you going to Mars. But we have to go. Now.'

She flung her arms around me, embracing me so hard I nearly dropped Ethan and our luggage. She sobbed, her tears soaking my neck. 'I should have believed you. That woman, the way she talked about Ethan. She was going to take him from us.'

I removed her arms from my neck and looked at her face. She was so pale, her eyes lined with red streaks and framed with dark circles, despondent from the realisation. Her dreams had been crushed. 'It's fine, Grace. But we still have to go.'

She grabbed a few more photographs, some cosmetics, and we left.

The Autocar came quickly and the hour to the airport whizzed by as Grace sat silently, white with shock. She stared out of the window at our building, at the fence, until it was out of sight.

'The evil. Reinforcing the Centre but not letting anyone in. And Ethan, *Ethan* ... At least we know why he's such a genius now.'

I stroked his hair and smiled at her. 'And why he's so gorgeous.'

The rain abated and the Autocar trundled along. We sat in silence for the rest of the journey. Grace had so much to process, and still so much more to come to terms with. I'd had years to understand and comprehend the maliciousness of the Centre. All the information had hit her like a smack in the face. I should have been honest. Should have trusted she was strong enough to shoulder the burden. Looking at her then, I saw malaise giving way to hope once again. She was stronger than I knew.

When we got to the airport, we had company. 4-09 was already there, as well as two others.

'This is Chris and Ester from the factory,' 4-09 said. 'They're coming too.'

Chris stepped forwards. He was clearly from the far Perimeter, and I recognised him as one of the factory staff I'd sacked. He shook my hand. 'More are on their way, those that are still able to come. Some were lost in the breakaway earlier.'

I nodded. 'We lost Archie and Amalyn. But we have enough, and the more the better. They can get on a flight tomorrow or the next day, whenever they can make it.'

The plane landed and Jerome stepped out, his face searching for Amalyn. He saw mine instead and I shook my head. He rested his forearm against his chest, holding his Golden Fifty tattoo to his heart. My eyes started to fill, but I swallowed the lump in my throat and got on the plane.

We all crammed in, Ethan on my lap, Grace nestled beside me. She didn't gawp at the finery as Amalyn and I had done. She buried her face in my shoulder, hiding herself from the gaudy opulence. The plane took off smoothly, without a bump. Silky smooth, Centre quality.

Jerome came and crouched beside me. 'More Golden Fifty are coming, I've heard. Amalyn got the word out. I'm so sorry she didn't make it. But because of her, many more will.'

I smiled and wiped a tear from my eye. 'Thanks, Jerome.'

Grace was asleep. Her face looked soft and untroubled. Perhaps in her sleep she had forgotten and would wake with regret. But for that moment, she looked peaceful and content.

Ethan stirred a little. 'Mummy, where are we going?'

I kissed the crown of his head. 'Home, little man. We're going home.'

28

Epilogue

I am alighting a solarplane, back at the Raft. Just a short visit. There is still so much doubt among the Golden Fifty, the lab staff, everyone who heard. Surely not, they say. It can't be that bad. There can't be *cities* out there. That's absurd.

Until they've seen evidence that the edge is crumbling away, seen the Mars rockets leave and not come back, until they've borne witness to what humankind has achieved off the Raft, nations working together, it cannot be believed. It's too alien, too abstract. Until they've seen the Tunnels, it's simply too much to comprehend. There's no life left anywhere – that's what they say. That's what they've always known. That one bit of information even the most cynical always believed. There is nowhere worth bothering with besides the Raft. It's easier to believe we are alone than hidden. Easier to believe that there's no one left rather than having spent years imprisoned.

It was all a Centre experiment. Mars had always been the plan. The Raft was temporary. A sterile country, insect free, all practice to see if surviving on Mars was possible. Rid the country of all non-human life, isolated from the rest of the planet. A sustainability experiment – that's all our lives have been. We passed the test, it seems.

Time wasted, relationships torn apart, technology and medicines withheld, and all for what?

There is no answer to that question. The never-ending streams of whys cannot be satisfied. *Because that's what the Centre Elite wanted to do. Because they could. Because we were all part of their big experiment.* Such answers satisfy no one. The truth rarely does.

My being at the airport is supposed to convince doubters to come and join us. I have photographs and videos. Just for Perimeter eyes, of course, those who have already been told. I have sent no more emails, as I promised. But I can't help word of mouth. Rumours spread. The Centre, of all people, should know that.

I also want to check if the fence gates are open, as the Prime Minister promised. They are, to my relief. And inhabited already. Plenty grabbed the opportunity to live in the Centre, assuming the fortifications will save them, or simply wanting to live out their final days in luxury. It's given them more time, at least. The edge is still crumbling – a lot slower now that the Blue Liberation aren't hovering over the explosives button, but the Raft is still being eaten away by the sea, bit by bit.

I left Grace and Ethan to explore when we arrived, for them to take in the wonder of it all. Ethan ran around, enjoying the space, laughing at the bald heads. Despite his sheltered upbringing, he isn't shy. He found some other children and befriended them immediately. Grace needs more time to settle, but she is adapting bit by bit. She left our room, ventured into the tunnels, spoke with other people. She's made friends, other mums. She's planning to start teaching again, face to face, like she wanted to before. Seeing the joy in Ethan as he ran around seeking out mischief has helped her feel at home. She hasn't mentioned the Centre. If she pines then she knows it's for a fictitious place. The Centre she idolised never existed. She's finding that the hardest thing to accept, that she believed the lies. I tell her it's fine, she saw sense in the end. I tell her I'm proud of her, that she'll get used to this life. She still loves me, I think, but I'm sure she hasn't forgiven me. Maybe in time, she will. The fertility treatment here is as good as it was on the Raft, and she is talking about having another baby. I'm not so sure, but if it would make her happy, then why not?

I was left with an awful and important task: to find Amalyn's parents. They were crushed, of course. I had not learnt from Penny, and my words were not kind enough to ease their pain. But could any words have helped? Their brave daughter was lost forever. True to herself and her cause until her last breath, fighting for what she believed until the end. Archie being there with her brought them some comfort. She didn't die alone. They died together, as in love as ever. I never told them she was expecting. Why make the hurt worse?

Jerome joined us in the Tunnels. Mars, the Centre, is no place for a man like him. He struggled to adapt more than most, missing the finer things. He wore his Centre clothes for some time before the stares got too much. Archie and Amalyn were right, it seemed. Not all Centre are pricks. He expects more to join us in the Tunnels soon. The ones that went to Mars have another agenda. Despite my promised silence, I doubt the Blue Liberation's reign will last. Maybe a revolution will come, maybe it won't. But the truth always comes out, eventually.

We didn't have to shave our heads. The Tunnels hadn't had

any lice in years, so it was deemed unnecessary. Nevertheless, they picked through our scalps when we arrived to make sure we weren't bringing anything with us. I laughed at how they saw *us* as risking importing filth, especially when they live in dirt and eat vermin. Filth is a matter of perspective, so the Prime Minister said.

Clementine's hair is growing in thick waves, as if she wasn't beautiful enough already. She adores Ethan. I hear him running down the corridor every morning to bang on her door. 'Come out and play, Clemmie!' He is thriving here with so much to explore, so many people to meet. Isaac has taught him to ride a bike. I still haven't learnt. Ethan says he'll pedal my trailer one day when he's bigger. He's grown so much already. He's still clever. Genius, though? I'm not convinced, but a bright boy for sure.

I haven't visited the library and the gallery. I considered it, but I'm sure it's not for me. Grace is thinking about it. I gave Isaac our father's book from our apartment to place it on a shelf, where it should be, complete with my mother's inscription at the back.

The lab is still under construction, but it's going to plan. We currently have three factory staff and have hired several recruits from the Mainland to learn. We hope still more will come from the Raft, those who believe us or haven't died already. We have some supplies with us, but we're rationing and are hungrier than we should be. I haven't yet dared to try the local food. Some have, though, and reported that it wasn't awful. Ethan liked it, so keen to try all new things and do whatever the local kids do. He gobbled it up without question. Maybe Grace and I will have to resort to it (I'm trying to learn not to call it 'filth') if the lab falls behind. But not yet. The insect larders are doing well. They had indeed been contaminated by the Centre, but it was isolated and they were saved. Thanks to Harold. And Archie, for hacking Harold's computer.

My heart aches when I think of all I have to thank him for. *Archie.*

From what I can tell, the Mars lab is functioning well. That is certainly what my Press articles say, and the Centre believe I am with them on Mars. Locked away, playing the role of the Prime Minister's prize. I'm still feeding their population poison, only it's just the Centre who read my toxic words now. Keeping the Blue Liberation in power, maintaining their control. From this distance, though, I feel detached and it bothers me less. Is that because they are Centre instead of Perimeter? I don't know. Maybe.

Marcus and Mabel are coping without me, although they have Lars as a boss now. Knowledgeless and with no expertise whatsoever, his teaspoon of Centre blood gives him the right to oversee their work. As furious as I was with Marcus and Mabel for their betrayal, I understand they were just trying to survive. I'm glad they did.

Mars has stockpiles of food, more than they'll ever need. The Select that live there have no idea they paid for it all and left their own people with so little. The Tunnels are functioning without them, currently anyway. Elections are happening. A government will be formed with representatives from every city. I'm looking forward to voting for the first time. Some candidates have strange ideas, and not all their new ideas make sense, but we're learning. Our community will evolve. We're progressing. That's the sort of progress that is paramount.

There isn't a day, barely a moment, that passes when I don't miss Archie. I can't drink a cup of tea without wishing he'd made it. I can't set up a joke without knowing his punchline. I can't look at a computer without imagining his glee. He should be here. They should both be here.

About thirty Golden Fifties have made it so far. That's Archie and Amalyn's legacy. Thirty more lives saved. Planes still go to the Raft to collect people as word spreads. The Golden Fifty aren't a quiet bunch. Some people don't want to come, and have accepted going down with the Raft. Some won't believe that a cohesive society exists. But for every person that does arrive, I know my dearest friends made it happen.

On the Raft, I make a quick visit to Maisie's old place. The haunting quiet of it makes me stop, expecting to hear Archie's voice making fun of me or Amalyn's excited squeal. Their drinks glasses are still discarded where they left them, marked with their fingerprints. Amalyn's hairbands litter the floor. Archie's vintage T-shirts are still in a box. I take a few. Amalyn's parents had some requests. Some photographs, an old toy of hers. Some keepsakes. I collect them quickly and leave. My heart aches. I can't bear the pain. The silence shatters me.

What would Amalyn and Archie have done if they were faced with my predicament? Would they have carried on with the lies to save their families' skin? I wish this story ended with the truth being revealed in its entirety to everyone. With Amalyn and Archie being here to revel in our success. For what is a society without truth? It is the whispers of the few drowning out the screams of the many.

I stop by my old place and collect the last of the MimikTea. The Mainland is lacking in that department and it's not a high-priority product for the factory right now, apparently. If Archie

was here, he'd say otherwise.
   I grab the tea, and I leave this book. Just in case.

A note from Emma

Thank you so much for reading The Invisible Kick. If you enjoyed it, please leave a review on Amazon or Goodreads. Reviews are so important for new authors like myself, and I promise I read them all. If you haven't already, checkout the first book in The Raft Series, The Poison Maker.

If you would like to get in touch, or be first in line to hear about the next book in The Raft Series, please visit my website www.emmaellisauthor.com.

Subscribers to my website receive a free e-book, Goodbye Flowers. A prequel to the Raft Series, it's set at the time the anchors are destroyed. It gives a little peak into the Raft before it started to drift, and delves deeper into the story of the Poison Maker himself, Peter Melrose.

The Raft is a crazy world I dreamed up whilst I was living among nature, as a full-time nomad exploring the great outdoors. How bland the world would be without nature. The endless grey of the Raft is my worst nightmare! Some readers of the first book in the series, The Poison Maker, have messaged me and told me what the Raft means to them, my own metaphors in these pages often being different to theirs. And that's okay. Our differences add colour to this world. If all our thoughts were the same, the Blue Liberation might as well be in power. What does the Raft mean to you? I'd love to know.

The last book in The Raft Series, The Final Fifty: Escape the Poison, is available now.

Acknowledgments

The Invisible Kick would not be in print without the help of my wonderful betas and critique partners. Thank you to Ansumana, Danica, Emily, Allison, Cherrie, Kate and Noah. Their time and honest feedback made this book what it is today. Thank you also to my editor Graham Clarke, and proofreader Alan Heal, for being so incredibly thorough.

Thanks especially to my partner, John, for giving me the space and time I need to write, for his support, patience and encouragement.

And thank you, for reading it.